Also by William A We

'Tales from the Stoney islands' children's
series of stories

Elliki Tangelena and the Sea Trolls

Hescat and Ixyweg

To Richard

from

the author

LETHELOREL

THE
LOST ELF QUEEN'S
CASTLE

----------o----------

BY

WILLIAM A WEBB

This book is a work of fiction. People, places, events and situations are the product of the author's imagination. Any resemblance to actual persons, living or dead, or historical events, is purely coincidental.

ISBN - 13: 978-1481089548
ISBN - 10: 1481089544

*To the one person I owe it all to,
my wonderful wife Jill,
who has borne the brunt of my highs and lows, was
always there, thick and thin, this is for you.*

Acknowledgements.

I have to add a grateful thanks to all those who encouraged me in the long journey this story took into
print.

Those D & D sessions with my son Ian Webb, his
friends Ian Grant, Michael Phillips and my daughter
Joanne Jordan spurred me into creating this intricate
web linking us with the World of Jodamia. I give
many thanks to them, putting up with my stories and
a DM father.

I am greateful to all those, including my son, Keren
Lilley and John Godwin and my wife Jill, who supported me by editing the book at various stages in its
life.

I add many thanks to everyone who guided and encouraged my basic artistic talent.

Illustrations

PART I

The Seeking

x

Prologue

Visions from Earth

$\mathcal{T}$he Scribe's hands clutched the ornate scrollwork surrounding the transparent tabletop as his horrified gaze looked through and watched the events unfolding beneath him. Somehow he knew who those in the tableau were, he did not know how he could see them or why… Helpless, he watched…

High above the valley the figure of the Sorcerer Aasphari sat on the great purple dragon Gouthbund, ordering his magic for one final burst of fury and hate at the beautiful Elf Castle of Lethelorel. Below him another fell plot was unfolding.

The elfmaid screamed and struggled, anguished and trapped. Her lover had vanished. He told her to meet him in this lonely clearing in the forest, but she only found a cruel bear trap-net stretched for her unwary feet to stumble into.

Hidden nearby, Heckke, the great Archdemon slavered, the anguish of the elfmaid was a sweet bonus, the trap within a trap was set, his vicious lascivious scheme was in motion.

"Scream, my beauty, scream. Look, here I am," he hissed. He appeared in front of her, first as her lover, his handsome face twisted in hate, then as his true awful repulsive self.

Her frantic screams echoed across the little valley to where her mistress, Eosilla the Queen of the Elves of the Star, rode warily amid her group of courtiers. The Queen knew that voice; Gerte, her empty-headed young ward. She was wilful and always disobedient, sultry and wanton, a danger to any elf or any other male.

But there was something in those screams, a terror that made a sharp fear slither down her spine. Instantly wheeling her mount, she bent forwards, gathering in her forces as she sped off. None could catch her when her favourite stallion responded to her command, a streak of living gold, its hoof beats like thunder, the trees parted before her and she covered the distance in moments. Her eyes flashed with anger and resolution, her unmatched beauty hiding her power and strength of will. Who was violating her valley?

Her bevy of followers, mounted on ordinary horses, were following way behind, too far, far too far. They were reckless in their attempt to catch her, to be her shield with their lives. Between the elf-maid's screams they heard with a heart-clutching horror their beloved Queen's cry of power end in a note of surprise. A gasp of frustration followed, cut off abruptly by a sound of a door somehow not of this world grating shut. Then there was silence but for the sobbing of an elfmaid. She knew that she had led her Queen into a demon's trap and so betrayed her.

The maid, the only witness, was mad with grief when they reached her; in her agony she snatched a young lord's dagger as he bent to free her from the net. Before he could stop her, she plunged the dagger into her own heart. Amongst the frantic courtiers, Lord Erliandol put forth his power to read the tortured maid's mind ere she died. He reeled from the horror he saw in those fleeting moments of re-membered agony.

That was not all; behind them the world they had known exploded in a pall of dust and debris, the ground giving a sharp lurch. When it cleared their castle, their home, most of their friends and family, had gone. Above, a great cloud formed in the shape of a Sorcerer and booming laughter bounced off the valley walls, and then that too cut off, faded, and was in turn blown away by the winds.

The year was 2300. It was called year of the Catastrophe of Aasphari and the last moments of the reign of the Elf Queen Eosilla. She was in the height of her powers, an Elfalee, perhaps more, a goddess of the higher wisdom, mighty in the lands around Westerland.

Of the Sorcerer Aasphari, there was no sign; he had vanished off the face of Jodamia, together with his victims. The great dragon Gouthbund flew on into the distance, for she cared not for her rider, nor what happened below her.

Hekke grimaced horribly, his attempt at a smile; Aasphari had called him into this world from his Abode of Horrors, thinking that he had control of the Arch-demon. He was wrong; the Arch-demon had him instead.

The demon, picking his jagged teeth, said to himself, "the scragmag of a spell pusher I will not keep, he can die for his arrogance, but I will play with the elves and the Elf Queen for a while."

The Scribe groaned as the scene faded, so that was what had happened. There was now nothing he could do. His group of young adventurers were on their own. He had sent them down into the hands of a great arch-demon and his victims. The Scribe released the table and found his hands were bleeding If only Brother Ignatious could be found?" he wondered.

"Fa thea dirigin!"

He said, passing his hand over the table, and a model of Lethelorel, the tall Castle of the Star appeared; a long ramp extending out from one side to a massive keep at its base. The Castle of the Star was the home of the Star Elves on the planet of Jodamia until that fateful day in 2300. His mind went back to earlier that evening and sighed. He went slowly over to the mantelpiece and took down a statuette of a lovely woman.

"Queen Eosilla, what became of you, O Elf Queen beyond compare?" he murmured. "Protect and guide these few, they are possibly your last chance, if you still live."

---0---

On Earth in the vault of the night sky, the stars shone above in the deepest black, then sweeping

4

downwards the heavens became tinged with dark blue, until the blue lightened to the horizon, making a vast twinkling bowl.

On such a night two figures walked resolutely on, following a line of houses on their right, curving over the top of the hill and down. They were on their way to bridge the gulf between parallel worlds, each joining with another identity on the new world.

Soon they were descending again, and turning sharp left, they could see the second road stretching away in front of them.

"Soon be there," Mark, the red-haired one whispered, apprehensively.

"Yep," replied Chris, the blond one and the taller of the two. Calmer, but even his voice was sharper than usual.

The Scribe described the world of Jodamia to them on the preceding day, so they had spent most of it rummaging through the ancient documents he had given them. He said they would find themselves in a frontier town called Mesquite between the well-ordered Westerlands and the wild lands beyond. There was a lot he had not told them; they could sense it in every word. Later that evening they had been measured up for their gear.

Now, as they walked down the road on the following evening, they speculated the moment in which the Scribe was to send them on their journey.

"I wouldn't put it past the Scribe to change things," Chris said doubtfully. "Nickolas would not be pleased."

"Nor Iyanna either," added Mark as they arrived at their destination, climbing up the steps to the front porch. On the door the number '27' glowed slightly in the dark.

The door opened as if by magic and there was Nickolas to greet them, his dark hair adding mystery to the scene.

5

"The Scribe said go on in when we wish," he instructed. "Iyanna is already in there, waiting."

They passed into the hallway and entered the room on the right. The size always amazed Chris; it was so much bigger than the house he had entered, like the hall in a baronial mansion. In the centre of the dimly lit room was a large model of a castle sitting on the oval ornate carved table. The model seemed there, but not there. There was an unusual transparency about it. On the far side of the room, on the left of the large fireplace, Iyanna was warming herself by the crackling fire. The firelight flickered on her outfit; her corselet was similar to dwarf-wear and she had a wicked-looking double-bladed battleaxe thrust into her belt. Her long brown hair, tight curled, waiting for the round iron-braced cap perched on her knee. On the floor, leaning against her carved chair, was a well-filled leather kitbag.

"All your gear is behind the screens over there," she said tersely, anxiety and a tinge of fear of the unknown creeping into her usually calm voice.

The screens took up almost all the left wall and behind them each found his clothes and weapons for the journey. Mark had the well-to-do gear of a wealthy Elf fighter from the Westerlands; Chris, had the battered but very serviceable banded leather armour of a half-elf fighter; and Nickolas had the off-white, flowing robe of a novice Druid.

Dressed, they assembled again around the table and the mysterious castle. The Scribe had said nothing about it to them. It stood on a flat-topped spike of rock almost as tall as it was, with a long sloping ramp to a massive lower castle gatehouse at ground level. Looking closer it seemed to be inhabited, alive. Then the reality struck them, they were looking through a window at a real place, full of live people. There were wains and carts climbing slowly up the ramp between the castles and soldiers patrolling the high turrets and ramparts.

The Scribe entered quietly, unannounced. He stood watching the four, pondering for a second or two and then waved a short thin stick. The model vanished, leaving an empty tabletop.

"Lethelorel, The Castle of the Star when it was last seen a long time ago," he murmured, regarding each person in front of him slowly, as if measuring them in some way.

"Good, very good," he added to himself.

"Are you all ready?" he asked.

"Yes," they chorused realising that he was not going to tell them anything further.

"Then on to Jodamia! The portal is ready."

He pointed to where the fire and fire-place should have stood in the far wall. Instead a misty doorway gaped in its place, with dark steps leading down. "Keep the order as I told you, Nickolas." As he turned, he paused and murmured half to himself,

"Fa thea dirigin," as he departed, leaving them alone in the room.

"Are you ready, Chris? Yes?" Queried Nickolas. He gripped his druid's staff tightly in one hand and then slung his backpack onto the other shoulder. "Then if you go first," he added, "I will come behind you, next Iyanna, then Mark is to follow on quickly."

"Good fortune! Jodamia awaits," The friendly but mysterious voice of the Scribe came to them from the door to the hallway as they went through into nothingness.

The Scribe's eyes belied the cheerful tone of his words, they were very anxious and sad.

Chapter One

Inns and Strange Stories

*T*he cloaked dark haired Druid had a second of blankness.

It was the year 4300 according to the Westerlands Calendar.

He was Nomaque Narafon and could remember his growing up in the Ancient Forest with his parents, brother and sister. The old forest in which he had played and grew up in had instilled in him a deep love of trees, which in turn, had led him to take up the druid's staff. His early instruction was by his parents and the local High Druid, but none since his gaining his noviciate. He had gradually drifted southeast to the frontier lands, and explored the great wedge of Westerland jutting into the vast oceans of south Jodamia. The main populated area of the whole continent, Westerland was mostly human but there were enclaves of the other races dotted about within its borders.

At this moment he was in the old walled frontier town of Mesquite, on the northeastern edge of the settled Westerlands. The devastated lands to the north, laid bare by the Goblin and Kob Wars, which ended in the battle of Nigreth Fond. Some miles into this waste area rose the bleak hills of the Mesquite Range, the dwarf kingdom of Delfteron was further north again. To the northeast lay the Ancient Forest, Nomaque's home and going on to the east was the elvish kingdom of Estamon around their great castle.

Nomaque was picking his way along a stinking, unlit alley, with its lowering dilapidated buildings.

Just around the corner loomed a larger, and slightly less crumbling building, the Old Duck Inn.

Accommodation was always a problem in Mesquite. Most inns were like this one, dirty and timeworn. After trying a few you usually picked the one you were used to, and didn't bother to try another. Over a period of time you were recognised as local enough not to be cheated, one of the lads so to speak.

This did not go very well with Druidic Orders but survival is a strong motive. Something would turn up every now and then for him to follow his calling. In truth most Initiate Druids did far worse than him, or so he had heard. He had continued in this way for a few years and suspected that if he applied himself once again to his studies he could attain the level of High Initiate or even higher. That always seemed so far away, and anyway, he now had good friends in the town.

He arrived under the familiar Old Duck Inn sign and turned out of the alley into the dark lobby in front of the rusting ironbound main door. Light streamed out from the smoky atmosphere, illuminating the familiar broad back of Chorky Endemion, a tall blond half-elf who was just going through. His slightly elongated ears showed as his hood rested down on his wide shoulders. Chorky turned and greeted him after they entered. It was a busy night and there was limited room, but as usual the crowd ignored the tall, white, cowled shape of the Druid and his companion. The torchlight glinted on his chiselled, young, but determined face, as he elbowed his way through. The ale barrels stood against the right-hand wall on a sturdy trestle, where the landlord dispensed his ordinary brew to any who had the courage to try it. Some of the ingredients were unusual and lumpy. The better ale was on the other side, where the buxom maid coped admirably with the regulars.

Nomaque and Chorky had been drinking there for several years and so collected their brew from the maid and made their way to the table where a lone elf sat. Nomaque thought he had seen him before; the red hair and the unusually powerful build reminded him of someone he thought he should know. He was clad in fine chainmail covered by a worn but intricately decorated jerkin, undoubtedly western elvish, and wealthy. He wore it in an unassuming way, which showed he was from a noble elf family, a fact that asked the question why was he there.

The rough wooden table was in the corner away from the crowd, where the elf could easily see trouble coming. The crowd was average, from the thieves on the table to the right, bent over and whispering, to the big table of militiamen nearer to the door, loud and bragging, who would doubtless disappear like smoke if a fight occurred in the Inn.

The elf leaned forward when they had sat down, and asked in a hushed voice, "Are either of you interested in old artefacts?"

Recognition dawned in Nomaque's mind. He asked, "You're the elf who is flogging an old rusty crown around and about, calling it an old relic, aren't you? Maltex?"

Maltex nodded, thinking 'no sale here', and sighed.

"Try Slimy Sid down in Lower Merchant Street; he specialises in old relics!" Chorky chuckled from across the table.

"Not the kind of relic Maltex wants, though. Those whores wouldn't want it, except to crown you with it perhaps," chuckled a voice on Nomaque's other side.

Nomaque looked around and was astonished to see a short impish-faced woman standing there,

10

bedecked in ring-mail and with a gleaming battle-axe thrust in her ornately carved belt.

"Go on look your fill," the apparition said. "I won't bite this time, human, but only if you shift over and let me in with my drink." As he regarded her he realised she was a gnome, although definitely a very good-looking one, her curved features giving her an exotic air. Her black hair was tucked into a dwarfish-style round helmet and partially covered her pointed gnomish ears.

"This is Ikin Galena, from a respectable family of miners west of Mayfle in Pickleyland," Maltex introduced, "I have yet to find out who these chaps are, Ikin. I'm Maltex Meraltion and by the way before you ask, my father is Nothernas Meraltion, the great General of the Guards."

"How did you escape the Westerland's great warrior's son's duty, Maltex?" Chorky asked knowing that the son was expected to follow on his father's profession, even more when it was a high rank in the Viceroy's Guard.

Maltex ignored the question, so Nomaque rose and bowed to the little gnomess.

"Little lady I am Nomaque Narafon, a half-elf, as is Chorky Endemion my companion. I come from the Ancient Forest to the Northeast of here, Chorky was brought up somewhere in the Westerlands. Bardonne, that's the place isn't it Chorky? So please don't call us human, Ikin." He smiled and as he sat down again, he made room for the gnomess. Taking the offered seat she replied cheerfully, "I won't if you don't call me little again; I'm regarded a shade too robust for a gnomess, so it rankles."

"You're unusual for a priest, Nomaque," she added some moments later when she had had a chance to size him up.

"That's because I'm not one. Haven't you heard of The Order of Druids in Pickleyland?"

11

"Oh! I thought they never went anywhere near towns, or alehouses for that matter, they stayed in and around trees." She carried on lamely, "or called their tree's spirits to guide them, or something like that." She was a little embarrassed and she felt drawn to this unusual Druid.

"Sometimes we do, 'go forth and experience the world, my son,' and all that. Then we return to the fold," Nomaque answered pleasantly, "I just haven't returned yet."

"Put your foot in your mouth there, Ikin. I was trying to interest them in the crown, but no-one seems to think it is worth anything," Maltex moaned disconsolately.

"How did you find the crown, Maltex?" inquired Ikin. "Do tell us the real version, mind you, not the one you give to the girls. I never did hear the truth of it."

"It was about a month ago now," began the elf. "I had decided to go hunting and so I set out northwards. I had travelled two or three days when I met four elves, Hons, Sorin, Nior and Vitn. Vitn was always moaning about something, a right pain to be with, his friend Nior wasn't much better. Anyway we all joined together to investigate a series of caves that the others had discovered previously near to the Range of Mountains.

We entered these tunnels three days later, and got ourselves lost as Vitn was supposed to know the way, only he didn't. The caves were unoccupied and dank, very depressing, not a sniff of treasure. Eventually I noticed a draught of air, we followed it, and before long we were in Goblin Land."

Several bystanders had joined the group of listeners, among them a couple of rangy elves. Maltex stiffened when he saw them, and looked less light-hearted. He paused for breath and waved his ale mug in a meaningful manner. The mug refilled, he continued.

"We must have come upon the inner secret chambers as, just after the first tracks in the dust, we came to a rusty old door. The old stick of a goblin was just about to cast a spell on us when Sorin caught him a wallop on top, and that was that. On the table behind him was the crown on a bit of old tatty velvet, so we picked it up and came home."

He rummaged in a filthy old sack and pulled out a round battered object, stained and filthy. It was undoubtedly an old crown, but very unusually made. Just above the dented headband a ring of small claws bent inwards. Set in the front was a goblin-like face, and flowing back from it over the top, four great talons curved back over again to end in two-inch claws pointing forwards.

"Goblin made, would you think, lads?" Maltex queried. Nomaque's uneasiness grew, he knew it was not goblin-make; they had not the craft. That was not what disturbed him; the object had powers hidden within it. He thought at first it was evil, but the more he teased it with a 'find evil' spell, the less it seemed to fit. He reached over to pick it up from the table, but it tumbled from his grasping fingers, sliding onto the floor with a clatter.

Maltex glowered at him and quickly retrieved it, putting it back into his sack. Nomaque was about to ask for it again when one of the strange elves elbowed his way forward and said loudly, "Not so fast Maltex, we have been waiting to catch you in a talkative mood, there are some odd things about that trip that ought to be heard."

"I know your gripe, Nior," Maltex retorted strongly, but with a little uncertainty creeping into his voice, "For some reason you hated me from the first. You made up that piece of nastiness about me leaving Vitn for dead."

13

"It's not only Vitn, there's Sorin as well," Nior replied sharply. "Hons here can back up what I say; you acted as though you didn't care a damn for them. The bloody treasure was all you cared about, and that worthless crown. The tale you have just spun, for example, was accurate as far as it went, but the rest of the adventure was more interesting. Even getting out of the goblin caves was a struggle. Obviously Maltex doesn't wish to tell it, so I will. If someone can bring me some refreshment, I will set the record straight!" he added in a sweetly vicious tone and giving Maltex a look of pure malice tinged with pleasure.

"No Nior, not you!" cut in the tall elf standing next to him. "You hate too much for your own good. If this is to be set straight without bloodshed, I must, much against my better feelings, tell you all what happened. Sorin was my friend, after all."

"Hons, what do you think Vitn was to me then? Still, have it your own way, it's obvious you don't trust me, so tell away."

"Right, when we left the old goblin for dead," started Hons taking up the tale, "we were still lost and so we wandered from corridor to corridor trying to find that elusive draught of fresh air again. The first turning we took led us slap into a band of five goblins, they were more surprised to find intruders than we were to meet them. One had more intelligence than the others and ran for it, yelling at the top of his voice that we were there. A lucky arrow shut him up, and we dispatched the others, not without Vitn being wounded. Nior, you said that he was a warrior when he joined us, didn't you? Some fighter he proved to be, always at the back, and quickest to plunder the kill. Anyway his wound was real enough, so we stopped to staunch his bleeding, and one of us found the sack of silver he had under his jerkin. You weren't going to share that, were you,

Nior, until Maltex reminded you? As you can see, everyone, we were a merry band. The way through the tunnels proved easier after that, as we could then feel the fresh air, we slipped out of one of the exits minutes later."

Hons paused to take a long drink from his ale, judging the reaction to the story as he did so. 'So far so good,' he thought to himself, and plunged on. "Skirting the mountains we came out in the wood-lands, and only stopped several miles later when we felt safe enough."

Chapter Two

The Legend of the Lost Elves of Estamon

A n hour or so earlier, under the shadow of the town wall, in an older, seedier inn, not far away from the Old Duck, the human farming community gathered.

They were there everyday, along with a few strangers, to chew over the happenings in the town that interested them. It was quite a rowdy occasion, and sometimes the only place where a lone figure can lounge without getting involved, was the bar.

This was precisely where the lone figure of the elf Eta Erliandol lounged. That meant in that crowded bar there were spaces on either side of him. Smoke from the cooking fires wafted across him, irritating his nose and eyes. He was also assailed by the sweet, acidic cloying smell of the group of unwashed farmers' bodies, as they ploughed through the ale, pot after pot.

While he had been there, the main topic was the recent goblin raids, which caused animated circular arguments of who was going to get it next. This really did not interest him at all. Some goblin king had started raiding to the north of the town, and there apparently seemed no reason or pattern to it; there had been relative peace with them for hundreds of years. They were turning out hapless farmers, bondsmen or even lords and giving their homes a going over, sometimes not even killing or torturing the former occupants.

16

This was an occurrence unheard of in the old stories. Eta felt that this was not an elvish matter, and had become bored with the endless farmers' problems. Then, just as he straightened to rise off the seat, a word from the conversation next to him at the bar caught his ear.

The topic had taken an unexpected turn. The word, which had captured this tall elf's attention was 'lost', especially when it was applied to a village. It opened up memories of his family history, which featured heavily on places being lost.

Over one and a half thousand years before, a handful of elf hunters had returned to their hidden valley in the mountains, only to find it not there; or more precisely; the people, the dwellings, castle and byre, all the livestock, had gone, leaving only the bare rock valley floor. Just as though they had never been there, and leaving a hole rapidly filling with water, with devastated groups of confused, mourning and bereft people. The shattered hunters, joined with all those who remained of a proud elvish kingdom, broke down and wept for their lost ones, because they too were lost. They did not know what to do.

Eventually they chose a leader from amongst the survivors, who charged them and their descendants to swear two vows to shape their lives from then on. Firstly, find a fair place to start again and build a second kingdom. Secondly the fittest and most able were, when they came of age, sent out into the wide world to try to find their lost ones.

Those brave few moved east and over the years built Estamon Star City, and occupied the fair lands to the East Sea. This was the land where Eta was born and grew to maturity. Being strong and able he was one of the one hundred chosen to go forth. This happened every 10 years, after the Great Games, which were held just outside the city walls. The hundred were charged to search, and only return in fifty years, they could come home earlier if they discovered some shred of evidence.

Only a handful of these young hopefuls had ever returned before their 50 years exile had elapsed, and these had all brought fruitless tidings. Many of those who knew the story called those elf seekers, the 'Hopeless of the Lost.' Even some of the elves themselves admitted that the cause was wasting the flower of their youth. This may also have been because from those one hundred usually only twenty to thirty ever returned after their exile.

Of course most of those who did not return had not died, but had, in their wandering years, settled in other occupations and communities all over the world. Wishing in their hearts to return but knowing they will never do so.

Eta had then been roving for 11 years of his allotted span and felt thoroughly fed up with the whole business. He had been over most of the land south to the sea, but never to the north. He had travelled east to the Erdish Grass Flatts and their western city, Vorsin. In the west he had visited the gnomes' peninsula of Pickleyland, and seen the glowering Starkhorn towering thousands of feet above the waves. How the gnomes could be so cheerful with a God living in such a place, Eta could not understand. There remained only to look to the north, a bleak and unlikely prospect with moors, bogs, goblin-infested mountains and wastes. There was perhaps the Dwarf Kingdom of Delfteron far to the north…

Lost… like a trigger, the word shot his mind into the farmers' conversation.

"Young Jablin, you know that scruffy lad as helps me off-times, had to go hunting with his uncle last week up to the north of the Mesquite Hills on the edge of the Merelands. Yesterday he came back bursting with a strange tale." Here he paused for effect, and to take in several mouthfuls of ale.

"They had just skirted the hills when they came upon a rough track where no track had been a while before. This perplexed his uncle mightily, who started to mutter of demons and things, seriously frightening the lad. I shall take it up with him when he gets back, I will. Now where was I? Ah! Yes, after a while Jablin's uncle decided to follow the track. Northwest around the hills he went, with Jablin following very cautiously by then. Mark you the lad was expecting to meet a devil at any minute. After a few miles the track had gone round the hills and turned towards the merelands, a mile or two more and the valley opened and there was a village nestling between them and the marshes. At this the uncle became even more afraid, and said something like,

'There's never in my life been a village here! Sorcery it must be!'

This really frightened Jablin. The old man decided sorcery or not, he would explore it, and off he went.

The lad cried out to him, 'No! Don't! Uncle? We won't be seen again, ever! I want to go back.'

The uncle came back in a rage and cuffed the lad across the ear. 'Any more whining and I'll box your other ear, come on you lazy good for nothing runt,' he said, and started down the track again.

Jablin had had enough of his uncle by then and so he took to his heels and ran back home. Jablin's uncle has not been seen since!"

The farmers continued on talking about the uncle and Eta lost interest in them, but the village was another thing altogether, a topic to be investigated as soon as possible. This was the first interesting thing to do since he arrived in town.

On his way to Mesquite he had been a soldier escorting some furs from the Port of Neldoretha, and in amongst the other hired fighters was Zeth, an easy-going half-elf, who might also be intrigued by

19

his discovery. The last time he saw him it was in the Old Duck Inn, a night or two back. Zeth had started off as an apprentice cleric and become an initiate, but his faith had fallen foul of the town and its many attractions, and he eked out a living at that time as a mercenary. Eta came to a decision, he would find Zeth that night and perhaps with one or two more he would go and seek out that village for himself.

The thoughts, 'lost village...lost elves... lost me,' kept going round in his mind as he picked his way absent-mindedly through the alleys to the Inn.

"Who have we here then!" a harsh voice rasped just behind him. He jerked out of his reverie to feel rough hands grasp his sword arm, foul breath and a knife at his throat. "A rich Elf by the..." The voice cut off and his arm was released sharply, and the knife forced away by the point of Zeth's sword.

"No you don't Scum!" Zeth shouted.

Just as the ruffians reached him, Zeth and another elf had come silently out of the shadows on the other side of the street and attacked furiously. The ruffians had been surprised in turn, giving way enough for the two to pull Eta away and bar the way with their swords drawn. Without doubt the other two saved Eta's life. He staggered round to lean on the wall behind the bloody battle. Two very busy figures were holding back quite a few ragged, though determined rogues.

As quick as he could he unsheathed his longsword and joined in the fray, his blade whirling a deadly arc in amongst the poorly armed gang. Faced with three good swordsmen, the gang became the ones in mortal danger, and so it was that three of the ruffians died on the swords before the four remaining could win free and run away.

Eta leaned against the wall, looked about him and caught his breath. He had had a very close brush with death, but for his friend and the other elf, it would have been fatal for him. He looked at Zeth and smiled a trifle wanly, the smile saying it all, and gestured towards the Inn door. Zeth nodded, pleased that Eta was obviously unhurt and thirsty. They went into the smoky room, where Eta led the way to the makeshift table at the side of the main bar. He called to the girl serving there to find three mugs of the best in the house, as well as asking her to tell the landlord of the three dead attackers outside.

While Eta was collecting the drinks, Zeth glanced around to gauge the mood of the night. His eye caught the way their new elf companion was watching a mixed group in the corner, he had a grim smile as though he knew them, perhaps with a touch of anticipation in the set of his body. Catching sight of Zeth's regard the elf turned and pointed towards the group he was watching and said,

"I have a feeling that's a tale worth hearing, and one I've come a long way to hear,"

He paused to take a quick drink. "Now that the ale's here, let's go and have a listen." The elf slowly made his way across the crowded room to the corner, smiling broadly all the time.

A tall elf with his back to the approaching three was recounting an escape from a goblin settlement. As this elf was speaking he was looking sternly at another broader built elf sitting on the far side of the table, as well as a shifty one standing next to him. The far one he addressed as Maltex, the shifty one it seemed was called Nior. Nior had an obvious dislike of the far one, verging on hate perhaps, judging by the way he sneered and fiddled with his sword hilt.

The nearer tall elf, Hons, continued, "We trudged on, not speaking, with one thing and another, we didn't stop at midday through bickering and sheer bloody-mindedness. The atmosphere you could taste. Anyway we went on like this for several miles,

21

until, still grumbling and arguing, lost in our own grouches, we walked smack into a bandit camp. I don't know who was more surprised, us or them. The five of them were making merry around a roaring fire, which was why they had not heard our approach. Leaping up, they grabbed for their weapons, and attacked. They were not having a lucky day,

In a trice there were three of them dead in as many minutes. They had no chance because of the foul mood we were in, the remaining two fled with their lives. We had a quick rummage to see if any of them had anything of value, and found a pouch with money in it and some little pots. The coins we shared out as best we could, and we then investigated the pots. Nior unfortunately tried one, he tasted the tiniest bit on his tongue, and then he collapsed. Fortunately after lying on the floor for a bit, he woke up without us having to revive him. Maltex threw the pot away onto the fire that the ruffians had going, where it exploded with a colourful bang. Whirring, the pot flew off to hit a tall boulder near the fire, bursting into a shower of sparks over everyone.

There was a great bellow of pain from near the boulder, followed by a blur of something large moving fast towards the fire. It was as though the whole boulder was moving, a knobbly great giant-like thing, covered in burning twigs and mossy rocks. It picked up Maltex in long lumpy fingers and held him by one foot, ten feet above the ground. It did not look happy as it had various parts of its anatomy on fire."

Eta heard a snort beside him, and turned to see the elf, who had come in with him, convulsed with laughter.

"That was the funniest thing... I have ever seen," he said in between gasps.

"The look on Maltex's face hanging there, dangled by a ramphorm giant," he chuckled, and went off into hysterics again.

"So you know those people?" Eta asked.

"Oh yes!" He said quietly into Eta's ear. "You will hear me mentioned soon, if they stick to the true story. Listen for Sorin, that's me."

Hons continued, "The boulder-giant jiggled poor old Maltex a bit, and bold as brass, it asked, 'Put out the fire, small people, and I would like no more fireworks, young elf. I was just waking up and getting warm when you go and spoil it.' He had a pleasant, very deep masculine voice, only the giant's shape was difficult to see, as he kept on changing all the time. His surface was not always rocky either, it was continually changing between, rocky, twiggy, furry or any combination.

When we got over our shock and finished laughing, we set about doing as the giant wanted, as he was bigger than us and he had Maltex by the...heel. Anyway as soon as he saw our intent, he put our taller friend down carefully, 'I'm so sorry, I got a bit heated,' the giant apologised."

"I knew you would make the most of it," put in Maltex, "I hope you enjoyed it! Now you can finish the saga, all the weeks of it."

"That's fine, especially as I haven't reached the part yet which you two disagree about." Hons went on. "The giant stayed with us that night on the edge of the clearing, but by the next morning he had gone, so we had a quick warm up around a good blaze before we broke camp.

Wandering north we encountered a sizeable village and hired rooms in the ramshackle inn. Maltex was as usual after everything that wore a skirt, which as usual got him into trouble, so we only stayed there one night. We liked the village, a mixed community, and we elected to sell the crown and see if we could buy or rent a house. We found a buyer and in a short time had ourselves a roomy cabin on the outskirts.

This proved a great success at first, as we got a good price for the crown, which not only gave us enough to buy the cabin but furnish it as well. There was a garden and a stable attached, but the previous owner had not elected to tell us of three night wanderers, which gave us a hell of a fright. They manifested themselves as armed skeletons, but as they fell over our gear, which we had been too tired to stow away the night before, we had warning enough to deal with them.

The next day we made a thorough search and found a treasure map in the garden. This was a fatal thing for us, the map described a room halfway down the well in a recess. Vitn was keen to go down, so keen that he and Maltex went off right away. We stayed behind for a while for some reason I cannot remember and got there when Vitn was down the well in the bucket. His voice floated back out of the opening some time later, saying very disappointedly that he had plumbed the complete depth to the bottom and found no recess whatever and was coming up. That was the moment when the rope broke, a wail followed and then a thud and silence. We quickly tied all our own ropes together to make them long enough and Maltex insisted on going down, as he felt some blame must lie on him for not checking the rope first. Whether or not this was true he went down into the well lowered by us. On the way down he kept a lookout for the recess but didn't find it.

He called back up to us that there was nobody down there, and Vitn had vanished. He was on the bottom and there was only the old bucket and nothing else."

"There must have been," burst out Nior, "people just don't vanish like that. You found him and took the opportunity to settle your score as he lay there wounded. Coming up telling us he wasn't there and so nobody checked. You're a murderer!" He shouted.

24

The talk in the bar stopped as if a knife sliced through it. The contents of the room began to sullenly gather around the table in the corner. The atmosphere in the room became lethal.

"You did the same to Sorin later." Nior lashed out verbally with every bit of hate he had nursed secretly, feeding on his own imagined wrongs. "You held back deliberately when we were attacked by those Hobgoblins just after. You let him take them on, taking your time, and so poor Sorin was mortally wounded. You were bending over him when we ran up, then he disappeared too. I'll bet you were finishing him off as well for his pouch, I wouldn't wonder." His words overflowed into flaring anger as he leaped onto a nearby bench. Drawing his long sword he glared at his foe, daring him to follow suit. The crowd around swelled visibly as everyone wanted to see the blood flowing, especially as elves rarely fought amongst themselves. Maltex levered himself up onto his feet and looked coolly at Nior, knowing that a wrong word would likely kill him.

"Why should I fight you, as I neither killed Sorin or your friend. I have thought a lot about Vitn, and long ago ceased to grieve as I think he did find the recess, but with a closing door. He then cut the rope and cried out hoping I would do just as I did. Later he came up with the loot, and scarpered, taking Sorin with him, because he saw everything, leaving you, his friend, behind."

"Prove that!" Nior yelled, still looking for blood.

"Of course I can't! But it's just as likely as your tale, especially as I would not have gained anything from hurting Vitn." Maltex replied heatedly, not really wanting to hurt or kill Nior either. Doing that would have partially proved the case against him.

This didn't please the crowd at all, they jostled spilling around the back of the table, their mood becoming very ugly since they didn't believe Maltex. A burly particularly nasty individual cried out,

"He's trying to wriggle out of it, just you call him out, we're behind you. We'll string him up outside before he can spin any more lies."

Seeing the situation turning to his favour Nior quickly pointed to the unfortunate elf,

"Seize him quick, but don't let him get to his sword or you will regret it."

A ruffian behind Maltex suddenly produced a cudgel from nowhere. He swung it to brain the elf, then leaped back with a scream. Blood poured from what was left of his arm, the wrist, hand and cudgel falling to the floor with a sodden thump.

Just in front of him, small but indomitable, Ikin stood and waved her razor-sharp battleaxe at the crowd. She yelled. "Any more with bits to lose?" No one had seen her move, but the result lay on the floor, and she was between them and the beleaguered elf.

At about this point a stout arm took Nior's legs from under him and he collapsed on the tabletop, the jugs of ale going in all directions. He lay there, out cold. The tall elf, who had accompanied Eta, climbed up onto the table in Nior's place.

He raised his arm and bellowed, "Wait! Before you all get too excited, I'm supposed to be one of the corpses that this bloke has murdered, my name's Sorin and I'm so dead that I've come to look for him and buy him a drink for saving my life. So just go away and let me do it!"

"Well met Sorin!" Maltex exclaimed. "Am I glad you came in tonight?" He was pleased and relieved, but even more confused than ever, where the elf had sprung from he had no idea.

"I also know he didn't kill the other one," Sorin added quickly to the crowd, "the excitement is over."

The crowd showed no sign of going away. The one-armed ruffian was clutching his blood soaked stump bitterly complaining, so Ikin picked up his lost arm and gave it back to him.

"Here it is," she said, "now you haven't lost it after all." This nearly started it all off again, as the mates of one-arm closed in around Ikin. This was prevented by the elves and half-elves all getting up and pushing forwards to protect her before anything further could happen. Faced with the wall of competent fighters, all those wanting blood wandered away. Reluctantly, nursing their grievances, they moved away and left the group alone. The focus of all the mayhem, Nior, recovered his sword from the floor and slunk away unnoticed.

Eta and Zeth joined the group at the table and sat down. After introductions and the story of Eta's escape outside the inn had been told, everyone wanted to hear how Sorin disappeared just after the hobgoblin attack.

"I was lying there injured," the elf continued, "the fighting having moved away from me, when Vitn chose that moment to climb back out of the well, tripping over me in the process. Yes, he had tricked you, he boasted about it to me later. He climbed out of the bucket into the recess, cutting the rope and crying out as though he was falling as he cut it. He cut it a lot lower than the recess so anybody following would be looking in the wrong place. He closed the door and waited, hoping that you would leave the rope dangling for him to climb out of the well later. You were fighting a little way off and had your back to us. Vitn was in a hurry and he persuaded me to go with him. Well, he stuck a knife in my throat and told me to keep quiet or he would kill me then and there.

So we hobbled away, while the fighting was thickest. We skirted the village and Vitn stole two horses, the loot and I were tied on one, the other he

27

rode himself. I feigned a fatal wound and after about four hours riding he cheerfully cut me off the horse, letting me fall on to the trail. He left me there still tied at the wrists, lying on the ground. Fortunately the knots were sloppy like the elf, and after a while I wriggled loose. There was no other option but to follow and hope I could catch him when he camped that night. I was quite weak from the first wound but I caught him. I don't want to describe what happened but I rode away with what remained of the treasure to share with you all. I have been looking for you ever since, although now there's not much left as I've been robbed more than once since."

Hons was still recovering from Sorin's sudden appearance, but said for all of them, "You've made my day, Sorin, I had thought you were lost, now you've come back. There must be some faerie blood in your family. Welcome back, Sorin old friend!" There was a murmur of agreement to this, and a short silence for a moment.

"If you sold the crown how did you get it back, Maltex?" Nomaque inquired.

"Well I might as well finish what I started out to tell. When Sorin disappeared, we all lost heart in our venture in the village. Later that week the previous owner came to us and demanded to be given his money back as he couldn't sell the crown, as there were very nasty rumours that goblins were searching for a dilapidated crown. Killing and pillaging too, so our former client was in a dither what to do, especially as the crown we passed on to him seemed to fit the description of the Goblin crown and looked old and grimy. Just like ours, curious wasn't it, but it was one of those things that was difficult to prove, it was very unlikely that the goblins could have tracked us. Anyway the chap could have made the story up just because he couldn't find a buyer. We swapped the crown back for the house and left the village. And after several scrapes returning here, I am still trying to flog this damned bauble! I shall go to the market tomorrow, and whatever the price, I'm selling it. It's getting too hot to handle."

"I think that a wise decision, just in case." Chorky added. "There has been a lot of goblin activity near here in the last few weeks."

Eta casually asked "That village, is it north of the Mesquite Hills? Did you notice anything strange about it?"

"Yes Eta, there was an odd feeling about it," Hons replied. "It was just as if it was either very old, or time had not passed as fast there as everywhere else. Why do you ask?"

"I am looking for a village in that area, reputed to be difficult to find, in order to trace what became of a lost branch of my family. If it is the one I'm seeking there may be either a lost city, or a lost castle, near-by. Did you hear about any such further north?"

"As a matter of fact there was some mention of a lost valley to the north, a weird place, a sort of crevice with sheer sides, and a ruined city overlooking it. Is that the sort of thing you mean?" Maltex queried.

"Something like that, it could be the old elvish city of the Necromancer my parents used to go on about. Right, that decides me, I'm going to go there and find out a bit more about it starting as soon as it's light on the morrow, and of course when I've got fitted out. Anyone like to come, there may be lots of treasure and a mystery to solve that has puzzled the elves for well over a thousand years?" Eta asked hopefully.

There was then much discussion lubricated with ale, but the outcome was that all of them had had enough of Mesquite for one reason or another.They decided to all go with Eta, elf hunting as Ikin put it, if he would put the departure off for a day or two.

Eta readily agreed, as it would greatly improve the chances with a larger party against the perils ahead.

Maltex sold his crown again and with a grand gesture fitted out the expedition from the proceeds.

The day after that was a feast day, so when they gathered in the inn the place was packed to the walls. Any departure was slowed right down in that air of celebration; and also while they were in the middle of deciding what to do, three burly elves in uniform, with a strong resemblance to Maltex turned up with a message for him. He apparently had to go home to a large family gathering. Rather unexpectedly his grandfather had died young at two hundred and two. This put the journey in jeopardy before it even started, as Zeth remarked.

"Not so," put in Maltex, "we can go in two parties to some agreed point. Name a time and place and we will be there."

"All right, say a month from now in the valley near the ruined city," Eta suggested and Maltex nodded reluctantly, he would have much preferred to meet in the town again, or the village as there were a few female acquaintances there he...

As usual with such arrangements it was doomed to go awry, as everyone found out much later, and their eventual meeting was probably more to do with divine intervention than chance.

Chapter Three

Village and Valley

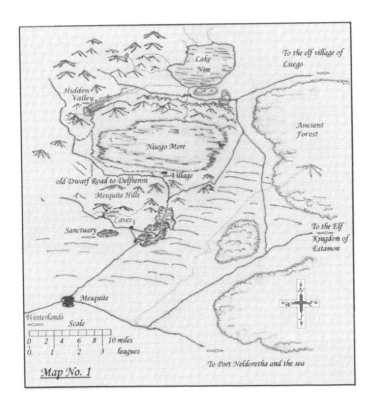

M altex left on his family business with Hons and Sorin that night, as it couldn't wait, the rest hoped they could make a very doubtful arranged rendezvous four weeks later at the mysterious valley. All those left set off the following bright sunny morning, well mounted and hopeful. The party consisted of the three half-elves, Nomaque, Chorky and Zeth, Eta the elf and the gnomess, Ikin.

For once the travelling was uneventful, a good interlude for the group to get used to each other and work together. The well defined track wide enough for a wagon, wound its way through patches of scrubby trees and denser woods. Going northeast at first, the track skirted the Mesquite Hills, and turned northwards. When the track veered east towards Estamon and Eta's home, they had to watch carefully for another trail going northwards, if they had not been expecting it they would have missed it completely. It was the old dwarf road to Delfteron, narrow and poorly defined, leading to a small gap in the hills. The vegetation had grown hiding it in places so any wagon would have had difficulty. It was the route that followed the story of young Jablin and as they topped the pass, the village was there in between them and the miles of dreary flat grey merelands, stretching out as far as they could see. The great battle of Nigreth Fond had been quite close to the west and no one wanted to live near to where so many had been killed.

They rode down into the village and the feeling that Maltex had described was most apparent. They felt its oldness, its not quite belonging in the present. The people seemed normal enough, carrying on as any village would. There was only one inn, The Bull. Typically there was no inn-sign, the name was in peeling paint across the wall nearest the muddy apology for a street.

"Sign must've fallen off a long time ago," Ikin remarked, "and got lost in the dust of ages," she added dryly.

They dismounted and tethered the horses to several posts. They all trooped inside and looked around. In the dim light the room looked filthy in keeping with the outside, with a shifty innkeeper. A sour looking establishment all round, but the only place to spend the first night, they would look further in the morning for better. There were rooms to be had, the innkeeper said, but not many, and the horses could go in the shed at the back. So they took two, using the floor as well, ignoring the patron's protests. Eta and Zeth had one, the other three the other, Ikin getting the bed when they drew lots, the others on their sleeping rolls on the floor.

They had a round of ale first before retiring, and surveyed the other residents, not liking them one bit. They were a ragged, smelly, loud and quarrelsome bunch, some had features not unlike goblins, pinched and angular. One person apart from these was the dwarf sitting in the corner. The dwarf nodded greeting and waved them across.

"I see you don't like our fellow drinkers any more than I do. My name's Clem, I'm from Delfteron a good way north of here."

The group introduced themselves and sat down. Clem was quiet and listened to the banter between the others, which carried on most of the time, not giving much away as to why he was there. Ikin got on with him though, as they were alike in many of their dislikes. After a while Clem rose and bid them a good rest, going off to his room.

"What do you think Ikin? Seems a good sort." Chorky asked.

"I think his heart's in the right place." She said thoughtfully "He might possibly make a useful companion, if that's what you mean."

They followed the dwarf up the creaking stair shortly after, the innkeeper leered at Ikin and wished them a good night's bed. Ikin put her hand on Chorky's arm and stopped any retort. Quietly she added, "He isn't worth it. You'll dirty your blade with scum like that."

33

"Nevertheless I don't like it one bit," Chorky replied through clenched teeth. "And given half a chance I will wipe that sneer off his leering face."

"Maybe in the morning." Ikin said yawning. They had reached their respective rooms and rolled in the filthy blankets, completely clothed, as the previous occupants had done the same.

"This place is as safe as a rat hole. I think we need a watch, if you like I'll take first turn." Ikin offered, to which the others agreed. Nomaque was second, and Chorky third. Chorky was feeling apprehensive so he went down the check that their horses were ok.

Ikin fell asleep, it was the first time that she had been on guard for some while, and she was dog tired from the journey, so the inevitable happened. Soft sounds came from the door, which unfortunately had no lock and Chorky had neglected to wedge. Smelly forms slid into the room, some rummaged in the gear on the floor, others bent over the sleeping shapes just as a fifth form materialised in the doorway.

"Banzak!" it bellowed and charged. The three shadowy forms darted for the door, hoping to evade the deadly axe-blade. More forms came along the corridor to the others aid, yelling in a weird tongue. The lone attacker desperately changed to defence, with his back to the wall. The room's original occupants forgotten by their attackers, brought sharply into the present, leaped up and laid about them all they could. The raiding goblins yelled to each other and made for the door as one, straight into the swords of Eta and Zeth, who stopped them in the open doorway. The goblins had little room to wield their weapons with their fellows pushing from behind. The front two fell in as many seconds, the next two fought hard, but their short swords were barely adequate to cope with the practised longswords of their adversaries. The hindmost died as he realised the dwarf was no longer against the wall. The remaining two died bravely, but futilely, against terrible odds, having no chance against six.

The torches were lit and the damage looked at. The three in the room were lucky, but for Clem's vigilance, they would have been the ones on the floor dead. The three all had minor wounds, knife-work on them by the goblins, small cuts on the face and neck that they woke up to.

Nomaque turned to the dwarf and held out his hand, introducing them again, fully this time. "We all owe you our lives, good dwarf. My name is Nomaque Narafon. Going around the room; on my right are Ikin Galena, next Chorky Endemion, then Eta Erliandol, followed by Zeth Zethion."

"Clem Sbandrin is my name, and I am pleased to be of help, but am I among fools? You are lucky that I am a light sleeper. Here you are in a den of thieves and you do not post a guard. I am speechless." Seeing Ikin's sheepish look he added with a sigh, "I suppose it happens to us all, once only I hope. I am going to check out the rest of the rooms for this lots gear, coming!"

Their temper flaming, the group stormed along the upstairs floor, checking to find the goblins rooms. They discovered one of their rooms four doors along, and in it, under a pile of bloodstained clothes in the corner, there were weapons and money belts. It was a thieves' hoard. Eta happened to glance out of the grimy window and then raced to his room to take up his bow. Throwing the warped wood shutter open, he aimed and loosed his first arrow at a fleeing figure, strangely like the innkeeper. A curse floated back and a thud as he dropped a sack in his hurry to get away. Two more arrows followed the first but the fleeing shape disappeared.

35

Eta, Zeth and Chorky ran down to see what he had dropped. In the sack was a suit of battered but light armour.

"We will have to draw lots for this, and the winner better not take part in any more treasure sharing for a good while!" Eta added.

As soon as they got back to their rooms, they put marked copper pieces in the helmet and drew lots. Chorky won, and tried it on.

"Great! It fits like a glove!" He chuckled, fully aware that the others would not like it to fit him at all.

"I have a feeling that it would fit anyone." Nomaque said thoughtfully.

"Why?" Ikin asked.

"It has a dweamer about it. Like your sword Eta," the Druid added quietly, much to Eta's annoyance, as Eta had kept that a secret for a long time.

"I'll thank you to not mention it again Nomaque." He grumbled, nevertheless with a grudging respect for the Druid.

"Do you want to join us Clem?" Nomaque asked changing the subject, turning to look for the dwarf, but he had already gone back to his room. "Let's sleep what remains of the night in one room, with a guard this time." This they did and Eta stood the first watch, he roused Chorky, who awakened everyone in the dawn.

When they had packed they went down to the main bar room and circled the innkeeper. Eta hung back in order to draw his sword to inspect it, Nomaque saw this and joined him quietly. The sword, which gave a faint glow of wrong, was more fell than it seemed, it had a special scrying power for any evil presence. Eta and Nomaque exchanged glances and joined the others. The innkeeper listened to their stories and sympathised with them for their disturbed sleep.

"We don't get the better people here nowadays, more's the pity. These bands of thieves get bolder every day. I will personally seek out these ruffians and call them to account. I will not allow this to happen in my inn." The innkeeper ranted on and on in this way, until they gave up questioning him and sat down to the stale bread and slightly off meat the innkeeper had found for them.

"Goodness knows what this meat fell off, but it died long ago." said Ikin, deftly dropping it onto the rubbish strewn floor.

"The lady has a very good sense of humour," the man said, "and a good appetite. Would she like some more?"

Ikin stifled a snort of mirth, and said, "No thanks, the beast it came off wants it back!"

A round of chuckling followed, and the innkeeper wandered away, muttering to himself.

"Lets get out of here, there's nothing here, food or otherwise." said Chorky, rising to go up to collect his belongings, the others followed and they all left the Inn.

"The bread was all right," Zeth muttered gathering it up and packing it into his backpack," a bit of a waste to leave it."

Outside they met Clem, "How did you sleep?" he inquired with a wry grin.

"We are obviously in need of a trusty addition to the party. Do you know any light sleeping dwarves in the vicinity?" Chorky asked, looking straight at Clem.

"I know of one, but he would need great assurance that they wouldn't act like young dwarves on their first excursion!"

"Well said!" Nomaque ruefully admitted, "We agree. Can you come with us straight away?"

"I'm packed," Clem added chuckling. "I thought you needed a nursedwarf. This may be important.

Just an odd thing, but do you know an elf, slight build who looks shifty. I know that describes a lot of people but...."

"Why do you ask? We may." Nomaque queried.

"Well last night, I had to come down later on after you had all gone upstairs. There was this fellow deep in some felony with people like those we argued with last night. He kept nodding towards the table you were sitting at. He's gone now."

"Well, well, it seems that we could have Nior to contend with. Nasty little toad."

The party, including Clem on his small cob, set off out of the village still following 'The Old Dwarf Road'. It continued on as a rutty overgrown track, skirting the large area of marshes. They had to dismount and lead the horses, which suited the dwarf as he did not enjoy horseback.

They made good time that day and had gone about fifteen miles before the halt was called at a place where the track went up a rise. This gave a view back along the route they had been following. They led the horses off the track behind some bushes. Three specks appeared in the distance which Eta then described, having the hawk-like eyesight of the elves.

"They look vagabonds mounted on sorry steeds to me. Let's wait and see. I like to know if I'm being followed. It's not Nior anyway."

"You would not know if he was tracking us. Sorin said it was his only real talent, unfortunately." Zeth added ruefully.

Minutes later Eta was proved right as the horsemen ambled past, all having the look of robbers.

"I recognise those beauties," Clem whispered, "they're from the Inn."

The party decided to follow, as it was always sensible to know where that sort of people were, as you could then avoid them. A short way further on the vagabonds stopped, searching the ground for something, one then mounted and came back along the track. Quickly and carefully the following group slid to the deeper cover in amongst the tree boles and bushes. The searcher came past slowly and disappeared around the bend in the track behind them. The remaining two ruffians continued on again making very poor time and the party decided to follow them. After two miles more the quarry turned off the track. This new route seemed to follow the edge of the marshes, rather than turning northwards and westwards into the mountains.

The pursuing party continued along the main track for a short while to the next corner and eased off to the east into the trees, calling a halt. Eta and Zeth returned to the main path to hide their tracks. Most of them were unhappy about the possibility of an ambush, and also whether the path the ruffians had taken was the one they had to take. They chose to follow the ruffians once again, this time with Eta and Zeth acting as scouts on either side. The terrain became more rugged, the two riders were nowhere to be seen amongst the brush, copses, and the turns in the track.

After an hour with no evidence of any travellers at all they dismounted. Two scouting parties went in the most likely directions, Nomaque and Chorky staying out of sight with the horses. Ikin and Clem, the first group back reported no sign of any activity.

Eta and Zeth returned quite a while later but with good news, they had found not only the two they were trailing but more around a campfire including the third ruffian who arrived while they watched. There was no sign of the elf Nior. The hunch that they were robbers was borne out as they had a captive tied up by the fire, who was being badly treated at every opportunity. They were sharing out some treasures, presumably from the luckless victim.

The scouts felt that the gang could be surprised, as the gang was getting ready for a meal and maybe some lethal sport with their victim, so hopefully not as vigilant. Following Eta's whispered directions they arrived at a hill nearby from which they could plan the attack and leave the horses.

As they had surmised there were no lookouts, and the gang felt safe. Nomaque had decided to use his skills to send any creatures into a frenzy within the area of his spell. These creatures would rush into the middle crawling over and biting the unsuspecting riffraff, who were more intent on their food and baiting the lone captive.

He started to chant in a very low tone and focussed a few hand movements firstly on his comrades so that they would be safe he thought.

They all approached silently under the cover of the hubbub at the fire and Nomaque continued to prepare. He knelt on the ground just on the edge of the clearing hidden by a lone bush to feel the forces there and focus them to his will. He probed for oak trees nearby, the steady strength from these trees helping him, since the oak was his symbol and a divinity of his Druidic Order. The lines of force flowed from him into the ground around the raiders and then he raised his hands making an encircling movement. There was stirring on the ground in and around the raiders as small shapes started scurrying about, trying to climb up and bite anything. He started on the outside of the circle he drew in his mind around the seething mass and moved inwards. The attacking party crept in the wake of this small but intense, writhing avance party.

40

One by one the raiders leapt up and tried to remove this creeping and biting tide, only to be deftly knocked out from the shadows. Three were tied up before the other three realised they were under attack, they then tried to escape the five closing in on them, but were stopped by the ring of swords and staff. They became desperate and charged their attackers, having to fight both large and small foes alike. Two of the remainder were unlucky, as they had unwisely left their weapons stacked away from the fire. The ones who would not yield were knocked out and tied, but the leader fought Chorky and Zeth until he collapsed dying of his wounds.

Nomaque sang the release incantation and the small creatures dropped to the ground, melting away to their burrows. This was to the great relief of the helpless captive who was well bitten. Quickly Nomaque collected his medicine bag and treated the bites on everyone, even himself.

"You will have to find another way next time Nomaque as we all felt that one personally", said Ikin grimly retrieving several wood ants from inside her leather armour after releasing the captive.

The captive stretched and massaged his arms to get the circulation going again, his eyes cautiously taking in his rescuers. He was tall and well built in a lithe powerful way, clad in a drab grey-green tunic, now somewhat ripped and bloodied in places. The raiders had been quite brutal and he was considerably bruised and cut, but not seriously and Nomaque could sooth most of these as well as the insect bites. He smiled and they knew that they could find an ally in those brown eyes.

"Thank you," he said. "My name is Tasherlon Tendralom and I am a woodsman. The rogues who captured me are only a small part of a larger band under a leader called Fredrika, who terrorise this area especially the dwarf road. He is either expected in

41

the morning, or they were to take me to the main camp in the morning. I don't know which, they hadn't told me that part.

They are looking for a giant, but here is the odd part, they insist it is able to change its shape. I know of the fable where the djinn tells you where the treasure is and can grant you wishes. Well they think this giant can do just that. Apparently one of these things has been seen near here and they are going crazy looking for it. Worst part was they thought I knew where this giant is and of course I don't." As he collected all his weapons and belongings he could find from the captives, he carried on talking, "The path to the main camp I know, it is the one through here. There is only one way through this area and this is it. You must decide whether to chance discovery here, or move tonight. Their camp is possibly in your way in any case."

"In that case I must rest," Nomaque added wearily, "as the enchantment has drained me very quickly. I shall need an hour or two to by myself to prepare and nap before I can use any spell again." He grimaced and added as they looked anxiously at one another, "but perhaps not that incantation again."

"We could move a short way to the side of the trail and rest a while, so long as the captives don't escape. But do we know that we have all of the ones at this camp?" Chorky asked.

"We didn't see any more when we were scouting but that doesn't mean that there weren't any." Eta added.

"There is one member missing, an elf, shifty looking." Tasherlon put in.

"Could be Nior I expect, I've been wondering when he would turn up. I wouldn't want to raid the bigger camp without Nomaque giving backup anyway." Ikin commented and made her way off into the brush on the denser side of the trail towards the low hill where they had hidden their horses. The rest followed her, taking their captives and hiding their tracks as well as they could.

"This won't fool Nior," Ikin added what the others were thinking, "it's the one thing he was good at, that and arguing, so Sorin told us." In the event they camped for the night about a half-mile to the north of the trail and used the captives to bury the dead. No one saw a dark shape flying away silently in the gloom. With the dawn they continued on, leaving the live raiders still alive but tied securely with dwarf and elf knots.

Topping a rise they saw the smoke from a sizeable fire, right on the line of the trail they were following.

Eta scouting ahead waved frantically to stop and come cautiously. They crept forwards and spotted a foot protruding from under a bush. It had elvish shoes on. Chorky parted the leafy branches and gave a gasp of surprise.

"Who is it," whispered Zeth suddenly anxious, wondering as to the fate of Maltex, Sorin and Hons. Ikin was next to look, easing past the seeming perplexed Chorky.

"I don't know why you are so surprised, the little toad must have had a good few enemies." Then she half turned to the others, "Nobody weep, it is or was our former friend Nior."

"It's why now and who that I worry about, Ikin," Chorky mused. "Nomaque, can you find out how?"

The Druid took his and Ikin's place and carefully searched the body and stood back perplexed. A moment later he bent and reexamined Nior's neck. He stood up and turned to face the rest.

"At first I could not find how he died, but it was very painful, his muscles are all clenched tight in terrible agony." He shuddered. "Then I looked at his

43

neck, a sizeable sting of some sort got him. Not an insect, too large, and..." He bent once more "and there are claw marks on the back of his head. Curious I have never seen the like." He knelt down and sniffed the sting mark, Nomaque's face drained of colour as he looked up. "Ichor! Dragon Ichor! Not very strong here, but it's a smell once experienced you never forget. We are in peril, both all around us and in front of us, we must be exceedingly careful from now on. You would not hear this predator, the first anyone would know would be the pain. This is no longer an adventure trip to find treasure. This puts a good slice of doubt on our survival too! We must have disturbed the creature, the body is still warm."

It was a subdued group that continued quietly towards the smoke in the valley.

Chorky looked about him suddenly, as he was sure he heard a 'voice' whispering in his ear, but he could see no owner to it near. The only living thing was a gnarled old tree with a few sparse branches here and there.

'Beware friends, they guard well. They in bush on this side. In tree to the other side,' the 'voice' said.

Chorky not quite believing the message but having no option, called a whispered halt.

He held a quiet conference, "I know you will not believe me but there is a hidden raider in that bush on the left and another in that tree on the right. We will have to surprise them if possible, or at least get to them before they give the alarm."

"Eta and myself could do that easily." Tasherlon suggested. "We could do with a bit of back up though, Zeth if you could cover Eta, and perhaps Chorky would do the same for me."

"Right, let's get on with it." Chorky agreed. The others nodded and stole away to circle the quarry in the bush.

'One in tree, watch road,' the 'voice' said in his mind. The voice had a peculiar quick quality, not elvish or human at all, fast yet understandable.

The 'voice' continued to keep Chorky informed of every move of their target. They were in the tree's shadow before the figure knew, and by then it was far too late, as his mouth opened to call, Tasherlon's arrow caught him in the throat.

"That was something I am not proud of, I would far rather fight in the open, instead of stealing around. Nevertheless very effective." Tasherlon sighed.

"No choice." Chorky consoled him as they crept back.

Eta had similarly dispatched the other guard, so the way was clear to creep forward. The sight, which met their eyes, was totally unexpected. Ten raiders were leading a heavily bound large giant at least twelve feet tall, into the clearing. Off to the left side a lone shaman was waiving a wand continuously at it, he was succeeding and the giant went down on one gnarled knee. As they ran around they bound its legs; so eventually it toppled over onto the ground near the roaring fire. It had numerous arrows sticking out of its body, some of them burning. Its arms and hands were writhing in agony although no sound escaped those tortured lips. Its old-seeming body was covered in skin, which was altering as they looked at it, from one moment to another its skin was changing. One moment it was rocky: the next, mossy, or twiggy.

"Oh my soul! The despoilers! That's a ramphorm as many call them. They are gentle giant-kind, I am no longer able to stand aside, the centre of my faith, my arbresoul is involved. *Oh Ash! Oh OAK! Come to my aid!*" Nomaque cried out as he sank to prepare himself for a supreme effort. "You may have heard of them in your elvish lore, Eta." Eta nodded as he and the others readied themselves for the battle to

45

come, the packs were hidden quickly and what little armour they owned was donned with haste. The only well armoured one was Chorky, who looked distinctly knightly. When Nomaque nodded his head they moved forward in two flanking waves on either side of him, a pincer movement, to charge for the best advantage. They were outnumbered two to one but Nomaque's obvious pain had fired them with determination to rescue this rare strange creature.

Nomaque sat with unwavering arms outstretched towards the malignant violence and let the force flow. The waves of earthly force could almost be seen leaving his fingers and leaping into the ground, which twitched and moved, quickly showing shoots curling up along the line to the target. This time the growth was strong and fierce, much faster than before, showing the agitation of the Druid. The raiders were caught completely by surprise as most of them had their weapons stacked by the fire, mostly swords and bows. Perplexed at being trapped by the feet, their cries became panic as the tendrils rose higher, gripping and strangling. On the far side the shaman came out of his trance and immediately started preparing a spell, but his feet became entangled, disturbing the flow of energy, the spell failing. Ikin watched helpless, unable to stop him starting again. Suddenly a small flying shape stooped on him and his figure crumpled to the ground. The shape scuffled away, seemingly unaffected by the growing vegetation. Only Ikin saw the event, and as it was over before she could blink twice.

The ones clear of the circle of growth were at first confused, but quickly caught up swords and axes and ran to the struggling vegetation. The rescuers then charged them. Three of the defenders fell in as many seconds leaving the armoured chief and one other. As Chorky was the only other person with full protection he leaped forward to try and contain the leader.

The remaining free defender turned and ran, Ikin seeing the fleeing figure, threw her axe. The figure collapsed with a finality that usually indicates death. Releasing her axe-blade she joined the rest anxiously watching Chorky's battle.

Chorky was outmatched and on the defensive. The leader was quick and deadly, intent on finishing Chorky off as soon as he could. At first Chorky was surprised that he chose to fight on against those odds, but Chorky soon realised that this was the leader Frederika. He thought he could kill them all. After a particularly close flurry of cuts the leader wounded the half-elf in the thigh, just on the joint. This worried Chorky as he thought his magic armour would protect him. Then the truth hit him, Frederica's sword must be special too. Concentrating on Chorky's wounded leg, Fredrika sliced into that leg again on the knee joint this time. Chorky nearly fell and opened his guard to his enemy. With a smile Fredrika swung to decapitate him when Clem stepped in and deflected the blow. Clem continued on from his parry to clout the leader of the ruffians a solid blow in the stomach with the haft of his axe. Following up his advantage the dwarf sliced open the human's shoulder joint with the axe-blade. Fredrika dropped his weapon on the grass and reeled back to be quickly pinioned by the others. Of the five who were trapped in the mat of vegetation, only one was still alive, and not surprisingly kneeled for mercy when he was released.

Nomaque freed the ramphorm, but it was groggy from some magic or poison and barely able to stand. Nomaque weak as he was, tried vainly to analyse its problem, but he had to give up apart from easing the burning flesh. Chorky's wounds were severe and dangerous out in the wilderness, but Zeth said he had some healing salves, which he applied with a prayer or two. The treatment seemed to ease Chorky's wounds, much to the half-elf's pleased surprise. The pain had gone and he could walk with a slight limp.

The question was what to do with the prisoners. They were loath to kill them, especially the lesser of the two, but Tasherlon reminded them that if the situation had been reversed Fredrika would have killed them.

They elected to leave the leader stripped of his weapons and tied on a long thong to the tree. The other one they released about a mile further back along the trail towards the main track when they were retracing their steps to collect their horses. Eta dropped to one side and followed the freed man just to see which direction he went. The ruffian watched the group for a short while and then went off towards where they had left the leader. Eta followed but lost a little time and arrived at the tree to see a figure departing limping heavily. Beneath the tree was the ruffian stripped and dead. Fredrika had killed him. Eta decided to follow. This was not difficult as the leader was bleeding badly. A mile later the elf found Fredrika dead of his wounds. Eta sighed and returned to the others who were tidying up and burying the dead.

They followed a faint trail northwards through the scrubland. This was the direction that the voice had guided Chorky to take. The voice was still there, sometimes faint, as though from a distance away. Chorky decided to tell the others about it whispering away in his head, but they had no more idea than he did about its owner.

The ramphorm had wandered away still a bit dazed, and as they felt it could now take good care of itself, they let it go. It had left the clearing before them so they did not see where it went. There was little they could do for it, even Nomaque offered no suggestions apart from praying to the oak to watch over the giant creature.

There had been a lot of plunder in the hoard from the raiders and so that night they decided to bury it midway between two tall marked trees. Also they had better weapons, armour, bows and a goodly supply of arrows. By popular decision Frederica's sword was given to Tasherlon who smiled.

"I have seen some terrible things done with this beautiful weapon, I shall now try to even the score somewhat. One good stroke for one fell one. I shall name it 'Shrivener'"

Ikin took a tarnished ring with a jewelled star emblem and some very battered shoes of a curious shape made mostly of wood, painted with curious designs and ornamental fabric curved uppers.

"Those become you Ikin!" They teased. "Battered and worn just like you."

"I know they look worn out but there is good wood in there, a bit like some sandals I used to wear at home." She said cleaning them off with a spare rag. "Lookey here, hidden in the heel there's a phial of something smelly. Any offers for this rare potion of green stuff?"

"Careful with that, as you well know, potions of any sort are dodgy. Is there any label or runes on it?" Nomaque said as he strode over to her.

"Keep your hair on, Nom old bean. I'll let you take charge, never fear. I have no hidden desire to turn into anything nasty, or have muscles as big as pans. Here you are, one ancient container with what looks like green paste in. No labels though, shame, you'll have to taste it. Best of luck for the future!" Ikin said as she skipped away in mock terror.

"Now there you're wrong, clever, there is a rune or two on the side, scratched by a jewel. Now let me think, the first means 'bad or wrong', and the second 'plants or vegetation'. So it is either rot plants or

49

kill plants. Not a lot of use to us, but you never know, I'll keep it anyway." Nomaque mused tucking it into his pack.

"Just what an aspiring Druid needs to protect him from carnivorous plants addicted to young druids!" Ikin put in.

They followed the path, which swung north through a pass between two high mountains. When they came out on the other side the valley turned to the east. In front of them was a forest, and behind it the towers of a ruined city. Rank upon rank of mountains climbed away straight ahead to the north behind the ruins. The path led towards the forest, about a mile away. This they covered quickly since the afternoon was wearing away and a camp had to be chosen. The trail split at the edge of the trees, one way went around to the west to the ruins, the other into the gloom of the trees.

The 'voice' whispered *'Not towards the towers, they deadly, you go through the trees.'* Chorky indicated the forested path to the others with some doubt, as the way was overgrown and unused looking. Still they followed it slowly, keeping every sense alert, and their hands not far from their swords or axes. Their eyes soon adjusted to the gloom and they found the path easier to follow. About a mile twisting between the gnarled creeper-festooned tree boles and they came to the light again. A partly forested valley stretched off to the east, the sides formed by precipitous cliffs over one hundred feet in height.

The 'voice' seemed closer now and directed them to the edge. Very cautiously Chorky parted the saplings on the brink, and saw a twisting track down into the trees below, starting twenty or so feet to his right. He guided the others to the spot with a warning of how wide it was. The horses brushed the cliff on one side, with its narrowness, barely two feet wide in places. The descent was made more treacherous by a small waterfall, which tumbled its way across the path. The sun was going down by the time they had negotiated the drop. The first clearing they came to had a stream flowing to the side, ideal for their campsite as long as it was secure. There was no comment from Chorky's 'voice' so the party stopped there.

As they dismounted, there was a movement in the trees and a tall figure covered in mossy and twiggy skin came out from the trees and waved.

"It's the ramphorm giant we rescued." Nomaque stated.

"Is it?" Zeth asked, "It could be another different one."

"True but another one would not welcome us." Nomaque replied in a tone that cut off all further doubt. "Anyway I 'feel' he is the same one, don't you?" The rest of the group looked at each other with questioning glances, they had saved the giant after all.

Nomaque said. "As far as I know these creatures are benign, so we could go with him without danger. The ancient books of Druid lore however tell us that, in their own homes, the ramphorm have ancient and strange powers, so we must go warily."

Cautiously they followed leading their horses. The tall lumpy figure led them towards the cliffs along a winding path, which seemed to open up as they went, oddly closing behind them. Near the side of the valley they stopped in a clearing and the figure indicated they should leave the horses there, which they did. They unloaded their packs and followed him as he started off into the trees. He continued along a path which wove its way through close thickets, the thin early evening light penetrating less and less. Clem apprehensively looked back and saw the trees had closed the path in behind them again.

51

A gap appeared in front of them as they moved forward, growing bigger until they could see they were about to enter a big clearing close to the valley walls. The ramphorm had stopped and was standing in front of them. In the cliff cavernous openings could be seen, one leading to what might be a stair up to levels above. The curving wall in some places formed a bench-like seat, where the ramphorm gestured for them to sit.

The ramphorm waited for them, and when they were seated, he spoke slowly in a deep rumbling voice, like a creaky clearing of his throat.

"Welcome to my home. I feel that apologies are in order as I did not thank you. My rescue was heroic and I am grateful. Druid, after your spells, I feel young again . Please accept the hospitality of my humble abode for the night. It is safe here. Make yourselves comfortable. I do not have any sustenance for you unless you can eat the mushrooms in the cavern. Water I have in plenty," he said and pointed to a small waterfall cascading over the cliff nearby.

His words were very drawn out and slow, spoken with the deep creaking voice, quite deliberate and understandable. He went out into another chamber for a while and the group waited. Some ten minutes later he reappeared, they were asleep where they sat.

The ramphorm smiled a bent smile, went over to them, and quietly looked at each one in turn as they slumbered. Seeming satisfied, he then moved out into an adjoining chamber, which was open to the sky with short grass and small fragrant star shaped flowers of *Lethelorel* growing in a perfect sward. He stopped still and became a tall pillar of stone as he stood watching his guests through the archway, as though he was shielding them.

---0---

Ikin opened her eyes from a refreshing drea-mless sleep and remembered the situation immedi-ately. The ramphorm bustled around his home. He inspected a minute crack, here and there tested the feel of the walls. The ceiling and walls were not dark, they had a translucent quality, especially in the mid-dle. Light filtered in through a very thin section of rock skin, and although dim, there was more than enough light to see by. The others awoke soon after her and he came over.

"I trust you slept well, Come into my garden and enjoy the air. I think it about time I introduced myself my name Is Ayay Ash Valli Elen. The place we live in is part of us. You may call me Ayay, and of course this is Elen Valley all around us."

He led them through the arch into the open grassy area. The air had a sharp vitality, giving them a strange refreshing feeling. Chorky described it lat-er. "The pain of my wounds just disappeared and the air made me want to leap around. The soles of my feet seemed to barely touch the ground. **"A breath for living and doing."**

The ramphorm wanted to know why they journeyed north, and so Eta told him that they sought for evidence of the elves former home.

"It is all around you and below you, there are the remains of the doomed city of the elves on the rim above us." he gestured up to the top of the nearby cliffs, where ancient walls and towers crumbled. He went on, **"There is little left to see on the surface. The nearest entr-ance is just down the valley at the stones. Light the metal disc, that will let you in. The horses will be safe in the valley, bury your spare equipment in the meadow where the horses are. From there you will find a path**

53

going east, follow it to the grass, the four stones of the elves are further down the valley." He stood for a moment gazing into the distance as if he was seeing the far future. He added sadly, "**Goodbye. I do not think we will meet again. But beware, dark are the clouds over the mountains.**" After giving them that grim warning, he strode off into the forest, a way through opening up for him.

---0---

Once again left on their own they followed the instructions, leaving the spare equipment and horses in the glade. After several miles of open forest they emerged into open grassland. Looking eastward they could just make out the tops of two stones in a little hollow to the north of the stream, even Eta's sight failed to see any more. They decided to check them anyway as there were no others in sight.

The two stones were massive, standing east-west, thirty feet apart. Making a triangle with them was a third stone, which was flat, sticking up from the turf only a foot or so, except for the central portion. The middle formed a rough curved wall of stone with a hole in the centre of it, over three feet in diameter. It took them another hour to find the fourth stone, which was almost buried, only a tiny bit showed midway between the two taller stones. They cleared the grass to find a metal disc six inches across let into the stone, with a tiny hole in the centre.

Clem got out his torch, lit it and held it over the hole to no effect. They were still puzzling two hours later when the sun came out and then when a mirror was used, things started to happen.

Chorky was at that moment standing on the third flatter curiously shaped stone when it started rolling ponderously over, pivoting about two of its sides, tipping off the half-elf. The hole in the middle of the wall became a way down into the ground, butting up to a flight of worn stairs. A cold dank odour rose out of the hole, very uninviting compared to the sunshine above. Now the moment to descend had come they hesitated a second, the bright sunlight seemed so much better than this dark path.

Tasherlon stepped up to the hole and looked in, an odd expression spread across his face. "Listen to me," he said. "There it is! Doesn't look much does it? I have a bad feeling about it!" With a pause Tasherlon continued, "I hate holes in the ground! You go ahead and I will stay up here for a few days and explore around the valley. If you all come out in that time you'll find me here. One of the horses is mine, and a portion of the funds, I'll take those if I don't see you. Good luck, underground isn't for me, I'm sorry I think my death lies in there… See you."

Chapter Four

The Places where dark things lie.

*W*ith that speech, the longest that taciturn Tasherlon had given them, he strode off, leaving the rest speechless, but not for long.

"There's gratitude for you," Eta reflected. "I thought he was coming with us."

"I suppose we never did ask him, did we?" Ikin observed. "We just expected him to share in finding out about the elves. Pity, I think he is a doughty fighter, even if an open air one. I hope we see him again…" She paused. "Right, let's go." With that she turned and descended down the steps into the darkness, her newly lit torch flickering in the draught.

The tunnel kept going down for a few yards then opened out into a cave, the steps descending the thirty feet length of the right-hand wall, until they disappeared into the far wall. On the left the cavern floor was some way below them, as the steps were high up the wall. There was no obvious way down to the cave floor.

As Ikin went down the others followed, the last, Chorky, stopped and wondered how the slab closed. That was until he held the torch so it lit up the back of the stone. The great mass began to pivot, slowly at first and then with a whoosh swung back to close hard against its seating.

"I think we may have to find another way out folks!" he said his words echoing around the cave. Meanwhile the others had gone on down to the far side of the cavern where the steps went into the wall.

From the end of the steps Nomaque's voice floated back as he scraped away at the wall, looking for a way on through into the old elvish caverns that the ramphorm giant referred to.

"There must be something like the other hole here but it's all covered in mould. Here it is, a bit clogged up though, let's see if the light will work. Yess. It's moving a little away from me. Several of us will have to push if we are to make a big enough gap."

Eta, Ikin, Clem joined him and pushed hard, the portal juddered and slid open with a grinding jar. They eased quietly and cautiously into a large rectangular cavern.

"Careful, don't push!" breathed Nomaque who had seen that the floor on the other side of the door was only a ledge on the edge of a wide pool. The portal entered in the corner of a large cavern, the ledge Nomaque spotted finished at the corner, not continuing around the corner to the left. The ledge in front of them was just wide enough to stand on, and looking right, the Druid could follow it eighty feet along the wall to the corner but he had to keep close in to the wall. The ledge at the far corner disappeared through an archway into a tunnel. The cavern was about eighty feet long by about fifty feet wide. Across the pool in front of them a series of stepping-stones led to the far left corner, where a pile of stone rubble sloped into the water. The stones and the surrounding wall were coloured an orange hue, but the top of the pile was blackened, just at the join with the crumbling roof. The rubble extended for more than halfway along the far wall.

Eta, before anyone could stop him, ran lightly across the stones to the jumbled rock and climbed up the rubble to the wall.

"I can see the tops of the old arches under the rubble here near the corner and there's another some way along the wall. This has been scorched, on top here, and the arch too, great heat. If I listen carefully I can hear a distinct rumbling, shall I call out?" He paused to take in a breath.

"NO! For all the gods sake NO!" Clem whispered heavily, "that could be something very large and very nasty. Its best left alone until there is no other option. We have another choice, the tunnel on the right. Lets go, and careful, I don't even trust the pool. I hope you haven't woken that rumble up!"

"All right, I'll come back across." Eta added.

"We won't be going far." The disembodied voice of Ikin came back out hollowly from the tunnel entrance. "The tunnel on our side's slipped downwards by the look of it." As the others came up to her they saw that the stonework of the tunnel ahead had indeed been wrenched upwards some eight feet by an earthquake, leaving only a narrow gap near the roof to worm through.

Chorky as the tallest of the party tried first but couldn't quite get through without help from the other side. He squirmed out again. Ikin clambered on to his shoulders and with a squeeze was through. Clem followed but he, being wider, found it only possible by taking off his clothes down to his jerkin, even then it was touch and go. With two on the upper side the rest made it through, although they too had to divest to do it, all excepting Nomaque. He was carrying no protective padding or armour, so he could climb through without help.

On the upper side the passage stretched away for some seventy feet to a dimly seen stair going up. After they had re-armed themselves, they approached the steps only to find the main passage went round to the left just before the foot of the stair. A sound of splashing came from the left. Intrigued they followed the sound around a right turn to a second bend, with an opening on the left side at the bend into a cavern with a pedestal fountain in the centre of the floor. The water jetted up into the high vaulted roof and back into the round pedestal pool encircling it, about eight feet across, the water looked murky and thick in the torchlight.

"Oh good, something to drink, my throat's dry as troll leather." Zeth had felt a sudden thirst and made his way towards the pool.

"Ugh! Don't touch that stuff, you'll catch something nasty." Nomaque said urgently.

"You're too squeamish," Zeth replied and ignoring the warning, went to scoop some to drink. Just as he stooped, a grey tentacle slid around his shoulders and neck from out of the pool. With a cry of loathing and revulsion, he struggled desperately, coughing at the smell as the slimy beast added another arm to the one already around him.

"Hold still and I'll hack it to bits," shouted Chorky running over to his aid. Chorky's sword bounced off the scaly skin under the filth. "I can't touch it, it's too tough!" He cried out desperately as he changed his tactics and jabbed down into the pool, with little success.

In the melee Zeth was inched closer to the water, even though the others by then had hold of him and were pulling against the creature.

Nomaque from the first felt the wrongness, and as soon as Zeth cried out, he started preparing his skills to help. Swaying with the effort of summoning his powers, the white form of Nomaque approached the poolside in sharp contrast to the struggling mass of bodies and tentacles on the other side of the pool. Whispering an incantation, which seemed to hang in the air, he sprinkled a handful of herbs over the thrashing water surface. The liquid seemed to take on a new life of its own, and rose up over the brim of the fountain, a grey tide pouring over to splash on the floor. Bubbles of noxious gas burst

59

all over its surface, followed by a great bladder, fetid and wobbling. Over-extended, it burst, showering all with grey water and pieces of stinking bladder.

The surface returned to level, and Zeth jerked back away from the pool as the tentacles disappeared. Instead of a fountain there was now only a pool of still water, with a centre stone boss standing up a few feet above it.

"What a repulsive thing," Zeth said, but he could not stop his body shivering with reaction to this narrow escape.

"Lets be a little more careful from now on, it seems a few beasties live here, and they feed on the unwary traveller." Nomaque chided as he wearily leaned on the wall. "I wonder what unwary traveller do you think?"

"Surely there aren't many of those in an inaccessible place like this, unless it is occupied. We haven't been all that quiet, have we?" Clem reminded them as he led the way out and to the right. Surprisingly the sound of water was even stronger as they rejoined the tunnel, which went straight ahead of them.

"Just ahead there are some openings on both sides." Ikin called quietly as she had scouted further on, "They're guard positions about three foot deep and there's something in them too. There is a worm-eaten skeleton in each opening by the look of it." As she approached and looked at the one on the left, she continued, "Look the one here on the left has an axe in its head."

As she checked left she failed to notice the skeleton in the right-hand niche jerkily come to life. It moved out behind her and swung a rusty sword to cleave her head. Her cap and the rusty sword saved her before anyone else could intervene. The sword broke in two over the crown of the little helmet, the force beating her down to her knees.

Mindlessly the bone figure continued to hit her helmet, and it was all Ikin could do to keep kneeling upright.

"Bloody, stupid, thing, I, can't, get, up," she gasped in between blows on her helmet.

Chorky raced up and hit the skull into the distance with the flat of his sword, but this did not stop the arm, which continued to berate poor Ikin. His second blow was hopefully more final, the arm, sword shard and the shoulder blade joined the skull somewhere along the passage.

The left arm fought on, joined by the left foot. Then there was a slithering sound as the skull and the other bits slowly returned sliding back along the floor.

"This ghoulish thing is enchanted!" Chorky said exasperated, stating the obvious, hitting the remaining arm to join its mate now halfway back.

"Allow me," said Zeth coming up to the frustrated fighter. "I will attempt to turn the beastie, so move back." He loosed the top loop of his jerkin and slid out a large beaded necklace of blue stones. Holding them in his hands he started praying. The bones immediately slowed, but it took a moment or two of concentrated effort by the novice cleric to finally quieten them down. Zeth beamed.

"That's my first turning of an undead!" he cooed proudly. The others came up quickly firstly to see how Ikin was, and finding her still more or less all right, slapped Zeth on the back.

"Well sorted Zeth, we couldn't have Chorky banging bits of the bones around for ever, could we?" Clem chuckled, relieved that there was no damage.

"That was a nasty setup, and I fell for it." she said kicking the other skeleton, which collapsed in a heap of bones on the floor. The skull, with the axe embedded in it, fell open to let a small remnant of parchment flutter to the floor. She bent down and her head throbbed painfully. She picked the scrap up, reeling a bit as she hadn't recovered fully from the punishment she had received.

In the flickering torchlight, Chorky caught a glimpse of a reflection in one of the recesses. He bent down and rummaged about a bit.

"I saw something in the rubbish, at the back here, and lookee here! Who's a clever Chorky then?" He straightened and turning, held up a battered helmet with two horns sticking out of the sides.

There was a gasp and chuckle from Clem.

"There's only this dent and it's wearable," Chorky went on. "These are only a bit loose," he said as he found the horns turned in their sockets. First a little, then with a squeal one horn turned right round, to point downwards. This was too much for Clem, at the point where the horn jerked around he doubled up with a snort, "You'll slay me!" He gasped.

"Don't mock me! There's more to this than I first thought." Chorky replied a little niggled at the dwarf's mirth.

"Yes. The helmet'll fall apart!" Clem wheezed, tears running down his cheeks. Chorky gave the horn a pull as if to prove Clem wrong and it came out in his hand. With a gasp Clem sank to his knees, shaking and groaning.

"You ought to be on the stage! Dwarves would come across the land to see that act."

Chorky went red in the face and walked away even more annoyed, and this made the dwarf roll about on the floor. The halfelf found the ridicule too much to take, and fiddled with the broken horn. What happened next was difficult to believe, it seemed that the rock surrounding them shifted a little, a judder went through everything. There was an odd quiver through Chorky's hands and the horn suddenly lengthened inexplicably three feet, reforming into a vicious looking military pick. Instantly mollified, he

62

turned back to the group. Clem instantly became serious and sat up quickly, as he did he yelled.

"Watch out! Take care Chorky!" Leaping up, he almost ran to the halfelf, wiping the tears from his eyes with the back of his hand.

"Look at this then," Chorky crowed, "I was right, the horn's turned into this fighting pick! *And* it feels light and deadly." He raised it for the others to look at.

"Now that's more like it!" Clem said recovering, reaching forward to take the weapon cautiously in his hand, testing its balance.

"Beautiful combination of elf and dwarf work that," he twiddled the tip which turned, the length shortening as he did so to change into the horn again.

"Marvellous," he said looking up at Chorky. "I humbly ask your forgiveness, you put me to shame. I was wrong to make fun of you, but it was so funny. Your judgement is very sharp, I would have totally ignored it in all that rubbish." He handed the horn back and took the helmet in his eager hands. "I have never handled one of these before, although I have heard about them. You have a rare treasure there, and I think you have only found one of the helmet's many uses. They usually do all sorts of things, depending on the power of the maker. There, look at the innocent seeming rivets on the rim and up the centre, some are press buttons to activate different things. Watch out for surprises, as there are usually a few nasty features too. Try it out in the open first and not on your head, as I think it is or could be something big. One blew a dwarf out through a window once, and another, I heard tell, sent a spike down through another one's head." The dwarf explained.

"I'll do just that, try it out in a bigger place perhaps." Chorky said, gingerly putting the horn into its hole and pushing carefully. A loud click was heard,

63

and it couldn't be moved. "Yes that's it for now." he said half to himself. It was very noticeable that he was a lot more cautious in handling it though.

The others were examining the scraps of burnt parchment, now all that remained of that piece Ikin found in the skull. Ikin, being a bit wobbly after her melee, had managed to singe the precious object in her torch flame.

"Sorry!" she said, annoyed that she had been so stupid. There was just enough writing left to indicate the existence of two secret stairs to caves above going from the alcoves occupied by the skeletons. They decided to ignore them and carry on for the time being along the passage.

A short distance further on the tunnel had a cross way then a split passage, the left one sloping steeply down, a rank odour coming from it. Watery gurgling and splashing sounds came from the right branch. Intrigued, they went right, a short way along the tunnel split again. Zeth, leading and not looking where he put his feet, fell into a pit in the middle of the junction. To his great fortune the swords which were originally upright in a rack at the bottom had long before fallen over, the rack was only pieces of rust, so he only had a bruise or two for his carelessness.

The others pulled him out, and they continued, turning left to follow the way to the water, which sounded through an archway just ahead. This time they went carefully and avoided falling down the five-foot drop in the entrance and across a section of the floor. It was as if a knife had sliced through the rock and the pieces had slipped. In the dim light they could just make out in the lower part of the cavern, two low waterfalls feeding three pools, the streams joining together and leaving the cave by another fall to the left. The roof, high and arched, was dark with many crevices. The party carefully climbed down to the lower floor and peered into the nearest pool.

"Well, who is going to have a look then?" Ikin asked, being the only one who couldn't reasonably be asked. They were reluctant, as this meant taking off their weapons, but as someone was needed to go on guard, Zeth finally got in and began to feel about in the sediment at the bottom of the streams. This only produced a leg bone not quite stripped clean. The next thing anyone knew was Zeth yelling and beating the air with the bone.

"Watch out everyone, there are some big biting things after me. Ouch! you little …, get off!" He howled, beset by the creatures, looking like very large flies they were settling on him and the bone. The ones on him were making a meal of it by the noise he was making.

Soon all the party were swatting the pests with what they could get hold of. Poor Zeth had only the bone, which they were perhaps more interested in. He did the only thing he could do, he dived for the nearest pool, drowning several of his attackers in the process.

Eventually the flies were killed or driven off, and the party counted heads, and found Zeth was missing. They rushed over to where he dived in and quickly looked in the pools almost fearing to look in case he was floating there, but there was no sign of the half-elf. They called his name, the sound echoing on the water. Then faintly they heard an answer from the exit tunnel.

"I've found a cave along the tunnel, but I'm coming back now." There was some splashing, which slowly came nearer, eventually he emerged from the tunnel on the right.

"Look here, I've found some amazing rope, see the weave, it's been in there god knows how long and yet it's still soft and pliable. Oh, and I found this

65

funny-looking object," he waved a curious case in the air. "Its purpose I cannot even guess, it was worth it to find the rope. There is a ledge along this side of the tunnel, I hardly needed to get wet." Zeth triumphantly handled the rope. Uninterestedly he gave Ikin the case, a hand-span round, with a flat side like a half gourd. Ikin deftly opened it.

"Careful...too late! You'll regret your haste one day, Ikin," Nomaque said, he was a bit peeved that he had arrived second, yet again. Nevertheless the object was spectacular. It was a complicated set of convex mirrors with many facets, made of finely polished white metal having a flat back with a small hook in the centre. When Ikin looked in, she felt she was being drawn in. Nomaque, noticing her odd behaviour, pulled it away sharply as her face went blank. Her knees gave way as he broke her eye contact. Swaying into Nomaque's steadying arm, Ikin raised her head blearily.

"Grief, is it dangerous in there?" she said faintly, in a questioning tone, her face showing how lost she was, the object had somehow drawn her mind into it.

"Yes Ikin, very perilous indeed!" Nomaque said, "I will keep this until you are yourself again." He carefully put the case back on, and tucked it away in his rucksack.

Having got in the mood Zeth was groping about with a vengeance, in first one pool and then the others. He had mixed success with several large gems along with the skeletal remains of various former owners, when his luck turned,

"This is better, it's about as big as that mirror thing but flatter," he said holding up a muddy flat object. He dipped it a few times and a large jewelled surface was revealed by a burst of coloured faceted light.

It was a gem studded six-rayed star, a large hand-span across, built up of two three-rayed stars, one behind the other. The front star was picked out by three rows of diamonds out from the middle, in the centre was an enormous single pale red ruby. The second star was arranged so that the lobes rested midway between the front ones and on each of the points a large solitaire diamond twinkled. Halfway along each lobe a rectangular, very pale blue sapphire rested, this rear star was constructed of a light silvery metal the same as the front one. The stones were arranged in the setting so as to leave the jewels raised above the surface, the gems and metal gleamed and sparkled in the torchlight. On the back there was a raised pattern of short pegs corresponding to the gems on the front.

"Very beautiful, we must draw lots for it when we have the time." Chorky said. "Shall we have a rest and a bite to eat here, seeing as now the flies have gone." With that reminder everyone suddenly felt hungry, and so they climbed up to the upper part of the cave and sat eating in the corner, resting their backs on the wall.

Ikin mused, "that jewel's like the little star shape on that ring I picked up from the raider's stash." They lapsed into the silence of their own thoughts.

Nomaque looked up. It was difficult to guess the reason why, some sense of presence perhaps. He had been dozing after his usual mental Druidic exercises, when he felt a touch of another mind. The white cowled figure stood by the exit near to them, seemingly not a threatening shape, and not evil. The Druid gently touched the sleepy shape next to him, Chorky, who, when he had recovered enough, did the same for Clem. Ten minutes later the shape had still not moved and by then all of them were awake.

67

"I bid thee welcome," the hooded shape whispered. "Why dost thou journey in these halls of forgotten glories?"

Surprising himself a little, Nomaque replied, "We, kind monk, seek those forgotten glories."

"Looking for Elvish remains, treasure or people, I venture to ask?" Quietly the voice continued, seeming to scan each in turn.

When his gaze reached Eta he spoke again.

"Well, well, thou hast the likeness of Liath Erliandol if I am not mistaken."

"How did you know of my ancient ancestor, goodly monk?" Eta queried, amazed.

"So the years have passed with a vengeance. I am pleased to meet you, howsoever you are called young elf. It seems just after all these years, well..." he trailed off half to himself looking as though into the distance. When he started to talk to them he was relaxed and quizzical but he changed as they talked. He became alert and anxious, "I have to leave you, but there are possibly some more trinkets not far from here, down a hole in a prison, good hunting!" he turned half away and stopped as though he sensed something else. He spoke again. "I see you have already found ...one or two," He chuckled and took a pace towards the tunnel, "but prithee do not play with one of them too much in here. You will have to find more emblems if it's the Old Elves you are looking for. Vodocanthey has a long memory, he may help, if you step carefully. If you don't he'll eat you."

"Who's Vodocanthey?" Chorky burst out, unable to contain his questions any longer, but the figure had already glided out of the cavern.

"Who the gracious, was that?" Ikin questioned, hoping for an answer but not really expecting one. Eta was quiet as usual, but this time he was just as confused as they were. He was thrown by the fact that the monk knew his ancestor."

"How long ago did your ancestor live?" Ikin asked.

"A bit over one and a half thousand years!" Eta murmured.

There was a silence while everyone tried to understand what the monk had said. Nomaque said thoughtfully, "We must go over all the things he said carefully when we have moment, especially as some of Eta's elusive past generations have connections. We seem to have stumbled onto something. Who was he? He was certainly helpful, if a little vague, certainly a clue or two. It looks as if we have been lucky and found the area where your Star Elves lived Eta. I've no chance of sleep now, but now let's get on, we have a prison to find, we'll go over the situation after that."

The others agreed and having searched the waterfall cave to their satisfaction, they went through the exit the monk took. They could only go a short way along the straight tunnel as it ended in a door. They opened it cautiously, but found the tunnel stopped five feet further on in a blank wall.

"Curious that, why have a door to a blank wall?" Chorky queried, scanning around for some reason. Ten minutes later Eta found a small brass plate let into the floor, a little way back from the front of the door.

"Stand back, I'm going to press it," he said, giving time for everyone to step away from the walls, and Chorky to stand in the open doorway. He then poked at it with his bow stave.

Nothing happened. They abandoned the attempt to find anything more and left the tunnel beyond the door. As he went past the plate Eta pressed it again, almost in disgust, but a little harder.

Click....Whirr. Muffled sounds and a slight rumbling issued from behind the door, Eta moved quickly to the door and tried it gingerly but it would

69

not open until the whirring had stopped. When it did open, a tunnel showed as before but this time it was longer and with a turning to the left. Without thinking he went through and the door swung shut behind him.

Around the corner in front of him came two elves, armed and ready to attack. Behind them two more came to stand with bows drawn to support their comrades. Eta held up his hand to ease the tension and to gather his wits.

"Who are you? Where do you come from?" One of the foremost pair asked.

"I am Eta, an elf from Estamon on 'The Search'. I'm sure you all have heard about us young elves of Estamon hunting for traces of our ancestors. I am looking in the old elvish settlements for them with a group of companions. Who are you?" Eta asked, confident that all elves knew about the lost Star Elves, and the search of the young for them.

The second one half-turned and said back over his shoulder, "Its one of the Lost." He turned back to face Eta and said, not unkindly, "We are four brothers from Lisego Village. We are looking for a comrade of ours who disappeared in this area over a month ago. What do you mean 'on the search'?"

As Eta showed no sign of answering, the third one, the youngest, said, "I think we should say who we are at least. I am Yanar, the one who firstly spoke to you was Lexar, the second to talk was Uslar and the silent one is Senar. The elf we are looking for is called Throndralon. Have you heard of him?"

"I thank you Yanar, no I haven't heard of him. Here are my companions now." Eta said as the door behind him opened, but no party of friends came through, instead a group of kobs, the larger and more vicious cousins of the goblins. Their sharp pointed ears bristling amid the tangles of their filthy thick black hair. These seeing a party almost as large as themselves and well armed, turned to run, but in turn were trapped as Eta's group came through the door in turn, fast.

Caught between the two parties, they attacked the elves with Eta with ferocity to force an escape and eventually they fought their way through, only to lose four of their number in the process. Shortly after the last kob disappeared around the corner, a clicking and whirring sound was heard followed by a sensation of movement. The parties looked at each other and went back quickly through the door the way they came. The passage was not the same as Eta had come in by, but the other elves recognised it, so they all went through. Uslar and Yanar had wounds, but they could be quickly bandaged for the time being. The parties then formed a truce and the elves showed the group the way they came in through a secret door at the top of some stairs in front of them. Unfortunately, the opening going in the return direction was not to be found.

The tunnel to the stair passed a turning to the right from which the sound of water issued, so the original group wanted to go that way. The decision had to be made quickly, as they were worried that kob reinforcements could arrive shortly, so they all went right. The tunnel led to a 'Y' fork with a pit in the centre of it.

"This is the pit I fell into!" Zeth said, "and there's the waterfall cave," he added, indicating the right-hand opening.

They turned left at the 'Y', passed the dank downward tunnel and came to the cross junction. The tunnel on the left led to a door, the one on the right went off into the darkness.

Clem suddenly waved to them to be silent, and many shod boots could be heard coming towards them from the passage ahead. He cried, "The door on the left!" and ran for the door and unlat-

71

ched it. With a creak it opened and they piled into an empty high roofed cave, with stalactites hanging from the roof. Hurriedly they closed the door and waited, dowsing the lights. The footsteps came closer, some even came up to the other side of the door they were behind. Voices in Kobish discussed coming in, one laughed, and then the steps went away, echoing into the distance. Clem looked around for his flint to light up quickly, he had heard enough to realise that they could be in trouble. Sure enough there was a startled stifled cry from one of the elves, followed by a choking sound. Clem's torch spluttered alight to show Uslar struggling on the floor, across the whole of his face a yellow membrane stretched. His body was arched and squirming in agony. The brothers desperately started to cut pieces off the mass with their knives, the bits wriggling away from them.

"Beware above!" Clem yelled, "there are more hanging chokers up there! *Prendicachk* as the kobs call them. Hanging chokers, good name that. They sensed his wound."

They all looked up, except the elves fighting for their brother's life, shuddered and then quickly moved away from the hanging *prendicachk*. Then a slight wobble in one confirmed Clem's guess. The elves had most of the horror sliced away except for the toothy-bit around his mouth and a tongue down his throat. With a sucking sound the last section came away, leaving the still white body of Uslar lying there, bloody blotches all over his face.

"Watch out! Move right!" Chorky cried as he swung his sword over the head of Yanar. The sword deftly sliced the arrow of yellow flesh, and deflected it to one side. "I was watching it, they can crawl across the ceiling. Ugh!"

The elves were trying to get Uslar's breathing going again and squeezing his chest at approximate breathing rate, at the same time Zeth was calling on

72

his powers to save the elf. He got up ten minutes later and said that he could do no more, and if Uslar was still not breathing then it had to be a necromancer or nothing.

Lexar slung his brother's body over his shoulder and everyone filed glumly out of the cave through the door.

"We will get out the way you came in if you will be kind enough to show us the way, our seeking must finish here." He said. They led the elves to the drop and helped them to descend. In parting Lexar said, when he heard their quest,

"The elf we were seeking was or is a prince of an elvish kingdom, who came out to seek aid in freeing his people from a curse. He came here to find some Emblems, as he called them, he didn't tell us what. That's all I know, but as you are seeking elvish kingdoms you must seek him. Oh, and he has a bright metal circlet upon his brow. Good fare and health in this foul place."

The others left, Chorky and Nomaque going with them to trigger the pivoting slab. On their return the companions despondently went back to the cross tunnels.

"Right now for some exploring, it has to be the left tunnel or upstairs." Chorky said grimly.

The tunnel went straight, and then turned left. As they reached the shallow corner, two doors showed on the right with another shallow corner further on to the left. They tried the doors of the two rooms and found them open, unoccupied, only rubbish in them. They moved on and turned the next corner carefully, every sense on the alert. The tunnel went straight on to the dim distance, a row of doors on the left, a large door just visible at the end. The first door on the left, opened with a protest loud enough to wake the dead, as Clem put it. Inside, the gloom cast a blanket over everything, the torchlight didn't seem to penetrate.

73

Clem went forward stealthily, followed by Ikin, with her axe at the ready. The spider landed full on the dwarf's shoulder and in a lightning reflex move, Ikin's axe chopped the spider in two leggy pieces.

"I hate spiders! Out Clem!" Ikin said encouraging him unnecessarily to get out of the room.

"That's one room we check last, if we have to." Clem grinning and slapping Ikin's back in gratitude.

The next room was visibly empty, so they went in to poke about in the rubbish littered on the floor. They found nothing but some broken boxes and empty barrels. The same for the next room too.

The door on the following room was locked, but by craning their necks they could see through the grille in the door. It seemed to be some kind of cell, with three scruffy bandits in chains on the left wall. Their weapons were stacked on the right in a jumbled heap well out of reach.

"They haven't had many breakouts here have they?" Chorky muttered.

"Shall we free them?" He wondered. "Let's have a look further on first before we release anyone, we may not have all that much time." He added. There were no disagreements so they proceeded to the fifth room, which was another cell. This time there was only one tall human chained up, a fighter by the look of his worn leather armour under a mail jerkin.

They passed on to the door on the end, which opened oddly when they pushed it, swinging to one side, then clicking back. The room was larger than the others and had a section of floor split downwards by five feet. It must have been a continuation of the rift in the passage and in the waterfall cave. They searched the room carefully this time, and as they hadn't found anything obvious so far in their search, they would have to look more thoroughly on the way back along the cells. Their extra diligence paid off, in the lower section there was a pot of liquid and a case of leather with what looked like a scroll in it.

Nomaque very cautiously opened the case and eased out the vellum roll.

It read in ancient elvish script::-

To whosoever it may Concern
The Wizard Lock may be broken
by a Party acting together
one being a Priestly Person
together with the five races,
and one other,
uttering the Word of Command
known by
LIGITZ The Unusual

"Well we almost have the requirements to unlock it, whatever 'it' is." Nomaque added after he had read the scroll out to the others.

"We need a human." Ikin put in, half humorously, but added in a more serious tone, "Of course, we could free the fighter? I feel there's something about him which has the look of a searcher."

The party had completed their search in the room so they left to go to the next cell where the human was. That is, all except Zeth, who had caught sight of something in the rubbish. He bent down and fished out a metal post, which he nearly threw back in disgust except he heard the others trying to open the cell door. He smiled and took it to the scene of action. It made short work of the doorlock and the fetters too.

Hectar Rolan, the human, was delighted to be given the chance to both get out and join in. They instantly took to him. His sword, a twohanded one, had been thrown on the floor in the corner of the cell by the kobs. He fitted it into a scabbard on his mail clad back, but he was totally against the release of the other captives in the other room. "I haven't anything urgent to do just at this moment," he said with a smile, "so I might as well come along. My sword is at your disposal. I do think that the others in the next cell are trouble and well worth forgetting about. They are worse than the kobs if that is possible!"

"We haven't searched your cell yet, but we don't want them involved in our hunt for tunnels." Eta commented as they tested the floor and walls for anything hollow to no avail. Finding nothing this meant they had to try the cell with the three cut-throats and release them. The men fawned over them, and collecting their weapons, went off down the corridor and round the bend.

"That's a relief anyway," Zeth said, as they looked for the tunnel. The search proved fruitless in that room and the next. Clem was getting anxious, he sweated with the thought of searching the room with the spiders, the one thing that really gave the dwarf the jitters. They heard sounds coming from the adjoining cell, the next one that they were going to.

A hushed voice muttered, "They think they've got us fooled, but they d'in't recon on us catchin on. Heh. But we better be lively though, just in case." One was saying in a whisper.

The party crept out of the cell they were in and to the adjacent open door, surprising the three ruffians.

"We was just lookin'fer somethin them kobs took from us," the nearest whined.

76

Seething, Chorky strode to the closest and took his sword from him, with Eta and Zeth doing the same for the others.

"Hey wot's that for. A body c'n look can't they?"

"A likely tale, anyway you made a mistake coming back, there's a secret here that you will die for, unless we tie you up again for your own protection. You would have fared better to have kept on going. It's a rope and the end cell for you my lads. Keep quiet or the kobs will get you!" They dragged the three off and left them as promised in the end cell tied up with some old rope.

"That won't hold them for long, it's old rope and they still have their knives, but we pushed them down the drop to delay their return." Eta said.

"I pity the rats!" Ikin muttered, although she did drop their weapons well along the corridor for them to find.

Without more ado they turned to the task of finding an entrance to the 'hole in a prison'. They were privately wondering whether the monk had sold them a bad one. The search revealed no hollow walls or slabs, but it was more difficult in this cell as the clutter was heaped everywhere.

Here there were old barrels, clothes mouldering in heaps, smelling revolting, and amongst it, other rubbish. They straightened, and looked at each other, decidedly they were reluctant understandably to search the next room with the spiders in. Nomaque's robe caught around a small barrel and he gave a heave to free it. The barrel toppled, falling off its resting place to the floor, but instead of a thump, the floor echoed hollowly.

"Well done Nomaque, we can always rely on you to solve the puzzle," Ikin said with genuine relief, bending to lever at the stone flag and to be assisted deftly by Clem. The practised hands of the gnome and the dwarf had it up quickly and they looked down at the dark narrow opening.

Ikin eased herself down into the darkness and found her feet came into contact with the floor of a tunnel when her head was just below floor level.

"The tunnel is dry, with a black dust covering the walls. The tall ones will find the height difficult, so I suggest that Clem and I go first. I can't say that I'm eager, there is a danger here, isn't there Clem? You feel it too. It smells hot and stuffy! Shall we lead them in, friend?" Ikin suggested.

The dwarf nodded grimly thinking that there was something odd about the black dust, the heat and the stuffiness, but he couldn't think what it was just then. He slid down next to her still wondering about it, but the narrowness of the tunnel and the unknown dangers ahead drove the thought from his mind.

"We must go in the dark as there could be just about anything down here," he added quietly. Turning, they disappeared into the darkness.

The others followed as well as they could. The tunnel ran straight as an arrow to a black open space, and gave access to a ledge, which ran along the rough-hewn rocky side of a large cavern. It was so dark that Ikin, with perhaps the best night sight of them all, couldn't see the other side or what was in it.

At the rear of the file of crouching bodies, Zeth listened. Behind him came a barely audible evil chuckle and the slab slid shut, their retreat had been closed. Ikin heard the thump, a shudder passed up her spine and the hairs on the back of her neck bristled. She felt a touch on the shoulder, startled, she jumped.

"Yes?" she whispered back to Clem, her heart racing.

"Something wrong here. I smell something very, very wrong." He breathed. "Stop pushing, problems ahead," Clem whispered back as Chorky moved forwards and bumped him.

Silence as deep as the thick darkness yawned in front of Ikin, she could hear the stealthy movements of her companions waiting behind her. Deep in the silence she thought she heard a regular creaking sound like very hard leather rubbing so, so slowly somewhere in that black mass in front of her. Ikin's sight could not penetrate that gloom even though she was desperate; she strained her eyes, again and again in every direction, but in that cavern there was no glimmer in the blackness.

Suddenly, without warning two large red lamps lit themselves directly in front of her. Shock flooded through her, the terrifying unknown was there in the dark, in place of nothing. Desperate to get away she jerked back but felt Clem behind her. Going beyond her terror, Ikin waited, accepting the horror and the following inevitable death.

Clem was as frightened as she was, but he knew very well what was there, embedded deep in his racial memories was the answer. This kind of creature and the dwarves had entangled throughout history, the dwarves always lost. Knowing very well that his next moment could be his last, the horror welled up in his throat. For a split second his voice seized up, and then he hissed,

"Oh Ye Gods! Dragon!!!!"

There was a lot of bumping in the tunnel as the word whispered back and until they realised that they just had to keep on going through whatever was ahead as Ikin and Clem were deep in trouble and would need their help. Slowly, because they could do nothing else they filed carefully forward, dread in

79

every heart, sweat pouring off their clenched hands on their weapons. As they each saw the horror they knew that they had no weapon that would even scratch the monster in front of them. They grew old in those awful, so courageous, moments.

The 'lamps', the dragon's eyes, lit the cavern in a ruddy glow. Ikin could now see that they were on a ledge 15 feet up on the side of a large cavern.

In the middle of it, sitting on a suitably large pile of bones, treasure, trinkets, coins and cups, was an ancient dragon at least sixty feet long, maybe more. Its scales glistening red-gold in the ruddy glow and its black-silver wings half raised above its spiked backbone. Myriad scratches and creases on the scales showed the age of the beast.

And there they all were lined up on the ledge looking at it, totally vulnerable, each preparing in their various ways to die. The dragon opened its mouth and the fiery throat lit the terrible scene even brighter in red. Furnace red. One spray of fire and they all would be cooked dinner. Tendrils of flame played around the blackened hedge of teeth ten feet in front of them. It breathed in. They tensed for the end.

"WELCOME, THANKS FOR BRINGING ME A FEAST, UNLESS YOU CAN DO A LITTLE SOMETHING FOR ME, THAT ISSSH." Rumble... Rumble...

A jet of steam issued from its nostrils and it was as much as Clem could do not to jump back, as hot eddies curled around his legs.

"ARE YOU TASTY THEN, NICE LITTLE DWARF?" Rumble. Rumble. "COME DOWN TO THE FLOOR AND WE WILL GET ACQUAINTED. DON'T BE SHY, THERE'S A SET OF STAIRS AT THE END OF THE LEDGE. DON'T FALL OR I MIGHT CATCH YOU." Rumble... Rumble... Rumble

The dragon seemed unable to continue speaking more than a phrase at a time, it then gasped a little. Nomaque said later that he thought it could have been its speech was rusty after so long. Ikin disagreed, she reckoned that it was laughing at their obvious discomfort.

"I HAVE A PROBLEM AND NOW YOU HAVE A PROBLEM. I'M SO HUNGRY AND I HAVE'NT EATEN FOR ABOUT... A LONG TIME...HERE YOU ALL ARE, PLUMP LITTLE CHICKENS." Rumble... THE REASON I'M HUNGRY IS THAT I CAN'T GET OUT;

IF I EAT YOU THEN I CAN WAIT A LITTLE LONGER." Rumble. Rumble...BUT IF I EAT YOU, I WON'T BE ABLE TO PERSUADE YOU TO HELP ME...Rruummbbllee....

Offered no alternative they filed down to the floor of the cavern, and stood in a despairing group. Ikin although frightened almost out of her wits, sensed the dragon's infinite sadness. It heaved itself off its mound and waddled to the further end of the cave spreading dented treasure as it went. It went through a high stone archway into another similarly sized cavern.

"FOLLOW." It hissed, and they followed, once again having nowhere to run.

At the far end of the cavern a sparkling opaque wall blanked off the whole cavern wall to wall. The dragon took in some breaths and an eruption of fire spewed out of his jaws with a roar, they raised their arms to protect their eyes from the searing heat, hoping it was not their last moment. The dragon after hesitating a moment swung its maw round to play the beam of fire not over them but across the opaque wall which crackled and flexed growing more solid if anything. The heat quenched suddenly leaving them all unable to see for several minutes. The dragon's bitter voice cut through the gloom.

81

"SEE... NO WAY OUT FOR ME. THE WARDING HAS BEEN THERE A LONG TIME. A WIZARD'S TRICK, BY LIASPHAR THE UNFAIR. HE'S LONG DEAD I IMAGINE...LEFT ME STUCK IN HERE."

Chapter V

Ligitz the Unusual

*T*he deep silence that followed was suddenly broken, and everyone turned to look at Ikin, who was distractedly talking to herself.

"Wiz, wiz, lock, that's it!" Ikin whispered brokenly, "the scruffy bit of parchment," she said louder, gaining confidence as she continued. Then turning to the Druid she added urgently out loud. "Get it out, Nomaque! The parchment! Get with it! Come on."

"Get what out?" Nomaque asked giving her a hard look, as if to say 'for gods' sake be serious for once'.

"That case-thingy, the writing, the rolled up scroll! It says something about a wizard lock, doesn't it?"

"Ah" Nomaque nodded understanding at last, and fumbled quietly about for the scroll case.

"I HOPE YOU ARE LOOKING FOR SOMETHING TO HELP ME DRUID...."

"I am looking for a rhyme we came across on our way here, O ancient dragon. It mentions wizards, and it may be useful but… only… if you keep your flame away," Nomaque tentatively replied, as to talk to a dragon was a skilled operation, and one rarely got more than one chance to practice.

"GOT A BIT OF GRIT, GOOD...."

'That went down well, good, now let's try something else' the Druid thought to himself recovering a little.

83

"It says something about Ligitz the Unusual. Do you know who or what it is?" Nomaque asked.

"WHAT DO YOU WANT WITH THAT PIDDLING LITTLE SQUIRT? OH! ALL RIGHT I WILL TELL YOU, SEEING THAT YOU ARE MAKING A REAL EFFORT. I KNOW OF IT BUT NOT MUCH. HE IS A DRAPTERA WHO CAME IN ONCE TO SCRATCH AROUND FOR FOOD. HANGS AROUND OUTSIDE SOMEWHERE, I DON'T KNOW WHERE, AS I'M STUCK HERE. GOT IT! "

"We need to go and fetch him as he has a part of what we need to get you out, O Illustrious One." said Nomaque warming to the task of talking to this living engine of destruction.

"DON'T YOU FLATTER ME AS THOUGH I WERE SOME EMPTY HEADED YOUNG DRAGON JUST OUT OF THE EGG!...HAVE A CARE, I'M TOO HUNGRY FOR SUCH THINGS."...Rumble...

"HELLO, I HEAR SOME FOOD COMING, NO VISITORS I MEAN, OF THE FOOD KIND. IF YOU WILL STAY IN HERE I WILL SEE IF I CAN CATCH SUPPER"....

There was a scuffling in the tunnel and the noise stopped. Kob voices whispered together on the edge of danger and went back up the tunnel. The slab could be heard falling in place, and then silence.

"CANNY LOT THOSE KOBS. DON'T CATCH MANY OF THEM. AND NOW YOU ARE STUCK IN HERE WITH ME. LUCKY, LUCKY."

Clem had been busy in the meantime looking at the walls of the cave. To the left of the ledge on the far side, the tops of the arches to the pool could be seen, blackened and fused from the dragon's efforts to blast his way out. Clem edged around the dragon and inspected the pile of boulders. He prodded, and kicked here and there.

"These have been melted tight, you sealed them yourself, O Dragon, its like rock. Now, there's a way if you'll agree to it, to break it open with dwarf-fire." He paused only a second before continuing "Firstly I will need some light from our torches, then, could we find a pick or something to hack out the bits of rock I'll show you, at this place here and over there under the ledge."

Totally ignoring the dragon he bustled around, and amazingly, the enormous beast put up with it and even seemed to look interested, if a dragon could achieve that state of mind. It even got out of their way several times as they carried boulders to a collecting area.

The dwarf found a long-handled military pick in the hoard and, with Ikin's help, soon accumulated a pile of debris. Now and then he would explain a point to her and she would nod in agreement. Then she found a war hammer from the same source and broke up the pieces to as fine as possible, making three lumpy powders, which Clem mixed thoroughly together. Clem tested the mixture between his finger and thumb, sniffed it, and pronounced it ready. He rolled the powder into a piece of rag and took it to the boulders. He stuffed the bundle in the deepest crevice they could find in the heap of blackened and half-melted rock.

Clem then told the dragon to direct a blast of hot fire at the spot, only wait until he said the word. He then hustled everyone to dive around the corner and cover their ears.

"NOW!" He bellowed to the dragon from cover.

WHOOSHHH...
KERA--BOOMMM...RRUUMMBBLLEE....

There was a flash, a deafening bang then the sound of a rain of rock pieces going everywhere. The

85

sound of a section of the roof falling in followed and a pall of fine dust eddied around them.

There were small noises at first, then sounds of rubble being shaken off and deep coughing.

"WOW... I NOW HAVE A HEALTHY RESPECT FOR THE MODERN DWARF! A RIB TICKLER AND NO MISTAKE... YOU CAN LIGHT UP NOW AND SEE WHAT YOU'VE REARRANGED." The dragon coughed again.

Clem slowly emerged and lit his torch, the others following. The whole cavern was full of choking dust and rock chunks littered the floor. It took several minutes for the cave to clear, the heap at first glance looked the same, maybe higher, but a large chunk of the ceiling had also collapsed back on to the pile. This meant that they could get out into the cavern with the pool, the second cavern they had visited on entering the caves. The dragon was determined to get through, he moved as much of the old pile as he could and with several good belts with his tail, the wall gave in and more of the roof colla-psed. When the debris settled once more, the dragon had achieved his purpose, and although he could sque-eze through to the pool and wash the dust off, he was too large to go anywhere afterwards.

"OH GOODIE A BATH!" he rumbled.

While the great beast was wallowing they climbed past it and made their way to the entrance. Using the torch they triggered the door and filed out, promising to find Ligitz the draptera as quickly as possible.

When the door slid closed, quiet returned. After the cavern with the dragon the next cave seemed dark, but they all breathed easier as the perilous creature was then on the other side of a stout stone door. Even so, sundry thumps still could be heard through the wall.

"Getting playful!" Clem chuckled. Turning they made their way up the stair. As he did so Chorky caught sight of the lower floor of the cave, spotlessly clean, no rubbish anywhere, a long way below them. He could not help wondering where the way down was. While he watched, a small stone, dislodged by someone's boot tumbled over the edge, idly his eyes followed it, expecting to hear a clatter when it hit the floor. Someone will have to go and clean the floor now, he thought.

He need not have worried, the stone passed soundlessly through the seemingly solid floor, and disappeared.

Clem who was following Chorky's perplexed gaze nodded to himself and said, "Some trap that, the elves always think big, even our friend the dragon would be in deep trouble here. I thought I heard a plunk afterwards, so there's water a long way underneath I think. That's not friendly, probably a deep water-filled chasm."

At the top of the steps, overhanging the drop to the right, standing clear of the wall at floor level, was a landing to a small recess in the wall. Access to it was gained by a small step off the stairs. It jutted out over the drop to the floor, giving access to the recess. It had a flower statue in its centre.

"Careful!" Clem cautioned as Eta stepped forward, "There may be a loose stone or pivoting slab around here somewhere." Linking arms they tested the stone floor to no effect.

"That does not mean there isn't one, it just means that it isn't triggered." Clem protested.

Oddly each time they had passed by on their way into the caverns, they missed it completely, even though they looked around carefully. The ornate greenish stone flower statue was a sturdy green leafy base standing over 3 feet high, topped with a large flower bud. The bud had a pink shade reminiscent of

87

petals, which became pinker and more translucent as they approached.

Eta looked thoughtful, "Nomaque," he mused, "When I was young something like this was in the old stories. A *Lianur* I think it was called. This could be very magical, but what it was I cannot quite remember."

"I am not surprised, look at the way it is changing as we walk up to it." Nomaque replied.

"The question is … is it friendly on not?" Ikin added.

"Nearly everything is dodgy down here, remember that fountain with the creature in it. I would not want to have a battle like that here," Zeth said looking over the rim of the landing down to the odd looking floor below.

"That felt bad, it oozed atmosphere." Nomaque asserted.

"The potential for something bad to happen here is far worse." Zeth murmured.

Nomaque had approached the pedestal and was looking closely at it when the 'leaves' or 'petals' opened out, showing an upside down cone with a flat top. It continued to widen to about two feet at the top and stopped.

Ikin had been looking about and found some little sacks of a silvery dust hanging on the wall nearby. "Do you think these have anything to do with it, Eta?"

"There was also a *Lianur Dust* which has magical properties in stories to open a person's eyes to something." Eta added cautiously.

"Did you hear that Nom…Nom?" Ikin asked tersely.

Nomaque was standing still preoccupied with his dilemma as to whether to touch the top or not. "What did you say then?" He murmured not really listening. Then he began to fit the pieces of the puzzle together. "Oh I see you are suggesting the two are connected."

"Why are you so dense sometimes Nomaque, of course," she added, "AND if they are, you can touch the thing, can't you?

"Right." he said and reached out to touch the lip of the cone top.

Several things happened.

Zeth said "Oops!" and dived for the floor. Closely followed by everyone except for Nomaque and Ikin who was holding one of the 'dust bags' in her hand.

"False alarm" Nomaque muttered, as nothing seemed to happen. He froze…"Wait, I can see something, the whole top is showing a view outside." He cried amazed, quite forgetting his irritation. Everyone scrambled to see, and there was careful confusion for a while.

The cone was like looking through a continuous mirror. It was as if you were standing looking around you, but above ground. When you walked round the view changed giving an uninterrupted panorama. Ikin replaced the bag and watched entranced.

A large bird-like object flew across the grass and sat on one of the stones in the foreground. Suddenly an arrow ricocheted off the creature's perch catching it across the body. It took off and flew away at high speed, seemingly unaffected by its wound.

From some bushes a good distance away a group of raiders emerged, not bothering to give chase. One had his hands over his ears. Further away more were beating the scrub along the edge of the forest, looking for someone or something.

"That's torn it, if that is happening now above us, I'm afraid either the ramphorm giant is gone or in trouble." Nomaque said pointing his finger at where smoke curled up from burning within the trees. "I hope he is long gone, there are too many for him, and us too."

"What did the dragon call the creature we are looking for, apart from a little squirt? It was a drap-something?"

"Draptera I think," put in Nomaque, "I haven't come across one before. I suppose it could be a littlel dragon maybe."

"That creature we saw flying off, may be a small dragon-like animal. It didn't have feathers, more like bats wings, but with more strength. It was very fast. If that's it, then we have to go out this way." Eta observed.

"Definitely not till dark," Ikin added, "But we can watch their movements till then. Neat this viewer isn't it, anything else around here, say, like a figurine with power?"

"There's this powder you found Ikin," Zeth offered, holding out the ancient drawstring bag.

Taking the bag, Nomaque gently poured out a tiny amount of the powder into the palm of his hand, the powder glistening strangely in the torchlight.

"I remember too the human tradition that magic mirrors tell the future if you sprinkle magic dust over the water uttering the magic words," Zeth added hesitantly, not sure that he had done the right thing in giving the Druid the bag. Nomaque could be a bit hasty with magic items sometimes.

"Zeth, Magician of Greater Mesquite, please utter the precious words for us, O Great One," Clem growled. "Nomaque any comments?"

"He may be right of course, there are symbols and words written here in amongst the petals. We could sling on the dust anyway, just to see?" He said taking a pinch, sprinkling it from his hand and blowing it over the cone's surface to everyone's horror.

Everyone except for the Druid and Ikin dived for the floor a second time. It became crowded. To defy all, Nomaque stood and looked at them mockingly.

"Have you no faith in my powers? What powers? You're right, move over I'm coming down..." He pretended to join them but as he moved, his gaze lingered on the cone and then stopped…

"Stop messing about. There's no reaction whatsoever," he remarked. "Wait!" He exclaimed as a flicker of a picture caught his eye, "there's a new picture forming! Quick, jump up and look!"

The view went opaque as if in a sandstorm then it cleared, a battle was taking place, and the scene moved as though the viewer was being carried just above and behind a group of knights as they marched forward. In the middle distance a lofty castle stood on a rock, besieged by a dark army a small distance in front of the knights. The knights drew weapons and charged into the sea of kobs, goblins and trolls, who up till then seemed unaware of them. The focal point of their view changed as they moved forward, it swept over the knight's heads to show the centre of the army ahead. Seated on a palanquin and ringed with large armoured hobgoblins, was a long tusked overlarge hobgoblin, festooned with jewels and fancy armour. On top of his head was a crown. The watchers gasped, the crown was identical to the one Maltex had in Mesquite. The scene began to break up and soon they were looking on the familiar view on the surface above again.

Zeth looked dumbfounded, shocked by what he had seen. Chorky and Eta too looked very disturbed.

"What do you make of that?" Chorky said more to himself than anyone else.

"Lethelorel," breathed Eta. "My ancient home, and under attack!"

"One of the knights had your helmet on, Chorky," Zeth said quietly, barely audible.

91

"The sky… I have never seen sky like that, it was a weird colour." Ikin observed. All the others became silent, wondering.

It took the rest of the daylight hours to prepare to go out. Then Ikin asked the question they all were avoiding asking themselves, saying, "I know we should go out, but where shall we go to? I mean where do we make for? When we are out we'll be without shelter until we return here, with enemies everywhere."

"The small dragon flew towards the cliffs." Zeth remarked.

"We should return this way only as a last resort, or if we have the answer to the wizlock question. This place gives us a refuge but once they know that we come and go from the stones they will be guarded and watched. I think it can only be of use if we know another way out." Nomaque replied, not really answering Ikin's question either.

"It's the cliffs then", she muttered.

When darkness fell all was quiet and there was no activity near the stones.

"Let's go!" Nomaque said waving his torch in front of the triggering hole.

"Dowse the light quickly." Clem whispered, "But keep in a tight group."

Trying to keep the light and noise down proved to be a lost cause as unfortunately the light had to be used again as they had to close the stone the way they originally opened it. Also to their dismay the stone swung back with a thump, which shook the ground. They froze to the spot and listened, and the silence settled around them like a blanket. Eta pointed to where it was just possible to see where the trees still burned within the forest, the light flickering on the far cliff face nearest to it.

Without wasting any more time they set off towards the nearby cliffs, almost silent on the springy turf. Hectar having poor night sight compared to the others paired with Zeth, who helped him be as silent as possible. At the rocks, more care had to be taken to be quiet because of the loose stones. During a particularly awkward manoeuvre while Chorky was edging his way around a large boulder, the 'voice' spoke to him again.

'*About time too, I hurt*', it said from just above him. Chorky looked up cautiously without loosing his hold, he was worried as he couldn't defend himself. Against the dark mountains he could barely see a small shape on the top of the rock.

'*Me*' the 'voice' answered his unspoken question. There was a flap and a part glide and a creature wrapped itself around Chorky's shoulders and head. The feel of its skin was not uncomfortable, and to his surprise Chorky sensed the creature needed his reassurance, it was not attacking him in any way.

Easing around the rock wall and on his feet again, he reached forward carefully so as not to alarm his passenger, and touched Eta's arm who was next in line. The amazed elf was about to draw his sword and attack it, when the draptera whimpered and Eta looked closer. He then realised that Chorky wasn't in danger, and relaxed. He moved forward and whispered in Nomaque's ear, drawing his attention to the pair. After negotiating the boulder they all gathered around the tall half-elf, speaking quietly and keeping out of reach of the draptera's agitated tail spikes.

"What shall we do now?" Chorky asked, his mind full of thoughts about his new companion, and not able to do much more.

"Ask its name," Clem said.

'*Ligitz*' it voiced, before Chorky could form the question in his mind. Then it squawked in agitation as it read Chorky's thoughts about the dragon.

93

"How are we going to persuade it to come with us to unlock the door?" Chorky asked the assembled group, just as Eta, who had been checking their rear waved them to be quiet. He had spotted creeping raiders moving in on the stones, so the retreat was now cut off.

Chorky put the question in his mind of ways into the caves. The voice gave him a picture of steps in the cliff a short way ahead up to a ledge with a great tree on it.

Chorky took the lead in order to save time and arrived at the steps, each of which was several feet in height. The draptera showed a picture of a ramphorm giant going up them. *'But not now, friend gone away hurt'.*

The group quietly scrambled up the steps to the grassy ledge, some seventy feet up where they had to squeeze past an enormous oak tree. The tree's roots had opened great cracks up and down a fault in the cliff face. As they went past the tree, Ikin noticed the figure of Nomaque seemed to straighten and grow taller.

'Most I in tree' the draptera's voice explained, *'when my cave no safe.'* There were several cave entrances opening onto the ledge and one of these the draptera was thinking of. The thought also came to Chorky that they were closed off at the back and gave no access to the caverns behind.

Partway up the cliff more holes showed in the dim light against the light coloured rockface, one looked as though it could be reached by climbing the tree, a stroke of luck as it turned out.

At about that time there was a snuffling to be heard below with muffled voices moving along under them, part whispers coming up to them from time to time. Instantly they realised they could not hide there for much longer without discovery, as their adversaries had a tracking animal of some sort, which would inevitably locate them. Their exposed position was perilous, especially if their searchers had bows, also Clem and Ikin were dreadfully slow clambering about in trees.

"If the gods had meant us to go up there we should have been bloody birds." The dwarf grumbled.

They had no choice, they were persuaded by circumstance, half pulled, half pushed, they scrambled their way up the massive trunk and wobbled onto the branch where they swayed while the elf checked out the cave.

"Its empty, but a bit small I'm afraid." Eta said on his return. The top of the large branch across to the cliff was well worn so something had regularly used this route. They felt even more trapped than before, caught between the unknown and the raiders. Ideally they would have liked to cut away the branch behind them to stop pursuit but this was not possible with the tools they had to hand.

The small dragon clung desperately to Chorky's shoulder armour, occasionally giving little chirrups of alarm when it was dislodged by anything. Unfortunately it was by then too agitated to give any help, in fact all its little mind was giving out was panic to its host. They milled around in the little cave getting in each other's way, until Chorky, exasperated by the situation and the need for his passenger, said,

"Eta, can you and Zeth defend the cave entrance with bow and sword? Nomaque and I will stand still in the centre of the floor. Clem and Ikin please explore."

"Good thinking Chork! Let's get organised," a female voice agreed.

A minute or two later a small exit had been discovered going further into the complex on the far side of the first cave, which Ikin and Clem entered after informing the others. Ikin went first, axe at the ready, and was the first to feel a tight grip of many pinpricks on her knee. With a funny little gasp she jumped back into Clem, who, after spotting what was wrong, tried to hit the creature on her leg with his axe-handle, partially successfully.

Stepping to one side he yelled back for a torch quickly, and tried to keep out of her way as she flailed at the centipede, fully over a foot long. It seemed an age later that Nomaque's head appeared in the entrance his features lit by the torch. He quickly gave the torch to Clem and disappeared, and Clem applied it to the centipede. The creature curled up and dropped off to scuttle away injured into the pile of rubbish on the floor to be attacked in turn by its brood. Nomaque appeared with another torch followed by Chorky and the others. Many boots and weapons were applied to removing the pests for good.

The new cave was similar to the last with an opening out onto the cliff. They quickly realised that they were spotted from below as an arrow sang in through the opening. Luckily it missed them, they did not realise they were in full view. Fortunately there was another exit on the far side of the cave further into the cliff. Clem and Ikin darted across and into it. As they ran through the opening they saw that the new cave was festooned with rope-like webs, over the ceiling, walls and parts of the floor. Seeing another opening on the far side they ran through quickly. Waiting for the others, Clem took a moment to throw a lighted torch back into the tracery.

"Ware spiders." Ikin called out just as Chorky darted into the smoking ruin. The little dragon launched itself off his host's shoulder and was in its element. Its first victim was a large spider, which was hiding behind its burning web on the floor. The arachnid had no chance before it was torn apart and eaten. With the torn webs and light, most of the remaining creatures kept well away from the people passing by. The draptera stayed on guard throughout killing several more before the rest of the party had all passed through, returning to Chorky's shoulder afterwards, much more contented. The exit from the cavern led into a tunnel, which made a sharp turn to the right. As they reached the corner the smell hit them.

The odour was of hundreds of unwashed bodies, or so it seemed, possibly some refuse pits as well. Just ahead was a 'T' junction with another crossing corridor. Very cautiously they approached and peering around the corner to the left, Clem watched a stream of goblins, kob females and children coming and going to a room in between them and the far end of the tunnel. They would have to go right even if there was a blockage, as none of them wanted to fight through the living caves of the kobs and goblins. Looking right the tunnel went a similar distance and seemed to end, no sense in waiting when they had all assembled. They charged around the corner and off down to the right, coming to a halt in front of a dead end after some fifty yards.

"Now what!" Ikin groaned. Voicing their collective thoughts. Quickly they searched, while curious kob females sidled up to a cautious distance of them to see what the group were doing, and after a while they started sniggering and nudging each other, while chattering away unconcerned at the situation. The group ignored them as they were a little way down the passage and not interfering at all, but the males at the back stood ready with their weapons drawn to fight. Eventually Clem found a recess in the ceiling, remembering caution he reversed his axe-handle and carefully so as not to cut himself he poked about in the hole. There was a clank and a screech as the end wall rose jerkily up a sword length. This was enough for the adventurers in the circumstances and they all crawled through.

97

Clem went out first fast, rolling, axe at the ready, as they had no choice but to go through. The other side gave access to a larger corridor. Clem came to his feet and stood guard. There was no enemy in sight so he cast about for a little recess in the wall like the one on the other side of the portal to trigger the closure of the door. He hadn't found it by the time the others had finished coming through, so he gave up.

They were in a fifteen foot wide corridor, to the right it turned away from them to a lighted section some fifty feet away, to the left after a short distance the tunnel went down a flight of stairs. Scuffling sounds came from under the door behind them, as the smelly and less cautious spectators peered through the gap, at the same time to the right more sounds of iron shod feet and lights were approaching. Hesitating no more, they quickly went left down the stairway ahead of the oncoming footsteps at a run.

The stair ended in the familiar tunnel by the now dried up fountain and going straight on they came to the drop down into the pool cave where the dragon left them. As fast as they could they scrambled down and into the newly altered cavern.

Sounds of pursuit came from the split tunnel, and a number of foolhardy kobs scrambled down to be cooked and eaten by the dragon. Others leapt back and ran for their lives scrambling up the drop, the lucky ones made it. Nomaque had to look away as several terribly injured kobs tried to scramble up the drop, but the dragon hooked them up on a claw and dragged them back to a gruesome end.

"AND YOU THOUGHTFULLY BROUGHT DINNER" the dragon murmured as he gulped them down armour and all, *"DIDN'T TOUCH THE SIDES"*. He sighed and looked at last at the audience, who had hung back a little.

"WELL, WELL A SIGHT FOR OLD DRAGONS. THIS MUST BE A RECORD FOR DRAGONKIND, I'M AMAZED, COME ON IN AND BE WELCOME GUESTS. I SEE YOU HAVE BROUGHT LIGITZ. warble, warble."

The dragon ended in a trill to the small draptera who replied in kind, but to a higher note. This discussion in dragon language continued for a short time, with Chorky getting a series of feelings from his new companion. The flow of thoughts registered firstly astonishment, pleasure and finally a hint of lost companionship. The little creature must have been lonely, almost as lonely as its massive copy, but even with these feelings it still clung to Chorky's shoulder as if it had grown there.

They all lined up in front of the opaque wall of wizardry, and Chorky asked Ligitz to give the word of command.

There was a silence, then from the very depths of that diminutive animal a deafening series of shrieks bubbled out and all around the caverns. It sounded as if the poor thing was being tortured. A flash of light went around the watchers, five races and the draptera. There was a swish, pop, and the wall faded away, one or two small stones fell from the roof but nothing else. The large tunnel stretched away up to the right.

"MOST DISAPPOINTING THESE WIZARD SPELLS, NO FLASH OF LIGHTNING OR THUNDER FOR ALL THOSE ENDLESS YEARS I SPENT COOPED UP IN HERE, IT JUST QUIETLY FADED AWAY. NEVER MIND I MUST GET SOME AIR AND BREAKFAST. DON'T TOUCH ANYTHING WHILE I'M AWAY, WILL YOU?
WELL...NOT MUCH ANYWAY...PROMISE?"

The dragon, after an experimental hop or two took off in the cave and whooshed up through the new opening, which swung away in a very large tunnel sloping upwards into the darkness.

They barely had time to move when down the tunnel came the sounds of a furious conflict. Grabbing their weapons they ran towards the sounds. The first deserted cave they entered through a wide shattered doorway, what remained of the door and frame lay amongst the scattered belongings and furniture. Disturbing sounds came from the large tunnel, which continued on the other side of the cave. As they hurried on, Eta strung his bow and the others gripped their weapons more firmly, called by the noise of battle up ahead.

There was a roar and flash of ruddy fire lighting up the arch, with steam spewing everywhere, then came the stench of burning flesh. A deafening roar followed, then heavy blows quivered the floor. The tunnel had widened out into a large cavern, in the middle of the floor the dragon was struggling with two ogres and a hill giant. Another ogre lay unmoving on the floor, twisted in the agony of the dragon flame. The giant was raining blow after blow on the dragon's head with a tree-sized club, while the two remaining ogres were holding the dragon by ropes around its neck. The ogress on the right had a terrible scorch mark all down the one side nearest to the dragon's head, but she was still holding on with grim desperation. The flame from the terrible jaws of the dragon lit the scene in a pulsing red.

As fast as only an elf can, Eta loosed arrows at the giant, while the others formed into two teams to harry the ogres. Chorky, Clem and Nomaque, taking care to avoid the dragon, took on the ogre on the left, Ikin and Zeth moved the other side to attack the injured ogress. The little dragon darted about the giant's head slashing it across the face with its spiny tail, very much in peril from the arrows and the giant's hand.

Chorky and Clem waded in, the one attacking

high with his sword, the other low with his axe, the ogre reeled and turned to defend itself from this new deadly onslaught. He let go the dragon and kicked Clem, sending him spinning, but not before the dwarf had sliced the ogre's thigh open to the bone. Chorky had to step back to avoid both of them and missed his second strike, but his first had opened up the ogre's chest. With his strength going the ogre still managed to grab poor Clem and start wrenching at his arm, which still held his axe. Nomaque gathered up his staff and with all his might brought it down whack on the ogre's head, just above the ear, where the skull in an ogre is thinnest. The staff, tested beyond its strength snapped with an explosion, and the ogre crashed to the ground.

On the other side Ikin and Zeth had wounded the ogress, but when she released the dragon she ran and picked up her cudgel, with which she was fending them off, and bruising them somewhat in turn.

The giant, his head and neck having three or four arrows embedded in it, turned to see what his new attackers were, in that moment the dragon launched itself, tail, claws and teeth onto the hapless giant. The dragon couldn't use its fire as the little draptera was in the way. Both monsters went down in a mountainous heap of bodies, rending and wrenching. The inevitable result was that the dragon would win, but not without injury itself. It was severely bruised, with one of its forelegs broken, teeth lost, one eye gouged and possibly more internal damage to its head.

Eta, finding no clear targets for his arrows, dropped his bow and drew his sword, running to where Ikin and Zeth were fighting. The ogress succumbed, soon after Eta joined in the battle, from the combined effect of dragon fire, axe and swords.

When the fighting had finished Zeth ran over to Clem, twisted and groaning on the floor. Clem was in poor shape, the ogre's foot had stovein three of his ribs and badly bruised his internal organs as well as broken his arm, and dislocated his shoulder making any movement agony. Zeth was doing his best to ease the dwarf's injuries, but they were at a loss as to what to do to help the dragon. It was contentedly eating large chunks of the giant, which made its treatment a problem to be solved later. It finished its meal and ambled back to its cave. The others looked around the shattered home of the Giant finding little. The dragon returned with a few trinkets including a scroll. It then carried on with it's munching

The quest was in disarray. Eta felt they had now lost their way, they were no further towards finding the lost ones, and he said as much to Nomaque.

"We have only found that jewel and Chorky's helmet of any importance towards finding the lost elves. I think we have missed our way somewhere."

"The monk said we were to find Vodocanthey, whoever he or it is, who could tell us more. We followed his directions and ended up helping the dragon." Nomaque replied.

There was a snort of derision from the feasting behind them,

"DON'T YOU THINK HELPING A DRAGON IS WORTHWHILE THEN!".. scrunch *"AS A MATTER OF FACT THE 'MONK', WHOEVER HE WAS, WAS RIGHT ON ALL COUNTS. HIS DIRECTIONS LED YOU TO ME, I AM VODOCANTHEY, AND I CAN TELL YOU A LOT ABOUT ELVES, LOST OR OTHERWISE."*

"Oh! Oops sorry Vodocanthey, but the monk didn't tell us it was a dragon we had to look for. Perhaps that was wise. We are looking for the elves and their castle that disappeared a bit less than two thousand years ago from around here. The survivors returned to their valley after being away the day it happened, only to find no trace of their kin's existence. Eta and young elves like him, descendants of the survivors, are sent out to scour the countryside for scraps of information about them." Nomaque explained.

"THE ELF KINGDOM; THE CASTLE, THE CITY AND THE VILLAGE TO THE SOUTH WERE ALL LINKED MAGICALLY AT ONE TIME. THEY SPLIT INTO TWO QUITE SOME TIME BEFORE THEY ALL DISAPPEARED.

IN A VALLEY TO THE NORTH, THE MAIN PART, WITH A CASTLE ON A TALL ROCK IN IT, STAYED TRUE TO THE LIGHT. THEY WENT FIRST. I CANNOT TELL YOU WHERE THEY HAVE GONE, BUT I CAN TELL YOU THAT IT WAS A SORCERER POSING AS AN ELFENE THAT DID THE DEED, AND I'M PRETTY CERTAIN THEY ARE STILL ALIVE.

THE PART CENTRED ROUND HERE, AS WELL AS THE CITY, BECAME EVIL. THE SORCERER'S SON WAS INVOLVED IN THAT AND CAUGHT ME IN THS CAVERN. THEY WERE FOOLISH AND MANAGED TO TRIGGER AN EARTHQUAKE AND DIED OFF.

OH, AND ANOTHER THING, I SENSE THERE IS DANGER BREWING FOR THE ELVES FROM THE CASTLE, A BATTLE FOR SURVIVAL ALL OVER AGAIN, AND MAYBE A COMING TOGETHER. THERE IS IN MY BLOOD A BOND WITH THOSE TIMES, AS WITH ALL OF MY KIN. IF YOU SHOULD ASK ME WHERE TO LOOK NEXT, I WOULD SUGGEST ANY LARGE LIBRARY, OR URDFUG'S MYTHICAL LIBRARY, IF YOU CAN FIND IT. FAILING THAT TRY ANY ELVES IN THE VILLAGE, ESPECIALLY FAMILIES.

LASTLY DO NOT WORRY ABOUT MY IN-JURIES, WE DRAGONS CAN HEAL OURSELVES BUT I THANK YOU FOR YOUR CONCERN."

"Who's Urdfug?" Eta asked.

"HE'S A SORT OF MYTHICAL PERSON FROM THE PAST AGES, IN THE BEGINNING ON THIS PLANET HE WAS THE ELVES' LIBRARIAN, YOU'D KNOW HIM IF YOUR PATHS HAD CROSSED, NEVER FEAR. IGNORE MY REFER-ENCE TO HIM, IF HE WANTS TO FIND YOU HE WILL."

"IF YOU NEED MY HELP IN THIS VICINITY, I MAY BE NEAR, SO JUST BLOW A BLAST ON THIS WHISTLE, AND IF I CAN I WILL COME."

The dragon held out his one good forearm and dangling from a four inch bloodstained claw was a silver chain with a small whistle suspended on it. Gingerly Nomaque reached out and took it, placing it around his neck.

"Thank you, Vodocanthey, the only library I know of is in Mesquite, where we started from. That's a goodish step for us from here, especially when Clem is injured."

"OH WELL, I CANNOT KEEP ALL MY SE-CRETS CAN I? HERE PRIEST ZETH, COME AND TAKE THIS SCROLL WILL YOU? READ IT OUT IN A MINUTE WHEN CLEM THE DWARF AND I GET SETTLED. PUT CLEM UP HERE ON MY NECK AND WEDGE HIM ON TIGHT."

They part lifted, part levered Clem onto the spiky back and wedged him in. Standing back, Zeth, not without some trepidation, unrolled the scroll and began to read.

The words, as with all scrolls, fool the speaker into speaking them. They sounded total gibberish to the listeners unless they were high magicians. This happens whether the spell is beneficial or not, also the speaker does understand what they mean, although he or she cannot do anything about it. This was the case with Zeth, he had doubts as to whether it would benefit poor Clem, but he could not stop reading.

With a hum of powerful spellcasting, the dragon and his rider swept up and out of the cavern. The words floated back to them.

"SEE YOU IN A MONTH. HERE."

Zeth held up his hand as if to ward off their comments before he could speak.

"I could not stop myself, the scroll put a geas on me not to cease speaking. The dragon, I believe, has gone to a dragon healer, so...Clem should be all right...shouldn't he?" He explained ending lamely with his own question.

"Do not blame yourself, Zeth, you had no choice. This was the best chance for Clem to have healing before he suffered permanent damage. What do you think that would have been if we had carried him all the way to the village?" Chorky reassured him. "The choice is either the village or the town. How does everyone else feel?"

"I think it will have to be the town again, there are several reasons." Nomaque counted them off on his fingers. "One, information, the library there is the only one near here. Two, Maltex, we could do with as many fighters as we can get, and we definitely have missed his help. He will certainly be on his way back to Mesquite by now. Three, the crown, I have a feeling about it, we should have held on to it. It had a lot of elvishness about it, even for the 'rusty iron' look. Besides the alternative is the village. That was a grim place, we had very little luck there,"

There was a silence as Nomaque had put their thoughts very clearly and had included all their own arguments in favour of returning to the town. Chorky felt a sudden loss and looked around for his small companion. He could feel no mind contact.

105

"Has anyone seen Ligitz, I can't feel him near."

"The draptera went with the departing duo, clinging to the dragon's tail. Do not worry it was not injured in the fight," Eta consoled. They packed up and rummaged about in the two caves. They found a sorry pile of tatty smelly clothes and sorry weapons near the treasure pile, which caused them to wonder about the fate of the three rogues. That was until Chorky saw a small pile of the treasure had been placed away from the rest.

"Breakfeast." He sighed.

The kobs being in the valley when they came out of the caverns to find Ligitz, they decided to leave the way the dragon went up the mountain. Some way up the tunnel, it branched with one tunnel going up higher, emerging near the mountaintop. Here they found Tasherlon and the other four elves. They had thought it best to rest Uslar for a few days and avoid the kobs. Activity down below had lessened a little and by then Uslar was able to hobble. The time had come to leave their hideout and make for Mesquite.

It took them a week to retrace their steps to the town. Journeying with the other five they were not bothered by raiders, as they were a respectably sized party.

Chapter Six

News from the Town of Mesquite

On their arrival in Mesquite the four elves went their own separate way, leaving the original party with the inclusion of Tasherlon and Hectar, to stay back at the Old Duck Inn.

They were disappointed as Maltex, Hons and Sorin hadn't been seen since they went off to visit their relatives. This was a turn of events that they hadn't thought of. They had already decided to stay on anyway at the Inn, also it was the most likely place in the town for any news of the three.

During the second day they set about finding some answers to their questions. Ikin went off to visit the gnome community in town, leaving the rest to find the library. The library proved more of a club for the wealthy traders rather than a place for information seekers. It was only the fact that Druids in general had an elevated position in town society that they were let in at all. When they discovered that Nomaque was only interested in 'books', the curious wealthy patrons left them to look for what they really wanted to find, although odd people sometimes hung around in the shadows.

The group felt that the elf secret was solely for them to solve, others would only take advantage of the situation and distract them. So they looked for answers, but openly, they were researching the histories of the different races in the area. The librarian Sioman was almost pathetic in his eagerness to please, as he was rarely asked for his opinions or treated with kindness. He offered to copy out any tome they wished to take away, an offer they very carefully considered. Unfortunately their requests to him, the one person who could really help, had to be varied to conceal the one of real interest in case he innocently gave the quest away.

The first few days they could only spend a limited time in amongst the tomes of the past, as the members found many ways to interrupt their search. Eventually most days they tired of the dim aisles and left after several hours, leaving a list of subjects to be looked at on the following day.

Ikin brought news of increased raider activity. Some attacks had proved to be a real menace to the trade in the area. All around the town the main roads were hazardous in the extreme and only large caravans were getting through unmolested. This had several effects on the seekers. The worst one meant that they would have to run the gauntlet to get back to the valley later in the month. Help in the form of hired fighters was very scarce, and only a few very mediocre individuals were available at all, and they preferred big caravans. Mesquite and some of the larger villages had at long last got together and formed a proper militia to keep the roads clear and protect the trade caravans, which were too small to look after themselves. There was of course a healthy tax put on any 'help' so received, a nice little gold spinner.

"Trust the merchants to think of a way to make a profit out of it," Ikin muttered.

By the end of the first week they were not much further forward in their endeavours. They had only at most seven or eight days left, and one was market day when the library was closed. A mood of deep gloom settled in that evening. There seemed no way forward and they missed having the dwarf about. The unexpected way he had left them, draped over

Vodocanthey's back had them all wondering whether they would ever see him again. One month it had said, what if it was longer and they missed him?

Tasherlon had healed the breach created when he refused to accompany them into the 'hole', as he put it. Really, they were pleased, as he had met up with the elves and helped them search for the lost elf Prince Throndralon. All to no avail, the elf had disappeared.

He also made up for it in another way. Some friends of his had begun a news notice, which was going to be delivered to businesses around the town every week. They sometimes kept copies lying about. He went off to see and visited the newly set-up inking rooms, with the rows of busy scribes scratching away. Someone located a copy referring to the recent goblin raids under an apprentice asleep in the back corner of the room.

GOBLINGS GALORE
Our riders have just ridden in from the lands near the Goblin Hills. Goblins have been going out in larger hunting parties of late, burning and pillaging any farm in their way. It is said they seek their Iron Crown, well I reckon yesterday they found it and went back to their black hills. There were a few bodies left behind, a bit mangled I'm afraid, in the usual goblin fashion. One short ugly stranger captured after too much sack and goblin 'amusement', was quoted as saying that they had found a rusty old crown at the back of his shack and he overheard that they were going to find out the secret of a lost valley with it. They were coming back to buy the town with the treasure of the elves.
WHAT A LOAD OF OLD GOBBLINGS NO DOUBT?????

Nomaque's mind went back to the viewing pedestal in the cave, he remembered the sight of the crown on the hobgoblin's head, and shuddered.

"Just think of the mayhem that crown is going to cause," he said thoughtfully.

The day following market day produced a surprise, when the librarian Sioman called on them first thing that morning with the news that they couldn't go to the building that day, as it was to be a members' day. This meant non-members, like themselves, were excluded. Two days lost! Despon-dency set in until the stout fellow produced a hastily copied manuscript of the elves' history. He had in fact been watching the books they looked into, and noted the one's they discussed most. He sensed that they were in a hurry and so he stayed up all night slaving over the task. Almost pathetically he asked whether the honourable researchers would accept his humble attempts to help them.

They were overjoyed and plied him with food and ale from their early morning table, as well as several gold pieces, which he at first refused. They could see he was poorly paid so they insisted and eventually he took them. He said that he copied the work as he was annoyed at the way his employers treated genuine researchers, and he said he would help them again if they called at his humble home the next time.

The leaves of vellum had been carefully bou-nd between heavier quality pieces, keeping them flat for travelling. The group were amazed at the diligence of the librarian. Amongst the pages there was the following story.

THE LOST KINGDOM OF THE ELVES OF THE STAR

One thousand years ago, some say as many as two or more, this kingdom was fabled to exist somewhere to the north of the city of Mesquite. Long before this the elves colonised this part of Jodamia journeying from the sea, coming up the River Glyda forming a settlement south of the river. They built a tall castle in a secluded valley and then expanded southwards some miles to another valley. Here they grew and created a city over many years.

The city expanded in and around the surrounding hills including another valley to the south.

One side of the valley was a fine city of trees, towers and another smaller castle. Across the valley to the other side were pleasure gardens and an arena for feats of skill. Once a year a festival of prowess was held similar to the Lisego Arrow of Gold, which as everyone knows, is held every second year in the village of Lisego on the way to the eastern elf city of Estamon.

The kingdom split apart, the northern and southern parts came under different kings. The southern one took the dark path, evil beings bred in the former beautiful towers, the arena became a byword for cruelty and death.

The Kingdoms were inexplicably subject to an enormous blast of sorcery some time later, which affected both areas quite severely. The cataclysm opened up a rift valley to the south-east and caused much loss of life. Many at the time were reported to have said this was a just retribution from the gods.

The whole area went wild, parts were said to have enchantments laid upon them, some of them were seen to disappear without trace. Another village to the south was reported to come and go at times. There were tales of elvish people sundered by the catastrophe, searching for their kin, but never finding them. There is much evidence that they moved eastward, to found the city of Estamon in a likeness of the former Castle of the Star. It is said that when the great jewel, the Star of Anhuaz, is placed in the tower of the Star Castle the area will return to normal. To this day no-one has traced where this site was, there are several possible reported ruins which could be it. The jewel has never been found, although there are regularly specimens given in to the Bardonne City Museum, none have been authenticated.

Another fabled item said to have some connection, was the so called' 'Iron Crown of the Goblins'. As antiquarian of some standing I was called to look at this artefact several years ago.

It certainly looked of goblin origin as there were claws around the rim and across the centre stretched four recurving what could be fingers with long nails. After special investigation, I could just determine fine writing on the inside of the rim of the crown:

'A joy to the peaceful and a gate to the lost' the inscription said in Elvish, this was odd as it was reputed to be the goblin's crown. The writing was well hidden and only the most powerful reveal spell I had could faintly show it. If of course it had some elvish spell on it to hide its real purpose the general shape would be similar, but the dweamer would bend it to its own design.

So hidden, it could easily be an elvish crown and maybe the Advisor's Symbol of Power of the ancient Elf King, which featured in the famous fireside story. The story describes how a crown such as this was lost to the goblins, and then found again changed by wizardry. In the story it was given to the king of that land, who, when he put it on his kingly head couldn't take it off again. It stayed on there, despite all the court wizard's efforts for most of the poor monarch's life. Eventually a poor old goblin prisoner took it off for him and was given a high place in that land, the king making him his chief adviser.

Extracts from Historian Reeve the Elder from his Magic, Investigations

113

and also other Various Histories,
Fables and Sagas of the Area
scribed elvenyear 3841
copied faithfully and truly by Sioman
elvenyear 4030.

They all gathered around Nomaque in his room in the Inn as he read it aloud, here was the breakthrough at last.

"That was our crown, definitely," Ikin muttered. "Unfortunately it's definitely gone beyond our reach. It was a shock seeing it on that goblin king's head in the view we had in the magic pool on that pedestal."

"The valley with the stones and the ruined city above must have been the elf city that went bad." Zeth observed. "We've got the right area then."

"North of that ruined city must lie the valley where the castle was before the Sorcerer blasted it." Eta murmured. "It's the monk I'm curious about. Did you have any feelings about him, Nomaque?"

"Possibly," Nomaque answered. "He seemed unconcerned at first but as we talked to him he became quite interested. He's real, and very powerful, especially as that was only a vision of him. I think it's a good chance that the big star shaped jewel we found in the waterfall pool is the Star of Anhuaz it mentions. Let's have another look." He went to his pack and pulled out a small cloth wrapped bundle. When he unwrapped it, the jewel was there for them all to see again.

The gem studded six-rayed star, a large hand-span across, was built up of two three-rayed stars, one behind the other. The front star was picked out by three triple rows of diamonds out from the middle, in the centre was an enormous single palered ruby. The second star was arranged so that the

114

lobes rested midway between the front ones and on each of the points a large solitaire diamond twinkled. Halfway along each lobe a long rectangular, very pale blue sapphire rested, this rear star was constructed of the same solid but light silvery metal as the front one. The setting of the stones was arranged so as to leave the jewels raised above the surface and constructed of a silver-white metal, reflecting the daylight. On the back there was a raised pattern of short pegs corresponding to the gems on the front.

"Would this be one of the Emblems the monk and one of the four elves, Lexar referred to? Do you think it was the one the Prince was looking for?" Ikin probed.

"Very likely," Nomaque agreed, "but the monk said that there are more to be found. Eta, is this Prince Throndralon, a high elf like yourself, from the castle, likely to be one of the elves we are looking for?"

"I wondered about that too." Chorky added.

"Yes, as far as I can tell. He must have mentioned the emblems to the four elves. Our present King Aurochus is an only child and has no children. There is no Prince Throndralon alive today in Estamon. He may be from some other group of elves though, the sea elves from the far northeast maybe. He definitely comes from a kingdom in trouble, and under a curse. Also from the picture in the mirror pool Lethelorel is going to be attacked too. Anyway, from what Vodocanthey said, it's clear we must hurry, he also knows more than he told us. Let's see if we can find out more when we meet him and Clem. Hopefully meet this Prince too! I think we have found out all we can here, let's go north!" Eta summed up their combined feelings and the meeting broke up.

The rest of the day was spent preparing to depart the very next morning. The manuscript had reinforced their need to return to the valley and continue their explorations, quite apart from their appointment with the dragon and Clem. They chose to go mounted and the innkeeper found them suitable mounts, at a price.

The gold gleaned from their rummaging in the giant's and ogre's hoard meant that they could well afford it, but they haggled anyway for appearances sake. In the giant's hoard they had found a large brass-bound chest with too much to carry back so they buried it in the lower cave exit onto the mountain. Nomaque arranged, with his druidic skill that no other person other than the group could find it. When they left Mesquite they asked the librarian to keep an eye out for other works too, paying him a retainer. This was mainly a way of augmenting the pittance he received from his employers.

Up to the point of departure, none of the missing members of the party had been seen, then the barmaid shyly came up to Chorky and haltingly said she thought she had seen the three elves going out of the town several weeks after they all had left. This made it all the more important to get away. They still left a set of directions for Maltex with the innkeeper, just in case the elves returned, then they took to the trail again.

PART 2

Goblins Known and Unknown

Chapter Seven

Curious are the ways of the Goblins

The setting sun sank down silhouetting the dark contorted tops of the mountain. Black and jagged, that rock gave off no light, it seemed to absorb the last rays of the disappearing orb. That orb, they would prefer it never to come up again. The blackness would reign forever. This is how the Goblins would prefer it. Black and jagged were the majority of their minds, but clever in their nasty and objectionable way. They would prefer it if there was no day at all. Deep in the caverns there were goblins with older minds and different ways...the ancients.

But the caverns had been taken over by Asphar the powerful Sorcerer.

Quillam the ancient, was explaining the real world patiently to a hasty young goblin, Paah, who was very much controlled by the upstart Sorcerer Asphar and his henchgoblins, the drivers as he called them, kobs from the nearby fortress of Nablutz.

"Day was necessary so Asphar's drivers said. Who are these Drivers anyway to know the wishes of the Great Ones of the Dark? These minions of the necromancer pretend to know these wishes in order to control us. You have to do all their jobs without them giving the cavern anything in return. They say they have to organise us so that we do not anger the Gods, that is their song. Go and sing it somewhere else, I want to go and sleep in my cave with my matan, Soohermi Neplin-iti during the lightness, it is not natural to work in the brightness. Things just do not work in that scorching, searing light, we were made for the dark, the Dark Ones would have made us differently if they meant us to do otherwise."

Aghast, the young goblin stared at the old goblin in front of him, there was nothing frail or rambling about the figure, old maybe but sharp as a knife.

"You will be punished." He blurted out, looking over his shoulder fearfully, "p-pegged out in the light until the dark returns again if you dare disobey him, Asphar, or his Drivers, or question his wonderful wisdom. He will banish the light and the dark will be everywhere, he said so almost a year ago." the young Driver's apprentice replied.

The old one sighed, "that is utter sludge talk, false words, you must know that inside you somewhere. We must live where we were meant to live and nowhere else, and not go poking around in

120

places we were not built to go. No good will come of it, you mark my words."

"You old ones are all the same, never want to improve things, only want what you already know, you cannot advance if you do not find out new things. Science and exploration are the things for any young adventurous goblin nowadarks. Go out and find new caves or make new ones in the new styles. Come and look at the new cavern Poggornish has built into the light. Isn't that wonderful? You must agree, Quillam."

"It's not natural I tell you!" Quillam replied, "It will collapse and let the brightness in. You will remember my words when we discover things that are best left alone. Out there in the light there are many creatures that we know little about, who at this moment leave us alone. They have a right to live the same as us. In my youth we tunnelled in good solid rock and found some spectacular caverns, they were something worthwhile to strive for.

Above us, not very far, there are open spaces so vast you cannot see to the other side, think of that, and fear. The roof, if there is one, is so far away that you cannot see it. It is said to have holes in it, as say the Books of Ghatz, and walls appear out of nowhere as you move along." Quillam went on.

"In my youth I travelled in the light. I think there is no roof out there at all, there is said to be nothing between you and that blinding spike that shows always in the light. It pierced my eyes, and sometimes I wondered if I was going to fly up for ever. At least in our caves we are protected. That is enough for me, this is my place, this is the place the Great Ones put me and I am content, with black walls all around me, snug and tight."

The young one remained silent, and having heard the speech before, he ignored it.

121

Quillam continued, "Do this and you will anger the Great Ones, Paah the apprentice, carry on the way that Asphar the Necromancer wishes and you will put the whole home cavern in dire peril. For all our sakes I wish it would stop. I, at any venture, am going to my rest, good day."

The old Goblin turned on his heel and stalked off, there was no weakness in his step at all. The hard life he had led and the experience he had gained, showed. The ancients were in fact the most skilful fighters the goblin home caves had. The mere fact that they had survived well over forty years in a community, where death from fights was quite common, had honed their prowess. It had given them wisdom as well, but it was not always listened to. The Ancients lived apart from the main community, in a quiet, deeper annex of caverns far away from the squabbling, scurrying mass of goblindom.

When he arrived back at his home cave Soohermi his matan, and Snoodl his daughter were anxiously waiting for him. Snoodl came forward to meet him at the entrance.

"They have taken two warriors from the over-world, Patah. The armoured one was horribly wou-nded. Matah wanted to go to tend them but I said to wait for you," she blurted out quickly.

"You know your Matah does what she wants. As she is the healer they will not hurt her but she needs a bit of support, so, could you go and help her, Snoodling?" asked her father.

Snoodl smiled and went across to hold her Matah's arm. Arm in arm they went off down the tun-nel, the younger one carrying the large coloured medicine bag over her shoulder.

Quillam smiled. 'That'll cause a stir in the ranks' he thought, 'good, they need stirring up!'

His relationship with his matan had been an unusual one for goblin couples, as they had stayed

122

together nearly all their lives. She came from another home cavern so she found it comforting to stay with him. He found the same not having to fight for a new mate every year in the spring. He became more stable and found wisdom earlier in his life.

Snoodl was born into this stable atmosphere and had united them even more, so they never had another little one. Now she was of mating age herself, she kept to herself, not finding any young male mature enough to interest her. The young males and scatterbrained females kept away from her, calling her names and picking on her. She grew up to be very tough and resilient, well able to defend herself with a sword or other weapon. Quillam was a trained and seasoned fighter, so he taught her care-fully as well as he could in that violent society. She found the others of her own age shallow and uncar-ing compared to her Matah and Patah.

Normally a youngling could not wait to get away from their cruel and selfish parents, living in the communal caves from quite young. They could not understand Snoodl's attitude living in the home cave. Actually she had her own small cave, now that she was older, so she did not crowd her parents at all. The most important benefit from living close to her Matah was that she had become Matah's able assistant and apprentice in healing arts, a position of trust in the cave.

This was the first time she had been allowed to treat prisoners though, as her Patah had forbidden it previously. This time it was different. These prisoners were outsiders. They would help Snoodl understand that there were living, thinking beings out there, not to be fought at every opportunity.

'Perhaps,' he thought, 'I had better go along too'. He put on his armour and strapped up sword and scabbard to his belt harness, a special belt with a strap going over his shoulder. This way he could draw the sword by reaching behind, over his shoulder; it also enabled him to carry a man-sized sword. His purpose in going was threefold, it would tell the outsiders to behave around his females, also stop any young ambitious goblins messing about in an important situation. More importantly than these reasons, it would show that the ancients had teeth. He would join the guard at the door. That would keep them quiet too, and not interfere with the proceedings. Afterwards, he would have to call a council of the ancients and discuss the new turn of events.

Arriving at the Keepcave, the two guards nodded to him, one giving a salute, the proper respect due to an elder-in-arms.

'One young blood and one of the older ones, he thought, appraising the guards. 'The older one's trained right, no sloppy modern methods'. He acknowledged them with a suitable grunt.

In actual fact, they were very surprised and the young one even irritated when the healer arrived and they discovered that the 'carrion' deserved to be healed. This was mollified, as Hjir and to a lesser extent Vart, were now thinking of taking young Snoodl to one side after duty. She was a Venta to notice, a looker and no mistake, a waste for the 'prisoner carrion' in there to be looking at. Asphar had said when they had taken the prisoners that they were only good for a bit of sport. Hjir had been even more horrified when Quillam arrived.

Vart, was undecided as to whether it was wise to stir up these large warlike creatures of the light. He was older and wiser; his attitudes were changing. Vart was coming to an age when, if he survived, he might be picked to join the ancients, also he would tend to think more carefully about his actions.

These thoughts rarely came to the male goblin until they passed the change at around 40 years old. Vart looked at his companions and realised for the first time how assured Quillam look-ed. Hjir was larger, but shallow, vicious, selfish, and a lot less war-crafty.

Groans issued from the part open doorway. Vart started to consider the raiding parties they had taken part in, and for the first time he thought about what it would be like to be raided by another cave in turn. The old ones butchered, the Ventas raped and killed, or worse still the little ones tortured; no, it was wrong, and it would lead to a dangerous end for the cave.

Looking up he noticed that Hjir was leering at him, obviously thinking of taking the Venta to one side, and wanting him to create a diversion. An action he would have done willingly a few moments before. 'Not now though', he thought as he shook his head negatively at Hjir, when the ancient was looking in the other direction.

Hjir scowled and looked mean, muttering to himself. 'He's too old for active service, that Vart, the sharp end of a sword would be a mercy, over the hill and no mistake.'

Quillam watched the interplay, out of the corner of his eye, not fooled for one tiny moment. He had a feeling that he needed to get about a bit more and there were a lot of things going on that he need-ed to know. It might come to the point where a physical rift ought to be created between the two factions, maybe actual distance as well. He did not want to have to move away but it could be necessary if Asphar had too much support. The young warrior in front of him illustrated the problem very well.

Snoodl put her head around the door.

"Can I have a bit of help?" she asked. "Oh! Hello Patah. I'm so pleased you're here."

Hjir leered and pushed forward, misinter-preting the request. Quickly Vart joined him to try and limit the damage.

Quillam wondered if he ought to go in too, but there was very little room and Vart looked as if he could handle the situation. He positioned himself in the doorway to see all that was going on, long sword now drawn.

One prisoner was manacled to the wall and had what seemed only a minor wound. The other lay on the floor with blood oozing from several places. Snoodl's Matah was struggling to take off the pieces of armour, but the elf was trying to resist her.

Hjir still had not realised what was going on. He drew his sword and swung it to finish off the prisoner double-quick, and then hopefully wander off with Snoodl. The sword rang as it was deflected to Hjir's utter surprise by a well placed knife wielded by Snoodl the Venta. She pressed home her advantage by taking the sword from him, throwing it into the corner in disgust.

Flaming with rage, Snoodl turned on Vart. "Well then, you as well?"

Vart stood his ground sword in his hand, but he showed no sign of using it. Confused and angry Hjir yelled with fury at Vart. "You finish him off then, weakling."

"No not me," Vart replied cautiously, sheath-ing his sword, he added, "you or your prisoners have nothing to fear from me." He moved to help Soohermi with the armour.

The raging Hjir went to look for his sword in the corner, only to find it not there. He looked around and found a quiet ancient figure standing in front of him holding his sword. He then made his second mistake of the day. Thinking that the ancient was a broken old goblin, to be trodden on without thinking, he barged forward, snatching his weapon he made to

126

shove viciously at the old figure, which was meant to put him in the dust of the floor where all the old goblins should grovel to the young.

The old figure wasn't there, and a quiet voice asked from the side, "Where is your respect for the aged, youngling?"

Hjir was now lethally vicious, swinging around with his sword in his hand, moving it up to finish this old bag of bones. There was a clang, as metal struck metal, and his sword flew out through the doorway, disarming him a second time. The long sword wielded with sure skill continued on to nick Hjir's neck.

"Leave us youngling," Quillam ordered, "you are relieved of your duties of the day. I do not wish to see you again, and I hope you will learn from this to respect older goblins' swords."

Behind him the elf on the floor had given up the rather one-sided battle now that Vart had moved in to help and allowed the two females to take over and administer to him, but his eyes were screwed up in pain.

---O---

For Hons, the other elf, the scene in front of him defied belief. He looked on with amazement as the young goblin girl deflected and disarmed the young burly soldier, then the goblin was again disarmed later by the sure ability of the old one. Not knowing more than a few words of the goblin tongue, the discussion that followed was gibberish, but the obvious affection of the two females for the old one belied all that he had ever heard of these folk. The other soldier after he had helped, went back to stand deferentially by the door, more guarding the inside than controlling the prisoners. These were an almost totally new type, a higher goblin folk with all the compassion and wisdom of his own village elders.

Normally goblins stood about 4 feet tall, with snarling and distorted faces, smelly and vicious.

127

These before him were quiet, loving and caring, still about four and a half feet tall, but quite comely, especially the girl. The ancient was slightly shorter but grizzled with close-cropped white hair. The real surprise was the old fighter's way of carrying his sword slung over his shoulder. This enabled him to wield a long sword, normally an elvish weapon. His skin was the blue-brown of the goblin folk and his mate had well cared for lustrous black hair. The girl's skin was a lighter hue of mauve-brown with wavy black locks, framing a round but pleasant face and large brown eyes. Her short figure looked trim, but full in the right places.

The girl bustled around her mother as she looked after Maltex, both having that deft way of healers with the sick. The whole thing was extra-ordinary. The veteran, after he had dealt with the younger vicious one, went over to the remaining guard and put him through a difficult grilling, which must have been satisfactory. He then took him out-side and had what seemed a weapons work-out in the passage near to the door. The guard must have passed this too, as he came in grinning, but worn. The responsibility of his safety was solely in this goblin's hands, a fact the goblin seemed to take as an honour, standing rigidly to his post half in and half out of the doorway.

---O---

Food was brought to the door and left, the guard bringing it in after whoever brought it went away. Maltex drifted into a fever and Hons was allowed near him, for his help was needed to calm the elf's wilder moments. The guard was relieved a few hours later by another ancient, even older and craggier than the first one. More ancient he was maybe, but he also had that veteran sureness about him. Obviously they were trying to take fewer chances and they were obviously protecting them.

About a day later the elves had a visit from a person who made their flesh creep. Dressed in the black robes of a sorcerer or wizard, he had the size and air of a middle-aged elf about one hundred years old but that was where the resemblance ended. His skin was dark and drawn tight, and his eyes deep and thoroughly evil, looked with loathing down on them. He had several thick muscular henchgoblins with him and things became desperate for Hons and Maltex, who were then beaten. The healers tried to protect the elves, but the brutes punched the healers too, and threw them into a corner. The evil wizard kicked Maltex until he realised that he was delirious, and then started on Hons, shouting in goblin at him and kicking him too.

He stopped suddenly as if remembering something long forgotten, then in a sneering elvish voice with a strange accent he demanded to know what they were doing spying on the goblins. Hons remained silent even though the Sorcerer put some power into the words to obey. When that got no result the magician drew a nasty little dagger with a toothed blade and closed in on him, chanting some spell on it. Hons started praying to Aloth under his breath, as the air around him grew thick with sorcery. He tried with every fibre of his body to resist but in the end his mind started to wander. It was in moments like those, that the elf's mind desperately reached out for familiar comforts, thinking of the sunlit woods of his home.

---0---

Quillam was slow, much too slow to guess the full power of Asphar. He had thought him a menace only, but as the hours went by after being called to the keepcaves, he realised his full stupidity. This was no jumped up minor wizard but a full sorcerer at the height of his powers, like his namesake of old. The home caves were in thrall to him, and so Quillam had barely enough time to bring together the Council. This quickly turned into a council for the desperate and the need to take emergency measures. In the space of several hours the inner core of ancients had decided to abandon the home caves and make for a secret stronghold known to only a very few, Quillam being one of them. The skilled veterans of many wars, the cream of the cavern fighting force, if the others stopped to realise it, put their plans quickly into action. The ancients armed themselves as of old, in their treasured war gear, from trunks and storerooms, arms and armour put aside and oiled for such a time as this. A score of seasoned fighters, with perhaps twenty younger ones verging on their change, as was Vart, a determined defence. They decided to take any enlightened females who were sympathetic, as well as their children, a group of thirty extra. The provisions were organised and carried on their backs, with the younger children. The arrangements were virtually complete when Snoodl burst in to the meeting, her temple bleeding.

"Asphar is with them," she gasped.

Waiting was not going to help them any longer, so passing Snoodl a short sword, Quillam gathered her arm and ushered her out of the cave, signalling a considerable force to come with them.

"What was the situation when you left, my Snoodling?" He asked as they jogged along in battle step.

"He was kicking the fevered one and the other was trying to stop him, Patah," she replied. "Matah was injured when they threw her against the wall.. Patah," she sobbed.

"Tell that to the others as we advance, Snoodling, they need to know. That is an act of sundering, I cannot remain, let's go!" With that he redoubled his pace.

The veterans swung into action and sealed off the keepcaves section. Before the Sorcerer's guards knew it they were rendered senseless, but not killed. The main force pressed on to the caves, and dealt with the guards outside the door. This they did by covering up their armour by their old cloaks and slowly shuffling up to the guards, surrounding them and then knocking them out too.

The cave was full of dark mist and the smell of wizardry. Quillam stopped just outside and gathered his thoughts, pulling out of his tunic a strange amulet.

"For such a moment you were made," he said throwing the glittering disc full at the back of the unsuspecting Sorcerer.

With a scream the figure leapt up, his spell ruined, trying to feel what weapon had pierced his mana-protection. Spinning swiftly he launched a knife towards the figure in the doorway. Deflecting the flying weapon almost casually into the door with a flick of his wrist shield, Quillam brought up the point of his long sword to the Sorcerer's throat. He then cried out to all those near.

" Asphar, as leader of the Council of Ancients I insist that you remove yourself. You have overstepped the hospitality of these caves, and the laws of this cavern. I hereby banish you by the Rule of Ancients and call down Brannisha upon you!"

Asphar laughed sneeringly and swept aside the four-foot blade.

"Council of Ancients! Pah! It is you and your decrepit band, who are cast out. You were worth keeping in the caves if you controlled yourselves, and did not meddle in the affairs of the cavern. If you stay I cannot ensure your safety. It is you who should consider going. For the moment I will retire from here, but leave the prisoners for me to deal with

131

later." The Sorcerer sneered, as he passed Quillam he whispered,

"You are the one who will regret this. Old upstart! Heap of rags! But *I* will come for you later and you will be the one in terror. *Fool!"*

Quillam was tempted to try to end the tyrant, there and then, but the ancient felt he was up against a foe beyond his limited abilities and he could not, after such a long time from battle, kill in cold blood. So he stayed his hand, and started to turn to clear the rabble from the cave. The Sorcerer passed the other veterans, barely giving them a glance, but they noticed him nevertheless. A lone voice, thin and reedy rose from the back of the group,

"One of power, you are at your most invincible now, but you who live by the power will die by the power. Beware clerics and Druids working together, they are more than a match for a sorcerer."

"Old seer, you are as blind as your friends." he sneered, and went on his way, wondering nevertheless.

Turning, Quillam stared in total disbelief, one of the henchmen was preparing to rape his matan as she was lying wounded on the cave floor, while the other ruffian blocked any intervention.

"A lesson to you oldings," the henchgoblin sneered while the ancient seemed to pause a second to take in the scene. Hearing another ancient behind him, Quillam started to give a signal behind his back with his hand. This was for the follower to attack the talkative one and go to the right, while he dealt with the other one on the left. His signal was stopped in a firm grip which guided his hand to the right instead and a young terse voice whispered passionately in his ear.

"This is females' work, Patah!"

So he feinted left and killed the guard on the right with one lightning blow, catching him as he fell and dragging him to the back of the cave.

A female shape slid silently by on the left, the movement terminating with a ghastly long drawn-out shriek. Quillam went over to the battered prisoners, and set about freeing them. Snoodl joined him several moments later supporting limping Soohermi. He embraced his matan tenderly, gently brushing the hair out of her eyes.

Close by Snoodl said, "Matah is all right, now...!"

"The stretcher is coming Snoodl," Quillam directed, "so can you prepare the quiet one for travel. We are going now, leave the 'carrion' behind."

He went out of the cave taking Hons with him. Outside he looked long and hard at the elf, thinking deeply. Then he called another ancient over who produced a tunic, belt and cloak and handed it to Hons, as he had been stripped on capture. He also handed over a short sword, but indicated for the elf to slip it under his cloak out of sight, giving him another belt with a scabbard in it. The poles and sling arrived for the feverish Maltex, and the females strapped him to it securely. The whole party left the cave without any more fuss and the whole operation had taken no more than 15 minutes. An hour later they were deep in the caves and tunnels of the ancient catacombs.

A fighting force forged ahead, a mixture of ancients and maturing goblins. The females followed, with children either carried or on foot, then the prisoners, with a vanguard following along after, clearing up and wiping tracks. They travelled a full day before they stopped, then only for a few hours, before resuming the march again. This took its toll of the weak and injured, Matah being one of these. Snoodl supported her on one side and Hons on the other. Eventually Quillam could not stand the torture to

133

Soohermi any longer and called a halt in a size-able cavern.

Quillam was worried in case the Sorcerer had planted a spell trace on them, and he needed a longish time in one place to sever any such possibility. Going to the entrance he traced a complicated pattern with his amulet over the tracks they had made coming into the cavern.

His skill in using this artefact had given rise to his name over the years, Quillamulent. Goblin's names grow with the owner during their lives, adding new parts with new skills or experiences. Practically it was shortened to Quillam. He then circled the group waving the artefact with a delicate precision, occasionally dipping the jewel in a liquid. When he had finished he sat down to rest as the effort he had used was considerable.

Snoodl went over to him to take him something to eat and saw how drained he looked. She reached out and gently touched his face lovingly. He looked up and smiled wanly, "I am not sure I shall be able to carry out the rite for too many more years, Snoodling. What are your needs?"

"It's just that you have only this minute finished powerful magic Patah, and this exercise is unusual for you. It will also take a little while for you to adjust to travelling again, now the years have given their blessing to you." she reassured him. "I need to find some fresh herbs to treat Matah, as the wound is not healing properly with the ones I brought with us. She also desperately needs rest. She will be lost to us if we move on again quickly. Are we near the surface?" She asked with a dread in her voice, as a fear of the open was instinctive in most goblin folk. Her need drove her much further than normal, as her cause was desperate.

"We are in an area where the surface is not known," Quillam informed. "We could send a party of the more adventurous with you to explore if you wish. Say, ten with the elf as well, he can help as muscle and interpreter if people of the open are encountered. Go after a half-day rest. We will be able to protect ourselves, never fear, but try to be back here in a day or so. We will screen and decoy if necessary, I am considering sending an ambush group back a little way at this very moment."

"But Patah" Snoodl observed, "won't that break your magic screen?"

"Oh wise young thing, of course. The screen will, I fear, have to be improved upon if we do as I suggested." He added. "But I will rest first now that the warding is in place. Go and get some rest yourself now."

Chapter Eight

Within the Dark Towers of Nablutz

*S*everal miles away from the caverns of the goblins the Sorcerer had been using the goblin artisan Poggornish to 'improve' the ancient fastness of Nablutz. Young goblins had been working for several years under absolute secrecy to make the towers impregnable. They had been using the new science under his instruction. Poggornish had disappeared from the main caverns about a year before and not been seen again outside the Sorcerer's halls.

"Neither had many others." Paah the apprentice thought. He had unwisely told Quillam of Poggornish's wonderful works in his fatal enthusiasm, the sort that causes young goblins to disappear, unfortunately for him.

Slowly, up one of the great tower flights of steps a rounded, bent and shambling form lurched, Nugth was wheezing every step and whispering to itself. A loathsome figure, rent and grimy garments hung from warty and slick limbs. From the sides of its twisted leathery lips showed two sharp fangs, which dripped a slimy drool. It was a blood wight, a thoroughly evil creature, extremely dangerous and absolutely silent when hunting.

"Drat that Poggornish, always had a need to build up, especially with lots of these blasted stairs. Won't build no more though, that's a certainty. I wonder if the lizards liked him, he did look surprised when I pushed him in. I did really like the way he squeaked when the vicious brutes snapped chunks out of him. Still that's what happens to surplus goblins when they are needed no more. Done their bit, and done in. Ha, ha, Hah, that's good. Never catch me being spare, especially if I do the feeding." The chubby creature muttered to itself and sucked its claw as it made its way up to the high chamber, thoughtfully it put up a seven-fingered hand and touched the circlet it wore low on its brow.

"I have your filthy circlet now, high elfling, but your blood nearly choked me, I couldn't get the taste off my fangs for days, ugh! Lizards didn't have you though, HE took you away," it shuddered, as if it sympathised with the luckless elf. It remembered the screams and shuddered again. It paused at the heavy panelled door and gathered its resolve.

The trips with the jeweled circlet always brought extra perks, tasty perks, but the gem made him uneasy in some way. Nugth could never rest when he wore it. The jewel seemed to have a life power of its own, drawing off the blood wight. The front diadem showed a star with six rays of diamonds and rubies. It particularly liked the rubies. They reminded it of blood, tasty red blood. It licked its thick twisted lips, and saliva wet its partially exposed stained fangs. It gave a little howl of frustration at the thought of several hours till its next feed. The voice of its terrible master came through to it as though there was no door there.

"Nugth, where are you, you foul bit of excrement. I wonder when I will tire of you, pawing around. Not yet perhaps, too many bodies to feed you. You have the casket, yesss I see it. I will remind you again though that if I ever find out that you've opened it, I will personally devise a special way to send you off, understand." The venom in the words slid along the unfortunate recipient's veins causing an involuntary shivering for several seconds.

"N-no… Great One n-never." It gasped. It quickly went through the door and dragged itself reluctantly towards its master. The figure before the twitching creature stood about six feet tall, dwarfing the now bent round shape of Nugth the blood wight. Asphar had the terrifying habit of writhing from one devilish shape to another when he was dominating his victims. Occasionally an evil tendril would caress the face before him as though he was tasting it for dinner. He did not use that form in the presence of the utterly controlled goblins. He preferred them to think of him as a dark evil elf, an elfene.

After long seconds he lifted the face before him and laughed, mentally squeezing the anguished mind a little, playfully almost carelessly hurting it.

"Now I have a task for you, which will test you to the limit. There has been a rebellion in the goblin ranks. No juicy chewing of the disobedient this time. This is more serious. They have gone, taking with them the two prisoners we took a few days ago. I must know where they have gone, I have a feeling I know, but the little runt of an ancient has hidden them. HE will have a very special end, similar to the one I promised you. You have to track them from the Keepcaves, do not let them be even vaguely aware of you or they will snuff you out. They may even know of your activities, yes even that. So you see, care where you go, bloodseeker." With that he propelled it to the doorway and out onto the stair.

Breathing heavily Nugth almost ran down the stair. It felt that it could stand only so much from the leader, before it collapsed on to the floor in front of him. The way to the Keepcaves was not long, so it went there first before feeding. There, a day or so old, was the corpse of Hjir, which gave it the snack it needed, to revive it. Moments later, collecting itself something to chew on the way, it was on its gruesome way, drops of blood trailing behind it.

138

It took several weeks of hiding, desperately close to capture a score of times, to locate the new quarters of the rebellious band under a valley miles away. As soon as it was sure they had settled Nugth had made its way back slowly, living off the land, leaving a ghoulish tale behind it wherever it went.

---0---

Some two weeks later and more reluctant than ever, Nugth approached the black mountains again where Asphar's fortress of Nablutz stood. It would have never returned, if it had not been certain that the Sorcerer would find it, wherever it was.

On its other trips using a circlet of power, it went to a strange world, like Jodamia but older and flatter, to another being, more violent but less evil and powerful than its master. The two were plotting a big take-over of a fabulous castle stuffed with booty and soft young elf prisoners.

"Nugth, so you have located them," Asphar hissed. "Gone off towards the old elvish valley, have they, no matter for you, you have done well. I will honour you, and make you one of my captains in the march we begin on the morrow. Yes, tomorrow we march on the Elf Treasuries. The plunder will be awesome. You must be proud that you are amongst the chosen to make such a journey. We will make our people one of the great nations, no longer will the overworld creatures look down on us, we will rule above and below."

"We will deal with the ancients when we have time for it, after the winning, it turns us too much from our march-path to bother with them now."

"Nugth, go and celebrate tonight, ready for the Great Vengeance."

---0---

The Sorcerer, after his hench-creature had departed, went over to his largest chest and uttered a complex series of sounds. He motioned a pattern

139

above it and it burst open. A deep hole went down into the darkness below. Opening another casket he took out a crown and examined it, looking for the marks he had put on it previously, 'Yes it may look rusty, but it really is the Crown of you High and Mighty Elves, one of the keys to reach you. Grand-father Aasphari, you will have your vengeance at long last, I will cast down the HIgh and MIghty Elves with their highest Crown. So very just! Use their own High Crown as the key to reach them in their fastness." he gloated.

Together with the Hobgoblin King, Kuk'I'mak, in the other world they would attempt to muster an army of over ten thousand, to be led by his warrior champion Impstalkish. His sorcery with a few trolls to sort out the gates, and a few other beasts, their combined forces will break the elvish Druids into pieces. He had just to crown the Hobgoblin King with that crown and there would be nothing to stop the army. He put the crown back into the casket and descended into the tunnel with it, descending by way of a ladder going into the blackness.

That blackness wrapping him around, the solace of his life, he was very much a creature of that dark. Born in an orgy wherein his fostering parents both die, him taking some measure of both, the humanoid cucoid. His real parent chose months before, carefully, cautiously and then seeding.

His first years were the agony of growing up in a village with his hosts, aunt and uncle of his elf foster parents, until the thirteenth year. Then he left, leaving bloody fear. Travelling by night he made his way to his kind and his legacy. He discovered his grandfather Aasphari was killed in the course of exterminating the hated elves, so was born the vengeance of his soul. Taking to necromancy naturally he became a master adept, following the path of his ancestor, at the same time probing into the

140

happenings in the Star Valley a long time before. Piece by piece he reconstructed the event and made it his great goal to complete his grandfather's mission, to annihilate the foul Star Elves completely.

The final piece falling into place came with the finding of the Elf Prince with the circlet, from the other world, in the tunnels. Posing as an elderly elf the Sorcerer gleaned enough in the first second of his victim's astonishment, before his victim realised that his mind was being read concerning the elf's quest and the circlet. Then the elf fought off his efforts until he was destroyed and his tormentor learned no more. Asphar smiled to himself and felt the threads were coming together, the elves would not escape this time.

There was another matter, which touched his base nature. Amongst his researches he found a statuette of a lovely elf-goddess, he desired to enslave her, more even than his vengeance, his lusting passion consumed him. But who was she?

He felt that she had something to do with the castle but he could glean nothing more. There was something blocking him. In the end, he would find her and control her. He always had his way, eventually.

Chapter Nine

Up on the Surface where the Perils Lie

*B*ack in the ancient goblins' camp, the small, but well armed party set off. The goblins had discovered Hons' elvish ability with a bow, so they found a smaller goblin equivalent and some arrows for him. The scouting party, which had been sent to look for a possible way up, had returned. They found a way through as far as a waterfall, but then they ran out of time and turned back. This route the surface party followed, they carried on past the waterfall for a while and then the tunnel went down steeply into a large cavern. This was a dead end, no way further could be found, and so another path had to be taken.

When the goblins returned along the tunnel, they found Hons standing by the falls, looking outward. He gestured through the water, perplexed, they looked too, but saw nothing, as they did not know what he meant. Seeing their blank faces he gathered himself and leapt out through the water and disappeared. The amazed goblins peered through the water sheet and they could just see him standing on a ledge a few feet on the other side of the water. He thrust his unstrung bowstave through, the tip protruding for them to grasp. With Hons help, the party soon passed through the falls and were soon on their way. The new tunnel showed many more signs of life, albeit only many piles of goblin and kobish bones. These were mostly very old and crumbled away at the touch, but here and there were fresher remains. These meant that there were some

142

feared predators around, as well as kobs and other goblins. They were slower and more cautious from there on, especially as the air now seemed dangerous to the goblins, and fresher to the elf.

They carefully noted their way by small marks on the walls by junctions, the elf taking a more important role now they were nearing the surface. The goblins who were feeling unsure of themselves, welcomed this turn of events. Apart from the animal's tracks and grisly leavings they did not see the animals themselves. Hons thought they were most likely to be large bears and were out foraging. This meant that it was daylight outside, and the elf was longing for the feel of the wind on his face. Later, soon after a large many-legged creature scuttled off out of the light of their torches, they could see the light streaming through the tunnel from the surface.

The goblins had a brief discussion about where Snoodl wanted to find the plants, in which Hons could have helped greatly. As he could not understand goblin speech he walked to the entrance and looked out on the sunlit valley. It was only many perils later in that seemingly safe valley that he found them for her. They set out from the cave and looked for shelter in the valley beyond, but it was meagre grassy scrub. The goblins were blinded by the light and could at first only stumble about in the cavern and they would have very much preferred to stay in the cave. Only the bears were due back and a meeting with them was to be avoided at all costs. The rest of that day was spent looking around the area, acclimatising their eyesight but none of the special plants were spotted. With the onset of night the goblins cheered up a bit, but they had to stop looking until morning.

The next day the party split up to cover more ground, Snoodl took four goblins to help her and Hons went with all the rest. Several hours later found both parties lower down the valley but they kept in touch every now and again when they moved on for safety's sake.

Snoodl had just found some promising leaves when suddenly a band of ten ruffians found them. She was held firmly before she could even drop the plants in her hands.

"Leave me and mine alone, humans!!" She yelled at the top of her voice, before a stinking hand came brutally across her mouth, after slapping her face. She struggled, but it was no use against the hardened muscles of the raider, who was enjoying her struggles. His foetid breath made her gag, his hands uncaring of her body. Quickly she realised open fight was hopeless and sagged, limp, onto the floor.

"Lookee here, we have some old goblins on a hike." The leading ruffian guffawed, "This lot's decrepit and no mistake. I can't remember when I've seen old gobbo's before, so let's maybe have a bit of fun. And looky there, say could that be a fee-male. I've never seen one of them either. Lets camp, and have some exercise." He said leering at Snoodl, her hopes for a quick rescue sinking as the time passed.

They never had a chance to defend themselves. They were surrounded and would have been killed without a thought if Snoodl hadn't made them feign being decrepit and ancient, also to put the raiding party off guard. This worked up to a point, as it saved the lives of the four males but it had its risks, unfortunately to her. She was at their mercy, there was nothing she could do, her foes being larger and stronger than she was. They stripped her and sat round in a circle eating their food, prodded, poked and handled her.

The other goblins they had tied up around a gnarled and twisted old tree, with the promise that they were next. In amongst them Vart struggled desperately, at the same time very uneasily, as the tree creaked and groaned as though it was about to fall on him at any moment. No warning or call for help could be sent as they were gagged with parts of their own garments. They could only wait it out, praying to their gods that the scum handling Snoodl would leave her alone.

Unfortunately they kept on until she could take no more, and collapsed on to the ground, refusing to move even when they baited and punched her. The mood changed, and the leader, who had led the events, gestured for others to hold her hands and feet.

As if the Gods had answered him, Vart felt the cords snap, and turned to find the tree branches bent down behind him. He brushed these aside carefully and moved to release the others but they were already free. With extreme caution two veterans moved to the pile of weapons and passed them back. Snoodl was by then, in dire straights as the leader was standing astride her, preparing to rape her. Desperately the four goblins charged into the ring of raiders, with little or no hope. The leader stood up and cast an eye over the desperate goblin veterans, he laughed and detailed four ruffians to 'finish them off'. He turned back to the little goblin girl lying defenceless and naked at his feet.

That was the moment the leader died, there was a slight whistle and his head jerked back with a feathered shaft protruding from his forehead. His falling body collapsed onto Snoodl. Her arms and feet had been released, she struggled to get out from underneath, the raiders holding her had turned to defend themselves from the unknown archer. They moved quickly to aid their comrades, because small though their foes were, the ruffians were having a tough time of it.

145

The ancient goblins had proved far better sword fighters than their adversaries were, and several of their large opponents were soon badly wounded or fallen. The arrows kept taking a deadly toll of the raiders, as they were taller than the goblins, they were good targets for Hons, the lone archer. He had had a premonition of danger and hurried back, arriving some time ahead of the others.

At that moment the other veteran goblins arrived and leaped into the fray, as deadly as their fellows. The battle now became short and very unpleasant for the renegades, and seven lost their lives before the remaining three made a dash for liberty. Only one managed to mount his horse and ride off, blood seeping down his jerkin and barely able to stay upright in the saddle.

Snoodl had crawled away to the tree and was sitting propped against it, crying softly, when Hons came up and gently slid a blanket from the raiders saddlebags around her shaking shoulders. A tremulous smile rewarded him, she caught his hand and pulled him down to sit with her. Much to his surprise she reached up and grasped his hair gently, he looked at her and she planted a shy kiss on his lips.

"Thank you, big elf." she whispered, her tear stained face and large brown eyes showing more violet then, transfixing him. He slipped his arm around her and smiled back. Goblin or no she was very beautiful in that moment, so he kissed her back very, very tenderly.

Hons had been through a desperate struggle, hiding in the undergrowth nearby, he had been on the verge of charging out several times, but knowing that he alone could not save her. He realised he loved the little gobliness. She was so different from how he imagined her race. It was only when the goblin veterans charged and caused the screen of raiders to shift enough for him to see the terrible events going on that he could loose the arrow. His iron determination did not waver even a fraction and his arrow sped true.

The rest had sorted out the bodies of the raiders and piled them to one side, wondering what to do with them. Vart looked around to ask Hons and spotted him still by the tree, partly hidden by the sparse branches, holding Snoodl. Vart sighed, as he was very fond of the Venta himself. His cough broke into their reverie, causing Hons to blush, and Snoodl giggle.

'Too late' Vart thought sadly, 'I've missed my chance with Snoodl. I don't know when, but missed it is. He seems all right for an elf, certainly has good taste in females.'

Hons helped Snoodl to her feet and grinned, but it quickly faded when he realised how battered she was, as she could hardly stand.

She burst out in tears again when she realised that in that condition she could not continue looking for anything. Hons gestured to her to show him what she was looking for. After several attempts she finally understood him and asked one of the others to bring her satchel over. From this she carefully brought out her precious herbs, selecting several leaves of each type. He gently took them and studied the leaves for a moment or two, handing them back to be packed away again.

Hons got up and pointed for two of the younger ones to go with him, leaving the rest to set up camp. He had garnered weapons for himself previously from the raiders' supplies, as well as a longer bow with many arrows, some in a quiver, the rest he put in his newly borrowed knapsack. With a reassuring smile to Snoodl, he left.

They ran as fast as they could down the valley to the lower grasslands where he felt sure the plants could be found. Even with a keen elvish

147

knowledge of the way of the open, he took all of the remaining day to find what he sought.

The little group rested during the hours of darkness under a thicket, setting out at daybreak to travel back. It was afternoon when they arrived at the former camp to find the party gone, with no new signs of a struggle. Motioning to the two goblins to stay where they were, he carefully paced around the camping spot trying to unravel the footprints. Then to his amazement he noticed the tree had gone, as well as the soil where it stood was flattened, and then the series of curious footprints leading in the direction he would have guessed the party had gone.

There remained nothing but hope that they were all right and that no further harm had befallen them. Gathering up their belongings once again the three followed the marks. The different tracks came together after a while, the marks, the goblins and the raider's horses, and then continued on together. Hons was completely at a loss, he thought firstly that they had run to the cave, but the tracks lead past there going further up towards the mountains, into groves of dark trees.

The forest, a mixture of conifer and decid-uous, occupied all the upper part of the valley and twittered with life. Further on, the thick forest gave way to orderly ranks of rowan, with the odd larch here and there. This continued for several miles, when suddenly it thinned, becoming a clearing of lush grass sward. On the far side stood what looked like some kind of habitation. The air was still and heavy with evening light, the deer browsed at the forest edges and rabbits ran where they would on the grass, completely tame.

Sensing the underlying witchery of the scene, Hons warned the two goblins not to try to capture or kill any creatures, and to stay on the path. This was totally unnecessary, as they were completely in awe of the place, it was a godlike park, to be revered not defiled.

Hons tried to recall the texts he had learned as a young elfling, but he was also totally confused by the building, it seemed wrong in that setting. Was it a dweamer creature, which had spirited the others, dreamlike to its realm? If it was he could not hope to combat such as there was in this valley. The feel of the power was benign though, he could not sense the smallest trace of evil, or so it seemed. As they neared the dwelling, very small figures emerged from the side where the doorway seemed to be. To his amazement, it was their companions. The scale of the house now looked vast, it was now that the size of the place truly revealed itself as it took some time for the goblins to close the distance. Snoodl ran unashamedly into his arms, and when Hons had his breath back, he returned her favours kiss for kiss.

"What is your name big elf?" She carefully said in elvish, much to his joy and surprise, cuddling up to him again as he told her.

He realised that he had been so worried about this wonderful armful, also now understanding that he could never willingly be far away from her again. She had claimed him, and he, her. Her being a goblin girl did not concern him overmuch as he had been used to living with all races from his early years, he had spent very little time in his home elf village. His parents took him travelling with them as they collected and traded all kinds of plants, from herbs to rare plants of power. This was why he could so readily help Snoodl.

The building as he had seen it, was no such thing. It soared up as a house of tended trees, the thatch being where the branches were interwoven in a leafy covering. All around the front and side the tree boles made a continuous wall, so they went around the side where Snoodl had come from.

149

Hons put Snoodl down and followed her lead into the arched portal of branches. An aisle stretched ahead into a central hall. At the far end a big fountain played, the water having a green tinged look. To the one side stood a gnarled tree-like figure, which he now realised, was the crooked tree from the clearing. Snoodl led them to it, where the other goblin ancients gathered.

"Meet Ele Aana Rowan, ramphorm giantess of the valley." Snoodl introduced. The enormous age of the giant could now be seen. "She has healed us and led us here last night for shelter while you were away." Snoodl asked Vart. "Did you find the plants?"

"Yes Snoodl," he replied, "we were successful but we had to go far down the valley. Hons has them in his pack." Looking over to where Hons was kneeling in front of the ancient giant.

"Ele Aana Rowan I bless thee and thy race." Hons murmured reverently, "Strong and gentle are the woven thoughts in this haven."

"Fair elf, your tongue is as free as your mind. The wise of the goblin folk have fled from tyranny I see. I must look to my valley, the flood may break over us." The giant replied in a measured mature whispery feminine voice.

Looking carefully Vart could now see through the tree camouflage to the giant inside. She was ten feet tall and roughly humanoid shape, her skin was a dark velvety looking brown. All over her body little tufts of tiny branches, not repulsive at all, but more like a garment, as human hair grows. Her arms, hands, and fingers sprouted little, longer branchlets, as well as the top of her head. When she was still, her legs merged into one to form a trunk, so you had to look very closely to see her. Her face was ruddy and mossy, with dark black eyes, which weighed you at a slow glance. The old tales were full of them, the

150

ramphorm giants, each being able to form into many surfaces but favouring one usually in their long lives. Nothing was known about there being young, but there was much speculation amongst the elves of old.

"Mother of the valley, it may prove true." Hons addressed her. "There are strange movements of people about, but I feel the goblins are ranging far and wide. Sorcery is about in its evil form and none may guess how far afield it will cause disruption and death, except by using sorcery."

She searched long into his eyes, as if feeling the depths of his soul.

"A lone monk known as Brother Ignatious is afoot and you can depend on him. But the story you tell me about Asphar is a rotten branch of another hue. I have felt something is about to happen for a little while now. So the wheel turns again, Aasphari in ancient times and now another Sorcerer Asphar to complete the cycle to a seeming evil end. History repeats itself all too often, but remember it is never the same end. Have you colleagues elsewhere?"

"Yes, maybe somewhere to the south and west, but possibly not too far I hope, somehow I was due to meet them." Hons replied. "We also have friends below, and a colleague as well, but several are sore wounded. They are the cause for the journey up to the valley."

"I think I can help a little there but not completely, my medicines are good but sometimes not all powerful. I am not mistress of life and death. You will see them all again, young elf, if you meet them before you are in need, you may wish to know that the key is written on the Labyrinth Gate, "

151

She reassured and then reached for Snoodl, to lightly brush her wavy hair with a mossy hand.

"*Remember that you must fear not for your mate, she is blessed. You must have hope although your paths are perilous.*"

They stayed the following night with her and then made their way back to the cave exit of the warrens beneath. This time they met the bears and had to fight to get past. They lost one ancient there before they won passage, but eventually they were past them and at the waterfall.

Not far after the falls they came upon a single set of seven-clawed tracks, which they all were at a loss to know what had made them. They seemed to meander about as though looking for something. Several of the returning party went off to investigate this creature, joining them later in the group's caverns with a curious tale, which was never fully known, only guessed at. The tracks to their surprise went right around the caves occupied by the main group and departed back the way they came. They found several grisly remains along the route, animals and sadly one small goblin with curious teeth marks around its neck. They rolled its poor battered body in a jacket and carried along with them.

As with all journeys the way back was shorter, so it was with this one. The remaining group quickly found the marks they had carefully left to guide them back, and located the main party quite easily.

The group was still in the cave as they left them, and had an uneventful time, apart from the two invalids slowly sinking into coma and the loss of one child. The mother was heartbroken but she guessed the fate of her little one. The outside party brought back with them several gourd-like containers of green potion from the ramphorm giant, as well as the fresh herbs. Snoodl immediately set about ordering the dosing of the patients.

Over the next hours Snoodl administered the draughts, and although both rallied, Maltex showed the most improvement. Although her Matah came out of the coma and was able to talk, as well as being more comfortable and at peace, she seemed drained in some way.

All the group were given small drinks from the green gourds, as a tonic, which dispelled some of the gloom that Soohermi's failure to recover was casting on everyone. After a further day had passed, Maltex was walking about slowly and looking a lot better. Not so for Soohermi, as later that day Snoodl's Matah died peacefully in Quillam arms. The sundering, the journey, and the vicious handling had all added to the burden of a life given up to other's healing, and could give no more.

It was a sombre party that a day later left the cavern where many hopes lay buried under two piles of boulders, one large and one small, blessed by everyone including the two elves. The elves had more than most to thank Soohermi's sacrifice for, one a Venta and the other his life. They stumbled on barely able to hope to reach their goal. Quillam and Snoodl were in a daze of grief, falling from quiet tranquillity to desperation in less than a week, and finding it difficult to come to terms at their loss. The other ancients moved around them and took over the running of the group, and working from the directions he had given them before. Time enough later to deal any problems when they arose, they had enough to cope with at that moment, without any more.

One improvement came from the fact that Maltex could understand and speak a little of the goblin tongue, this was especially useful to Hons who cajoled him into teaching him as much as possible. The affair between Hons and the little Venta was a surprise and a shock to Maltex. He fully realised that however beautiful Snoodl was, there was the

153

prejudice to be borne when they returned home, and he was not sure that Hons did. There was always going to be hatred from the young goblin community too, as elves were hated in most places, rightly too, as there had been a history of fighting between them for centuries.

There was also the problem with Ikin, her race hated goblins just as much as the goblins hated them, how could they be brought round to accept Hons and Snoodl's love. There was no denying it, they were hopelessly entangled, and no infatuation either, Maltex had had plenty of those to draw experience from. Anyway it was a problem to be faced later, like the other ones, day to day living was enough to deal with, like teaching goblin to an elf. And teaching elvish to a Venta! Snoodl was quicker than Hons, she had a thirst for it, almost desperation, as her love for Hons helped to fill the gap left after her mother died.

It took that next week to arrive at their destination, to the elves it was just the same as the rest of the caverns, very boring. This was a complex of caverns, which was previously occupied long ago, and remained empty for a considerable time before they arrived. There was a good supply of running water near the living quarters, with sizeable caves for growing a mould and fungi farm, which was needed to produce part of their diet. Foraging parties went out to explore the surroundings, and brought back any eatable denizens that they could catch, but kobs were seen on occasion, so utmost care was exercised to hide their new home. Maltex and Hons went out with them, as now they were accepted members of the little community. The spearhead of any attack on or by the ancients was Maltex's ability with his sword and Hons's skill with a bow, now that he had one more to fit his size. The elves made a bond in those days, which lasted many generations

154

from that date, and did much to heal the wounds between their races.

PART 3

Journeys to the Unknown

Chapter Ten

The Mesquite Hills

When the main party left Mesquite they took the Old Dwarf Road again as they were going to follow it as far as the Mesquite Hills and then cut eastward around the Nisego Mere. This time they wanted to avoid the goblin raiding area reported on the western side of the Mere. The new route went through rolling wooded country and hopefully came out onto the more used roadway going north-east to Estamon and the Elflands.

That morning they saw no sign of the raiders, although there was ample evidence of them in the burnt wagons, bones and graves by the wayside, half hidden in the bushes and grass. Midway through the morning, a large party of militiamen passed by, galloping the opposite way. They would have liked to ask them about the dangers ahead, but as they were ignored, there was no opportunity to inquire. Soon afterwards they saw the reason, just to the side of the track was the remains of a caravan, obviously attacked only hours before. The personal belongings of a fairly large group were scattered across a clear-ing, and sad crumpled bodies left hastily pulled into the bushes. They set about the grim task of burying the dead in a shallow communal grave and tried to guess who the attackers had been. Tasherlon ruled out goblins and as all the bodies had been robbed but not mutilated, the most likely cause was a large party of raiders. When they continued on they nervously followed their original intended route along the track, but they felt obviously much too vulnerable to attack for comfort.

It was with some relief when at midday they pulled off the track and headed into a scrubby area for about a mile. There they then discovered another disused track leading westwards to the mountains. Moving a good way further into the trees, they quietly stopped for food, not knowing when they could next safely eat. There were too many disturbing events going on.

They started again one hour later, but as Eta started to move off he suddenly held up his hand for silence. Nerves on edge they waited while the elf and Tasherlon slid forward to investigate. As they listened they could hear the crack of whips and loud guttural voices, this was quickly confirmed on the return of the scouting party.

"There is a well armed kob caravan with four or five goblins tending the animals and eight fighters as escort at present. There could be others of course scouting around like us." Eta said, taking his bow from his pack and stringing it. "The noise I heard was caused by a female slave trying to escape, we must move fast if we are to prevent her being hurt, even so we may be too late. If we attack with bows first we can perhaps draw off some, to reduce the odds and maybe prevent most of the damage to any slaves. Right? Lets get at it." The fact that there was some-one desperately in need of their help triggered them all, quite apart from saving them from an uncertain future as a slave of the kobs, who were merciless with captives. Also they realised that the kobs, being so close, could attack them at any moment.

"Wait a minute, if Zeth, Ikin, Chorky and I go round a bit and get ready to charge on horseback from the left side," Hectar suggested, "then we wait until Eta and Tash have shot a few of them, we should have the edge."

160

Zeth, never happy on horseback at the best of times, quickly added, "If you are going to get Ikin and I to charge on the backs of these four-footed monsters you are better than Gods. No, let's change that, you and Chorky charge them on horseback, if you want to, we two will come in on trusty foot from this side." Ikin, who felt worse than Zeth about horseback, if that was possible, turned and nodded thankfully to him. There was a short silence while the change sunk in, then that was the end of the battle planning.

Eta and Tasherlon crept up quickly to within bowshot behind one of the small areas of scrub on that side of the track. They waited a while to allow the others to position themselves and then opened up on the caravan. In a very short time one kob and one goblin were seriously wounded, as well as one mule. The mule caused havoc, and being tethered to the other mules it disrupted them too. The two cavaliers swept onto the scene and took out two more on their pass through the ranks to turn and wait their chance to ride in again. Eta and Tasherlon, after loosing another volley of arrows, joined Zeth and Ikin to charge in from the front. Hectar and Chorky rode back again, Hectar leaping off near the slave and the mules. Chorky took the horses away and returned to join the others in the main melee.

The female captive was tied head down across the back of one of the other mules, with one kob moving to kill her. Hectar made a desperate dash to get in between, only just in time to fend off the kob with his shield. This action upset the mule behind him and he was kicked forwards into the kob, falling down on one knee just as the kob slashed with his sword. The cut went astray and sliced the human's thigh. A second later as an arrow appeared in the kob's neck, it fell over Hectar, black blood running down his tunic.

The three kobs remaining standing threw down their swords and cowered against the mules,

161

realising that they stood no chance. Of the rest of the goblins there was no sign.

At that moment from out of the bushes stepped Sorin, holding a wounded goblin in front of him. "I found this one creeping away, a stray of yours maybe?" he said jokingly.

Sorin's arrival took them all by surprise, even more as he was obviously without his companions, Maltex and Hons. His face was bruised down one side and his gear was badly battered.

Hectar, despite his wounded leg, was busy freeing the captive from the back of the mule. She hung on him a while as the circulation returned, until he stumbled, then she noticed the blood seeping down his thigh. Looking up she gave him a smile of thanks, and gently freed herself from his arms. Nomaque came across to the two of them.

"I hope they didn't have time to harm you, Lady of the Trees." The Druid said, noticing that her torn garment was in fact a Druid's cloak.

"Too much, Half-elf," she replied, her voice hard with pain. Hectar turned and saw in her eyes dullness associated with great loss, and gave a little gesture to Nomaque to be gentle. This was not needed as the Druid had already felt the mental agony the woman was going through. She looked far away for only a moment then bent to examine Hectar's gash.

"I have some healing skills, Friend of the Oak, enough to heal this brave man anyway. I am called Riva of the Wind, may I ask to whom I owe my life's debt? Is anyone else wounded?" She asked.

"I am Hectar Rolan and human like you, as is Tasherlon Tendralon over there. The attractive gnomess is Ikin Galena. The rest of us are Half-elves, Nomaque Narafon here, Chorky and Zeth over there with the prisoners, except for our elves, Eta and

162

Sorin by the mules. You see we are pretty well mixed. Where were you captured?"

"In the Ancient Forest, Hectar, it has been a wearisome journey. Does anyone here have some herbs and simples?" She asked.

"Zeth and I have a few," Nomaque replied. "What do you need?"

Riva reeled off a list, and he went off to see what he had in his saddlebags.

"Hectar? Can you hobble a bit, as I have to go over there to where those elves are rummaging in the baggage." She asked tersely.

On arrival Riva said brusquely "There are some things from my home somewhere in those bundles, elves. Rather painful mementoes, but important nevertheless. May I remove them as they come to light? Where are the kobs you have already dealt with?"

"The piles of sorted articles are just over there, but we have concentrated on these two chests only. There are a lot of other things on the other mules. Have a look by all means. Oh, and the dead kobs are laid out over there." Eta said after a quick look towards Hectar who nodded.

Riva left them and began to unload the next mule in line, not at all interested in the finery the other chests held. The chests contained clothes for a large fat person and made in the richest cloth available. Velvets, cloth of gold, damask, gold ornament everywhere. Separate from these there were smaller outfits, a parcel held capes and clothes of jet black for a tall slim figure. In amongst the black garments sparkled a glittering magician's robe, every bit as expensive as the golden ones.

"Gaudy ain't they. A very rich person with no taste wanted these. Pity they've gone astray. No use to us, we're going the wrong way. Here Nomaque, I promote you to chief thingmy of the order." Ikin said,

163

picking up the magician's robe and throwing it to the Druid as he returned with the medicines for Riva.

"O thank you, your highness, most gracious Madame." Nomaque replied, handing over the medicines to the Druidess. He tried the robe on. "Good Gods. This is not what it seems, it reeks of power, I shall keep it if no-one objects."

"It becomes you." Riva wryly commented, observing the unbelieving smiles of the elves, as they repacked the chests.

While the others opened up the unexpected treasures, Zeth mused over the fate of their prisoners.

"I have no stomach to kill these, although they would have not hesitated to kill us had we been taken." Zeth commented, looking at their kob and goblin prisoners.

"We will have to take them with us or tie them up then, and the first, I don't fancy." Chorky replied. "They seem to belong to some sort of organisation, look at the badges sewn into their tunics. A 'K' with wings, most unusual, kobs are usually an undisciplined rabble, so something is welding them together. An unpleasant thought, that something is the owner of the costumes maybe."

"These kobs weren't the ones who captured me." Riva stated bluntly with the pain showing in her voice. "I was taken to a transit camp, and sold there." She shuddered and took a breath. "This caravan came the day before yesterday to the compound and collected me. They already had the rest of the goods, but I recognised one of the bundles from the raiders who captured me. I think this lot are a kind of dealer or carrier. On the whole they were not bad to me until I tried to escape."

"Tie them up it is then," determined Nomaque, rummaging about for the necessary rope. They put the bound kobs in a particularly dense patch of

164

bushes, and were soon on their way taking the mules with them. They looked for a cave to put the goods in and a river to hide their tracks.

"There is a cave about four miles west from here," Sorin called up from the back of the mule he was riding. Sorin and Ikin had elected to ride a mule each, as there were not enough horses to go round. "I passed it on my way here, and it may throw off the pursuit, if any. We could go along the track the kobs were taking."

The company halted and discussed the idea. In the end they went back to the main track turning northwards towards the village, as they felt that Sorin's idea was too long a detour. Soon after they started they arrived at another junction with another track coming in from the west. They continued on northwards through thick forest following the well-defined way. On that side of the Mesquite Hills the forest flowed away from the heights out onto the plain for about four or five miles. The way went through the great trees, producing a favourite spot for ambush and a place to harbour large numbers of raiders. On this occasion they were left alone. Once the eaves of the trees were reached the group stopped with a sigh of relief and the two elves went forward to scout.

While the others rested, Chorky kept a sharp eye out for anyone following. As he was looking, a flitting shape moved ever nearer, making for the forest from where they now watched, quietly Chorky alerted the others. There was an audible gasp from Riva. The party still had not quite accepted Riva into their midst, as she had only been with them a day at most. She had deflected any probing for further parts of her story and they felt uncomfortable at her obvious recognition of the figure following them.

"Shall I shoot, Riva?" Chorky said waving his bow in a meaningful way.

165

"No please don't, Chorky, please. That's my son," she gasped with a desperation that made the half-elf squirm with regret at his ill chosen words. As she looked at him, he saw suddenly a frail woman, very close to breakdown. The gods alone knew what she had suffered. The events of the past weeks had worn her to a fragile desperation.

"Don't worry," he said quickly. "I was only testing to find out who it was. I didn't mean to hurt you or your son. Call him before he passes us."

Riva rushed out to her boy and brought him back. "I'd like you all to meet Onaroah of the Sky. I think he has always wanted to soar like a young eagle."

The boy was about twelve or thirteen years old, lithe and going to be tall. He had his mother's black flowing hair and dark complexion. His longbow of yew was strapped on his back, but as he came towards them, he held a short sword in his hand, unsure of the group around his mother. He had been watching their attitude towards her and their suspicion was obvious.

Riva quickly motioned for him to sheath the weapon and join them in the boscage, away from the roadway.

Eta and Sorin joined them soon after that with the news that the way was blocked three miles further on by a large group of raiders, over a hundred strong. They would have to retrace their steps to the turn and take the other way around the mountains, it would cost them many days delay. It then was decided to use the cave Sorin suggested to camp in overnight, as it was on the track going west.

It was late afternoon when they arrived at a promising cavern. It gaped large in the side of a spur off the nearby hills. In the entrance there were too many tracks of all sorts going in that direction. It looked like a common route for too many things to be safe. But there was a breeze coming out of it.

Sorin explained that the cave they were looking for was about two or three miles further on, and Eta, Chorky, Zeth and Tasherlon crept up to the gaping opening, while the others stayed back. It was very fortunate for them that they did so, as, sensing their presence outside the cave maybe or hearing a slight noise, out from the cave came an ogre. It stopped and looked around, sniffing the air, very alert and looking straight at them.

The creature stood nine feet tall, knotted skin and bone. They were always mean but not always stupid. It looked surprised at the size of the group and bellowed something back into the cavern, which caused uproar inside. There were obviously many more of the brutes. This was too much for the forward party. They glanced at each other and ran. The ogre bellowed again, but only advanced a few steps and waited. Arriving at the horses and mules, they scrambled on as best as they could and every-one went off as fast as they could get the mules to go.

They had gone several miles like this when they began to hear the crashing of pursuit. At the speed they were going they could not reach the next cavern entrance in time to avoid a pitched battle, without at least one of their number killed.

"There's a ruin over to the right on the hill top," Sorin called out.

"It's our only hope to avoid a battle or at least have a little cover," panted Nomaque. It took them precious minutes to reach the knoll, but the way to the top looked choked with trees. Riva began to sing to the trees, low at first, to weave a path through to the rock. Miraculously a path opened for them to the old entrance arch of the creeper-covered ruin. They wearily squeezed inside.

167

Watched by Eta and Sorin from the dark of the trees, the score of ogres had stopped and gathered in a huddle some fifty feet away. Undecided, they grunted and jostled each other for a while around a large dominant male. He waved a knotted club at them in frustration and then they all disappeared off into the gathering dusk.

The entrance arch gave access into an outer courtyard, where they stood waiting. When Eta called to them saying that their pursuit had given up, there was a silence while everyone wondered what they had ridden into. Over the doorway to the ruined halls there was an ancient script chased into the curved lintel, Nomaque read the badly worn letters out.

𝕾𝖆𝖓𝖈𝖙𝖚𝖆𝖗𝖞

"Sanctuary it reads. There was a welcome here long before our problem ogres moved into the district," he added. "Let's go in and see what's left."

They filed in after tying their reins to the old rusty iron rings around the walls of the yard. The ancient hall still stood, the floor strewn with debris of the centuries, even with large rents in the roof it was still shelter and very welcome. They cleared a space and put the first load of bags on it, going back to the horses for another lot until all was unloaded. They elected the watches for the night, the first watch moving off to explore the outer walls. The others explored the ruins. The only building intact was the main hall, all the others were in varying states of collapse and in a dangerous condition. So they decided to stay where they were for the night.

"This would make a fine place to come back to, after," Zeth said dreamily. "With a stout band of clerics and others, we could remake the order to protect travellers. That's a task worthy of anyone."

"If I survive and have not found another worthy task, I will consider joining you." Sorin said.

168

"We all know that task, don't we? That barmaid, daughter of the innkeeper could have a connection, maybe!" Eta called from the archway, where he was on watch.

"Some watch, I don't say!" Retorted the much-maligned elf. "Put those long ears to better use."

"You will have to let women into the order then, and bang goes the idea of a beer-free hostel. There will be an inn here in three seconds flat." Chorky put in.

"What's wrong with having women about the place, Chork eh!" Ikin said quietly, a dangerous gleam in her eye.

"Absolutely nothing where you and Riva are concerned, lustrous Ikin," announced Eta, ducking quickly as a rock clattered off the masonry close to his ear.

He went off to patrol the outside, while the others rummaged in the rubbish lying on the floor.

"There's a loose flagstone here." Ikin called across. Quickly the others joined her, and with a heave it was lifted, showing a flight of steps covered with dust. Cautiously with a shielded torch to light the way, Zeth, Ikin and Chorky made their difficult way down the narrow stair. After some twenty feet it opened out into a crypt, with coffins and chests here and there. Everything was broken open and the contents scattered about. Someone had plundered the dead, a long time before. The chests held the, once expensive, vestments of the order, and a few relics. The bones of the occupants of the coffins hung half in and out of the boxes, so in a moment of thoughtfulness Zeth started to put them back as best he could, the other three joined him and soon the bodies were put to rights, their lids ill-fitting but tidy.

"That's better, I hate to leave the dead in such a state. We can bring the stuff down here out of

169

harm's way. Few will find it, especially when I put back the flagstone properly."

Tasherlon's face appeared above them, "There's devil of a lot of activity going on around this hill, so dowse the light and come up for now. We may have to fight for our lives. Eta and Sorin have gone to scout out the menace after we saw stealthy movements just beyond the trees."

There was a rustle and Eta came through the archway. "There's an army out there!" He whispered as Sorin appeared beside him. "The whole of goblindom and kobdom's on the march, Hundreds and hundreds of them with other things in amongst them. They seem to be holding a meeting beyond the trees in the moonlight. We are lucky we weren't spotted before we put the lights out. I have muffled the animals as best as I could, not perfect I'm afraid."

Riva and Nomaque became deep in discussion, the others waited. It was wise not to get in the way when the Druids looked serious, unusual things happened. Long moments slipped by before Nomaque turned to the others.

"We are going to attempt a mist warding. The trees here are ancient and have no love for the goblins. They will help. If we channel their enmity and both of us put forth all our force, it may be enough. When we finish wrap us up and let us sleep. It would be as well if you could do the same for a while too, this is complicated and powerful so don't move from the building until morning, when I think the danger will be long past. Eta and Sorin can you do a small task for us first. Here is a bag of powder, all we have, can you circle outside the buildings, sprinkling this powder as you go?"

"When you want." Sorin answered taking the offered ornamented bag.

The two elves disappeared, returning some twenty minutes later. Handing the nearly empty bag to the Druids, they retired to the sacks on the floor. Standing facing opposite ways, back to back, the Druids called forth their arboric essence, chanting in a lilting harmony, the sense of power in the air could be felt, almost tasted. A swirling mist started from them and whirled around, circling until it filled the hall, the two figures the middle of a spiral of haze. Then out from the archway it billowed racing around the trees a little way and onto the grass, forming an isle of mist, silent and forbidding.

The enemy streamed past, in the main not even noticing the mist. Some more bloodthirsty, hatred flowing through their purple veins, turned aside and essayed in. Their cries as they came to an unknown end trailed off into the distance, not the actual distance but a dimension to do with the ethereal hearts of the trees. No others tested the unknown, the fear of the wood ran through the host like a bitter wind at the sound of the cries.

It was about one hour from dawn when the Druids collapsed in a silent heap. Ikin and Sorin laid them as comfortable as possible on the sacks put nearby for that purpose, and covered them as the morning was going to be a chill one. Then they carefully made their way to the entrance arch to stand guard. Everything was peaceful, there were almost no signs of the night's exodus, it could easily not have existed except for a bloodstained sword lying on the ground nearby. It was a grim reminder in the early light.

When the dawn broke they let the Druids sleep, the elves and Chorky reconnoitred towards the tunnel they had passed by before, to see if that could be the way to go, now that the way both east and west were blocked. One direction was blocked by the goblin and kob army and the other possibly by the raiders. They could only go over the hills, or turn back across country towards Mesquite. The hills had an evil reputation and were cut with cliffs and gorges.

Tasherlon came up with a third option. "I have heard of a route through these hills starting with a great cavern. We could try the one Sorin saw. I don't fancy going past those ogres again"

The sun was high in the sky when they set out to attempt the caves, the recce party had reported it was clear of either goblins or raiders to the entrance so they determined to at least try it. The horses, packed light made good time to the entrance, they had turned the mules loose and rode double on two of the animals. The horses would not go into the dark recesses of the cavern, so they too had to be released. Riva went some way away with them, stroking their necks, urging them away. Tasherlon murmured, "I know how they feel, although I must come into the cavern deeps this time."

Chapter Eleven

Way Beyond

*T*he tunnel was large and it went through a series of caverns, each one going deeper until they reached one cave which dwarfed the others. There they decided to rest and eat, leaning against the wall and whispering to each other. Another whisper of sound caught their notice, looking up they realised that a party of hobgoblins had been creeping up. They were larger and more ferocious than ordinary goblins, standing almost man height, wielding maces, cudgels and large notched swords. As they charged, chaos ensued.

The two elves, Chorky and Zeth leapt forward drawing their swords to form a defensive wall, while the others held the flanks, Ikin, Tasherlon and Noma-que on one side, Riva, Hectar and Onaroah the other.

This time they were lucky, the hobgoblins broke and ran, leaving three of their number on the floor, disappearing into a small tunnel on the far side of the cavern. Not slow to leave the spot, the group packed up and continued as much of their meal as they could manage. They took the large tunnel on the other side of the great cavern, which seemed to be continuing on from the one before.

More cautious than before, they continued on with a low rumbling sound coming from the way ahead. The tunnel went on for another half mile before they emerged into the light once more.

The roar of tumbling water was all round them as they came out onto a narrow rocky path beside a mossy-sided river gorge. The narrow pathway going both ways tucked into the rocky wall with the fast flowing river roaring along some twenty feet below. The waters poured over a falls fifty feet to their right, the path to the right stopping there. Turning left they continued on up beside the rushing river to where another path came in sharply from the left another half mile further on. Undecided, they stopped for a breather and to work out the way to go, but at that moment rocks began to fall around them. Breaking into a run they ran on up the gorge and shortly came to a rope bridge over the river, which took them away from that side. As fast as they could they stumbled across one at a time, hoping that the mossy ropes would hold them. Only pausing to look up when the reached the other side, they could just see flitting figures high on the rim above.

The ledge on the far side became a narrow path which wound up the side of the ravine, after several zigzag bends the path went into another large cave mouth.

The cave entrance was very wide at first but in a short distance it narrowed sharply to a ten-foot tunnel. Careful this time they approached with drawn swords and bows bent. It was well that they did, for out from the opening came a large band of goblins with spears and armoured hobgoblins. The smaller goblins were pushed on into the fight by the fear of their larger colleagues coming up behind. The two elves loosed off as many arrows as they could at the bigger opponents before joining in the fray. There were too many against them for the Druids not to be involved in the hand-to-hand fighting, so they had to use the weapon that made them feared and left alone by one and all, the wand. It consisted of a short rod about a foot and a half long, ridged wood braced with metal for strength, and well laced with power. Each Druid danced, deftly avoiding or deflecting blows, delivering counters, which the opponent rarely got up from. The ends of the wands barely seemed to touch for a telling blow to be delivered. Even Onaroah accounted well for himself, and they put the attackers to flight a second time, although alas not without wounds.

Hectar's previous wound had opened again under the strain, Zeth, Tasherlon and Sorin had slashes on arms and body. Feeling tired but unable to rest where they were, they moved forward into the tunnel. It ran on gently curving upwards for several hundred yards to another cavern. This they wearily approached even more cautiously. This time they were also expected, so when they arrived there was an odd reception group of four goblins with spears and shields standing in the centre of the cavern in front of them. On seeing them they stamped and shouted at them, but they also cast furtive glances behind them and off to the right. The air seemed hot and suffocating, with an odd tremor in the floor. Yells from behind the goblins came to try to drive them on but they still seemed to be on the point of running away. Confused, the group of travellers came on slowly, doubly alert. It was only when they had taken a few steps into the cave that they realised what the trap was.

On their right was another tunnel, and coming up that tunnel at a furious speed was a fire-breathing dragon.

"Gods breath!" breathed Ikin, "A bloody Dragon, just what we need, and definitely not going to chat this time!" she added to herself. As one they took to their heels and ran across the cave to the next tunnel round from the dragon's, running full speed into it.

"This is getting to be too much of a habit, we must stop doing this," Ikin gasped, who never liked running at the best of times. They passed several side tunnels and out from one of them another group of hobgoblins issued, cutting off their retreat.

"What's next?" spluttered Zeth, wondering where they were being headed, and whether to stand and fight, before the odds became too uneven.

Chorky, who ran on easily in front, was thinking the same thoughts when with the next step, there was a sensation of not belonging for a second then he was himself again. The tunnel had changed. He ran on for a step or two and stopped. Turning he saw he was alone, and the tunnel behind him was also different.

Eta suddenly appeared, running on to stop by him, looking equally perplexed. He too turned and waited. Before long all the group were standing in the new tunnel, panting but ready for whatever turned up next.

Suddenly a running hobgoblin appeared in the tunnel, who on seeing the group waiting for him, scrabbled to a stop with a screech of fear. Before anyone could do anything, he turned and ran off into the new tunnel away from them. He disappeared around the corner into the darkness, moments later there was an unearthly scream of terror and pain. The screams grew in intensity, again and again, on and on. Eta drew his bow and nocked up an arrow, cautiously creeping to just in sight of what was happening, he slowly and with extra care loosed the shaft. The screams cut off as with a knife.

"We should not hang around here," he muttered running back to them, visibly shaken and face waxen.

"What was it?" Ikin asked as she ran along beside him.

176

"Don't ask," Eta replied. "At least not for a good while anyway."

They passed another cavern but went on through it, taking the exit opposite, and on through another short tunnel into a vast cavern. They climbed up on the boulders well to the side and rested against the wall. Away from the path, they could eat a frugal meal and begin to breathe more normally again. Riva and Zeth set about treating some of the wounds taken in the previous affray, trying to make as little noise as possible.

They thankfully rested for some hours and had another snack before setting out again. Their way wound along between great slabs of rock fallen from the roof out of sight above them, but was a well-defined path. The great cavern seemed to go on endlessly, the steps echoing back from the walls out of sight on either side. They began to imagine a dismal flapping overhead, which they whispered about to each other as they went along. They crept along quietly, walking with their hands on their swords, hoping that the creature had just had dinner and was not interested in them. In silence they went the remainder of the way through that enormous cavern, the creature passing overhead with a whisper of sound and a slight creak of its imagined wing beats, whatever it was.

The tunnel at the exit was not long and soon they were in a similarly sized gigantic cavern on the other side. An unpleasant odour filled the cavern, reminiscent of the smell of the kob dens. The path carried on across the floor coming to a circular space surrounded by roughly man-sized blocks of stone. They were using the torches sparingly, but Eta caught a glint behind some of them.

"Ware ambush!" he yelled. The wall was not far to the left, so he started to edge towards it. The group closed up around him, moving with him they

177

took defensive positions to cover all sides. They felt very exposed to the figures emerging from between the stones. They were cave dwelling tribesmen like the ones to the north, wearing animal skins, with slings, clubs and spears. There were quite enough of them to do permanent damage. Things looked bad as there was nowhere to go other than to the wall, and perhaps die there, as more and more foes gathered until well over a hundred foes stood in and around the stones.

Nomaque, looking around, saw further along the wall they were approaching some darker shadows which to his desperate mind seemed to be the shape of a monk. The figure seemed to wear a habit with a cowl pulled well down so no features could be seen. One arm seemed to beckon them. Nudging Riva to follow him and calling the others, he charged full for the figure. It took a second for the others to join with him in a phalanx. Caught by this unexpected move the tribesmen gave way, at least allowing them to reach the wall by the figure. At the point when Nomaque was doubting his eyesight and wondering whether the manoeuvre was wise, the wall and monk dissolved in front of him showing a previously hidden entrance. He raced through, turning and waiting just inside the tunnel to defend their rear. The others followed suit and were astonished to find the opening closing itself, and the tribe on the other side prostrating themselves. They were calling out again and again, "Eoophi! Eoophi!"

Totally perplexed the group looked at each other, and then saw at the far end of the straight well-hewn corridor, once again there was the figure of the monk, beckoning.

As they started towards it the figure dissolved and was gone. Only the heavy double wooden doors at the end were visible. Given only one way to go they approached the doors, which proved difficult to open. They managed to force them open wide enough to squeeze through, but when they let them go, they firmly closed with a click. Hectar who was the strongest tried to move them but to no avail.

They looked around, they were in a circular chamber, the walls decorated with a random pattern. In four places around the walls, there were doors similar to the ones they entered by, and as they were all locked tight they obviously weren't going anywhere fast.

"There must be a way, you elves are renowned for solving this kind of puzzle, as well as dwarves," Nomaque observed and sat down, his back to the wall. "So I challenge you to do so."

"Thanks!" Sorin replied wryly and began to examine the walls.

Joining Nomaque, Zeth asked. "Those creatures the tribesmen were calling 'eoophi' perplex me. What were they?"

"I have been wondering that myself, but I think they are a form of creature similar to the ones which form stalactites and fall on people, *Prendichak* the kobs call them. These seem a much more intelligent type and could act in a very precise way. I seem to remember the elves have a name for the creatures like that, *eomorphim*, I think. There are quite a few different forms, some intelligent, some very nasty, even one type that was telepathic. Most feed on mould and fungus found everywhere."

"I have it!" Sorin cried, indicating little holes in the wall central between the doorways. "These holes have little levers in them which I think probably operate the doors but there are usually traps too. We need the longest sword held by the longest arm. Then his belt held by someone who is looking all around and ready to pull him away.

179

They tried this with Hectar and his sword, but with a rope around his waist. The lever refused to move, so Hectar afraid to break his weapon, gave up.

"We're completely lost, so any door will do," Chorky commented wryly. They plumped for the one on the right of the entry door, and tried the haft of Ikin's axe in the two adjacent holes. The levers old and brittle broke off in the first one tried, but in the second, with a jerk of disuse they managed to move it a little. Encouraged with this small success, Zeth moved to help Sorin on the axe-handle. Giving a hefty pull this time the lever jerked several inches and stopped. There was an ominous rumble and the floor the two were standing on dropped six inches. They were pulled to safety and with utmost caution the doors were then tried, the rest of them stood frozen as in a tableau. It was still locked. Sweating visibly the two tried again, and again, each time the floor sagged a bit more. The fourth try proved the best, with a click the floor rose up again and the door opened. With speed they ran through into a long corridor, which stretched off into the distance.

When they arrived at the other end of the mile long corridor, there were another pair of doors. To their surprise these moved to their touch, and gave access to another circular room with four doors as before. Holding the door, they filed in.

Ikin spotted the red pool of blood first, definitely not goblin blood, on the floor near to the door going to the right. Rushing over she touched it with her finger.

"Its still just wet!" She exclaimed, "Lets to it, I'm for the rescue. Who's with me?"

"Hold it! You will be a dead rescuer in a moment. Lets get this door open. As before, rope and axe-handle." Nomaque said firmly. Following his lead the procedure was repeated, but the lever was well oiled and glided across with no trouble, the doors opening without a sound.

In the room a sickening sight welcomed them. Chained to the wall were six small humanoid people, all in a terrible state. They were about the same size as Ikin's race but built in a lighter mould, in most communities of larger folk there was a small community of these quiet people. They had a variety of names, seftlin, oddlin, gnomlin, or neftlin as they called themselves. Three were lifeless, hanging in their chains, but the other three showed fear of their entrance and moved closer to the wall.

"Right! Chorky and Eta, guard the door we came in." Riva ordered. "Zeth, Hectar, the other door. Come on the rest of you, we need to get these three off the wall, pronto. Backs to it, axe-handles to the fore, lets pull the shackles out, never mind the rest." More than willing, they laboured feverishly, fully aware that the lives of the small people were slipping away. Records were broken that day in the dungeon and the freed little forms were carried back into the circular room as they could hardly walk. The group elected to try the doors opposite to the ones they originally came in as there was a whisper of draught coming through cracks in the doorframe. Their decision was proved right and the doors gave rise to the outside, a wide valley opening up before them.

Leading the way, Riva made for a small oak wood about a half a mile away. The others streamed after, some carrying the still forms of the seftlin. The seftlin were a little but comely people, very quiet, mostly living to the far west. Twenty minutes later they were passing the great gnarled trunks of Nom-aque's chosen oaks.

"They will be our walls," He said to Riva as they set the burdens down onto the leafy under carpet between the trees. There, inside an outer thicket of briars around the perimeter, between the

181

aisles of trees, the scrub opened out leaving only the banks of leaf mould collected over the ages. The Druidess, in her arboreal element once more, wove patterns of healing over the seftlin, a thickness of power pervaded the air all around, giving the others a balmy relaxed feeling too. She knew nothing of the seftlin, where they were from or how they were captured. That would have to wait until later. She suspected they were from the elf village of Lisego where a small community of them lived.

Eta and Sorin were also in their element, the forest being their loved haunt, kept watch. In the distance a cloaked figure strode along, coming their way.

"He has armour on under that cloak, I'll wager." Eta sounded eager all of a sudden, "He's got a definite Elvish air, High elf Lordling. Wait, I've seen that device on his helm before. It's very like the Star Jewel, the one we found in the pool in amongst the waterfalls. Tell the others while I stay here and watch."

Sorin slipped away noiselessly to rouse those available, and presently everyone except Riva came back. This was fortunate, as when the lone figure was nearest, out from the doorway to the caverns they had escaped from, crept twenty goblins.

"We will have to help, but lets run around the trees and come from behind them. That should keep our injured hidden and we may still catch them before they get to him."

"Good idea Nomaque!" Eta cried running back in order to carry out that manoeuvre. They followed and came in time to rescue the lone elf. Yelling at the tops of their voices they charged the goblins, eager to get at the ones who raided the weak on the road, torturing their helpless victims. Surprised, the goblins turned to give battle, stopping well short of the lone figure.

182

Even though the numbers were better than two to one in their favour, the goblins showed little fight now that there was a real likelihood of their losing. They immediately turned and ran for the caves, encouraged by several well placed arrows in non vulnerable places. Their assailants, having no stomach for the slaughter let them go but followed right up to the cavern portal. The goblins shut the doors firmly, followed by locking noises which came from the inside.

"Right, we can help you goblins there, lets get those old tree trunks from over there and wedge these doors tight." Zeth suggested. "Then we can all sleep soundly tonight." No sooner had he mentioned it than it was done, with the extra insurance of driven wooden wedges crafted on the spot with Ikin's sharp axe.

Their former adversaries shut up tight as a drum, the group then turned to greet the cloaked, armoured figure coming up while they were blocking the doors.

"Greetings and my thanks, a very convincing rout, I obviously could do with an escort." The elf knight observed. "It's a very unfriendly land. I have just come west from the village of Lisego looking for a party of five elves who were going to meet me along here. Have you seen them?"

"No. We haven't been here very long. Would you like to join us for some food, and a rest for a while." Eta added quietly. "We can look out for your friends from where we are hiding."

"That sounds good." The new arrival suggested. "Let us leave introductions until we are away from here."

They made their way back past the forest until out of sight of the goblin's entrance, just in case of watchers, then doubled back into the trees. As they busied themselves with their camp tasks Eta went over to the elf knight and introduced everyone.

"I am Eta Erliandol, an elf as you are, but we have nearly all the races represented in the group but some are absent at present. Nomaque, Zeth and Chorky over there are half-elves, Riva, Onaroah, Hectar and Tasherlon are human and Ikin is our lady gnomess."

"Call me Encathalon. I've only been in this area for several months. I'm very much a stranger here."

Throughout that uncomfortable meal both the group and Encathalon tested each other. This started innocently but soon they were deeply entangled in a web of intrigue.

"Will you answer several questions for me?" the elf knight asked as they rested after eating. As they said nothing, he continued. "How did you come across that ring on your finger, lady gnomess?"

"I found it in a raider's hoard." Ikin replied. Something had attracted her to it in Fredrika's Hoard. She was going mention its uncanny resemblance to the Star Key when they found it, but the moment never seemed right whenever she thought to say anything. "I see it has a similar emblem on it to your helm device. I would very much like to know the origin of that double star pattern."

"I suspect they came from the same source." Encathalon commented. "Why should you, a group of mixed races be interested in the affairs of elves?" He countered more cautiously.

"Are some of the elves who you seek named Uslar, Senar, Lexar and Yanar?" Nomaque inquired quietly. A group of four elves was unusual under any circumstances and it could just be the others they met in the cavern complex on the previous trip.

"Why yes! How did you know? You must have met them before I came along. At a guess?" The elf

184

retorted a little put out, as the group knew a lot more of his affairs than he wanted to be known. His journey had to be secret. So many lives depended on it.

"As you yourself have not seen them, how did you know that they were around here?" Nomaque asked sharply. The others gasped, the Druid must be out of his mind.

Then Ikin nodded and said, "I see now, yes, I would like to know that as well, Elf. In fact I would like to know when you met them."

The others stirred expectantly and wondered at the verbal onslaught, but were sure that their two comrades had worked it out. Encathalon sighed and carefully scanned each one of the group in turn. There was strength in that searching look that went farther than desperation, it showed a deep inner power.

"You are very cautious," Encathalon replied after a pause, "and I should be too, but time is running out for my brother and I. We have few friends and those four kindly elves helped my brother Throndralon. What do you know of the elves who used to live not very far from here a long while ago?"

"We know they were the victims of terrible sorcery and the survivors suffered greatly." Nomaque answered. "They have been seeking a lost elf castle and its inhabitants for hundreds of years to no avail. Eta here is descended from one who was left behind and is one of those searching. We decided to help him in his quest getting on for a month ago now, and have been hunting with him ever since."

Encathalon turned to Eta, "Do you remember any names of the survivors of the castle?"

Eta ruefully shook his head and then had a thought. "One of my early ancestors was named Erlian Erliandol."

"I shall have to trust you as you seem to know of us." Encathalon decided. "I am the younger and more cautious brother. Have you seen the elves you named near here today?" He asked in return.

"No, we haven't seen them here today, or your brother." Nomaque replied. "We have only arrived here today ourselves. Also we are a bit uns-ure as to where we are anyway. We saw those four elves nearly a month ago in some caverns near the old elf city, I think they were trying to find your brother then. We have never seen your brother, I'm afraid, and you still haven't told us who you really are, we have heard of Throndralon but not yourself."

"Throndralon and I come from not very far north of here." He replied quickly. "I am really surpr-ised to see so many races together, it must be a worthy cause you follow, as you are all so united. The future bodes well and your... Oh, Pestilence!" He muttered to himself, stopping suddenly in mid-sentence.

Encathalon was at a loss as to what to do. He was at a turning point, he had to decide whether to trust these strangers or not. He had tested them and there was no evil in any of them. They had passed every trap he could think of on the spur of the mom-ent. It seemed that they were the very people he needed to contact. If not, then he had nearly let himself down. These well intentioned travellers could be just treasure seekers after a quick raid. Where did the little gnomess's ring really come from? Did she understand the significance of it? 'Possible,' thought Encathalon, 'she did seem protective of the other elves. The Druid now, I cannot read him at all, but I must probe deeper. The elf Eta has to be a high elf from the lost castle and probably related to me.' Sighing, Encathalon realised that he must trust them as Eta was in the party and he desperately needed to

186

know more. They were his last and only hope. He had to explain.

"I'm from the Castle which went from here-abouts a long while ago, as was Eta's ancestor. My home castle's emblem is that star pattern that you have on your ring, Ikin. It was the emblem of the first elves coming to these shores, many thousands of years ago. We call ourselves the Elves of the Star. Later it was the emblem of a lost queen."

"Where is it?" Eta probed, the careful mood catching. "Elves have been looking for the original settlement for countless years. I am surprised that we haven't seen any about. I mean, where is the castle now?"

"The valley where the castle was should be a little east of here and a good few miles north. We are a few miles off a track from Lisego village to the town you mentioned, Mesquite is it called? I believe on past Lisego it goes to Estamon City where you come from Eta. This track leads to the elf city as you call it."

Encathalon paused still reluctant to tell any-one his real secret. They were still fencing verbally with him. He felt Eta's cautious mood similar to his own. He went on, "you are quite close, especially to the old elvish city. How did you locate it after all this time?" He asked still needing reassurance.

"In the caverns where we met the other elves was a monk, who directed us to an ancient dragon." Eta said fed up with all the subterfuge. "Then a scribe in a library in the town of Mesquite south of here, found some more of the story. Also some came from my ancestors. First clue was a lost village. A village which was there sometimes and gone others. I thought that the village fading in time might have a link to the castle's disappearance. I thought when I saw the … design on Ikin's ring it reminded me of the Lost Queen." Eta in his frustration almost gave away

187

their biggest secret, the Star Jewel. Not something to talk freely about to strangers on the road.

"What lost queen? Is that the Queen of the Elves of the Star, the Queen of the High Elves in the castle in trouble?" Chorky asked, he was vexed as the task of putting the pieces of the puzzle into place was bad enough, without an unknown lost queen popping up.

Eta stopped. The flow of what he was going to say was broken. He looked blankly at the half-elf for a moment and seemed to gather his wits together.

"Didn't I tell you about Queen Eosil? No?" He scanned the faces in front of him and they all showed blank. Encathalon was grinning with relief, as he knew then that they were genuine friends.

Eta explained, "Queen Eosil was a queen of the elves in the ancient past and in time has become a goddess to us. We think that possibly a reincarnation of her was reigning when Aasphari unleashed his sorcery on us causing the catastrophe all those years ago. Anyway that double star is her emblem and that of the castle too, as on Encathalon's Helm.

"Never mind the Queen, most important is that the Castle's in extreme danger." Nomaque relented. "We have been told from our various sources, it either is, or will be beset by a horde of evil races bent on plunder. There is a link with the goblins and kobs from near here, we were caught in the way of the horde as it passed by a day or so ago. The goblin's crown is involved." Nomaque went on to recount the more relevant parts of their story as he decided to get the answer to some of the questions that had been building up in his mind for some time.

"Could you sketch the crown?" Encathalon asked, the mention of the Queen Eosil meant that they were already tangled up with the fate of the castle. Their involvement with a strange monk

188

clinched the accuracy of their story. The monk had weaved his way through his story too. "It may be an important elf crown that was lost long ago, and could well have the power to take the goblins to the castle."

Anxiously they gathered together, and Nomaque in a short while, scraped a reasonable drawing on a piece of bark with his knife.

"The crown had a dweamer on it to make it look old and rusty, it has four golden feathers which could seem as great claws. That looks very similar to the drawings I have seen at home." Encathalon groaned. "Oh my poor home! The evil forces of both our times are combining to ruin us. We already have troubles with the goblins and orcs in the other place too. My father sent us out to find the answer to riddles set by a monk. We have not any answers, unless it is yourselves. I have lost contact with Throndralon and I fear for him. I have accomplished nothing else, I too have lost a treasure of our castle, I lost the Sword in the hills to the north. I cannot go and look for it now, it is too late, my time has been wasted fruitlessly.

I must go back immediately and support my father the King, I have a means to travel to the castle too, only Throndralon and myself set out from home, as only two could come that way. Also few could be spared. I beseech you all to look for my brother and tell him what you have told me. I have a terrible fear he has fallen, and is lost. Look out also for two Weapons of the Star, an axe such as you have never seen, and a sword of similar lineage. I will sketch them. These we brought with us to protect us, but as with everything, we lost them, and our way."

"I don't agree with you, how about this?" Ikin said producing the curiously shaped mirror in its case. "I think this may be from your castle or the Star Elves' city."

189

"Yes, but unfortunately the way of using it has been lost, it's another thing that I have only seen a drawing of. You seem to be tangled up in our problems. Have a care though, the present position of the castle is now extremely perilous, you risk your lives to go any further in this matter."

Nomaque came forward and unwrapped the large Star. The elf Prince gave a gasp.

"You don't go in for half measures do you? So the Greater Star has been found. Treasure it, Druid. Only the crowns have higher honour. I believe that Jewelled Star could bring you, if you so wish, to us. The Ring also. Maybe the sword and the axe too; if you can find them. The two weapons, the two star jewels and the Greater Crown were called the Emblems of the Star, in years long past. I will stay in your shelter this night, and then go forth, a happier elf, knowing at least the jewels have been found. Then I must return. Any who wish to, may come with me." Encathalon offered, "It seems that you all have a choice to come to us if you so wish, but into strife and perhaps death as a reward. Fate or the monk has chosen you as well. So be it. Be aware that there is little or no chance of return. My father and I will do everything in our power to help you but our own future is not written either."

"We need to go to the nearest village, you mentioned Lisego earlier, how far is it?" Riva asked. "We are not familiar with this spot. We came here in a rather unusual manner through a complicated underground journey. These seftlin are in desperate need of more healing than a roving Druidess can provide."

"Lisego is the nearest I think, ten miles or more back the way I came. There are small people there I believe. Maybe if I show you, you will accompany me back to the castle? A trade, one care for another." Encathalon bargained light-heartedly, but

190

seriously, not wishing to undertake the journey home alone. The separation from his brother in this strange land of his fathers, and finding help again after being lost and friendless, led him to seek their companionship.

"I would be happier if Ikin would come with me bringing her ring, then at least one emblem will return," He added thoughtfully, "I ask but humbly, and you are in no way beholden to come."

"I come willingly, this is a turning point in my life," she said determinedly, realising fully the knife-edge the quest followed. "I will not fail until I live no more!" One by one they pledged themselves to help the Prince who seemed to straighten, his shoulders going back and a determination showing in his eye.

"You have given me my faith back, may the goddess Eosil bless you all. I will not fail you." He turned and with a sigh knelt in front of them.

"There is one question I have not answered and I should before you come with me or go to the Castle. I am sorry to mislead you, but I was afraid to discourage what I see as vital to my people...," Encathalon humbly explained, "also mostly because I do not know myself. The Castle is in a strange place, the sky is strange, a slightly different colour, and you may feel heavier. Whatever that means, I just sense it is not linked to here at all. Some of the plants are different and the castle is on a great plain."

"That explains the odd sky in the vision in the magic pool!" Zeth exclaimed.

"That settles it, we come." Ikin decided for all of them.

They discussed the situation and they decided to split into two parties. Ikin, Riva, Hectar, Onaroah and Tasherlon chose to go eastwards the next morning to the village and then on to the castle with Encathalon.

Eta, Nomaque, Chorky, Zeth and Sorin would go westwards back to the caverns to meet Clem, and if possible look for the weapons and the ancient route that Throndralon was looking for through and under the mountains when he disappeared. The only clue that Encathalon could give was that it started from somewhere near the old city.

Chapter Twelve

Major magic is where you least expect it

"Nomaque? Why did you call out Encathalon?" Zeth asked later when the other party had gone.

"Didn't you realise that it was not likely the other elves would be here to meet him," Nomaque explained. "They did not mention Encathalon at all, so where did he pop up from? We left them back in Mesquite, and they were adamant about not going back to the caves. They felt that Throndralon had gone or was killed, so Encathalon did not tell us the truth. I'm not really sure why, but I think it's to do with his being cautious in another time and place with enemies all around."

"We had not better tell Clem about the Magic Axe or he'll be wanting to stay until he finds it." Chorky added.

"About the same as you and wanting the Sword, eh! Chorky." Nomaque retorted, realising Chorky's ambition almost before Chorky did. "You haven't even investigated that helmet of yours," Nomaque added.

"I must protest, I haven't had any time to mess about with it. Right, seeing that you mention it, I will have a closer look now," Chorky replied.

"This track is well used by the look of it, we had better be on our guard." Sorin reminded them all, but no one was listening.

"Do you think there is enough room?" Nomaque joked, looking up at the clear sky. The half-elf stopped and lifted off the helmet. As they all gathered around, he began to examine the rows of studs around the brim and over the curved crown.

"What did Clem say? Press the studs. Nothing happens. Look, not a flicker." He had continued to press one after another all round the rim. Then he started on the row going up the curve of the crown. When he pressed the third there was a small sound and something fell to the ground. He picked it up, and discovered it was a small piece of parchment. He could just make out faded elvish letters.

ZINFLAX'S EXPERIMENTAL HELM ---use with care

Underneath the writing were several diagrams, curved arrows and he could not make any sense out of the numbers. Turning the helm upside-down, he looked inside and discovered a little trap had opened, obviously letting the writing fall out. He put it back and pressed the stud again, the compartment shut again.

"Last time I fiddled with the horns. Perhaps I inadvertently pressed a stud too." He pushed a stud at random, and held it while he tried the horns. The left horn pulled out with a screech, and stopped tight, and nothing happened. The horn could turn. He eased it forward, still nothing, disappointed he jerked it back, and disappeared, magic haze enveloped where he stood.

When things cleared again Chorky had been replaced by not one, but two solid looking metallic legs. Nomaque looking up gasped, the legs belonged to a monster of metal. He looked up and up. So did the others, utterly dumbfounded.

"I'm up here," a disembodied voice called from somewhere above. It was like half a ball with legs, the legs were at least twenty feet high, the whole thing towering well over thirty feet up. The grey metal was streaked with oil and dirt, bolt heads showing in patterns everywhere.

"There's loads of room up here, come on up," the voice added, coming from the monster over them.

"How?" Eta asked. "You're in a half-ball on legs thirty feet up in the air!"

"Oh I see. I'm in a sort of room, the metal comes about halfway up the sides and you can look through the rest. I wonder what this does? There's a panel with more buttons and levers up here, with a little cup in the middle of it. I wish you could get up here. It may be safer. Heigh-ho, lets try this bottom stud farthest right."

There was a clunk from somewhere inside, and a trap door flew open in between the legs, nothing else happened. Shrugging his shoulders he tried the one on bottom farthest left. Eta gave a yell as the whole metal creation disappeared, leaving a swaying Chorky holding on to the helm by one horn. Everyone else had leapt backwards a step or two.

"Didn't I tell you? There was a little drawing under it," added Chorky. "It must have been a helm-et."

"That's one way down," Sorin said moving forwards again, "But there's no way up yet, maybe except with a rope. If you took some up with you, some of us could climb up with you."

"What do you want to do, Chorky?" Nomaque asked. "This needs to be understood a bit better. There are times when this could be very useful, if you found out how to control it. Any chance?"

"Well... There are over a dozen studs, levers, dials and pointers. We need to try a few of them..." Chorky replied thoughtfully.

They all looked around for somewhere to go to be out of the way. To the north were some hoary trees and underbrush, which was good cover for a thirty foot monster. They all trooped over and made camp in a large clearing a good way in.

Adopting Sorin's suggestion the half elf slung a coil of rope over his shoulder before he attempted to recreate the monster. After a little fumbling he performed the transformation, threw the rope over the side, and then tied it to a ladder going down inside. They climbed awkwardly aboard, holding the rope and walking carefully up the leg as it was quite slippery.

"Quite some Chariot you have got yourself here," remarked Eta admiringly.

The top was spacious, a good fifteen to twenty feet across. All around there was a rail to hang on to on the circular wall, seats in the centre and another for the controller in front by the curious panel. At the back a hole led downwards to floors below. A curved transparent screen with arrow slits came over their heads to about eight feet, the rest was open.

Chorky settled himself in the control seat and called for the others to hang on. They stood in the centre, gingerly holding onto the seats. He flexed his fingers and looked closely at the panel. There was a dial, pointer and a scale with numbers on at the very top, two levers and four rows of studs, a cup in the middle and another pointer lower down.

"I don't know what any of these studs do except for the something round and small, perhaps the button on the front opens it to let the things through into the inside. Any suggestions? No? return to helm one. Ah yes, there is a little helm sign there, it's just under it." Chorky called out. "The little pot in the middle must be important. Wonder what you put in it,

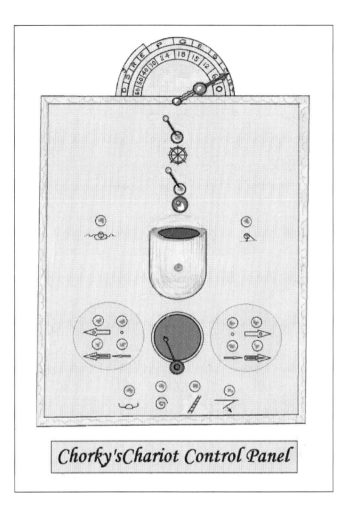

Chorky'sChariot Control Panel

Then I will press a few buttons. I'll try the next one in from the right it might be a ladder. The marking under it looks a bit like it."

There was a clanking from below, and the sound of something hitting the ground. Sorin went down inside two floors, came back amazed but no wiser as to the noise. "Can't see out from inside on the second floor below. There's more seating and a store of large arrows and metal balls in racks on the

197

wall, and on the third floor below again there's a good bit of seating space." He explained. "But no way out."

Eta slid out over the side, clinging to the rope while he looked down. There was a ladder resting from the bottom of the machine to the ground. Eta signalled to Chorky to press it again. The ladder retracted. Pressing it once more to put the ladder down, he remembered the trap stud.

"I am a right idiot, sorry everyone I forgot the trap door!" he confessed and pressed the stud. The trap opened and Nomaque climbed down. He scrambled back up, Chorky retracted the ladder and closed the trap.

The last stud on the fourth or bottom row gave a clunk but nothing seemed to happen.

Above that bottom row in the centre there was a blank dial with a pointer across it. Within marked circles on either side were the second and third rows of studs, making two identical sets of four studs in a square formation.

"I'll keep on the left side," Chorky decided. "Next one!" He tried the second one on the left on the next row up, with what looked like an arrow below it. This time there was a much more protracted clanging from the floor below. The dial in the middle went fuzzy and buzzed, Chorky jumped back and waited, but nothing more happened.

"One of the arrows has been moved, from the rack to a tube on the left side of the second floor. That's all." Sorin called up, as he had decided to stay down and watch. Very cautiously Chorky pressed the same one again and the arrow returned to the rack. The dial went blank again and he heaved a sigh of relief. The next button on the left proved to do nothing obvious although there were two arrows shown, one inside the other.

Next came the second one on the third row with a small circle over it. That proved to load a ball, its function was the same as the stud below with the arrows. It also buzzed him, making him jump again. Chorky replaced that ball too. They were very formidable weapons and he was not going to go any further before he knew more about the panel.

Leaving that row he looked at the first row. There were two studs on either side of the little pot, with odd markings under them.

"These look confusing I think I will leave these for another day too." He had had enough of complicated signs and left them for later, a lot later.

Up from the pot was a dial with a small circle in the centre, it was unaffected by him prodding it, so he left it alone and grasped the little lever just above it.

"I'm trying a lever, be prepared for anything!" He called out. Fortunately everyone had by then had made sure they had a handhold nearby when Chorky moved the lever left. With a lurch the left leg shortened, and frantically he reversed the lever. That leg extended back to level and then the other leg shortened and tilted them the other way. More carefully and with a few minor jerks he brought them on even keel again.

"That shortened the left leg, and then the right leg." He muttered noticing the little circle in the dial below moved right, then left again to centre. "Why did it do that?" he wondered, getting confused.

"What about if it's on a sloping hillside, won't you need one leg shorter than the other?" A voice piped up from below.

"Maybe." Chorky said. "Could be that's how we go around corners, over them or round them." He took a deep breath and tried to be calm, but his heart was thumping. 'Lets get this over and done with' he thought gritting his teeth.

"Last Lever, it seems important" He moved the lever just a little and nothing happened.

199

"Perhaps turn the top lever on the dial t..o..o…!"

The machine immediately waddled forward in the direction he moved the lower lever. Luckily every one was wedged in after the last shake-up. The machine marched right, straight for a respectable sized tree.

"Hang on, a tree is attacking us!" The shaken half-elf shouted, grabbing at the lever, missing and trying again jerking it to the left just in time, but still trundling on at the same pace. Branches of the tree were breaking as it shot past at a reasonable trotting speed for a horse. They were through the gap in the trees and out, onto the open grassy valley, Chorky breathed in a gulp of extra air. Calmly he brought both levers back to where they were to start to bring things to a stop.

They all emerged battered, from the corners where they had clung.

"Impressive. Now take us back to the camp." Nomaque said, and they all groaned as Chorky reached to move the levers. He grinned and waited until they had braced themselves. Gently, he very carefully, and in smaller bursts, eased it on its way back into the trees, testing what each lever did. The top dial was for speed and the lower lever was the direction. Twenty feet away from the camp it stopped on its own. He pressed all the buttons except the helm return without any response. This last he then pressed and they were immediately standing or sitting on the ground in a group around him.

Chorky sat there a little stunned holding the helmet in his hands. He was just pleased to rest, he had had enough of the walking machine for the moment.

"Now I know why there are padded seats down below." Sorin put in, rubbing his elbow.

"Listen, there was a band of horsemen approaching when we returned into the trees," Nomaque observed. "I don't know whether they will investigate us or give us a wide space and go past as fast as they could. I know which I would do, but they are not me. Perhaps Eta you could take Sorin and check. If we could gather up all our belongings in readiness for whatever, we will not be caught napping." Nomaque suggested.

When they returned, the elves reported that the group of horsemen were having an animated argument about something, half a mile from the trees.

"We can't stay here then. I would feel safer in the Chariot whatever." Zeth added. "Even if it won't move, the height advantage is good and there are those loopholes in the see-through stuff. Get that helmet working and let's get in." He entreated.

"Unfortunately a good idea," Chorky added groaning, taking off the helmet again. "As long as we stay put." He triggered the Chariot and operated the ladder and trap.

They scrambled up inside, loaded their gear in and he closed the trap, this time taking their time and looking around them. Chorky came down and joined them in examining the rooms, firstly the sitting area, and then the armoury. There was some speculation as to how the arrows and the iron balls were shot, and how to control them. They felt that Clem would have been able to come up with the answer. In his absence and that of Ikin, they floundered with these practical weapons of war.

There was a ring of mounted raiders riding around the legs, calling on someone to come to see them or they would attack. But apart from brandishing their swords, they were obviously wondering what to do. Nomaque answered them, and told them that no one was going to come out and to go away before he squashed them.

They took exception to this and several tried to throw ropes up the sides to wedge on the top while there was the sound of a hammer hitting the metal leg. Then an arrow or two bounced off into the trees. Nomaque severed each rope as it lodged, Eta nudged Sorin and disappeared down to their bags He emerged with their bows, followed by Zeth and Chorky with their bows and spears. Eta watched for a moment and drew back his bow to let fly at something in the tree nearby. There was a cry and a body fell out.

"You had better take him away when you go, too." Nomaque called down.

With that demonstration, the riders pulled back out of bowshot. Another arrow loosed from ambush nearby glanced off the clear top. Those further away couldn't see the gaps in the topping so it looked like a magic wall that protected them. All seemed to grow quiet, as both sides took stock of the situation.

Nomaque went below and came up wearing the fancy robe they plundered from the kobs. The sun was sending shafts of sunlight down through the trees onto his glittering presence.

"I felt the need for a bit of persuasion." He added waving his arms in a highly magical way, encircling the chariot as though to be warding it.

Inside in the armoury, there was a deep discussion going on as to why the thing stopped so suddenly, and whether they could bring the arrows into use. The first question, they felt, was there for them to work out, the second they left alone. The cup was the key.

"What would fit into it? Stones, beads, jewels, no it can't be. Coins perhaps. Lets try all those apart from the jewel of course." Chorky muttered as he and

202

the others trooped up to the light. The stone went through the bottom of the cup onto the floor, so did the bead, but the copper coin stopped where it was. It was then taken inside when he pressed the little stud on the front of the pot. Chorky popped a few more in for good measure and called for them to hold tight. Braced against the back rail, Nomaque gestured when he saw Chorky move to operate the levers, and then off they went with the expected lurch.

'Very imposing' thought Nomaque, trying to look in control, all the while hanging on for dear life, 'that should give them something to wonder at.'

---0---

The raiders stood and watched the disappearing apparition going off down the valley and showed a lack of enthusiasm about pursuing it.

"I think we were lucky there," one said," it pays to leave powerful mad magicians strictly alone. They are very unpredictable."

"Very rich though," another mused, although he was pleased at not taking it on. 'Very nasty too' came to his mind as he thought about the deep footprints in the turf. "I didn't like the word 'squashing'."

---0---

The four copper pieces took them the better part of a mile before the chariot stopped. They put in four silver coins and carried on for another fifteen miles. Chorky found the big lever showed what he thought their speed and found he could increase this up to the top of the 'S' mark. There were a lot of complaints and Zeth was sick through the trap in the floor. They were all feeling a little queasy from the curious waddling gait of the chariot. The forest closed in again so they elected to carry on by foot. The afternoon was drawing in as they picked their way through the trees.

"We must find somewhere to camp." Eta called to the others, "perhaps over towards the cliffs, there's a lake the other side. They went on a few more miles northwards, and came to a dell cut into the hillside, with a stream tumbling down.

"Just the spot." Nomaque mused, unstrapping his pack. They spent the night there, lulled to sleep by the sound of the little waterfall

Undisturbed and well rested they set off the following morning. The sound of a major cataract soon came to their ears as they went westwards. They kept to the north of the main trail and approached the roaring waters carefully. The gorge was spanned by a very substantial rope bridge, and big enough to take a cart. Looking a little closer there were kob guards on both ends of the bridge.

"We have to pass on foot, the bridge probably won't take the chariot. If you looked at the tracks we left behind, the metal feet sank quite deeply into the ground with the weight. It's either all out attack or the sneaky way. The two sentries on our side will prove no trouble, but the hut with all the others and two on duty on the far side, are a different matter. They would see the attack on the first two." Eta observed.

"We don't know how many there are over there. We had better watch for a while and try to count them, meanwhile everyone else think about it." Nomaque put in.

Half an hour later Sorin came back saying that there were five armed guards on duty. There were signs that there were many more kobs off duty in the hut.

They decided that to brazenly approach the bridge was a solution all right as a last resort, but a decoy action would be better. Chorky would go a little into the woods and produce the monster for the guards to see, they would rush across to investigate, leaving the bridge unguarded. The others would be ready to slip onto the bridge and hold it until Chorky nipped around to them. They would retreat leaving the kobs in disarray.

That was the plan. Chorky created his monster and caused a panic as predicted. The two guards on the near side couldn't see it, but the other three on the far side could. The three rushed across and all five stood on the end of the bridge and trembled. The Chariot party on the ground couldn't see why but the kobs could. The front of the chariot seemed to have a great mouth with rows of teeth showing on it, the effect was devastating. When Chorky changed back, the guards were still standing there, arguing what to do.

Chorky circled quietly round and joined the ground team.

"Now what, any ideas?" He said.

"I could..." Nomaque began when they heard the drumming of horses' hooves. They edged back into the trees and waited. Into view came the horsemen from their previous encounter. There was animated shouting and the mounted warriors galloped off over the bridge with anxious glances back towards the trees, leaving those at the bridge to their fate. These few guards gathered in a knot by the bridge, waiting.

The group decided a charge from the side was the only way, to try to push them out of the way. To this end they assembled in an order of march. Nomaque chuckled.

"Let's go as if we were being pursued by the chariot. If we come at a run, dishevelled and afraid, telling of horrors, we may nip through yet. But, if not, our swords are out and our bows strung ready." Nomaque explained.

They started from about a hundred yards from the chasm, out of sight, racing forwards into view, straight up to the frightened guards.

"Get out of the way, a frightful monster off the hills attacked us. Get out of the way, cretin, or you will be mauled too! It got two of our party before we ran. It stamped on one and ate the other, argh, bits all over the place. Well, while you are trembling, I'm off." Nomaque snarled in kobish. Barging the kobs aside and walking quickly off across the bridge, without a backward glance. The others followed and they were over in a trice.

"Where do you scum think you are going in such a hurry?" A resplendent guard captain and three guards with bows drawn faced them. "You've woken up the whole damned infested country with your yelling. Running away, my prizes? What have you got for me, or you will be down in that river feeding the fishes." He boasted. They had run into trouble. While they thought about what to reply, the other guards joined them, totally distracted, they yelled.

"Tell him what you told us. We saw it so we believe you. I've never seen anything so horrible." The trembling guard called out.

"We're running for our lives, don't stop us, for the black demon's sake! There's a creature as big as those ruddy trees on the other side, its eaten one of us and stomped on another. It went off so we ran like hell for the bridge. The river might stop it, but if it doesn't, the dark one help you all. Let us pass! Prepare to defend yourselves, the beast is coming! Our arrows just glanced off it." Nomaque snarled in kobish. The Captain wavered as he saw his men were mixed up with the group, to loose arrows then would set his own men fighting him.

"We saw it, its mouth was a big as our shed. Over there in those trees it was." The most disturbed kob yammered. The captain looked at another of his band standing with the group, as though to confirm, but hoping that the guards would disarm the group. He was doomed to be disappointed as the second guard nodded in agreement with Nomaque. More than that, all five guards standing with the group started to mutter amongst themselves as they felt threatened. Nomaque quickly realised what was happening and shouted.

"What! You don't believe your own chaps, and are still going to shoot at us all. You must be slavering mad. Right lads, lets sort them out. We can't stand and get trampled first, that's what he wants, save his own damned hide, that's the way with these captains. Come on lets get'im." And all of the group moved forward taking the kobs with them.

The captain panicked and shouted, "Shoot! Shoot the deserters! Shoot! You cowardly scum," all the while edging back from the front line.

This action was just what Nomaque wanted, "Coward, look he's running away, I told you, cowardly scum. Get the others to do the dirty work, while he keeps his hands clean. I know his type, weak all the lot of them."

Caught neatly, the captain screamed his orders again, but the guards put up their weapons, but not before their captain sank to the ground with an arrow in his back. He was shot by his own kobs. Nomaque shouted. "Well done lads, he deserved that, cowardly worm." Leaving the kobs to gather around their fallen leader, the group quickly disappeared into the trees, determined to put as much distance in as possible before dusk.

"That was neatly done, Nomaque, a worthy victory that! They still don't know what happened to them, and possibly never will. The chariot is now 'the monster of the Chasm,' and that guard duty will be very unpopular amongst kobs." Eta chuckled. "The kobs will, if they are clever enough to make the captain a 'victim', get out of it almost unscathed," Nomaque added. They went several miles before they stopped to camp, a goodly distance into the trees. They were sitting around with Sorin on guard when the elf cried,

"Ware intruders!" They dived for their weapons and came up ready for action, they were determined to sell themselves dearly. Five kobs stepped into the clearing, in fact five kobs recognisable from the afternoon's fracas.

"Don't jump, friends, some of us lads have had enough of guard duty and followed along for the fun. Got any grub? We had to leave in a hurry," a tall kob explained.

"What happened then, did the monster return?" Zeth asked as he too spoke a little kobish.

"Oh! A little argument over who killed who. No monster came. Only a few of the dim ones bleated about that. I think too much rout, before standing too long in the dark. Where are you goin?" the kob asked.

"We are looking for a kob leader with a magical axe." Eta couldn't resist adding.

"Oh, there's one in a valley fifteen miles further on," one of the kobs replied, glared at by the first speaker.

"We plan to go north along the track to the sisters, in the night, so as to avoid any patrols from that valley, after a bite." the first kob proposed.

"Did you see the monster?" Nomaque asked.

"No I doubt there was one." The first kob replied.

"Sit and have a bite then, yes, but true there *was* a creature thirty feet high roaming about, we should know. Nazir and Sthim were killed by it. It ate Nazir, but it seemed to have somebody controlling it. We ran like hell. Don't laugh, it could be near, if it crossed the ravine." Nomaque told him.

The party of kobs seemed uncomfortable, but accepted the dried meat and water, leaving them a little while later.

208

"We need to know where they have gone. Sorin and I will go scout about but you will have to provide a way for us to slip into the trees unseen to give us a chance." Eta said in a rare dialect of elvish that Nomaque knew.

"All right, we will dowse the fire accidentally and when we start it again it will seem as though we are all be asleep in our blankets. We will actually all be on guard and in sight of each other, hidden in the trees.

The two elves departed leaving Nomaque, Zeth and Chorky lurking in the trees. True to type about half an hour after all was quiet the kobs came creeping back. Zeth was the only one with a bow and the two elves still had not returned, so they had to take the intruders on three to five, hoping that Zeth could kill one with his first arrow. Straight and true flew the shaft, catching the kob in the throat. Being the nearest to the trees the gurgle was not heard by the other four. His second arrow unfortunately pierced an arm and the kob let loose a shout which echoed about the trees. Turning, the kobs saw the three closing in on them. With a laugh the tallest kob whipped up his sword and beset Chorky, driving him back. Two leapt for Nomaque and the third approached Zeth. Very soon the two found the Druid no easy victim to their cost, his figure seemed to float out of the way of their blades. Both were soon limping badly, one with a broken arm. Zeth and Chorky's opponents were good fighters, and so they formed three groups of battling figures in the flickering firelight.

The inevitable happened and Nomaque ran out of opponents, his two lay sprawled dead on the ground. He then closed in on the kob with Zeth and tripped him for the half-elf to finish, otherwise Zeth would soon have been wounded, as he was tiring visibly. Both Chorky and the other larger kob were

209

cut in places but neither had the advantage. Both were well armed and armoured. Deftly parrying a cut from Chorky's sword, and seeing that he was the last on his feet, the tall kob span away and ran into the trees. Nomaque quickly followed to discover him bending over two bundles on the ground. Throwing his wand, he caught the kob behind the ear, stunning him. Several swift blows and the kob was groaning on the ground. To the Druid's relief the two elves were bound but only bruised. He released them, but by the time he looked for the kob, he had vanished. Fortunately Eta's and Sorin's gear was piled nearby and the kob had no time to pick it up.

"We were ambushed and bundled up," Sorin recounted. "The tall kob Nachik stopped any torture 'until after'. When you came just now he was going to kill us, he said, 'now you two chickens it's your turn.'"

"Close, thank you Nomaque." Eta added when they were back in the clearing. "Anyone hurt. No? Thank the gods. I feel badly about this, we let you down. Sorry again."

"We won't get any more sleep tonight, but we can rest awhile." said Nomaque as he tiredly sat down. The two elves took the first watch but Eta's first question to Sorin had them all propped on their elbows listening.

"Sorin?" Eta mused, "You never told us what happened before you appeared at the kob caravan. Or what happened to separate you from Maltex and Hons."

"Sorry I should have told you all sooner but with everything happening I clean forgot. We made good time back to Hecalin, attended the grand burial and were back in Mesquite within a week." Sorin began, "Not wishing to stay too long we grabbed provisions and went off. We didn't even go in the Old Duck Inn, Hons said that if we did we would never get to the valley in time as Maltex would find

210

something or someone to distract him. Too right! So we hustled the said elf through the town and out again double quick. The route we took went across country due north to get to the valley as soon as possible, I think that Maltex felt that there was something very unusual about this trip and did not want to miss any of the action. There were goblins and kobs everywhere. This became worse until we cut across the eastern end of the Mesquite Hills and found the kob fortress. We were in real trouble, there were troops everywhere."

"We went to ground, hiding at night and moving carefully by day working slowly eastwards into the hills. Those hills are grim travelling. Canyons and gorges cut across the line of the hills east to west. We climbed in and out of more than I can count. Then we were ambushed by the goblins, at least twenty of the little... chaps. In the melee I fell down into a gully and wasn't noticed, or left for dead. People it seems always leave me for dead! Anyway Maltex and Hons fought like mad, unfortunately there were too many I suppose."

"I was knocked out cold when I fell and so I missed what happened next. I awoke with a thumping headache and cast about to find them but there was no sign of them. There was nothing apart from a lot of trampled bushes and a bit of blood here and there. Not any bodies, goblins or elves? Odd, very odd, they are usually not fussy over things like that. There was a leader with those who attacked us I think. Anyway I crept away and came across a track. This helped and I made good progress. About a day later I found a raider encampment in the ruined village of Nigreth Fond, you know, where the last great battles with the goblins took place. There were both kobs and raiders there and a lot of slaving was going on. Then I saw the kob party assembling with Riva in chains. When they departed I followed hoping to sneak her away. But they were too well organised and no opportunity came until your ambush. Boy was I pleased to see you all, and no mistake. I suppose the other two are in the clutches of the goblins, at the time there was no chance to track them in the condition I was in." They all sat silent for a while and the grim mood banished any sleep there was to be had that night. The chances of the two surviving was slim, no-one could recall anyone who had escaped alive once taken prisoner by the kobs, apart from Riva in living memory.

The next day they reached the hilly country on the edge of the valley with the caverns. They camped near to the rushing waters in a gorge. It was good cover and so they spent a quiet night, catching up with their sleep after the previous night. The path was treacherous down the gorge, but well defined. It took the rest of the day to reach the valley.

The quiet little valley was quiet no more. Kobs and raiders had joined forces and made the beautiful valley a place marred. A large number of the trees were felled, and several log cabins sat on the track, which traversed the length of the valley. Kobs and raiders were everywhere.

"Well? Now what? Where on earth is Clem in all of this?" Nomaque mused.

"We are a day or two before the month is up, we might have to wait for him." replied Chorky standing by his side in the trees, a bit back from the rim.

The stones were there still, but they were quite close to the huts as well as a regular path up to the cliffs. The group had to get in somehow, find the axe, sword, and get to their destination. It was a tall order indeed.

Chorky then heard a 'voice' inside his head, '*me help*' it said. Grinning with pleasure, the half-elf told the others that his little friend had just talked to him. The 'voice' told them to skirt the valley to the south in the dark and climb up the mountain on that side, and it would meet them. It was shot at if it approached the valley. This they did, following those directions they were directed to a cliff face above the valley sides. After a while the little draptera joined them.

'Others come soon, told wait here or in cliff cave. If go to top of mountain there another way down too.'

They spent the night at the base of the upper cliffs, sleeping fitfully. The next morning they looked up at the cave in the cliff and decided that the mountain top could be the easier route. They set out, reaching the cave a little below the topmost crag in the afternoon. The tunnels joined up in the mountain, leading down to the caves where they had previously vanquished the giant and the two ogres. The picked, crunched and blackened bones of the carcasses were scattered about the floor. The rest of the caves were as before, there was still a heap of treasure on the floor. The tunnel on the far side of the now scummy pool was broken and stopped up.

"The dragon protecting his hoard I expect." Chorky reflected, hoping that was the truth, but those picked bones troubled him. He framed a question in his mind for his small friend, who had flown off somewhere,

'Has the dragon come back while we were away?'

'Dragon been get better, come back with us.. EEGH. IT'S NOT? HELP, I ATTACKED...I FLAMED .OOH I HURTS,' the little creature's thoughts shot lightning fast from one picture to another and then blotted out. It was now in deep pain and very frightened.

Chorky felt helpless to aid the little creature and was extremely worried by the fuzzy sobbing thoughts from Ligitz. Then he heard the cheery voice of the dwarf calling down to them. They looked up and saw the familiar short figure come walking unhurriedly along the tunnel towards them.

"Vodocanthey's not far behind. He left me in a hurry to catch some raiders, they are in for a hot reception and no mistake. His fire was really up as he swooped down on the huts in his valley."

There was a disturbance in the air of the tunnel and a little fire scorched creature was in a whirl around Chorky, the draptera had arrived, to land and desperately cling to Chorky. The poor little thing was in a mess. There was a burn mark all along his one side. He was incoherent with pain as he wrapped himself tight around the half-elf's shoulders.

'A DRAGON HAS FLAMED ME!!!' the small voice screamed from Chorky's shoulder.

"That's definitely NOT Vodocanthey, that's why this has been made into a lair again, FOR ANOTHER DRAGON!" Chorky shouted and started running up the tunnel to get out.

He was too late, roaring and rumbling was coming down the tunnel. Skidding to a stop they all ran back the other way, with desperate speed they pounded down to the inner cave, up on the ledge and scrambled madly into the little tunnel. They just made it, Clem feeling very hot around the heels for the second time in his life.

Chapter Thirteen

Pawns on the Seas of Fate

*B*last after blast of superheated fire bored into the small hole, the rocks melting and flowing down onto the floor of the cavern. The surrounding rocks began cracking with the great gusts of flame. This was no ancient, this was a mature dragon in the height of its power, it was absolutely malevolent. They would be snuffed out in a trice if caught. They hoped that the old friend they saved escaped, this one would definitely kill him. There was a rumbling far above them, and then silence. The blasts stopped and the rock in the tunnel between the cavern and them collapsed in half molten slurry. The red-hot dust was rising in a ruddy cloud, illuminated by the glow from the molten stones.

Crouched in the end of the tunnel they waited for a chance to try the trap above them without alerting their foe. The chance came with the roof collapse. Very slowly with wetted cloths over their mouths they tried the trapdoor above them, desperate with thick choking air. Drawing their weapons they made ready to fight their way out. The two tallest Eta and Zeth heaved on the slab. Firstly there was not any give at all. Perseverance paid off and slowly the stone rose, there was a thump and then the slab went up with a rush. There had been something standing on the top, which had toppled over. They poured out of the hole gasping great lungfulls of cavern air, all the while looking about for kobs. The door was shut and everything was quiet. The cell door was not barred, so after checking cautiously, they were on their way.

They chose the stair to the upper level as they felt that was where the trouble would come from, even though it may have been diverted by the attack by Vodocanthey on the raider's huts. As they raced along they noticed the half-open door slab they had crawled under before. They carried on past, turned the corner and raced into the kobs guardroom. The three kobs sitting at the table and the two standing on the attacker's side of it, had no chance, but the remaining three tried to run. One made it to the doorway but was brought down by one of Eta's unerring arrows.

"No axe or sword here," said Zeth as they searched the bodies and racks of weapons. "I will gratefully accept the donation to our funds though." He added collecting the odd purse. Chorky was hampered by the draptera, but short of prizing the animal from his shoulder there was nothing he could do. There was a minor advantage, the little dragon breathed a hot breath into the face of his last adversary, putting him off guard long enough for the half-elf to run him through.

Not pausing long they hurried on. Opening another door they came on two more kobs, who were dealt with. This was another guardroom and racks of swords and spears adorned the walls.

An exclamation came from Zeth as he waved what looked like a knobbly spearshaft in the air.

"A staff of something, I've always wanted one. Oh goody this is my lucky day."

"Nothing else, except a suspicion that this wall is not what it seems. There's something in the middle of the wall." Eta poked and pried at it, a moment later there was a click and a section opened.

"I told you so, easy." Eta crowed. The door gave onto a passage with another door almost opposite. They tried this and it opened. As they opened it the sounds of pursuit came from behind them and many mailed feet stamping some way back along the corridor.

In front of them was a passage, which went into a room, exactly half of a circle, the two exits being equi-spaced around the semicircle. The room was deserted, but the door they had just come through burst open, and a horde of kobs poured into the room. In front of them was a greatkob. The drool dripping from its fangs and its black bloodshot eyes both showed rampant madness.

With a scream midway between agony and bloodlust the leader charged Chorky, above his head he whirled an ornate battleaxe. The axe moaned and glowed thirstily as it descended, the half-elf was only just able to deflect the blow. A jolt of power shot up Chorky's arm from the contact with the weapon as it still hit his helmet a glancing blow.

"Not another magic weapon?" Chorky groan-ed shocked and worried, as this one was much more fell. Battle royal ensued, knots of fighting figures staggered about the room. The newcomers were equal in number, but the room wasn't wide enough for more than two engagements across. The great-kob's next blow was hampered by the wall and went astray, which Chorky returned with all his might. His blade slid off the breastplate into his adversarie's thigh. It bellowed and stepping back awkwardly swung at Chorky again. Suddenly the draptera launched itself at the greatkob's head, this caused the axe to come down awry, giving Chorky time to dodge and go in for the killing thrust. Surprised and shocked, the kob tried to look down past his little attacker, at the sword transfixing him, and sank to the ground. The little dragon, realising the kob was dead, panicked and leaped back to Chorky's shoulder, as the half-elf bent forward to wrench out his sword.

217

Deftly side-stepping Chorky and his fallen adversary, Clem swept up the battleaxe as it fell from its former owner's nerveless fingers. He gave a great shout of triumph as the power of the weapon surged through him. Hewing left and right he cleaved a path through the demoralised kobs. They broke and ran back to jostle in the doorway, crowding each other and unable to defend themselves. Several escaped running back up the passage calling for help. Severely demoralised the remaining kobs succumbed quickly to the blades and Druid stick wielded by the group.

"Is it the Axe, Clem? It looks ornate enough. I thought Chorky was in for it then." Nomaque asked as the dwarf was leaning against the wall resting. He pulled himself up and looked more closely at his treasure.

"Yes I think so, there are seven stars in a circle set in electrum in this white silvery metal on each face of the electrum blade, the metal's the same as the Star Key Jewel, and by gods its powerful. I can sense some things through it. I feel an urgency to travel northwards when I grip the shaft. I also can sense your Star, Nomaque, possibly Ikin's ring also, but that's very faint. There's no feeling of any Sword or anything about the other Prince, not that I would be able to tell. According to this there's no reason to stay around here." Clem suggested. Faintly they heard sounds and shouts in kobish back the way they had come.

"That's torn it, our way back is blocked," Nomaque muttered. "Somewhere there must be a way out."

They tried the other door and found it open, so they all went through, wedging it after them. The tunnel bent a couple of times to the left bringing them to a pair of curiously swinging doors. Immediately suspicious Eta started looking for another secret exit, he had a feeling that there was a trap of some kind ahead of the doors. Clem agreed. In a short while an opening was found into a second corridor, confirming Eta's reasoning. There were three doors along the right side of the passage. Zeth was just about to try the first when Sorin heard a groan coming from the third door. Investigating this he found the door ajar. Inside a prisoner lay in a pitiable state, part on the floor and part supported by his shackles to the wall. They ran over and saw he was almost gone. Chorky took out a flask, gently easing some water over the man's parched lips. The man opened his eyes and amazement showed at first and then gratitude, his eyes clouded with pain.

He smiled a cracked smile and croaked, "Aagh, I see the kob chief is no more.The only way out is the chair...," then he shuddered and died. Chorky sighed and laid the tortured body back against the wall.

"What chair?" Clem mused. Seeing no further need to stay in the room, they left and tried the second door. That was when they realised what the tortured one referred to. In the next room with its backrest leaning against the wall, stood a highly ornate chair. The back and sides were painted panels of various scenes around a castle on a plain. The armrests were carved, ending with griffon's heads. Clem wearily mounted the dais on which the chair stood and eased himself down in it.

"That's nirvanaaaa… "

The dwarf just faded away. Totally dumbfounded, the others looked on.

"Quickly, let's follow quickly as fast as possible, before it changes!" Nomaque yelled, as he pushed Zeth into the chair after the dwarf. No sooner had he sat than he went too. Not knowing where they were going the others followed, taking no little courage, especially Sorin who went last but having no choice.

Going off into nothingness…

Chapter Fourteen

Somewhere Unpleasant to Somewhere?

*I*n the pitch-black quiet of the cavern nothing disturbed the body of the Elf Knight as it lay at the bottom of the scree slope of old bones. The sharp ambush had left no hope for the lone elf, powerful sorcery struck him down, torturing his mind to the end of his endurance and murdering steel had finished him. His helm was torn from his agonised and dying head and the circlet of ancient power ripped off. Disposed of in the timeworn way and the body had tumbled down a steep slide of bones to rest forgotten in the dark. Creatures had plundered his weapons but the bright metal of the armour had been too *painful for them to touch.*

---0---

A gasp broke the silence, a scrabble, and another body tumbled down the slope to join the silent knight. During the course of the next moments five more joined the first, along with a dwarfish voice admonishing all the dwarf gods past and present in the darkness.

"Clem, I would know your cheerful tones anywhere, well met old friend."

All noise stopped and all eyes which could turned towards the words, spoken with an elvish smooth slur.

From an archway a dozen feet away came a dim light, which partly illuminated a figure standing there.

"What have you found now, Maltex!" another familiar elvish voice muttered.

"You would never have guessed in a month of godsdays! We have a heap of adventurers. Clem the dwarf, our old friend is under the lot of them, by the sound of him. Somehow he has joined up with Nomaque, who has rolled onto a skeleton nearby, and by the look on his face, finds it a little lumpy. Come on Hons," he chortled, "and see a sight you will never beat as long as you live."

"So, we have guests." Hons added. "Welcome to the caves, wheresoever they are."

"Chorky, what with the horn on your helmet and the teeth of that animal of yours, there's no way I could tell which way up I am, let alone what stone floor I'm being squashed on! Maltex?…Hons?. If I knew you knew this bunch I'm with, I wouldn't have joined them. Don't you know where we are either, at least you're not in this pile, are you?" An exasperated dwarfish voice rose up from the pile of arms and legs.

222

"No. Neither Maltex nor I know where the gods we are. We have been through most of our journeys underground. Seeing you all I hoped you would enlighten me, but it seems we are to be disappointed. I must admit you seem to have a 'just arrived look' about you all. Who's that you are sitting on, Nomaque?" Hons mildly teased. "Oh hello Sorin old friend, how did you get here, we thought you were dead."

"I ran into this lot not long after we left Mesquite looking for you two." Sorin retorted.

"I knew the two of them would turn up, looking well fed and unharassed. It feels about a year ago when we were in that inn." Nomaque cut in. "As to this character I'm sitting on, he looks like a knight in armour, bring the light over lads........... Good gods, I have seen this armour before, haven't you Eta? So this was where the other brother died. Look at his face! What terrors did he have to endure before he died? ...I present Prince Throndralon, of the Elves of the Star. Sent to find this," holding up the Star Emblem to flash in the torchlight.

"And lost this," Clem waggled the axe, not quite free yet from the tangle of bodies.

"Do be careful Clem! That axe is razor sharp!" Nomaque muttered, rolling painfully onto his knees to look.

They looked down on the beautiful elven features, distorted hideously in death, but there was still an undefeated air about that terrible mask of agony.

"Where is our absent friend, Ikin?" Hons asked, only just able to count and identify those assembled.

"She has gone off with this dead elf's brother, Encathalon, another way round with some more Castle seekers." Nomaque explained. "Possibly a flanking movement, we could call it, while we make the frontal assault. If we can find the way, that is. By

223

the way the whole of goblindom and kobdom could well be in between as well."

Hons started, and went quiet, wondering what to do.

"Asphar, no doubt." Maltex said to himself.

"Who?" Queried Nomaque.

"A particularly nasty sorcerer who is responsible for the plight of some friends of ours, and nearly our deaths," Maltex explained, and added. "He is mobilising the goblins and possibly kobs to go and fight some elves somewhere."

"Yes, we may have come across them. There is some involvement with the crown you were bartering in Mesquite. It will probably let the horde of goblins and the Sorcerer from here attack the castle and the elf people that we are looking for." Nomaque quietly added.

As the truth sunk in Maltex staggered slightly. "Ye Gods! What have I done this time!" Visibly shocked he breathed deeply for a moment and sinking to his knees, he groaned "Ooh!" again. Another agonised pause followed then he continued, "By the gods above and those below, I must try to atone, if I can." His voice was in a terrible state that the Druid had not heard him utter before.

"Maltex's changed a lot,' the Druid mused listening to the two new arrivals while he got his breath back, 'it's difficult to tell with Hons, but he's different too. There's something here that needs telling, I smell it.' He went quietly to the kneeling elf, "Maltex, I know you blame yourself, but there are other greater things happening here which you cannot know about or be responsible for."

"Where are you? My Elf? Maltex?" A small but deep, female voice called in elvish with a curious accent. Hons turned away from them and walked back along the tunnel he and Maltex had approached from.

'Ah ha! I knew it! Female interest,' chuckled Nomaque to himself.

"Snoodl, my love, we have special visitors. Come and meet them, they are all friends and won't harm you or your guard." Hons's voice carried back. Maltex' face looked apprehensive and worried.

"Have a care everybody, Hons's heart and mine are involved with these people. They are not what they seem, Clem keep iron control!" Maltex said low and vitally.

"As if I'd hurt him or hissssssss........" Clem muttered and ended in a slowly expelled breath, as Snoodl turned the corner into the light, surrounded by her ancient goblin bodyguards. There was a quiet moment while they all took stock of the new situation.

Always the first to deal with a crisis, the Druid walked slowly forward and held out a hand to the pretty little gobliness. Realising that whatever his feelings were, they were eclipsed by the anxiety in the lovely eyes in front of him. In them he could see the love for the elf by her side. Smiling he said, "I have waited a long time to see such lovely eyes! So you have captured Hons's heart, have you?"

There was a releasing of tension, and the group took her into their hearts too, even Clem. Amazed, he took Maltex to one side and asked him the question blazing in his mind.

"These are not the goblins I know, are they another race?"

"I would not have believed it myself if I hadn't been saved by them from others of their own kind. Her father saved both of us from Asphar himself, and lost her mother in doing it. Some goblins, if they reach an age around forty, undergo a complete change, becoming as our elders. Sort of Coming of Age and a Change happens. Veterans or ancients as they call themselves. Normally they would guide the colony, but when powerful sorcerers rise, the goblin

225

young flock to them. The ancients either die or flee the caves. These just made it."

"I like their bearing, doughty, like dwarves. Introduce me, I will try to bridge the gap, for I have been in ignorance, and would like to fill it." Clem strode over to the four veterans and extended a call-used hand to take each of theirs in turn and warmly welcome them. Maltex followed quickly and interpreted. The language was mellowed too, it was not as harsh, just deep.

Hons looked over to the dwarf and the old goblins, and smiled down at Snoodl. "Look what you've done, I would never have believed it," Hons said expelling his held breath gently, 'that only leaves Ikin to face' he thought. Snoodl chuckled happily. She went and talked to the ancients, and a little while later came back over to their group.

"I have sent two of them back to prepare some food in your honour. Please be our guests in our new caves. You will all be taking my elf and Maltex away from me soon, so allow us to welcome you." She suggested.

There was general nodding and agreement, as their rations had been meagre for a while. A good spread would be great. Their curiosity also got the better of them.

'Good goblins?!!' Zeth wondered and shook his head as if to clear the vision.

Leading the way the gobliness twisted and turned through old goblin caves, finally arriving at a spotlessly clean hall, in the centre of which was a large table. Goblins of all ages were happily bringing food of all sorts and placing it on the table. Everything froze for a second on the entrance of the party, but the veterans, after casting furtive glances firstly at their leader and the newcomers, especially the doughty dwarf, everything started again. At the head

226

of the table sat a venerable old goblin. He rose and bowed.

"Welcome to my hall, you will always be welcome as friends of our tall brothers. Sit and rest, we have a brew, which will refresh you, and food to fill you. Welcome, Man of the Wood we are honoured. Welcome doughty dwarf, of whom I have heard many times, may all the stone brothers be joined in friendship."

As they began to sit Snoodl came up to Chorky and looked at his charge.

"Your draptera is badly injured, look just here, and also there. He has been deeply burnt." She gently scratched the little dragon behind the ears. "You poor little thing, got yourself into somewhere hot. It is very upset as well, isn't it? Do you think it will allow me to treat its wounds? I would prefer to do it away from the table, so if you can hold back your hunger for a while we can go to my room and treat him." She led Chorky away out of the cave.

The others, overwhelmed by the hospitality unlooked for, sat, ate, and drank until very content. Chorky joined them after a while, without his draptera, and ate his fill too.

"I have left the little chap in Snoodl's care. I hope it will stay. The thought of taking an injured creature into battle worried me." The half-elf mused, "from its thoughts I think it understands."

When they had finished, they were shown several cool chambers and slept well, recovering for what must be their greatest challenge yet.

The first task was to bury the Elf Prince Throndralon, with as much ceremony and honour as they could, in a rough tomb of rock in a cavern near to the goblin ancient's halls. The only personal effect left apart from the body was an ornate locket, this Nomaque took with him in the hope that he would eventually see Throndralon's parents.

227

On the way back to the cave Quillam gathered them all around him and asked. "Will you please carry our infinite sadness with you to the King and Queen at the great loss of their son?"

The next day was spent mostly in discussion, meals came and went, the table was the focal point for the exchange of information. The goblins themselves were not sure exactly where they were, and could only give them vague directions towards the valley in which the castle once stood. This tied in with the feelings Clem had with the Axe. The ancients didn't know what the group had to face, apart from their own young led headlong by Asphar. This topic was of course completely omitted. It was too painful for all. The group's task was to help swell the forces opposing the Castle, and try to take the Emblems back to their rightful owners. Quillam, Snoodl's father, asked them to take two prospective ancients with them, to help in a small way to redress the wrong their youth was doing.

Vart and Venric were their names, with their swords strapped over their shoulders and covered head to foot in fine ring-mail, they presented themselves just before they all gathered to go on the following morning. For Hons it was a particularly wrenching farewell, and he was to look back many a time and sigh lustily over his fair gobliness.

The new group was larger and better able to cope with problems on the way, having many diverse races' experience to draw from. Eta, Sorin, Hons and Maltex made up the elf contingent, and Nomaque, Chorky and Zeth represented the half-elves. In addition Clem brought support from the dwarves and Vart and Venric, from the goblins.

They went back to the tunnel near to where they met the two elves, and searched about for a tunnel going northwards or Axewards as Clem described it. There was a large crossroads twenty feet further down the passage and this was where their search centred. There was no obvious tunnel going that direction. The ten of them hunted, deter-mined to find a way through.

Clem first spotted it, there was a crack that defied the eye. So narrow that he thought it wouldn't allow anyone to go down it. It went off in a close to northward direction.

He gathered them all together and as no-one else had had any luck, he showed them the crack. It was very difficult to see, almost as if it didn't want anyone to go along it. After a while they decided to try it, and filed in. Once in there was no going back, as the ones behind stopped retreat, and Clem thought back to the first encounter with Vodocanthey, going down the tunnel to his cavern. The narrow tunnel opened into a large cavern, with a doorway on the far side. The doorway was set into an arch with a wide edge. Into that edge were six brass studs.

Without any other options the studs were pre-ssed, carefully. There was a heavy slithering sound and a door on their right opened and in slid an enormous snake with an almost human head, all of thirty feet long. It swayed, looking at them all. Eta later told them these creatures were always found near some important place to control it, they were called naga spirits or guardians.

Slowly, taking an age, it surveyed all of them in turn, turning their minds inside out, seeming to look for evil. Everyone afterwards said that all the wrong they had done was taken out and examined. The goblins felt exceptionally guilty. So did Maltex. The naga focussed on the unfortunate Maltex who jerked as a puppet under another's control. He had sold the crown for base desires, and put in jeopardy hundreds of people. He reeled back in agony, at the scenes the naga was portraying for him.

229

Then just as slowly it released Maltex and made him walk to a small shelf in the wall. He lifted a circlet and placed it on his own head, it lodged on the centre of his brow.

"YOU ARE TO AID THE ELVES OF THE STAR
IN ALL WAYS, UNTO DEATH,
OR,
UNTIL THE ELVES ARE SAVED.
OR,
UNTIL THE ELVENKING RELEASES YOU FOR
DEEDS OF VALOUR.

.....

IF YOU FAIL YOU ARE MINE. FOR EVER."

It turned from the rigid Maltex to the others, who froze expecting the worst.

"I AM THE KEEPER OF THE FIRST GATE.
MY TASK IS TO GUARD THE PAST'S FUTURE
THROUGH THIS GATE.
ARE YOU WORTHY?
YOU MUST PASS BACK OR YOU WILL FADE.

.....

The seconds went by, no sound penetrated into that chamber.

....

I HAVE SPOKEN AND JUDGED.
YOU CAN ALL PASS TO THE
LABYRINTH GATE.

......

The creature had a force of presence, which they had all recognised instantly. There was no changing anything, what it said was true and would happen. The naga nodded its head and a second of cold and dizziness enveloped them.

As they recovered they saw that she was no longer there. The room seemed the same, but the circlet on Maltex's brow was real evidence of her presence there moments before.

230

"I think that was a little unfair on you, Maltex." Zeth said.

"No, she was very fair. It is a just task for me to do. In a way I asked her to." He replied.

"She?" Sorin queried.

"Yes, they are all female." Maltex replied firmly.

The door through which they entered was gone. The only exit was a stout double-door to the north, They went through and found themselves in a short corridor to a crossing tunnel. To the right the tunnel had collapsed. The left stretched away into the near distance, but the sides had an unusual silvery shivering look. The way in front led to another doorway with an archway over it. Taking this, they approached the archway. Inscribed over the arch were the words,

DOORWAY TO LIGHT.

Seven brass studs just showed in the stone of the arch. Nomaque pressed these as before, and the doors swung open to give access to the next chamber. This time there was a large archway, highly ornate.

In the centre was a double set of gates, terminated in a series of terrifying spikes, which matched those on the lower edge of the stone of the arch. The writing on the arch was in ancient elvish Which Nomaque translated for them.

LAST GATE TO REMAIN... FIRST GATE TO PASS TO...

There also were rune letters inlayed in electrum inscribed in the stone above these words. The group spent some time examining this edifice with little idea as to how to open it. Clem it was who found their way in. He noticed that in the centre of the gates was a symbol, consisting of dots and rods. Nomaque then remembered that the Star Emblem had similar lumps on the underside, which he had wondered at

231

before. When he tried it slipped in easily, and the doors slid open.

"Doorway to light," Hons said thoughtfully, "I remember now, the ramform giant's last words to me were of this, and she mentioned we had to pass through the 'Labyrinth Gate.' That presumably was that gate. Though what she called it 'Labyrinth' for I cannot guess. The key was on it she said."

"We are about to find out, no doubt!" Eta retorted, as they filed out of the cavern on the other side of the 'Gate' through another doorway and into a tunnel and yet another door. The door refused to open. This set them all searching again for holes, but they found none. Zeth found the press stud in the floor about five feet in front of the door. He pressed it and there was a loud 'Click' from the other side of the door and a 'whirring' sound, then silence. On trying the door they found a tunnel showing a bend to the right. On they went and found another door like the one they had come through just around the bend. Like the other one it would not open until another floor stud was pressed. There sounded the 'Click-whirr' and the door would open. They went through and instantly recognised the tunnel coming from the Labyrinth Gate.

"Your Labyrinth, Hons!" Eta said ruefully.

"I felt a movement when we were in the space between the doors. The Axe felt wrong somehow, too. When we travel north it feels right, I cannot explain it, it just feels awkward. So let's go in again and test this out." Clem suggested.

"We have another clue as well," Nomaque observed, "When we were in the other caverns, before we found Vodocanthey, we were caught in something similar. That was a revolving 'L' shape, operated by door studs, just like this one. We should be able to work it out now."

232

Hopefully they opened the door, and found a blank wall. They operated the stud again, but had to close the door as it would not operate unless the door was closed. That, when opened next, showed another wall again. All for giving up Clem tried one last time and this time found the tunnel going right at a bend.

"Here is where we came in," he said, and a little hesitantly stepped in past the door. They all followed him and operated it again. This time they just checked the corridor. They were back where they started if they went out. But if they stayed in the bend they could ride around with it. Once more with the stud and Clem felt sure they were pointing north. They trooped out of the door to approach another identical corridor again. Everyone groaned. The operation of the door this time had the bend going to the left, which confused them. It was only the dwarf's north sense that extracted them from the 'Click-Whirr corridors' and out into a large chamber with tunnels going off in all directions.

There were bones everywhere, armour, very large beetle skeletons, rubbish heaped all over the floor. It was mainly in a heap in the centre, around a high pile of what looked like old rope. After a look around they started to pick their way round to the other side. Something stirred in the centre of the cavern, catching the memory of the two goblins about the same time. Leaping up, they yelled at the top of their voices for everyone to get down and threw their torches at the heap of 'rope', dropping to the floor. Maltex and Hons, understanding some of what they shouted, warned the others as well as they too dived floor-wards, although the others had understood and had acted already. It was well that they did, the rope pile was an ancient creature, which preyed on the unwary, and could reach all parts of the cavern. The whole seeming pile in the middle of the chamber was

233

a wreathing, flailing, burning maelstrom. Anywhere within a circle of ten feet radius anyone would have been caught in the toils of the monster.

The dry accumulations of waste had caught alight. A few more torches were tossed in for good measure, to keep the rubbish burning. The monster had been waiting for all of them to get well into its reach before striking They all uttered their thanks to the aspiring ancients, benefiting from the knowledge of both goblins and dwarves in the underground caverns. After the burning had slowed they crept out and across to the tunnel most north, and slipped away, from the choking smoke and lack of air.

Only a short way into the tunnel the air was still. A bit further on they saw the reason why, rubble filled the tunnel completely, floor to ceiling. Seeing that they had nowhere to retreat to they set about finding whether the fall could be cleared. Clem declared that he could feel the faintest draught, so it was possible. They started straight away in shifts of two or three, to roll the rocks back.

In two hours of hard toil they made an opening to see through, in another hour the goblins were through working on the other side to enlarge it for the bigger ones. It was not long before all had wriggled through, into another large cavern. That too was strewn with debris. The only exit was in the wall facing them and it was partially blocked. Cautiously they crept along, scarcely making a sound so as to not cause any more roof to fall. For some twenty feet they managed to get through, but at that point the rubble rose again to the roof. Not wishing to retrace their steps they slowly started again to dismantle the pile. They had been doing this for half an hour when they thought they heard some movement on the other side. They stopped and rocks could be heard being shifted on the other side. Then that too stopped. Heartened they attacked the pile sure in the knowledge that there was a way out on the other side. Small hands were seen soon after, broken and bleeding and obviously desperate.

"Who you?" a small strange voice asked nervously in a quaint but recognisable elvish when the hole was big enough for a small body to slip through. "We afraid...."..... "You help?" The voice fearfully asked each question in rapid succession.

"Have no fear, small people, we will help." Nomaque answered in elvish. "Can you get out the other side with our help?"

"NO out! We trapped for long time, many meals have passed. No out this way," the diminutive high-pitched answer came back. With a sigh Nomaque said,

"You had better come this way then."

Getting everyone to turn somehow and go back. Wearily they stumbled back the way they had come to the ropy creature's cavern. With torches held high and very slowly they crept out on to the floor. There was no movement in the heap of blackened rubbish but there was no telling how injured the beast was. Taking the next tunnel round to the left they quickly left the cavern behind, breathing freely again. The tunnel wound around in a rough northerly direction eventually coming out into an enormous cavern.

Here they stopped for food and to properly get to know the little people they rescued. There were six of them, smaller than gnomes, but obviously adults. The leader squeakily introduced himself as Sassanidi of the Neftafi. He explained that they lived in great caverns similar to the one they were in, but further to the west. They had been looking for a new cavern to spread into when, the roof fell in and trapped them completely.

They wore rough one-piece garments of a smooth fibre, stained in fairly drab colours. They see-

235

med to have no metals, only stone tools made of fine flint. On their heads they had varying hats with wide brims, Sassanidi having the most ornate one. Given their very weakened state they were hardy little folk, and were quite cheerful, skipping around Chorky in his armour. They appeared to find the half-elf fascinating, calling him Shiny Man and getting in his way. When he inevitably trod on one, the little person apologised for putting their feet under his.

Littered across the uneven floor were lumps of rocky material, bent to fantastic shapes, and ten or more narrow exits went off from the cavern, mostly on the far side. They sat on some of the lumps and shared their dwindling provisions out, not knowing for how long they had to last. After a while they found the pieces of rock they rested on were sagging down, some of the group ended up not much higher than the floor.

"These rocks are melting!" Clem exclaimed, getting up from his squashed seat. The seat rumbled and rocked a little. Other seats joined in as the group staggered up off their bent perches. The cavern echoed with the rumbling. Elves, half-elves, goblins, dwarf and neftafi all stood where they were, unsure as to what to do, or whether any threat was present.

"It's the second time we have found moving stone, last time they were animated by something else." Eta remarked in a hushed voice, not knowing whether the lumps could hear him.

"It's the second."....
"time we have."...
"found moving stone."...

The voices echoed around the cavern, different voices and position each time, some faster, some slower. All were deep and deliberate, as though they were trying to understand the words.

236

"Do you understand us, cavern dwellers?" Nomaque asked slowly and carefully.

"Do you understand?"...

"us cavern dwellers?"...

At that Nomaque didn't know whether to answer 'No' or not. The lumps began to move, easing themselves to one side of the floor and form up together in a group, becoming roughly humanoid in shape.

"We are visited rarely by others," one of them in the front rumbled. "*We did not know how to greet you.*" The rumbling continued.

"Dwellers of the cavern, we greet you in friendship. We have not talked to your like before, and so would be pleased to know what your race is called." Nomaque continued diplomatically, wondering how much they understood.

"*We are the gemorph. We know of you, Fast moving creatures of the open. We look from our cliff. There are many cruel ones in the valley now. They war on everyone. We also know of the neftafi and would help our friends but do not know how.*" The spokes-creature said.

"We would also like to help your friends, that is why we are here. These neftafi were caught by a rock fall, which has also blocked our passage too. Do you know the route to their caverns and out into the valley?" Nomaque explained.

"*Come, we will lead you to the little ones' caves. Come back to us when you are ready to go out and we will help you as much as we can.*" The gemorph speaker answered, turning he sprouted two legs and walked to one of the openings in the left of the cavern and slid into it.

They quickly picked up their belongings and followed. It led them along a winding narrow crack to emerge shortly out into a well-hewn tunnel, part of an

237

older system. The right going into the distance and the left, the way it took them, to blank wall.

"*Through there are your caves. It is a door which we cannot open.*" The stone like shape retreating back down the tunnel. They were surprised for a moment, wondering what would happen next. Clem started looking at the wall surface looking for clues. Not finding any he gave the stone several hefty kicks in frustration and sat down in disgust.

Eta tried next and after studying the stone for a little while, said. "I think the doorway has been sealed for so long that the marks are filled with muck and dust," "Look here there are small dents, no... holes in the rock. Got the Star, Nomaque." Nomaque quickly produced the article in question and slipped it into the wall. With a groan of protest a whole section of the tunnel wall cracked revealing a portal shaped line. Clem's boots added to the feet pushing and soon the gap was several inches.

The dwarf felt a tap on his arm and the neftafi moved up to the crack.

"Must go first, people frightened of you. We prepare them. We too don't see new races. We go. Wait little while, then come in one at time after Shiny Man." Sassanidi explained, and gave the door a good kick. Slowly it eased open and the six little people went through to a silence, and then cheering and much merriment, there were cries of "Sassanidi!".. "Sassanidi!". "Sassanidi he is back! Hooray for Sass-anidi!" And then a lot of speech the group didn't understand.

Then Chorky pushed the door further open, stepping through the gap. Some twenty little neftafi looked up in horror as he stepped through, some taking to their heels to the far side of what looked like giant mushrooms, dwarfing the small figures. The cavern was huge, containing many of these fungi, which were actually lived in by the neftafi. There was a small village of them. Several giant beetles could be seen scurrying about with neftafi riders, some larger ones with a box on their backs.

Sassanidi was welcomed by most, but a few yelled at him in obvious fear of the newcomers. Blaming him for their arrival. One younger one was performing cartwheels in joy. "That was Englodidi, my grandson," he explained.

They found they were a bit large to get into the mushroom houses, but politely looked in and praised their owners. They set up a sort of camp alongside the overshadowing fungi and next to the wall. They felt quite safe in their new company so they soon all rolled up in their blankets and slept while the little people went about their business quietly around them.

They were woken by the sound of small very curious squeaky voices,

"Shhhh"... "It moved."... "It's very big..."

Clem, who entered into it with a spirit of fun, gave a growl. The little ones scampered away, twittering twice as much. With a chuckle he sat up and looked around him. The others were rousing as well, and soon they were all watching the neftafi going about their daily duties. They were watched in turn by the young ones, peering out from behind the massive stalks of the nearest mushroom houses. A delegation approached them bearing large dishes full of steaming food.

"We like share food with Shiny Man. Guests like try food?" A shy neftafi maiden laid down her dish near to Chorky for him to try. The others waited.

"For goodness sake Chorky try some, or we will never get the chance ourselves." Clem muttered good-naturedly. Gingerly the half-elf picked up a piece and put it into his mouth. With an effort he pronounced it very good. Then the other dishes were given out. The cooked fungi tasted rather bland, but

239

nourishing nevertheless, a welcome change from the travelling food they had with them.

After eating they were shown around the domain of the little people. To their surprise the community was quite large and packed into the three enormous caverns. They could see the need for the continuing exploration for more caves.

They also became very aware that a large part of the population, were extremely afraid of them.

"Why are your people so worried by us?" Chorky asked Sassanidi, who had the job of their guide.

"Long time ago, big people like yourselves drive Neftafi out of their homes. So we hide away, so no find. We live like this long time on own. We pleased Shiny Man come to show the new caverns, and new friends. We talk to Grocki after you show. They make new way and stop off other ways out." He explained, but the group still had no idea who or what the 'Grocki' were he was talking about.

The little people seemed to regulate their day by meal times, no reference to 'Day' or 'Night' was made. Only meal times, three of the gaps between were to be awake in, and one for sleep. They had completely forgotten the outside world.

It was during the wake period after the next meal, that Zeth spotted the monk again. He was beckoning them as before, when they were in a dire straight. Zeth quickly gathered the others and went to the spot where he last saw the figure standing near the wall of the cavern. Nomaque remembered that they were close to the doorway through which they entered the neftafi caverns. The monk appeared again and opened a different portal in the wall. They followed quickly when they had told their hosts they would be back soon. The monk closed it behind them.

The vague figure led them through many ways, but eventually up a long stair onto high cliffs with a misty view. The monk passed his hands across in front of them, the mists cleared and they were overlooking a valley. In the centre of the cliff bound valley, about a mile wide, stood a tall castle on a rock pinnacle. A road zigzagged up the rock from a gateway and bastion at the base.

Eta gasped. "Lethelorel!" He sighed. "That's just like an old drawing my great-grandfather brought with him from the Castle of the Star showing the valley as it was."

The monk pointed to the tower, the elves could see it was riven by a great split for fifty feet from the top, and it looked deserted. There were no fields around for tilling food for the community, everywhere was desolated. "That's different," the elf commented, "it wasn't a ruin in the picture."

The figure waved his arms again and they then overlooked a misty plain. The view magnified and they looked further out across the flat expanse. A castle came into view, the same castle on the rock pinnacle as they had been seeing in the valley except that it was whole. It was the one they had seen in the *lianur* magic pool, surrounded by foes. It was shining in the sunlight, and they could just see a pennant fluttering in the breeze from the topmost tower. The monk waved his hands and the misty cliffs returned.

The monk then led them back to the caverns and disappeared without uttering a word the whole time he was with them.

---0---

"Why do you suppose the monk led us up the cliff?" Zeth asked.

"I'm afraid I don't know. If the first one's now, the castle in the valley is not being attacked at this moment that's certain. It must be back in the past, or somewhere else, or both. The question is, why has

241

the monk brought us here when the battle is somewhere else?" Nomaque argued. "Unless it IS just the time that is wrong. I suppose I had better stop guessing and wait like everyone else, it's just that I don't like not knowing things when there are large armies about somewhere," the Druid grumbled.

"Or some when near here." Zeth added confusedly.

"The second castle's position is the one we saw in the lianur, isn't it? Perhaps that is where both the castle and the goblins are right now! Where we, or people like us, were charging the whole goblin-kob host. Sorry Vart and Venric, but it is your people. We respect your need to assist us and value all the help you can give, but it will be very difficult from now on." Chorky said.

The goblins rummaged for a while in their packs and brought out bright white covers for their armour. "We will wear this on the battlefield." Vart said. "It speaks of shame and dishonour for the goblin race. We will wear that to atone, as Maltex wears his circlet, until the elf king takes them off." Venric nodded firmly.

"I don't think we are quite there yet." Clem put in. "There must be another gate to pass through. The mate to my axe is close and is calling me. I have a feeling that the monk will come for us again soon. We had better be battle-ready, I for one must do hard serious preparation."

This proved to be a great spectacle to the Neftafi, and in most cases they joined in the exercises with great enthusiasm. A new interest was born for them, games, but they did not want to know anything about the battle. Nomaque used two caverns for getting them ready. The nearest one, they had games with the Neftafi, to toughen thems-elves up to an attempt at battle fit. This would not be enough but it would have to do. In the other cave they used their weapons, and trained as hard as they could, the little people leaving them alone in there. It frightened them and reminded them of the cruel world outside. Zeth's staff of healing was in demand to heal their many small wounds that their lack of weapons practice led them. The walking and travel helped, but it was nowhere near enough.

The memory of the sight of the battle in the *lianur*, and how close it could be to happening the next day, shocked them into action. Talk of battle, and tactics became the topic discussed and of course when it would happen.

"We need as much time as possible to get ready, another month would not be enough." Chorky moaned wearily after a particularly bad day as Zeth strapped up a thigh wound.

"I think a week is all we are going to get maybe less, so be a bit more careful and concentrate more on the point of all this." Nomaque grinned.

"Ho ho you slay me!" Chorky added cinically, "any more humour like that and we will all hide… from you! Perhaps you could shout it at the kobs and they will all fall down, cut to the bone."

They spent the rest of that day and another day with the little people, and as Clem predicted, on the following morning the monk beckoned again.

As this was expected, they were ready. The cloaked figure had opened yet another portal in the side of one of the caverns, which they went through into a wide tunnel. The little people clustered around the opening of the tunnel, the sound of their farewells came to them as they went around the far corner. The cowled figure strode briskly ahead of them, Clem almost having to run to keep up with his long stride. They turned several more corners and came to a doorway, which the monk opened and they were ushered into a long cavern, barely wider than the tunnel. As they passed him in the doorway, he see-

243

med flesh and blood, no longer the ghostly figure of previous encounters.

"I am Ignatius," he said. "I have been waiting a long time for this moment today. Not far away a battle is raging, through which you must pass. The other side of the enemy, you are needed to fulfil a prophesy. When you go from this cavern through the doorway, you will step out onto the plains to the rear of the enemy forces.

Chapter Fifteen

Trials by Elf, Gnome and Goblin

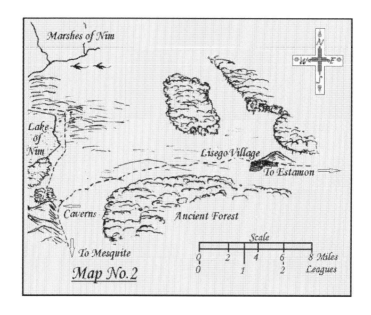

Marshes of Nim

Lake of Nim

Lisego Village

To Estamon

Caverns

Ancient Forest

To Mesquite

Scale

0   2   4   6   8 Miles

0   1   2   Leagues

Map No. 2

I kin and the party going eastwards took all day to
cover the ten miles to the elf village of Lisego,
this was because the one seftlin who could walk was
only able to travel at a slow walking pace. As it was,
the other two had to be carried all of the way. They
staggered into the village just as the guards were
closing up for the night.

"You lot will have to go in the second hut, as
there is no room in the first one, and anyway you're
too late. Late-comers are all to be put in there to stew
overnight," the officious guard stated.

"When I was in this village a few days ago you weren't so unwelcoming." Encathalon tersely replied. "What has happened to change your attitude? You turn even your own race away now."

"I'm told to put everyone in there and by gods I will, without being questioned by any stray knight of the road. I will call the guard if I hear any more from *any* of you!" The guard retorted, sharply indignant to be so questioned. He was a little wary of the richness of the prince's armour showing under his cape.

Seething with this offhand treatment, Ikin bustled forward. "So your mightiness will call out the guard if we demand any more of your time, will he?" None of the party she was with had known her when she was in Mesquite, so they didn't notice the danger signals, neither did the guard.

"It's bigheaded dim bullies like you that become night guards. Do you know why?" She asked.

The guard looked down at her in a 'Get out of my way or I'll squash you' glare'.

"It's because the ones with the intelligence know it's the most dangerous time to impose stupid rules, they're not here, they survive, the thick ones don't." With that she brought her axe, which she had drawn from her belt unseen, around and across. The guard leaped back, not before the haft of his spear was riven in two by the whickering blade.

"Help! Foes in the village! Cut down the invaders!" he cried running back to the stockade gates, ashen faced and trembling.

The village perimeter at this point had a double wooden palisade. In between, there were three huts. The late-comers were herded into these huts until morning. The two nearest to the village gates had their own smaller stockade around them. The favoured ones were placed in the nearest hut, which had guards at the entrance.

"I think we have just burned our boats, Ikin." Encathalon said tersely, rebuking the little gnomess.

"Oh go and polish your armour, if that's all it's fit for." She retorted, fed up with his cautious attitude.

Out of the gate ran a dozen guards, brandishing their spears, and a few more with bows coming from the other direction. From their rear came a more finely dressed individual.

"Thelin, come here, and point out the invaders to me," the resplendent figure asked.

"Them over there, Sir, especially the little one with the axe. She broke mi' spear."

"A likely story, they look innocent enough. Put them into the first hut and double the guard."

Riva strode forward, her white cloak fluttering with her purposeful stride, behind her, but keeping pace ambled Hectar, his hand not far from his sword handle.

"Captain?" She called clearly, "We have sick amongst us who need urgent attention."

"I'm afraid the healers have all gone back to their homes now, so you will have to wait until the morning, Madame Druidess."

"I'm told you have a seftlin community here. We have three of their number, hurt, to be returned to their homes tonight." she persisted quietly.

"Not tonight they won't. No-one goes through this stockade after nightfall. And that's all, Good-night." With a gesture of finality, he turned on his heel and strode off leaving them to be ushered into the hut nearest the highest palisade.

"Of all the unreasonable elvish snottyness..." Riva muttered under her breath and felt utterly helpless against such stubbornness. The huts were divided into compartments meant for four but they all crowded into one, not wishing to be separated. They all thought that there was something going on in this village which did not ring true.

247

Ikin sat with her back to the wall, her feet hurt, the boots she bought in Mesquite were developing blisters. She unlaced them and sighed. Sitting absentmindedly going through the things in her pack, she came across her wooden shoes, the ones she had found in the caves. She tried them on, and to her surprise they felt light and comfortable. Getting up she took a few steps forward and back. She felt lighter still. Looking up she saw a rafter high in the roof, and sprang. She reached it easily and grasped it, pulling herself up. Ye Gods! How do I get down again?" She said a little frightened.

"Drop, and I'll catch you." Hectar chuckled. He got up and came under her. When he raised his hands up towards her, they looked near enough, so she slid over onto her stomach and let go. True to his word he caught her easily.

"Those shoes? I haven't seen them before." He queried.

"I can fly like a bird now, a rather dumpy bird." She said ignoring his question.

Riva called her over and she examined Ikin's shoes very carefully. After, they whispered together for a while, Ikin nodded a little unsurely. After a while Riva called the one mobile seftlin over to join the group.

"I have had an idea." Riva explained to everyone a little later, "If Ikin can jump the stockade with her shoes, maybe she can take a seftlin with her. They could go to the others and bring help. Here is Pippa Longstride, she is the least injured. She will try the jump with you and then show Ikin the way across the village."

"I am sorry to be such a burden to you folks." Pippa said. "I feel we are holding you up from your quest, we have talked amongst ourselves and perhaps you could just leave us here. We will be alright with the guards outside."

Ikin cut in, "No there is no way we will leave you here in this poorly defended hut, at the mercy of the rest of the rifraf and balshy Guards. Please let us get you all home and then we will be on our way knowing we have helped in some way."

"Ok. Thanks to you all for saving us." Pippa added. "We will remember you all should you come back to the village another happier time. We wish you luck with your Quest and you all come through it safely."

"We will need every bit of luck there is." Hectar added a rare comment from him, although he realised why Ikin looked apprehensive about the leap.

They had to cut a hole in the roof to let them out as the entrance was guarded. Ikin leapt to her perch again and Pippa was half pulled, half lifted up to her. They cut a hole and then went through the hole into the night. It was dark enough for them to creep down to the eaves and slide down to the ground. The wooden palisade was not far away from the base of the hut and they quickly crept across the intervening distance. Pippa clambered onto Ikin's back, the little gnomess gathered herself and leaped. This time she put power into it and they sailed over the stakes, flying a good long way inside the walls. They landed with a thump and rolled over. Ikin burst out chuckling, partly with the exhilaration of flying, and partly with the release of tension and the realisation that they were all right. Pippa, who had been jolted off her back, joined her. They lay there laughing quietly, getting their breath and wondering whether anyone had noticed. After a moment or two, Ikin felt they should move. Rolling over they cautiously rose to their feet, and melted into the dark village.

Back in the hut they soon realised why the village had these strict precautions with visitors.

During the night fights broke out in the other huts, occasionally cries were heard, and suppressed. The night wore on, but their hut stayed quiet. Because of this, back in the hut the injured seftlins were holding their own, and just stable.

Ikin arrived back about one hour before dawn, with a terrific thump on the roof. She had forgotten that without the extra weight of her passenger she would fly further. Unfortunately this awoke interest from the other occupants of the hut, the unwelcome ones. There were stealthy movements near their doorway, and then, all of a sudden, they were besieged in their room. Forced to defend themselves, they stationed themselves around the injured seftlin. Any attempt at entry was severely dealt with as the long hour dragged away. There were even attempts to come through the light wall from the next room.

The eagerly awaited dawn arrived, and the main gate to the village burst apart with most of the community's seftlin pouring through, decidedly in no mood to be put aside. Bows bristled, small swords, axes and anything that was handy, was brandished by the horde circling the hut. The guards kept away, clustering in the main gateway, very outnumbered, trying to pretend that they weren't there. They were frightened by the unexpected reaction of the seftlin whom they previously thought as harmless. The entire hut was stripped of people in one minute, including the besieged. As Pippa was there in the forefront, the group were the only ones who were allowed to keep their weapons. Tom and Sam, the wounded seftlin, were carried away on stretchers accompanied by Ikin's group. They went briskly through the gate and on to the little collection of holes and the unusual round houses of the Lisego seftlin.

They were made welcome there, and were assured of a welcome whenever they were in the village, even though the rooms were a little small for the larger members of the group. Although pleased by their welcome, Encathalon felt that the time was pressing, and so they departed back westwards that day after sharing a bountiful meal or two with their hosts.

Ikin had her feet salved, and was given a pot of medicine by Granny Heatherfull, the matriarch of the community, to put on every day. Her wooden shoes went back in her pack next to the magic mirror, carefully wrapped, now amongst her prized possessions. She felt that they had more potential, given time to experiment, but that would have to wait. That night they camped in the woods, in the eaves of the Ancient Forest, hedged about by Riva's magic. They felt that they desperately needed a good night's rest   before going off into the wilderness. The next morning they found the faint track going northwards in a small patch of forest, after the main track turned south. The landscape changed quickly after that becoming more open and rolling, with quagmires here and there in the hollows to watch out for.

Not long after they started the following morning they reached the great misty Lake Nim, this they had to skirt and then go round the mountain behind it. The lake was bordered by low hills covered with a thorny scrub, forcing them to the tracks, discouraging cross-country walking, and perfect for an ambush. To cheer them all up Encathalon told them that there was a lot of goblin activity when he came through the week before.

Notwithstanding the terrain, they made good time cutting around the side of the lake, and had left it behind them by the late afternoon. A river roared through a gorge half a mile away to the west flowing into the lake.

"Soon we will have to cross that river," the elf explained, turning to Hectar who was in the file just

251

behind him. "The crossing place is a few miles further to the north."

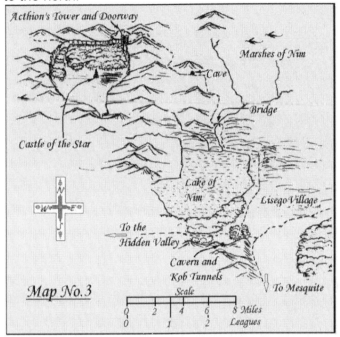

Map No.3

"You won't be crossing anywhere *soon*, matey." A low growl came from the bushes next to him. Looking again he saw the scrub all around was seething with heavily armed gnomes.

"Well you can forget any thoughts you had of ambushing us, this party is gnome protected, so shove off!" Ikin's 'tread carefully, dangerous' voice came up strongly from the back. "While the rest of you are thinking about it, Eager here can keep his hands off, or he will be trying to put one back on his arm again!" She said as one tried to grab her, he only just avoided having his arm sliced.

"This spitfire back here won't submit," the gnome she called Eager indignantly cried.

"Too right, any more grabbers wish to taste my axe," she said.

The party had by this time drawn weapons and made ready to fight. Riva began to weave a mystic net.

There was a yell from the bushes, commanding the gnomes to pull back as the Captain of the gnomes came hurrying up. He gathered the gnomes up and took them off to a clearing a short distance further on. Ikin followed quickly on their heels and spun the Captain around.

"Why did you ambush us, fool? Idiot? Then an apology is in order." Ikin demanded.

The Captain looked awkwardly about, embarrassed by the appearance of an attractive warlike gnomess. He looked around hopefully for some support from his band but in vain. The whole band were making themselves very busy finding things to do urgently around the clearing, pretending not to notice their Captain's predicament and very sensitive to the presence of Ikin. Female gnomes were a difficult problem for the male of the species.

"Well! I'm waiting! A right lot of bozo's you are! Instead of helping, you HAD to attack us. Hasn't anyone got eyes. Or do they breed blind gnomes around here!" She laid into them with her tongue. They became even busier if that was possible. A lot of polishing weapons, oiling bowstrings and examination of garments industriously was going on.

Hectar and the party quietly eased away from the direct line of verbal attack, trying hard not to burst out laughing, the gnomes looked so crestfallen.

Ikin managed to keep a withering barrage up for a bit longer and then came back to the party.

"I'm sorry to inflict such a regretfully thick bunch of my kin on to you, but there they are, in all their glory. This is the male of the species. They had

253

better escort us through this next bit or else!" She threatened.

She approached the captain and ushered him to one side. With very little persuasion, he agreed to accompany them to the edge of the mountains, but there they had to turn off, as their route went east. Having the escort was fortunate, as they were all ambushed in turn when they reached the gorge. A considerable force of goblins hurled themselves at the party at the narrow bridge.

The gnomes, spurred on by a 'Female', surprised the ambushers by counter charging into them so furiously that the ambush wavered. There was some spirited resistance in the goblins, but they had to give ground when the party joined in, hewing over their companion's heads. This proved decisive, and a force of twice their number was routed, fleeing across the arched stone bridge, elegantly spanning the wide chasm. The eager gnomes pursued their quarry into the scrub on the other side, returning with grisly trophies.

There was an amazing transformation in the gnomes, their faces were smiling and cheerful, the previous incident forgotten. They milled around Ikin, oblivious of the efforts of their Captain to attract their attention.

"WE are in goblin country!" the captain shouted, to try and bring order into chaos.

Ikin held up her hands, and waved them to be quiet. She then turned to the Captain and said, "You said something."

"I just felt we should keep an eye out for trouble, that's all." he said, defeated. "We are in hostile territory, and there must be more goblins about than those we scattered. The routed ones are probably telling them about us about now. Lets get moving."

"That's a good idea, we have a lull now, let's make use of it and put a few miles under our belts before night." Tasherlon suggested, swinging his pack up to his shoulder in readiness to move off. The gnomes bade goodbye to Ikin and went off eastward to their homes, one weeks' travel away, to what they called the 'Gnome Iron Spike'. This place was referred to in a secretive whisper. When questioned further on that subject they tapped their long noses and said 'Secret, Gnome Business'. They would have liked Ikin to go with them, but she would have none of it.

Turning north the scenery looked desolate. The mountain skirts ended in marshes stretching as far to the right as they could see. To the left, or west, a ridge of jagged mountains rose in a severe wall, snow showing on the tops in amongst the high summits.

"We have to go round that mountain in front, then head more westerly up a long, dreary valley, into the mountains." Encathalon explained. "It took me the best part of a week, to come the other way, as I had to hide a good part of the time from ogres, dragons and the like."

"Great travelling, ogres, dragons and the like. Sounds wonderful. For a second helping, a full scale battle. Can someone tell me why we are here. No, I'm not surprised, I can't explain it either." Ikin said missing her kin. She looked down at her jewelled ring, glittering in the gloom, refusing to be dulled. It penetrated the gloom in her mood in the same way, and as she glanced up, the others could see a new glint of determination in her eyes.

The broken terrain continued, excellent for potential ambushers who knew the lie of the land. It was difficult for the travellers, as the track had to be followed. All the same, it was no surprise to them when there was no attack, as it would have been very difficult for any goblins hearing of their presence to outflank them through that country. They still could hear the river, as it was still in the foothills, a twisting lively course including several waterfalls. A complete contrast to thirty miles or more further up when the waters meander lifelessly through the Upper Nimlith marshes. The light was beginning to fade when they sought the slopes to make their camp for the night. A cheerless affair, without a fire, but most managed to rest fitfully. The dawn broke over the same dreary landscape, a drizzle started, driving in from the north, so breakfast was reduced to a frugal effort. They plodded on into the mists of the wetlands.

They crossed the next valley northwards, and saw the trail turned and went west, following the side of the mountain ahead. Some way along there was a large cavern, so large it was clearly visible from where they were, several miles away in the lowering gloom of the day.

As they neared the great cave the elf knight whispered, "It was near here that I encountered ogres."

"Ideal for them, we only have two bows, we could have done with some of your doughty race, Ikin." Tasherlon said, stringing his bow.

"You'll have to make do with little me!" She said mincing along in front of him.

"Stop turning the male's empty heads, Ikin. You know they are very vulnerable in that area!" Riva chuckled.

Ikin stopped and rummaged in her pack. "You carry on I'll catch you up in a moment," she said, an idea forming.

A little reluctantly they went on slowly and carefully. The trail wound its way along the strip between the marshes and the foothills, so it wasn't long before Ikin was out of sight. They closed in on

256

the enormous cavern entrance. The big boulders littering the landscape nearby gave the only cover.

They crept on until the cover ran out. Here they watched for a while, crouched behind the last of the rocks, to wait for Ikin. There was a shout from behind them, they turned and heard a guttural bellow of frustration. Around the corner swept Ikin, almost flying, just ahead of a large ogre. Flitting along in great strides, she was just too fast for him, and every stride made him more mad. He stopped and hurled his club instead. This was very nearly her undoing, she had not noticed his change in tactics and was enjoying baiting the creature. The weapon, twice as big as her thigh reached her just as she was taking off for the next leap, and took her legs from under her. With any other shoes on than the magic wooden ones she would have sprawled in the ogre's path. Not so this time, she just continued on up, tumbling and turning, her feet waggling about in a confused way. The ogre stopped and perplexed, scratched his armpit thoughtfully, and finding something there he investigated it.

Ikin landed in a heap, not far from her concealed friends but in full view of the cave. She sat up and shook her head to clear it. Of a sudden, two gnarled hands grabbed at her. Having only a split second in which to react, utter panic set in. She instinctively leaped, and the hands missed. An equally large female ogre and a three-parts grown male one had come out of the cave, seen Ikin's landing and thought that her mate had thrown the little gnomess there for them.

Ikin went on up, this time fully in charge of her magic. A happy peal of laughter came from over-head.

"I knew it, I knew that there was a key to these. I have it, the secret. Oh! There you are, peo-ple. Oops, careful, Ikin," she said to herself, "you will

257

land the others in it." She flew out of sight back over the absorbed male, who was still nibbling on little vermin and did not notice.

"Do you reckon the ogres have monster fleas, mum?" whispered Onaroah, grinning, but gripping his sword more tightly nevertheless.

"Probably more like beetles or grubs feeding on his mess. Ugh! Son your mind! You've been talking to the men again. They will corrupt you yet." Riva muttered, half amused.

"Mum, it's not their fault, I'm not little any more." The boy explained seriously. "I like Hectar, Mum."

"Do you now! What's that supposed to mean?"

"Nothing, Mum, just that you like him too, don't you? I know he's not a patch on dad, but, he's nice all the same."

Riva kept quiet, thoughtful for a while. She missed her husband terribly, the way he lost his life saving them from the goblins still lived on in her every moment. But, the tall forester looked after them as well as he could in the circumstances, gladly lending his strength to hers whenever she needed it. He got on with Onaroah too. Her reflective mood was broken by the return of Ikin, quietly from the side.

"Everyone all right?" Ikin whispered.

"Yes, we were waiting for you. What do you think of our chances of sneaking past?" Tasherlon asked.

"Not very likely, they are quite sharp, that female especially. Their attention will wander soon I hope. The one to watch is the youngster. He would rouse the other two, he will be aware long after the others, we must look out for him." Ikin mused.

"I don't fancy killing him, if we can avoid it. Couldn't we decoy him and knock him out. Say trip him." Riva replied.

258

"I can act as decoy, without any fear. But the rest will be up to you." Ikin added.

"Better the other way round. If we decoy him, trip him, and then Ikin clobbers him from above. If that fails we can let him have it before he cries out. A trip is a good idea though." Hectar observed.

Ikin agreed and flew off to find a boulder she could carry. When she came back they would organise the decoy, Riva and Onaroah wandering past, a threat that the youngling would not be frightened of, and investigate before calling out.

The plan was good, but both the male and the youngster came out. The young one rushed forward and fell sprawling as it tripped over the rope. Ikin changed her direction of attack and swooped on to the male, her boulder hitting it heavily on the side of the head with a sodden thump. Stunned, it collapsed in a heap on the ground. Hectar had picked up the male's club, and swinging the enormous knotted bludgeon, he caught the young one a solid blow. The rope handlers wrapped the rope around its legs, and it fell over. Hectar hit it again and it subsided into a heap.

They made a rapid retreat after untangling their rope. They were a half mile away when the ogress found her companions. A long plaintive roaring cry cleaved the air.

"I hope we were gentle enough." Riva said sadly, life, whatever it was, was precious. They passed on, never to know the answer.

The air cleared and the view opened out before them. Far out above the mountain in the distance, big specks were wheeling about the high peak. The trail went between the two smaller mountains in front of them.

"Those dragons can see phenomenal distances, we must have a care." The elf knight said, wrapping his black cloak tighter around himself.

259

The track, sometimes difficult to find, swung round towards the endless marsh, but after several miles turned westward, to skirt around the dragon mountain. They journeyed in stages when there were no dark shapes in the sky. The rest of the time was spent hiding and the long miles seemed endless up this featureless valley.

Three days later Encathalon led them into a forest of tall trees of great girth.

"In a short while we will be at Acthion's Tower and Doorway, I hope the journey's end," he explained. "When we have entered we will have to descend many flights to the Outer Doorway. Just before the Doorway there is a room where we must then prepare ourselves for the worst as we will pass to other times and places when we go out through it. We will have then arrived in my world. That was how I arrived here. There may be a battle nearby, or it may be already over, Gods forbid." His voice betrayed an element of doubt.

The Tower of Acthion loomed up out of the trees and he sighed with relief. The doors opened to them and they all filed in. It was deserted and dusty, Encathalon's doubts returned. Finding old torches on the walls they lit them and descended the flights of stairs cautiously. At the bottom of the stairs was a large dusty room, in the far wall was a pair of large very ornate doors. As Encathalon entered the room changed, it became an armoury similar to the one Nomaque found days before. Encathalon seemed distracted while the others explored the walls, he could see the shadowy figure of Ignatious the Monk and hear him in his head.

"I cannot be there as I am needed elsewhere you will have to follow the instructions I am about to give you and go out through the doors onto the plain before your home castle Prince. There is a great battle going on and you are needed desperately. You have arrived only just in time. I am on the cliffs in the far distance. God speed." Then his emanation disappeared.

Chapter Sixteen

The Dark Host

*F*rom myriad warrens streamed the dark and misshapen warriors. This was to be the plunder of the times, as of old when the first dwarf kingdom fell. Contingents of goblins, kobs, hobgoblins and trolls assembled in the Great Caverns of Asorg, and the surrounding ones as well.

On a dais the Sorcerer Asphar addressed them, using his considerable powers to cajole the trolls, persuade the hobgoblins and terrify the goblins into fever and frenzy. This was the beginning, and several times in the following days and nights he would have to stop for similar gatherings. To stir up war and dispose of the few dissenters in various very nasty ways, it was spectacular for sharpening discipline and terror.

They came from most of the mountain communities, several hundred strong from the Sisters of Wrath Mountains, five hundred from each of the Wall Fortresses in the Upper-Glyda Valley and the Mesquite Hills, small dark goblins from the Nisego Mere and the Bitter Seeps Range, many hundreds from the forest of Neldoreth, all joining in agreed meeting points, swelling the numbers. There were over three thousand by the time the Valley of Sending was reached.

Mostly the migration was not visible on the surface as it went through deep tunnels, but the foraging companies were merciless. The wild life, the communities and villages were all wiped out along the line of the march.

An ancient valley hidden deep in the mountains was their meeting place a week later. The tunnels had eventually issued out into a pass about a mile from the valley. As they filed down from the pass, a roar went up from the thousand who awaited them on the valley floor, as they came over the lip into full view. Asphar was dressed in full regalia on his palanquin, spearheading their advance down the hillside. From high up on the crag to the side of the valley came a terrible cry, and a great black winged shape rose over the host.

"GOUBBLAT." Thousands of throats roared again and again.

Asphar held up his staff and called the creature bred in the lightless pits deep under an ancient city of the elves. The city had turned to evil, and trapped and defiled Gouthbund, a scion of Golden-Ursam, the Golden Dragon, to become mother of that mutated purple brood, child of which flew in the sky over them on that terrible day.

"COME DARK ARROW
AND WELCOME ME!
GOUBBLAT THE GREAT!"

Asphar cried in a clear voice that carried out over the sea of heads. Asphar readied the magic to send the host into battle. The sky boiled and the world changed around them.

PART 4

Limbool, the Land of theLost

Chapter Seventeen

The King of the Lost

On the world of Limbool, a long way away from Jodamia and perhaps in another time, the Elf King Alaimane sat looking out over the misty grassy plains surrounding his castle. For nearly a thousand years, he and his elf forebears had sat surveying that scene, wondering when, if ever, they would find the way back to their home valley on Jodamia. Their ancestors after the catastrophe, which brought them to this spot, had decided that they were probably on another planet; the sky was another colour and they had felt heavier. That terrible event had happened in the year 2300, the king estimated that the year in Jodamia, could well be approaching 3300. He wondered what had happened to his people who were left behind and if they ever wondered about the Castle of the Star.

The succeeding kings had also thought about the battered piece of parchment that he held in his hand for nine hundred of those years. In the year 2400, one hundred years after the catastrophe, Bertold the Thin, the Arch-Druid of the castle, thirteenth of that name, put forth his power to look into their problem. He produced a telling, which had been very much discussed ever since. As with all such documents they never approach the problem directly, and this one was no different from the others. It described a scene from a battle and as Bertold did not live through the ordeal, he was not able to interpret the words his scribe carefully recorded.

The king looked down at the spidery writing...

I, Bertold, Arch Druid
of the Star Castle foretells......
by appointment to the great
KING AZIM 1

It is foretold that after
the Catastrophe of Aasphari,
there would be a period of isolation
pain and toil.
Some will be sundered from us and
start anew.
Do not despair,
there is a thread of hope in the far
future.
I, Bertold the Thin in a supreme and
final prophesy, using all my
remaining physic and strength,
have seen what could be the end...
I see....
Appearing from the West and South
by secret ways and peoples
two bands of adventurers.
They are arrayed in shining
armour,
wading through our enemies

to our aid....
I see a Flaming Sword, a Singing
Axe, a Starred Cloak,
kindled arrows
arching into the enemy host....
The host divides, the arch-enemy is
Revealed out of the darkness.
Oh no...
He wears the Greater Crown.

The small band stop and look,
there is something hidden there that
I cannot see.
A thing of fear,
aiee...Red Fire leaps opon them..
there is ..a great flash..
Is it of molten metal?...
all is dark now,
I.. cannot see any more, I am not
given to know more,
The Great One is calling me, I go......

The places shown thus.........
were where the High Druid
stopped for a moment.
Scribed verbatim, Indricolatm.

Scribe to the King, Year 2400

---0---

The King sighed, he found it all very perplex-ing.

The first sign of a new turn of events was the appearance of a mystic figure, a monk, about six long months before. It happened while the King was studying some ancient tomes in the far corner of the Library, and had picked up the prophesy in his hand to study it yet again. The King started as he looked up, sensing another mind. An ethereal cowled shape was standing next to him by the library wall, compl-etely in shadow.

'Seek ye the Doorway to Light, after the
Doorway to Dark,
And after that the emblems of the Queen,
And those ones that come.
The circlets of Golden-Ursam
will let your Scions pass.
Guard them well.'

The voice spoke directly into his mind, and there was no doubt that it came from the figure in black. With those words the shape faded away lea-ving the dumbfounded king standing there.

Much against his better judgement he summ-oned his sons, Throndralon and Encathalon, and told them of his visitation. They looked at each other in joy, this was what they had been waiting for all their lives. It was a chance to solve the riddle of the Catastrophe. This was their only clue they had to follow, even if they lost their lives in doing so. Their father watched sadly, unwelcome tears lurked behind the stern exterior, he had a very strong premonition that, if they went away, he was not going to see them again. No-one came back home again from beyond the far mists.

They went the next day, adorned in their bright mail, shield and helm emblazoned with the castle's device. Throndralon the eldest carried *Gridor* the Singing Axe, Encathalon carried *Incizor* the Star Sword, as they went they looked every inch the Princes they were. All eyes watched them as they strode off into the distance, a figure of a monk joined them and they disappeared. They had promised to be back in two months at the latest, six had now passed and still no word.

Elf Queen Hermione joined him, and they watched together from their high tower. His mind went back to when his kingly sire told him stories in the flickering firelight of the Father of Dragons, the first-born Golden-Ursam and the airborne chariot. In those early days in Jodamia the King and Queen flew in a flying chariot that the Great Dragon carried. The circlets that his sons wore were made from that light marvellous metal of the chariot, as were the weapons, jewels and the crown.

That was when the castle in which they sat was built in the Star Valley, in the first year of the elven calendar, long before the Catastrophe. He looked up at his Queen and saw gentle tears were flowing down those wondrous cheeks.

"We have lost a son, my love, in some dark, dank place away from my arms," she whispered brokenly. He gently put his arm around her and drew her to him, his tears flowing with hers in the pain of their suffering.

Chapter Eighteen

Onset of the Hosts

*S*everal days after, the Elf King and Queen stood in the tower grieving, they once again sought the high tower balcony and watched as the first ragged refugees came to the Castle across the plain from nearby villages on the heath, telling stories of kob hosts and burning. Winged and foot messengers had already been sent to the dwarf kingdom in the north, the doughty dwarves under Nenderailt, as well as to Prince Brithael of the Elves of the Mists.

The Castle of the Star in Limbool

"It comes, the end for good or ill." The King observed to the Queen as they watched. "The waiting is over for us, my dear. We must draw in what provisions we may to add to the granaries below. We will

272

undoubtedly have many more mouths to feed ere this all ends.

"That I have in hand, dear, all the near fields are at this moment almost cleared, there remains only the far stores to finish the gleaning. Alas for the poor dispossessed who arrive here, only the lightly wounded and unhurt escaped, and mostly they were forced to leave dear ones behind." The Queen replied, the two of them couldn't help thinking of their own sons, their stout hearts, and their loss to the Castle Guard, who idolised them. Both were going to be trapped outside the ring of the enemy, unless they came soon it would be too late.

The castle troops numbered only five hundred, with seventy more in the King's Own Guard and the Elitan Guard. They were hardly a sure defence against the oncoming hordes. In the follow-ing days no message was received of the Princes or of their ill fated mission to go back, no monk came to give them any solace from the bitter seeming truth. People streamed in from the outlying districts and swelled the numbers of potential fighters by almost a thous-and, but these were ill armed and untried against any foe.

--- 0 ---

Two days later the castle was surrounded, the enemy had come to the ancient Castle of Lethelorel, but there was no effort to attack, the enemy seemed to be waiting for something. The horde stopped just short of the Lower Keep out of bowshot, and chanted.

"KUK'L'MAK!..........KUK'L'MAK THE KING!.......THE KING!"

The gross King of the Hobgoblin-kob Hosts, borne on a palanquin by four great trolls, slowly approached the Lower Tower and stopped. Surrounding him his bodyguard stood, fifteen large slavering hobgoblins lolled in various attitudes of anticipation. The misty sunlight glinted on the sea of weapons of the great army, and showed clearly that across the heath a large area was being cleared, many hundreds of yards across. Placed in the centre was a small ornate tower. When this was ready the Hobgoblin King blew a curious horn three times, the small tower burst into red flame and they all waited. Quiet settled on the whole scene, totally unreal, the enemy expectant, and the besieged, wondering. This curious scene ended as a roar erupted from the thousands of evil throats as the cleared space suddenly filled with warriors, these moved out to one side and the area was filled again. This time in the centre another palanquin bore a tall human shape; above him black, seething clouds blotted out the gentle sunlight and rapidly spread out across the plains. The watching elvish eyes could make out the swarthy dark tan of the almost elvish face, surmounted by a crown. The leader seemed one of the evil elfene subrace of the elves who sought the dark ways while they lived in the ancient elvish city, becoming tainted and twisted, hating all who lived and laughed in the beautiful Castle of the Star.

The Elf King gasped, the crown was a garish copy of the Lesser Crown of the elves but under this on his brow he wore one of the circlets his sons had worn when they departed on their quest. He reeled and with a great effort he straightened, the strength of his lineage coming to bolster him in his hour of need. Inside a part of him wept for his son.

The second litter moved up next to the other one in the front of the evil ranks while thousands more warriors poured through the magical gate to swell the hordes around them. Both palanquins were lowered to the ground and the elfene carried an iron-bound chest to the other's side. Opening the lid he took out another crown. He raised it over the Hobgoblin King's head and cried out in a clear cruel voice,

I, Asphar, Arch-Sorcerer, reincarnation of Aasphari the Bane of the Star-elves, am come to finish the task of my predecessor. The crown of the self-styled Elves of the Star I raise and crown a new King of all Star Elves and of all Jodamia. You, in the castle...Throw open your gates and bow down before your Lord and Master."King Kish'l'mak, New Lord of the Elves."

As the words left his thin lips he lowered the crown on to the hobgoblin's head. The enemy host roared and chanted,

**'King Kish'l'Mak,
King of the Elves,
King of the World.'**

The Elf King groaned inwardly, he knew that the enemy host would, given the time, reduce the castle of his forebear's undoubtedly to rubble. He knew he faced a worse foe than the assembled hosts, starvation and hunger were the greater.

While anyone stood within, the mighty walls of the castle had never been breached by an enemy. The appearance of the Greater Crown was not a surprise, the crowning of that foul being before his walls, was. Livid he projected his voice out from the gatehouse to the perpetrators of the besmirching of the fair. It could only have been thought of by an evil mind of another elf, as foul as the other fair. The cruelty was subtly eating at the Elf King, attempting to belittle him. He sent his voice out across the assembled host and they covered their ears.

"I WILL NOT REST UNTIL THE PERPETRATORS OF THIS DEED ARE

275

DEAD, AND YOU, SORCERER ARE SENT TO THE PLANES OF HELL WHERE YOU BELONG."

His voice strong with the force of an Elf Lord, the host before him quailed back a step, not ever having experienced the full power of an Elfala in wrath. The Sorcerer fleetingly winced, but having no little power himself was proof against the daunting.

"Your words will blow away before the wind of our armies, deposed Elfking. Await your doom."

The elfene cucoid Sorcerer replied putting forth his voice lofted by magic to every corner of the castle. The elves in the castle received an involuntary feeling of being slowly pulled limb from limb if they did not give in.

From some way down the ramp there was a creak and a thump, and out over the Lower Tower sailed a small bag. Unknown to the King the Arch-Druid had a trick or two and felt the situation had become too one-sided. Working with the Castle Artificer Themil they had calculated the range for a small object from a small mobile catapult. Just as it reached the group around the two palanquins, the Sorcerer pointed a finger and a ray of power lashed out to hit the object, which then burst and a rain of many thousands of irate red wasps and their nest descended on the occupants of the palanquin. With a howl of anger the principles of the enemy beat a limited, but hasty retreat.

Not for long, the lone figure of Sorcerer Asphar and a group of dancing kobs walked around the castle, at six points he stopped and performed a sacrifice, the screams of the elf victim echoed around the great towers in front of the elves watching in anxious watchfulness. Over the dead body he set a fire of purple flames. When he completed the circle he stopped and faced the castle over the first fire. Severing a burning limb he used it as a wand, conjuring an arcane spell from the blackest pit.

All those in the castle felt it, a wave of despair and force of sheer evil. They felt exposed and unable to defend themselves to the will of Asphar the Great.

The ground shook lightly at first but it increased in intensity, the Castle Tower juddering and swaying. Then he sent blast upon blast of sheer power directly at the Great Lower Tower. There was no way it could withstand such punishment, even though it was created by the greatest Elven builders who ever lived. But it did. Screaming his spell again he sent a hurricane of force straight at the front gateway. All around the ancient stonework dust and rocks hurled themselves in a maelstrom, there was a rending rumble as though the very earth was coming apart and stones flew out in a great cloud.

The Sorcerer cried out in his victory and called for the trolls to rush forwards into the maelstrom. Not even waiting for the cloud of debris to clear to see the damage, he was so sure.

A desperate wail of rage rose up and the wave of troll bodies crumpled as those following were squashed against others halted on the murk of ruin. Slowly the advance failed and the dust cleared.

The Tower stood tall and untouched, the portcullis down, the gate strong. The difference was that there was an enormous pit in front of it filled with struggling and screaming troll bodies. The Tower had withstood the attack, the ground in front had not.

Undaunted Asphar dropped the limb back into the fire and took out a sparkling wand, which glowed evilly in his hand and the fear returned to all anywhere near. He waved it in a pattern and incanted to form a ball of blackness twenty feet in front of him. It pulsed with energy, not ordinary energy but some

277

other form from the deeps unimagined except by a few like him. Raising it up he sent it towards the Lower Tower, at the last minute it passed by, and swung around to plunge into the great rock basement under the castle itself. Leering with pleasure, as he really wished to completely dismember the castle stone from stone, preferably with all its occupants in it. Ground to pulp as the fabric of the castle crumbled on them.

The earth exploded and everything in the castle and surrounding it for half a mile lurched. No one remained standing, they were bowled over with the wall of force as it swept out from the explosion. A great cloud rose over the site. The opposing army was bowled over in heaps, nobody except the Sorcerer kept his feet. The fires were put out, their debris spread out over the plain. The pits in front of the Lower Tower were gone, their struggling contents of trolls buried alive. The gateway to the Tower had lost the approach roadway and was some forty feet above the ground.

In the Castle of the Star the King crawled to his feet, surprised that there was any stone under his feet at all, but there was, solid stone. It was very firm and reassuring. Everyone around him was rushing about checking and reporting to him. In all cases the castle was still there, some minor damage where the masonry had fallen but all gates had amazingly survived.

"They built well in Golden-Ursam's Time!" He grinned. The occupants though not broken were quite shaken up too. There were a lot of injuries from being thrown about in a stone box. But there were no deaths. He then thought about their escape and realised that it was likely that the castle would survive such an attack as it had survived the journey to the plains hundreds of years before. He was perplexed though. He could have sworn he saw one of his

278

knights standing on the path of the ball of hell just before it hit. He shrugged and put it out of his mind, he must have imagined it. He was not the only one to have imagined a strange knight that day; a soldier on guard on the Lower Tower also thought he saw a knight standing before the rock walls before they too were struck by the hellish sorcery.

The Sorcerer's Army was in not fit state to continue and so they retired to a ring of steel half a mile away and set up camps. Of the Sorcerer there was no sign but ominous black looking clouds started building. The clouds, which now spread across the horizon, rolled towards the beleaguered castle, and within seconds of the withdrawal of the palanquins, the threatened rain squall struck the white shining stones. The evil-smelling wetness was not just unpleasant it sapped the defenders will, the rain settled down to a steady drizzle reducing the visibility across the plain. Misery and evil had arrived at Leth-elorel in abundance.

The hosts held off until nightfall and then hurled themselves forwards carrying thousands of stones and earth. They feverishly rebuilt the ramp and by morning the whole area was back to its former level, perhaps higher. There was little respite and the evil army flowed against the Great Lower Tower and the high walls on castle side, protecting the base of the great ramp. They had been made by artisans thousands of years before and were outward curving, resisting all sorcery. During the night the dead piled up in heaps, the relatively few defenders praying for the morning, and the light. With the dawn the enemy legions pulled back, fresh troops moved up to keep sending withering flights of arrows at the defenders from the new wall and hastily constructed hide shelters.

Within the castle, as well as the trained troops, there were over a thousand elves who could fight and others who could be some help manning the walls, but even so, the future for the Star Castle and its beleaguered occupants looked grim. All through the night the training of the auxiliaries went on at a feverish pace, so the regular troops could be given respite. No sorcery had been evident during the night, apart from the incessant rain, a fact surprising all but the Arch-Druid Bethalon. The Druid guessed the nature of the Sorcerer Asphar, he was an elfene, a race of evil elves or worse, a shape changer or even worse a cucoid. These infested one of the elf children in an elvish family taking over and killing them when they became fully grown, there were some reputed to be in the elf city. Asphar would always prefer to torture his victims, and as he felt secure in the knowledge that his forces far outnumbered the Elvish forces, a slow wearing down of the garrison was more to the enemy's liking than a relatively quick victory.

Chapter Nineteen

Even though all the ranks of the enemy stood betwixt us

C horky and the others stood in the bare cavern the monk had brought them to, there was nothing there, it was totally empty with no exits. Perplexed they stood waiting. The monk Ignacious turned away from them and passed his hands in front of the bare walls. It was as though a screen had been pulled aside and instead of blank walls on either side there were now suits of armour and racks of weapons. A small side door led off to the left, and on the far end wall two great brassbound doors stood closed. The suits of armour were of a white shiny metal, together with helms and shields.

"Please put them on quickly." The monk urged, "These are for you, except the Druid, who has adequate protection already. Your cloak of protection will be best hidden under a robe along with the Emblem you already bear."

The armour was light but very strong of elven make, the helms were all similar to the one Encathalon and his brother wore, with the device of the castle emblazoned on the front. The monk came forward and presented an ancient sword and scabbard to Chorky.

"This is *Incizor*, the Sword of the Star, take it and wield it with honour. It is the mate to *Gridor*, the Axe of the Star, the dwarf holds. They both have some of the metal in them brought across the sea

281

and sky from far elf worlds before the founding of the Castle."

Chorky's hand grasped the hilt of the ancient sword and as he unsheathed it, he became aware of it, and he knew its name as though Ignatious had never told him. It became part of him, it was much lighter to hold than he expected. It was a joy in his hand. He looked across at Clem and the dwarf nodded, knowing the amazing sensations he was experiencing.

Ignatious continued, "I have a black bow for you Eta Erliandol, it was your ancestor's and passes to you, it too has great lineage. Everyone else take whatever you need from the racks. Your own clothes, arms packs, and other goods you cannot take, place to one side, as no-one will set foot in here again but yourselves. Yes, probably the horned helm is better, Swordwielder." He said to Chorky who was loath to part with his magic helmet.

""Are we ready? The host will not see you and this will continue until the Sorcerer spots something is amiss. With good fortune you may win through almost to the outer gates without being noticed. I will be aiding you, and you will be able to see me on the cliff top in the mists, if you look behind you to your right."

"Then good fortune go with you!" He said in a ringing voice as he swung the great doors wide and watched the gleaming band of knights move through into their destiny. The future of the castle rested on a very slim chance that these few could turn the balance in some way against the thousands of enemy assembled on the heath before them.

---0---

The valley had disappeared, instead an open grassy heath stretched before them to the mists, or it would have had it not been full of armies and thick rain clouds. Half a mile away, a castle rose above the throng, tall, white and powerful, dominating the scene. It was the same castle and view as in the mirror in the caverns but now the scene was real, they were there. The tall Castle of Lethelorel sat on a volcanic spike of black rock, the sides sheer except at the side towards them, where a causeway zig-zagged down a curving rock ramp to the massive Lower Tower. Of the gates or cliffs they had come through there was no sign, or of the mountains encircling the valley apart from an ethereal shadowy outline of the cliff edge where the lone figure of the monk watched. They could see in the murk off to the left, nearly a mile away, tall wooden towers were being constructed. There was just a sea of foes between them and the great Gateway.

As the safety of the walls and the cavern were gone, they took deep breaths, gripped their weapons firmly and ran across the open heath towards the throng. On their arrival they pushed their way in between the loose throng, calling out in kobish to let them through. At first, the enemy was confused as though they were not aware of the knights in their midst. They were treated as fractious rebel troops, not as enemy at all, the enemy not knowing what was opening them up. Every now and again tempers broke around them as the knights barged through with their shields, and occasionally a knot of the foe would turn and attack. This was gruesome work as they found the foe could not see them and it was little more than slaughter. They all hated it, Nomaque more so being a Druid he felt all life was precious. But their only chance was to make the castle walls and gain entry as fast as possible.

---0---

The Lower Tower and the adjoining lower rampart up to the Castle, had come under the full force of the attack, the waves of the host broke before it. The weaker winding upper rampart was

283

less strong, and this was where the large trolls were set to climb the almost sheer obsidian face of the cliff and the smaller wall. Blasts of sorcery hit the wall, which, with its polished stone deflected the power back onto the trolls. Impossibly the trolls, mountain ogres and kobs slowly climbed up towards the castle like a black blanket covering the stone. The first ones attempted to hammer in foot and handholds as they went, but it all bounced off. The defenders would now and again pour foul liquids down on them, searing a triangular patch all the way to the rocky base. Screams of those it touched floating up above the great din of battle. There were a few large war machines up to the front of the battle, the thump-creak of the arm hurling boulders at the walls, punct-uated the general roar of fighting.

The Captain of the Elitan Guard, Esaldur, scanned the scene from the top of the Lower Tower. He called his fellow officer across and asked him to take a look.

"Over there to the south, Themil, coming towards us, a wedge of nothing. What do you make of it?" The armoured figure of the Castle's Artificer beside him watched for a moment and smiled.

"That's no kob trick, that's something new to them. There's flashing within it. What it is I couldn't guess. It needs watching, it makes for us... Look I was right! The Sorcerer has spotted them and has cast down their shield of invisibility. Oh Gods! It's a group of fighters attempting to get to us!"

"In our armour too! Any of the lads out before the mob came, Themil?"

"No, all accounted for. Could it be the princes, I wonder, coming back but that would be only two. The King would know, there he is now, could we ask him?"

The King was making for them anyway, so they drew his attention to the knights coming towards them. The King stopped still, his heart sank as he knew it was not either of his sons, but he did sense the sword *Incizor* and the axe *Gridor* in anger, but there was more there, hidden. Unbidden the words of the seer's prophesy came to him,

'two groups of adventurers will come,
a flaming sword and singing axe,
through the host,
aiee the host opens up....'

The King started, there was just visible a flaming brand, or sword. The group seemed to be protected by something from the bolts of fire flying from where the King deemed the enemy wizard to be. The bolts just bounced off into the enemy's own troops. Esaldur nudged his arm, and pointed to behind the host in the mist. Showing through the rain in some arcane way, was a long shadowy outline of cliffs. On a vague promontory a lone figure watched. "The monk!"

The king gasped in surprise. "We must prepare to sally to retrieve these knights, they are the key, to be preserved at all costs!" The captain gave a sigh and went off to strengthen the gate defences, and assemble the Guard on horseback at the Lower Tower to sally out at a moment's notice.

---0---

The wedge's progress was slow towards the castle but almost relentless. It seemed impossible for such a group to survive in those conditions, but forged by elven smiths long before, Incizor and Gridor formed their cutting edge, and were invincible. Flaming with a white fire they flowed into the enemy, carving a way, leaving a swathe of bodies. Clem and Chorky never felt so inspired, the blades were like thistledown, and they were hardly out of breath. Eta and Sorin held the front flanks, then came a rank of three, Zeth, Nomaque in his magic cloak and Hons.

285

Behind again strode the goblin ancients and Maltex held the vanguard. Heroes were born that day, in the mass of the enemy.

Desperately the enemy captains tried to cover the living thorn piercing their vitals, but all the crack units were in the main assault and only auxiliaries held that part of the field of battle at that time. The nearest were attacking the Lower Tower walls, so the Sorcerer pulled these back from the castle and set them to rush back to attack the intruders. They were hampered by their own troops. The mass of auxiliary soldiers were caught between the enemy and their own elite troops and panic set in, and a hole began to form as they broke and surged back from these two forces.

Realising his mistake the Sorcerer took steps to fill the vacuum. Fifty yards from the gates a blackness formed right in front of the group of knights. So great was the wave of fear that even the trolls rushing across slowed and halted. The cloud took shape, forming into a black horror, a creature from the foul places under the earth. The loathsome thing stank, oozing a black fluid, which scorched the ground. There were many misshapen heads, different sizes, some with teeth and some spitting out venom. It rose up in front of the valiant band, forcing them to stop. On the flanks it immediately became desperate as the kobs attacked them from the rear and sides. They were trapped and their foes screamed for their blood.

Gripping their weapons firmly, Chorky and Clem braced themselves to attack the creature, realising their chances were slim, as they hewed at the awful heads in front, the other heads at the sides could catch them undefended. As they prepared to step forward in the attack, they heard the rest behind them fighting madly to keep from being overwhelmed.

286

With no warning, the ground suddenly erupted in between them and the creature, cutting them off from the horror. A dark mound built up and up like a seawave of breaking earth, causing the nearest kobs on either side to go recoiling back, and raising up the gallant band on its back, giving respite to all. Expanding upwards over the heads of the watchers, the mound grew, then, when it reached some ten feet in height, it started curling over the thing in front of it. Mindlessly the horror piled into it, biting, hissing and screaming, trying to overwhelm it and having no effect on the now black glistening earthy substance.

Under Clem's foot, this structure had an underlying rock-like hardness. He then realised that the monk had brought in the gemorphs from the caverns. Higher and further the wave of black bent, right over the oozing thing, quenching and squashing it down into the ground, leaving only the mound. Steam and vapours shot out of the sides, but of the rest nothing was ever seen again.

Grinning, Clem ran off the smoking pile, calling out in an archaic language. "Thanks old ones!"

"Go on and conquer, courageous ones." Rumbled at their feet.

Chorky, followed by the others, quickly came down behind, taking care to avoid the gasses, and charged into the fray again.

Horn after horn rang out, the great gates of the Lower Tower swung open. Mounted knights clad in castle armour poured out in full charge, scattering their disorganised foes like chaff. The enemy, squeezed beyond endurance melted before the combined attack, and the cavaliers quickly reached the small band. Reinforced, the group withdrew through the archway in the ancient battlements and the great gates of the Lower Tower boomed shut behind them.

287

The heroic little group rested on their shields, as they stood completely oblivious to the stir they caused. Outside the great gates the goblins and kobs howled in frustration, and the trolls stamped and yammered, throwing themselves once more on the great strength of the massive doors of the Lower Tower.

One of the mounted knights came over to the resting group in the small courtyard of the Lower Tower.

"I am Captain Esaldur of the Castle Guard, will you kindly follow me?" The Guard Captain grated, still suspicious of them, as they were clad in an ancient form of the High Armour of the Castle. Only the Princes had the right to wear it, his own troops wore a similar but not so ornate version.

The mounted guard preceded the group up the steep covered, part stepped trackway, curving up through the structure of the Lower Tower, very much a castle in itself. Wearily they followed, their progress was slow as they had to make way for the teams placing stout timbers to help support the great gates, and the bustle of war. Out onto the steep open way in between high ramparts they went, climbing steadily, joining the stream of casualties up the winding roadway and narrow ramparts up to the Main Castle.

A stir spread through the defending forces, wondering rumour flowed along with them, "Knights from the past." "Look at their armour!" "But so few."

Everything to defend the Lower Tower had to negotiate the roadway, a line of wheeled carts going to the walls with containers of seething noxious mixtures, companies of troops moving to the walls and battlements, covering the gaps as they went down; moving along with the injured, the battle-weary soldiers dragged themselves up to the castle through the pouring rain. Nearing the top of the ramp the murky view over what they could see of the plain showed the size of the attacking host and the visitors were daunted.

The Barbican Tower loomed high above them as they reached the top of the roadway, out onto a viaduct over a sheer cleft deeply cutting through the complete width of the ramp. Walking over this dizzy bridge four hundred feet over the battle below, made Chorky's head spin, this was made worse as he turned and looked at the Barbican Tower in front of the castle with the castle main keep soaring behind. He looked up and then up again. The castle proper towered six hundred feet above him, firstly a great Barbican Gatehouse keep, then the turreted keep above, then placed on that again, the topmost tower. On the top was the symbol of a star and a pennant sagged in the drizzle. The viaduct came to an end and the massy drawbridge led into the portal of the one hundred and fifty foot high Barbican Tower, virtually a castle in itself. They carried on through the archway past the great gnarled metal-laced Outer Gates, proudly bearing scars of ancient wars.

Clem paused to touch the workmanship of these ancient elvensmiths, marvelling in their skill, then on only to be brought to an astonished stop as he came out from the back of the Barbican Tower. They had not yet reached the main castle, a second drawbridge gave access to the sheer daunting face of the castle proper towering above them. Under this second drawbridge yawned another dizzying drop to a still, oily encircling inner moat. The workmanship of the castle and the stonework left him awed. Crossing over Clem saw the even more massive Inner Gates. Never broken, this supreme elfcraft of the ancients defied all. The visitors came through the arch of the Inner Gates into the covered Main Courtyard. Five massive columns held the enormous weight of the castle above, one in each corner and one in the centre, each hung with the ancestral shields of the

High elves. The grey light of the sky shone in on either side under great arched roofs, and under this were the stables housing the horses for the Guard.

A tall richly emblazoned knight strode towards them and stopped in front of the centre column. The Captain dismounted and bowed his head in respect. Realising that it was the Elf King standing there, the new arrivals also bowed. Their escort guard split up, some led the horses away, and some retired to a protective distance to one side, leaving the little group in the centre of the Courtyard with the King. For a moment all those present, troops and others stopped and watched as the King raised his hand.

"Welcome to my castle, Wanderers. Your deeds are impressive, and in recognition of your prowess I formally give to you the armour, shields, and weapons, yes, even the Sword and the Axe of this Castle, you have earned them." He said clearly.

Chorky looked at his companions, gathered himself up, and addressed the King.

"I have come, your majesty, as have my companions to aid your cause in any way you think possible. We are but few, but if you will accept our fealty, we would be greatly honoured." As one they kneeled before the King and bowed their heads. He smiled, and bade Chorky give him the Sword *Incizor*. Taking the Sword the King straightened as its power flowed in to him. An iron resolve fleetingly showed on his young-old face as he walked along the line of kneeling armoured figures. Then putting forth his will as an Elflord or *Elfala*, he perceived many things about them and their journey and judged them worthy, touching the shoulder of each with the Sword. As the King came to the two veteran goblins who were bowed low to one side, he saw their great hearts and was moved.

"I will, here and now, create a new Order of Knights, once and for all time. Swordholder,

Axebearer and Druid I name thee, Knights of the Star, all others in the group shall be Esquires of the Star. Bear your arms lightly, I dub you before the assembled soldiers in battle. Fight valiantly my Knights, Only when need arises, kill, be merciful otherwise."

"Arise... Salute the Knights of the Star! "

Cheer after cheer rose above the din of battle and the hearts of the defenders lifted. The great weapons of the past *Incisor* and *Gridor* had come to them in their need. Sir Clem and Sir Chorky drew them and raised them above their heads, they flashed with the power of the great keep around them. Down on the heath the thousands of the enemy heard and wondered what the accursed elves had to cheer about.

The battle continued, and gradually the Elves grip on the Lower Tower weakened, day after day the defenders held out in terrible odds. There was little respite in the day or at night as the enemy put forth new fresh troops. Against them, where the defenders desperately rotated shifts to cope, slowly, inexorably, their numbers dwindled.

The Knights fought with their hosts and earned their respect, the enemy ruing the day when they let the Sword and the Axe pass through. Maltex was assigned to the mounted guard when they discovered his ability to ride a horse. Exploring the stables he found to his amazement twenty graceful flying horses, the pegassi, and two hippogriffs tucked into a corner in one end of the courtyard that no one would go near. Seeing a chance to start to atone, he volunteered to ride the hippogriffs that no surviving elf could ride. Seeing the underlying determination and the wide shoulders of the elf, the High Druid, the head herdsman and the horse master were called to find a way to introduce him to the beasts. The last hippogriff riders had been killed in an accident and

291

everyone else had since left them strictly alone. They said that it took an idiot or a very brave elf to even feed the creatures. Maltex immediately started by feeding them and getting into their confidence slowly, he always had had a way with animals so he only just managed in the beginning. The second day he mounted for the first time and thanked the quadruple leather leggings when the thing tried to bite his leg off. By the end of that day, he was accepted by the beasts, so Captain Esaldur decided they could make an airborne attack on the enemy the following day, if his training continued to improve.

The Captain's former doubts about this powerful elf had evaporated as he watched the diligence with which Maltex carried out his training with these very dangerous creatures. He decided that with Maltex's new skills he could now talk to the King about a daring plan, which was forming in his mind.

The Elitan Guard in addition to horses, each was assigned one of the pegassi, the graceful flying horse from the far fastness of Heradon. And now Maltex was showing command of the hippogriff. It was a weird creature, with what looked like a horse's body with an oversized eagle's head, and a one and a half foot long beak. The feet all were padded with five-inch retractable claws, and a bare tail hung down at the rear. Two very powerful wings grew out of the shoulders, strong enough to carry a large rider into battle. Unfortunately they were doubly dangerous in a fight, as without iron control they could attack their own troops. Perhaps thought the Captain he could use an aerial flight to harass the enemy? Unknown to the Captain, Asphar had other plans, which drove all thoughts of the flight out of the Captain's mind.

As night fell that day the Sorcerer wove a spell of darkness about the Lower Tower and in the darkness of sorcery, he brought up a massy weapon of power to the Great Lower Gates that he had long been building in the fastness of Nablutz. The boom of its evil might shuddered through the fabric of the lofty castle. Time after time the highelven workmanship survived the explosion of force against it. Nothing could be seen through the evil cloud surrounding the Lower Tower.

There had been a furious assault with ropes and grapples hurled up to the lowest parts of the ramp all afternoon, then as dark fell a mist of sorcery rose up and over the Gateway. The defenders increased their vigilance, knowing some devilry was about to happen. Then the booming of the fell weapon on the gate started. Eventually even the mightiest must be riven. The Sorcerer put forth his strength and finally the structure rent asunder, hanging crazily to be brutally crashed aside. The trolls, waiting just for that chance, poured through, killing twenty brave fighters trapped in the rush, before they could escape. The surviving defenders retreated back up through the Lower Tower, pouring volley on volley on the advancing enemy where the inner ramp circles the inside courtyard twice, rising all the time before it is high enough to reach the exit of the Lower Tower to the Castle. High up in the Lower Tower, just before the point where the ramp curves round to meet the outside ramp, there was concealed an inner drawbridge. This was pulled up leaving the trolls and kobs howling in frustration on the edge of a great deep pit. The outer ramp and most of the inner parts of the Lower Tower was still then in the elves control. Chief Artificer Themil, using secret hidden levers within the walls, collapsed sections of the inner ramp inside the Gateway, this prevented the weapon of power approaching the inner drawbridge. The evil cloud sapped the will of the defenders, and confusing them, not knowing where the enemy was going to strike at next.

293

Sir Clem, Vart and Venric became suspicious as the trolls had stopped attacking the outer ramp on the castle side of the Lower Tower and went to find Themil. Collecting a detachment of twenty of his elves, as well as the three, they climbed up the stair in the Lower Tower.

"I must blindfold Vart and Venric here." Themil ordered.

"Myself too," added Sir Clem. "If there is to be secrets between us then it must be all of us!"

"So be it!" Blindfold, the three were led through several dank and echoing tunnels and down a stair to a cavern hewn in the basement rock where the three were allowed to see again.

"We are deep in the ramp here," Themil explained, "nearby this point the enemy was launching their assault on the ramp, just through that rock." Themil took what seemed to be an unusual key from his jerkin and walked up to the wall. He examined the rock for some moments, inserted the key in what seemed a crack and turned it. A small section of rock opened.

"This is one of several listening places in the ramp, in the past small elf children were trained to crawl in to hear what was going on outside. Vart or Venric, could either of you understand what was said if you crawled in?"

Vart nodded and took the first turn in the tunnel.

"The trolls on the other side seem to be bringing *taraxlevn* to the rock wall made of timbers." Vart described. "Whatever *taraxlevn* are is not clear, but they are large and need at least four trolls each to move them. Also there are a lot of them, the trolls are in great difficulty over numbers over twenty and they are talking about twenty-twenty and more, towards twenty-twenty-twenty. All is not going well, two have been killed for slacking. Oh, and one *taraxlevn* has collapsed killing a few more."

Venric took his turn and reported that the voices were becoming fainter, but confirmed all that Vart had said, but added that a chief had arrived and the muttering had stopped, only commands like, 'tie this,' 'move that way,' 'faster or the morning will be here.'

"So they are building something up that wall." Themil bustled, locking the hole quickly and ushering them all out of the chamber, and up the stair. "You three were right, let's get back. I apologise for the blindfolds, we won't need those on the way back. We must move quickly or everyone will be caught in the trap. They are trying to outflank us and are well on the way to succeeding. Let's hurry." The information proved too late to save the loss of the Lower Tower but it saved all those in the Lower Tower being trapped, as the withdrawal was well under way when the attack came. The enemy surged silently over the wall of the ramp in a black wave at that point near the listening place. This would have isolated any in the Lower Tower but thanks to the warning they met a wall of armour, the combined might of the Elitan Guard and the Knights of the Star. This could only hold for a time and the defenders retreated slowly under the sheer pressure of numbers.

Amongst those retreating were Vart and Venric in their new armour that Themil found for them, originally belonging to some young elflings in times long past, their tell-tale white atonement scarves fluttering with every movement of their small bodies. They had declined to accept the Esquire status as they felt that they were unworthy, as there were so many of their own in the enemy host. The King had dubbed them Elf-friend instead and gave them the Freedom of the Castle. They fought like little demons, many a troll learned to its cost that

295

these fighters were perilous to be near. One minute they were in front of their quarry, and then in unison they swung around its legs and stabbed up into its vitals, quickly darting to one side as the large figure toppled groaning the floor. They were the main reason that there was no rout amongst the retreating troops. Holding the resistance together, they gave ground only when it was safe, preserving life to fight another day. Those with them grew to respect and honour these stalwart fighters.

Chief Artificer Themil and his elves harried the advancing enemy up the ramp every step of the way, until they had to clear their own dead to advance. Nearly every death-dealing device lurked in those ramp sidewalls. Spikes, darts, screens of knives, scythes and drop hammers, pits and traps of blocks dogged their path, but slowly they cleared it with awful losses. The Sorcerer drove them on mercilessly, wasting them in droves, his power giving them no respite from the agony of their existence. Baulks of timber blocked the worst of Themil's devices in the end. The time gained enabled the defence to consolidate in the Barbican Tower. The desperate band led by the two veterans harried the enemy all the way up to the ramp and on to the viaduct. Eventually when the last fighter leapt back and the drawbridge in front of the Barbican Tower raised, the elves regrouped and poured missiles down upon the enemy on the viaduct and lost roadway.

The new day dawned drearily, with continuous rain, there had been no let up in the downpour from the beginning, blotting out the sun. In the dawn the light barely changed as the enemy began to bring up the towers and great beams of timber to span the gap to the Barbican Gate they had constructed on the heath. They were luridly painted with sorcerous symbols placed upon them, smoking blackly in the early light. That was the night when the enemy started the attempt to mine into the basement under the castle, the boom continuing as a knell of doom in the dark, troubling even those who were trying to sleep. It seemed to penetrate the innermost depths, spawning ill dreams to the tired but valiant defenders.

During the morning the elves morale slipped down to the lowest it had been since the war had begun. The enemy trolls brought up an enormous battering ram, faced with a grotesque bird's head and beak from some evil den. The misshapen head was dripping with blood from its necromantic rites of birth. Symbols were scrawled all over it, calling forth some arcane demons. This massive weapon had to be hauled by fifty trolls it was so heavy, that was until the Sorcerer put the power into it. Afterwards it rose up under its own malevolent will, making the trolls writhe who had to wield it. Now the defenders could see the cause of the loss of the Lower Great Gates and the Lower Tower and the same terror was moving up to and on to the creaking timbers over the chasm supported by the evil malice of the Sorcerer.

At that moment, a strong breeze came across the heath, and nearby a trumpet blew. A great blowing of horns followed and the mists and foul murk cleared from the south east. Hearts leapt, as into view out of the clearing mists, rode an Elf Lord in full fury, Prince Brithael, his armour sun-bright ahead of his host. Six thousand elvish fighters from the neighbouring kingdom of Ethan took the field that day to try to save the Lost Castle.

Out in front, covering the ground in great leaps bounded a great Golden Dragon, wings furled but flaming as he came, his scales brilliant gold. Riding on him was the Elf Prince Brithael his armour almost blinding silver in the sunlight. The light had come with the Dragon.

The enemy cried in fear, and a cry from the battlements went up.

"Prince Brithael is here! Asfamnur the Fair is here! We are saved!"

The elf host although smaller in numbers, was nevertheless a cruel blow to Kuk'l'Mak's supremacy, breaking the siege and prevented him from dominating the field of battle. The fresh elvish warriors streamed forward to engage the hosts' southern flank, piercing deeply and fanning out, following the swathe cleared by the terrible flame of Asfamnur the Fair, the great dragon.

A great cheer rose from the castle as the sun shone through. The massive Barbican drawbridge was dropped with a crash onto the already overloaded temporary bridge the enemy had barely constructed. At that moment the Sorcerer's thoughts were distracted in fear of the great dragon's wrath, the Sorcerer's malice holding the timbers faded. With a groan the timbers bearing the birdram gave way to tumble off the viaduct to clatter off into space. The Birdram screamed in its fall, exploding in anger hundreds of feet down on the hard obsidian rock of the castle basement. Captain Esaldur, Sir Chorky, Sir Clem, the Guard and most of the Esquires charged over the drawbridge. The trolls having lost their leaders' mental support at that crucial moment, as his will was bent elsewhere, were dismayed. The trolls were bowled off the causeway viaduct, to join the Birdram amongst the remains of the timbers down to the rocks below. Cheering, the sallying force poured on down the ramp towards the Lower Tower. They cleared any assault towers as they progressed over the heaps of dead enemy.

The Sorcerer was calling his champion forth, Impstalkish, the Champion of his forces, an enormous hobgoblin creature. His mount too was a dragon, Goubblat, not quite so large as the great golden dragon, but a more vicious purple variety. It was bred for war from the last of ruined third-born dragon Gouthbund's eggs found in the pits of the old elvish city and filled with hatred for the creatures of the light. All down one side the dragon was burned, and blind in one eye, from an untimely battle with Vodocanthey, the ancient dragon. With uttermost quiet Goubblat floated over the heath, coming from the west it glided towards its adversary from the cover of the castle. On the castle, the elves manning the towers gasped and died, as this monstrous thing in flame seared the stonework in passing.

Perceiving its mortal enemy before its rider, the golden dragon, with all of the power of a first born, rose to its defence. The Sorcerer, immediately assailed the Elf Lord sending blast after blast at him. The purple dragon feinting to the side also directed the full force of his flame at the Prince and Asfamnur's back. Bending his thought to his own defence Prince Brithael became caught directly in the path of the flame. Even an Elf Lord in the prime of his powers could not withstand that combined attack between the dragon's flame and the sorcery. The Prince was scorched in ruin, falling to his doom amongst the kob host just before the Gates. Asfamnur the Fair, unable to catch his rider again, spun in his own length mid-air, its wrath terrible to behold, stooped all along the back of the purple dragon and its rider, killing and searing as it went. As it had seen its enemy had been blinded and burnt along one side previously, Asfamnur turned on that side and raked the burned Impstalkish off, to plummet down to crash lifeless on the ground. Goubblat, realising that he was mortally wounded, wheeled, and fastened tooth and claw on to Asfamnur in mid-air in a biting and scorching melee. Unable to both defend and fly Asfamnur folded his wounded wings and dropped. The two great beasts tumbled out of the sky to fall where the Prince had fallen just before, close to the Lower Tower. The purple dragon's death cry rent the air even before the weight of the golden dragon landed on top, the last vestige of life crushed away. Asfamnur the Fair fared not much better, crippled too, it eased itself up, at the mercy of the Sorcerer, trolls and kobs of the enemy. In its loss, and realising that it was too injured to fly, it gave one defiant bugle of heart-breaking anguish and flamed a big circle of circle of foes. The Golden Dragon, Asfamnur the Fair then disappeared from that place forever.

Chapter Twenty

The Light, the Dark and the Fire

*E*veryone on the battlefield was stunned, the whole aerial battle had only taken a minute, and the chief warriors on both sides were left ruined on the ground. The grim fighting for survival continued, the castle forces having gained a costly advantage from the dragons' demise. The force coming down the roadway, had swept a path again to the Lower Tower, taking advantage of the disruption to destroy the *taraxlevn,* the great scaffold of timbers up the side of the ramp. They relieved any of the elves still fighting in the Lower Castle and reoccupied it.

The elf host from across the plain, incensed by the loss of both the Golden Dragon and their prince charged into the press, more fell in their agony and pain, seeking death. The enemy host reeled and Kuk'l'Mak poured in troops waiting for the next assault to save a rout.

At about this time by lucky fortune, the army of Limbool dwarves under Nenderailt, charged into the battle from the west, two thousands strong, the traditional enemies of the evil host. They had come to the summons of the Elf King, and had force-marched to arrive in the nick of time. Tempered by many wars against these same foes, they had crept almost into hailing distance of their foes before they were discovered, the battle hardened fighters carved their way into the press but they had a wide swathe of enemy reserves on that side to deal with.

Reeling from the dwarfish assault, Kuk'l'Mak committed his last large group of his reserves into the fray, pouring several more thousand goblins in from outlying camps around the castle; committing his reserves to cutting off the dwarves from the castle. Even so he still held on the north-east side of the castle a force of rock-trolls from the high peaks. They were in readiness for a final assault on that side with a force of about a thousand other races with climbing skills. Deliberately he pushed them further to the east, holding them there on that side, away from the defenders, the elf host and the dwarves.

At that moment, unforeseen, over the heath towards that area in which the goblin king had just placed the special force, swept a small but determined company. Ikin, Prince Encathalon and the small band that went with them entered the battle. Behind them were a company of one hundred gnomes under Chief Grindalwald of the Mace, flanked by two companies of elves from the nearby villages to the north and east. As with Chorky's companions all Ikin's group excepting Riva wore Star armour, but they carried different shields, these were highly polished with a circular boss in the centre of each.

High in the castle in the Main Hall, Elf Queen Hermione, working with the healers, was tending to the wounded coming in. As she paused to straighten her weary limbs, she felt a surge of hope for the first time in weeks. Then she realised, she could feel the presence of her son. Prince Encathalon had returned home, somewhere out there he was fighting. She smiled to herself, a tear of joy trickled down her lovely cheek. She turned once again to the injured with a new vigour after she had sent an urgent message to the King.

---O---

When Ikin's party had gone into Acthion's Tower with Prince Encathalon, they had descended into a tunnel room much the same as Nomaque had with the others. Arriving at the lower hall, Encathalon gave suits of armour to everyone, except Riva who took a light corselet and a many-coloured cloak, similar to Nomaque's. They chose their weapons from the racks, but the elf brought some special shields out from a storeroom nearby.

"The monk Ignatious has just appeared to me. The battle is raging and we are in time. He also described these ancient shields, worn long before my time by a detachment of the army called the Company of Light. They have a small copy of Ikin's Lens in the centre of the body of the shield, which can be pointed by the wearer's hand." He then hand- ed Ikin a similar one, but with a blank in the middle.

"Fit your Lens on, Ikin. This is the master shield, when the sun is in the sky, even on a misty day, this is supposed to be terrible weapon. I was told it creates a beam of light terrible to see. All races find the beam hot and blinding, in addition, those races who live more in the darkened caverns are said to find the beam mind blinding. The lesser shields must direct their light beams onto this one, and somehow it produces an awful one, which Ikin can direct where she wishes. Have a care where you point that thing Ikin, I think it does no good to our own troops either, it will blind them at least. If we keep all of the centres with their covers on until we're quite near the enemy, they cannot run away or outflank us."

They emerged through a set of great doors and found themselves on a heath, not far from the Castle, with it shining in the thin mist. Ikin thought she saw a ghostly figure of a monk standing alone on the heath out of the corner of her eye, but when she looked again it was not there. Neither were the great doors or the cavern. They were on the heath, armies all around them in the thin mist.

303

Coming up to them were several companies of Limbool elves and gnomes, wondering how to reach the Castle, with the host of the enemy in between. Collecting this new force together quickly, Prince Encathalon arranged the shield holders in the centre, and let them practice the operation of the shields, while he welcomed the new arrivals. He then arranged the gnomes in between, but just behind Ikin's group, with the elves in roughly equal companies on either side to cover the flanks in a large wedge. They came up to the side of the great enemy host cutting firstly through thinly spread enemy until they hit the hidden hand picked climbing troops of the goblin king. Then they charged, tearing off the covers of the mirrors as they went. In the centre of each shield flickered an intense bead of light, at first the beams flashed in discord, but quickly they gained control and then from Ikin's shield in the centre of the group blazed a terrible ray of incandescent light. Each of the lesser shields reflected light too, forming a circle of brightness. The master beam burned everything that was not metal and even the metal melted after a second. Ikin found she had to keep the beam low or on the ground or else it could hurt anyone in the castle looking their way. It was awkward to maintain, as the lesser shields could not always point correctly.

The beam array caused every kob or goblin it approached either to crumple up protecting their eyes or fall to the floor in burning agony. It devastated the enemy forces in front of it, opening an immediate gap of crippled bodies, further back the enemy peeled back in horror onto those behind. The pockets of kobs and goblins who survived ran to the sides completely disorganising the flanks who could have attacked Ikin. This was lucky as she and her group needed time to learn how best to operate the lens in battle. Moving forwards quickly Ikin passed the overcome enemy having left gaps in between her shields, the gnomes then dispatched disoriented troops before they could recover. The elves on the flanks swooped around, catching those on the sides, a lethal killing machine. In a short time there was a considerable swathe cleared over the heath. The backlash of the enemy fleeing back came up against those fighting the dwarves and severely hampered them. There was little resistance to them until unfortunately Ikin's force came up against the rock-trolls. These were outdoor mountain bred trolls, covered in stony-scaly skin and used to bright sun-light reflected off ice and snowfield. The beam had no effect whatsoever on them, unless it irritated them.

Readying their weapons Ikin's relatively small company covered their mirrors and prepared to make a stand, although their chances were poor against such lumbering creatures the size of barns. The elves without the shields, tightened up their formation and they all prepared to sell themselves dearly.

Chief Grindalwald burst through their line with the entire force of gnomes and raced for the towering creatures, everyone else thought them berserkers, but one of his men told the rest of the force to close up but not to engage, the gnomes had a plan of action against these creatures. Apparently the mace that Grindalwald carried, he told them later, was a fell weapon out of the mists of time, passed down from chief to chief's son, as far back as the tribe could remember. The Mace *Earthcrusher* could shatter the bones of large creatures if skilfully used, and when they fell down the company finished them off.

The gnome chief darted about toppling the trolls, catching a scaly knotted knee here and an ankle the size of a young tree there. Before they realised what he was doing, he had many felled, half of his band followed on behind, catching the fallen creatures before they could defend themselves. The

305

other half, fifty strong, with Prince Encathalon and a few picked elves attacked the remaining trolls, nimbly dodging out of the way of the enormous clubs until the Chief could get to them.

Ikin had reformed the lens formation, and attacked again to the side of the main battle, cutting into the reserve forces of the goblin king between the dwarves and the castle. The reserves were caught in a pincer movement. This force, although small, demoralised a large part of the enemy, who thought that the force was an advance guard of a larger army coming around the castle. But the enemy host was vast and those killed were replaced, slowly and at great cost forcing Ikin's company back towards the castle.

Four hundred feet above them the black cliffs rose sheer and above again the white castle walls gleamed, Ikin then began to wonder how they were going to get inside. They had been so involved in fighting, that they had not given it a thought. It was only when the cliff loomed up close, they realised also that they were in the castle's shadow, they could no longer use the lens and that the gates were on the other side with the enemy host in between. They were trapped themselves!

---O---

On the other side of the Castle the knights won the passage down the ramp and commanded the Lower Gate again, although the gates, once strong, hung shattered and a shelter no more. The elf forces both on the heath and in the castle, gathered for the assault they knew was about to come from the massing enemy.

Captain Esaldur watched the enemy host and realised that their forces were more balanced, and for the first time the elves had a chance. He went to the King with his perilous plan.

306

"If you are determined on it, I will not forbid you. There will be no rescue for any of you on this mission, you realise, and as the battle can go either way at this point, your abilities are irreplaceable. I cannot command you to go on this mission." Seeing there was a grim determination about his Captain, he added, "Still no battle is won without risks, so go with my blessing. If you are successful your force could turn the battle our way. The red-haired elf and the hippogriff wish to go with you?" The captain nodded. "Good, he will produce chaos," the King added and gave a rare smile.

Before he assembled his troop, the captain went out onto the Twelfth level balcony where the High Druid watched the events unfolding before him. The two shared the command of the battle. The Captain controlled the troops, and the High Druid tried to control the magical forces, countering the Sorcerer when he could. The High Druid fully realised that the power of his enemy was the greater, and if it came to an out and out magical confrontation, he would lose. There was of course, the monk...

"Have you seen the events in the north?" The High Druid inquired.

"I saw the arrival of the dwarves, very reas-suring, they are progressing, I hope? I have been involved with the retaking of the Lower Castle, High Druid."

"Well, you ought to know that there is another force out there, what it is I cannot tell but although few, they have decimated the climbing troops the Goblin King had tucked out of the way for his final blow. They have the appearance of gnomes, Cap-tain, In their midst I think I can discern more knights dressed as Sir Chorky's group with a slightly larger force of elves from the villages. About three hundreds all told, shattered over a thousand picked troops, as well as fifty rock-trolls! There is some fell weapon at work there, very bright light seems to flash in front of them. So bright that I instructed our men on the battlements to have caution looking that direction."

"Where are they now?" The Captain asked, looking down.

"I think they are in the shadow of the base-ment cliff, and are out of sight. I feel in their midst is one of my order so I will guide them towards the dwarves who will be reaching them soon, hopefully they could need help," the Druid added, but he had a niggling worry that it might be too long. The weapons that the three hundred used may not be used under the castle in the shadow, and so the small numbers may be vulnerable. Still they may be able to hold a while longer. This became desperate as a message came from the Queen about their Prince. His anxiety was well founded as that moment the evil captain of the enemy troops mining the castle basement had seen the small force approach and held off as long with the light weapon causing such havoc. Seeing it fail he charged with all the kobs and trolls he could muster.

----0----

Up in the castle the Captain outlined his plan, asking for magical help to deflect the Sorcerer. The High Druid agreed the timing would be good for such a venture, but felt much the same as the King. Also privately he felt that if both commanders of the Castle forces, the Captain and himself, were involved in it then who would deal with any other problems? Reluctantly he watched the broad back of the elf disappearing and sighed, the little group with the Prince below would have to fend for themselves for a while. He then scanned across the valley to the phantom cliffs where a lone figure stood watching, and sent a guarded thought in that direction.

The scene in the courtyard was all bustle, but there was a space where no-one went, that was near the still figure of Maltex astride the vicious looking hippogriff. The pegassi were led out of their stalls at the other end of the stables and mounted. The order was given and they all rose up and out over the battlements, swiftly clearing the castle and diving down the side of the rock base. The sight of the fliers in the late afternoon sun uplifted the defenders hearts. Cheering inwardly, they kept silent, thinking, 'Gods go with you!'

The hippogriff flew in front, with the others forming a wave on both flanks. They sped very low, skimming over the heads of their enemies. Flying in a curve, which was designed to fool the watchers for as long as possible, they arrived over the palanquin of the Goblin King. They then stooped sharply straight onto the great hobgoblin and his bodyguard.

Maltex landed in their midst, his hippogriff causing havoc. The red-haired elf of another time leaped from the back of the hippogriff at the hideous hobgoblin King Kuk'l'Mak. Almost caught off guard, the gruesome king held his own for a while, but the superior fitness and cold determination of the elf told, and it was not long before the King's body sank headless to the now scarlet cushions of the palanquin. The Elitan Guard swiftly followed Maltex in, taking advantage of the chaos to attack the bodyguards, slipping off their mounts into battle with the practised efficiency of trained warriors.

Maltex turned and leaped for his mount, dangling from his hand was the severed head, still with the Elfcrown upon it. Taking off immediately, he led the surviving guard back. They had killed King Kuk'l'Mak along with most of his Guard in a short but devastating attack for the loss of two of their number and two pegassi. Keeping their mounts as low as possible to avoid the many arrows directed at them, they skimmed home over the heads of the shocked host screaming for their blood.

The story of Maltex and the Elitan Guard would be told as long as the elves lived. Triumphant they returned, to deafening cheers as they cleared the castle walls to land in the courtyard, the severed head of their enemy held high.

Things had been extremely difficult for the Druid, who had, at much risk waited until the Sorcerer noticed the flight, and then unleashed a bolt of pure plant essence at the Sorcerer, the sticky substance trickling down and totally preventing him from blasting the aeronauts out of the sky. Furious, at being caught unawares, the wizard vaporised the ooze and sent blast after blast at the unfortunate High Druid. The Druid, expecting a reply of that nature was not there. The Monk from the other direction quickly enshrouded Asphar in a thick mist and rained boiling water down upon him, as though the Druid sent it. The Sorcerer quickly revised his estimate of the High Druid's power and blasted the tower again. Getting no reply he grew into a great shape to see over the mist cloud. Simultaneously the Monk and the Druid unleashed bolts of energy at their enemy. As soon as the attack was released, they defended themselves as quick as thought. Seething, but more than a little puzzled at the apparent abilities of the Druid, perceiving that the Goblin King was dead, the necromancer laughed viciously and said in a voice that carried to his opponents.

"Now you will see what a master sorcerer can do,

I didn't need the fat fool of a King anyway,

Laugh now if you can!.

Now!"

Right in front of the Gate there was a shimmering, and then a cloud of blackness, the kobs

310

there stumbled over themselves to get away, the wave of evil emanating from the cloud engulfed firstly the Lower Tower and then shortly afterwards the whole Castle, terror and fear stalked abroad in the chambers. Everyone rushed to look at what was happening and there was an awful lull in the fighting.

The cloud grew until it was some twenty feet across, and then from its darkest centre two red orbs, two red eyes looked out with such malevolence everyone shuddered and wanted to run. Caught emerging from the Gate, Sir Chorky stood and waited, the bravest thing he had ever done in his life, while the creature from the Abyss Core slowly took shape in front of him.

The High Druid groaned as he realised the danger, he was unable to get down to aid the half-elf in time. He mentally called to Sir Nomaque, who was close-by to the lone Knight. The younger Druid, being of a similar order, could gain some support from him. Support flowed too from the Star Emblem on a chain around his neck resting on his chest, reacting to the evil in front of them.

The heat was building from the red fire rippling all over the tall bestial shape, most intense in the sword it held. Sir Chorky was more worried about what it held in the other hand, a black net. The creature opened its mouth and a stream of fire shot towards the luckless Knight. The half-elf raised his shield hopefully, but realised it offered little protection. But the Sword was a different matter, from it sureness surged within him.

Sir Chorky suddenly felt a presence beside him, and heard the familiar voice of his friend Sir Nomaque saying, "We stand together, to the finish. Its fire will hurt, but not damage us, I have protected you. Give him a taste of the sword!"

Greatly buoyed up by his friend's arrival, Chorky took a long pace forward and smote with all his might. The sword suddenly roared with a white flame as it hit the terror. Numbness shot up the half-elf's arm as it hit the red fire, and played around the helm turning it black. He staggered back a pace to be supported by Sir Nomaque, mind reeling. He was amazed, the helm and the sword had protected him and he was still whole and upright. He rested for a second to gather up some of his shattered will, and then he charged forward again. The black net streamed past and over the two of them, Sir Chorky cut a piece out but Sir Nomaque was entangled. The dweamer of protection wavered and the heat became devastating. The net melted from Sir Nomaque's chest outwards, and the heat lessened as the druid renewed the spells.

There was a whirr from behind and the rest of the net was shredded. The familiar short but doughty figure of Sir Clem had joined them. Gathering up his druidic essence Sir Nomaque put forth all his power to ease the heat for them all, and stepping back he let the two take the field. The half-elf and dwarf were standing side-by-side, dealing blow after blow at the creature. The Abyss Lord was faced with a pair of weapons it could not withstand, born of the light, they were slowly sapping its strength, slicing through its contact with the world, and drawing him away. Desperately it summoned forth his remaining powers and leaped high in the air, up over their heads, in order to come crashing down in amongst them, but behind the Sword and the Axe onto Sir Nomaque. Desperately the two knights spun around to try to defend the Druid but they realised they were outflanked and prepared a desperate last suicide attack to try to save their friend as the creature came down.

It hung in the air and savoured the treat of taking their lives, and licked its twisted lips, little puffs of black fire played around its nostrils and a gaze like the pit to hell gloated down on them. Fear and heat beat down on Nomaque, and his control of the shield of protection for Chorky and Clem wavered and held firm.

They would have been at the creature's mercy, had it completed the jump, but at the highest point of the leap a beam of incandescent pure light struck it, enveloped it, a timeless moment when dark and light mingled, and the last of its contact with the world drained away. Its fire was snuffed out. It vanished with an explosion, the force of the blast bowling over all in the vicinity. The Sorcerer, with a thin wail, faded too, as with those who do not give a victim to those of the abyss, the summoner is taken instead. The force of its leaving the planes of life came back along the light beam buffeting Ikin's Light Company and turning the shields black with soot.

Ikin's force had been in a desperate fight, but unexpectedly a secret battalion of well over a hundred elf veterans led by Themil, the Castle's Artificer issued out from a hidden portal in the rock basement. They had been waiting for just such a moment to pour out onto the mining kobs and goblins. With this valiant force, Ikin together with a dwarf elite corps had been able to fight off the kob captain, and Prince Encathalon defeated him in the shadow of the castle. Reforming again they fought their way round to the Lower Tower. Ikin had begun to employ the lens again, just in time for her to catch that terrible leaping figure.

Getting to their feet, Sir Clem, Sir Chorky and Sir Nomaque were doubly overjoyed to see the little gnomess again, as they had missed her.

"We must give up meeting like this!" She chuckled grimly, as she eased herself off the ground where the blast had thrown her. She had fully realised that if her aim had faltered, she could have lost three close friends and the enemy would have

313

had the Castle at their mercy. A tear of relief trickled down her battle-grimed cheek.

The dwarves, elves and gnomes had formed a wall in front of the Gates around the valiant few. They then drove the demoralised enemy hosts back. Slowly at first but when the Lower Gates burst open and the mounted Elitan Guard led the castle forces out. From the Castle above them, Maltex flew out on his hippogriff flanked by the elite of the Elitan Guard on their pegassi, stooping to harry the enemy. The enemy host cried out in dismay. Losing both their leaders, and their champion, and then suffer continuous airborne attack was too much for the remaining attackers, who turned and fled, leaving the battlefield piled with their dead. They scattered through the plains, the ones coming from Jodamia were stranded and drifted, to die totally disoriented, at the mercy of wild animals or as slaves to other kobs and goblins.

The defenders and their allies met just outside the Castle, at the place where the Prince Brithael died, and Asfamnur the Fair fell. It was one of those occasions when there was cause for rejoicing and grieving at one and the same time.

Sir Chorky, Sir Clem and Sir Nomaque didn't stay long as they were burnt by the fell creature and needed treatment. Ikin and all the other members of the group followed, as the position they found themselves in was strange, and in unfamiliar situations friends congregate together. Slowly they climbed up the roadway past the reminders of war, and could not but help feeling the sting of life. There they were alive and more or less whole, when all these unfortunate elves lay dead on the cold stones. With all their genuine feelings of sadness for these poor people, they were only too pleased that they had managed to survive, when the others had not. The problem was more acute for the Druids, as they were by nature neutral, and tended to dislike killing on all occasions. They all felt tarnished, especially Vart and Venric, who had completed the final part of their transformation into ancients and could see the futility of the young goblin's actions.

As they reached the Barbican Tower, the tall form of Maltex strode to meet them.

"It seems a long way and a long time ago when I saw you last Ikin, but my eyes do not deceive me, you are prettier than ever." He said with a wry grin, a very different Maltex from the one they knew in Mesquite.

"A wiser Maltex, it seems, but I am relieved to be able to greet you again, I missed you." She said serious for once.

Riva, seeing the drooping figures of Sir Nomaque, Sir Chorky and Sir Clem, bustled all of them into the Castle, and called one of the healers over. The healer, Zachiel, and a beautiful elf lady came over.

"I think these three desperately need help," Zachiel cut in immediately, and asked the lady. "They have been touched by deep evil flame, I can see a transparency about them, where ma'am, can we take them for treatment?"

"I will take them to the healers in the hall as you have your hands full," the lady replied sadly. "Maybe the High Druid will wish to come too. If you see him send him up please." she added, he nodded deferentially, and she lead them up to the level above where many more wounded were being treated. The outer parts of the Great Dining Hall had been partitioned off, to form dormitories for the injured. Beds lay in serried ranks across the floor, figures in white robes tended to them. It was to one of these that the elflady took them, asking Riva to explain their needs. All those who had minor wounds she led off as they were quite a crowd.

315

"Are you all known to one-another then? What started your journey to us?" She asked.

"It was Eta here's fault, and a missing boy, if I remember correctly, your majesty," Maltex enigmatically explained. "I don't think you have been introduced to us all. I would like to introduce Ikin, Hectar, Tasherlon, Riva the Druidess over there with the others, and Onaroah, Riva's son."

Chapter Twenty-one

The Aftermath and the unpleasant Truth

*P*rince Encathalon came up to them just as Maltex finished his introductions.

"Mother, there you are, do you realise that Ikin here was the wielder of Ziphra's Lens on the north side, and the cause of the final end of the Abyss Lord. Maltex, I haven't met you before but I am astounded by your feat, same as I'm amazed by all of you. When I met you in the other place, I did not realise the meaning of you all holding the Emblems. Fate, it seems did. I must have seemed aloof and distant, for this I apologise. You have put me justly in my place, you came to my home and saved us. Thank you all, I feel honoured to have fought with you." Encathalon said, bowing low.

"Hold on a minute, Prince," Ikin retorted, "you fought just as hard as any out there, on our way round the Castle base, your majesty, your son with Grindalwald was our saviour. He fought like the true Knight he is, getting us out of a tight corner, protecting us and making space for the lens to work again. We must honour you."

"They met and decided to help us months ago, mother, and following a long trail, found me. I was without direction until they told me you were under attack, then I came home. I don't think I would have made it without them all, especially Ikin. Sorry Ikin, I know you don't like to be praised, but this time

317

you cannot shut me up!" The prince replied and smiled at her. She shrugged and shook her head.

Queen Hermione smiled and led them away to wash and rest before they would be required to come down to the evening meal. They wearily followed without a murmur.

The sun was setting on a stormy day, one in which a great battle was won. The Castle thankfully rested, apart from the teams who laboured long into the night with the gruesome task of clearing up. The bodies of the kob and goblin dead were piled into several mounds some distance from the Castle base, the elvish dead were placed carefully in another much closer to the walls as there was not enough fuel to burn them. It was named the Watch Mound in later years in memory of the fallen. Light meals were taken by those few who still had energy to eat, while the rest of the Castle slumbered.

The following morning all the allies gathered outside the Gate to give thanks to their different Gods, burn the trappings of war that littered the landscape, and generally tidy up. Support wagons for the elves and dwarves began arriving that morning, so all was prepared for feasting. Open-air kitchens were set up for the roast meats and hot vegetables, cold viands and wine flowed from the marquee set beside them.

The sun had barely dipped from zenith, when the King climbed up wearily onto a large oak table.

"Before we start to enjoy ourselves, I have several duties to perform. Battle Honours are given to the war-flight of the Elitan Guard, would they step up here to receive them." After they had walked forward to receive their colours, he then continued through his list, honouring the heroes of each stage of the siege.

"Next, I come to our allies, in recognition of their help I give this electrum axe to the dwarves of

Nenderailt, to the gnomes and Chief Grindalwald this cup of gold and amethysts. To the elvish villages I give each a bow and quiver, which has been laced with enhanced prowess. I cannot express the debt we have to you. To the elves of the South, I am grief stricken at your loss, there is nothing I can do to ease you of your burden, but I can bestow an heirloom of our far shores upon you." The King paused while a team brought a golden *Lianur* across to the elf visitors.

"I have passed to you one of the three *Lianur of Light*, to be found on this side of the oceans of air. We will be able to contact you through the ages, as we have one other in the tower of the castle, the other was lost in the City of the Star I believe.

"LET THE HONOURED BE PRAISED
PRAISE THEM!!!"

The assembly cheered and those honoured bowed to them.

"Lastly I am going to increase the order of the Knights of the Star, Sir Maltex Meraltion, step forward."

Maltex stepped up to the King, and bent his head. Clearly he replied, his voice ringing out over the gathered throng.

"Sire, I am unworthy. I, in part caused this attack, by my foolishness. The crown that you now wear, I had in my possession in a town in our times. I sold it, and by various means the goblins gained it. And thereby gained an access to you. I repeat I am unworthy. I also wear a circlet of control to atone justly placed by the Naga of the Labyrinth Gate."

"I know all about the circlet," the King replied, "and also it is for me to judge when you have served sufficiently. I remove it with honour, and bestow on you the full rights of the Knighthood of the Star. Wear the armour with pride... Lady Ikin Galena step forward, I have never had more pleasure in the best-

319

owing of an order. Your feats match your friends in all ways, I dub thee Lady Ikin Galena, Holder of the Ziphra's lens and Knight of the Star. Your companions I name Esquires of the Star. Step forward Esquires, Riva of the Wind, young valiant Onaroah of the Sky, Hectar Rolan, and Tasherlon Tendralom, wear your armour with pride from a grateful King. All the Knights, Esquires please rise.

"LET THE HONOURED BE PRAISED, PRAISE THEM!!!"

The assembly cheered again and the Knights and Esquires bowed to them.

The King continued, "I have been saddened by the wishes of the gallant two Elf Friends, Vart and Venric not to take the honour of the Esquire of the Star. Will you not change your minds?" He looked to the two goblin Ancients who fought so heroically for the elves cause.

They looked at each other and nodded in agreement, "We cannot, honoured King, our kin have caused too much havoc here and elsewhere, for us to be content."

The King thought for a moment and strode forward, grasping the soiled white armbands that they wore throughout the battle, he eased them off the two shoulders. At his touch they changed, suddenly gleaming white softest elf cloth where the cloth was and rubies in place of the bloodstains. Turning he raised them up to the assembly, and cried out, his voice thick with emotion,

"These sacred badges are more to me than if they were of the purest gold and platinum, they represent true honour, selflessness and good. Wear them in my gratitude and of all my kin. I dub you the King's Ancients, welcome here and in any part of my kingdom, free of restraint.

PRAISE THEM BOTH!"

The cheering burst wildly from every throat as their deeds had been many and valorous, when it subsided a little, the King continued, turning to all the Knights and Esquires,

"I would deem it an honour if you kept your weapons and armour in memory of us, valiant ones!" The grateful Elf king then called out joyfully.

" THEN LET US EAT".

The assemblage then merrily cleared the tables of food, and with full stomachs settled down to a storytelling as the sun set in the light from the few fires. Later the group were asked to tell their adventures on their way to the Castle. The joyous mood continued until the tale came to the finding of the dead elf Prince in Castle armour, which Nomaque left out. Everyone went quietly to their tents or Castle when the Knights finished or soon after, both sad and pleased, bittersweet tasting victory in their mouths.

Sir Nomaque sadly approached the Royal Chambers and entering in, gave the royal couple the locket from their son and the knowledge that he was buried with honour in that quiet cavern in Jodamia. Unfortunately that was how the King and Queen heard of the sad end of Throndralon in a lonely cavern.

In the following days the dwarves, elves, and gnomes of the surrounding heathlands of Limbool departed. The latter making a great fuss of Lady Ikin and wishing she would go with them, but she remained adamant on staying. That gnomish Lady had captured a host of gnomish hearts and those of many other races, and her not going with her kin almost caused a rebellion. Lady Ikin was not amused but Prince Encathalon and the rest of her party were. Wherever she went she aroused gnome male passion.

They went to see the King several days later, to discuss the next moves.

The King and Lord Bessarte, the Senior Lord met the Knights, Esquires and King's Ancients up in the tower.

"We came to help you to return to your own times," Sir Nomaque explained, "and we thought that the reappearance of the emblems all together would trigger this. It does not seem to have done so,"

"We in turn do not know the answer either," Lord Dessarte replied. "We have an old prophesy that roughly described your advent on the scene in the battle, and infers that you will be instrumental in the change back. I feel that the solution must lie somewhere in the Castle Library. I also think we do not have the power to send you back to your own times anyway. The Sorcerer must have used the crown, but provided the power himself. The monk is the only other one to do this, as he sent the Princes to your times, with their circlets as guides. So you are here until we find the solution to the riddle.

---0---

The next week was hectic, but even so the group felt themselves stranded. The most affected were Hons and the two veteran goblins. To ease their pain, Encathalon approached them six days after the battle, with a faint hope.

"I have been searching for a way to get you home. I think the only artefact, which will help the transfer, is this circlet that I wear as Prince. I have asked my father, and he has given me permission to act as I think fit. The High Druid will try to summon the Monk when you go, and wearing the circlet he will come to you. This is a very risky path, and I only offer it as a last resort because I know your fear that your relatives and loved ones are vulnerable. Do you wish to take this route?" He offered.

The three readily agreed and Encathalon gave the circlet to Hons, Esquire of the Star. On the seventh morning they set out across the grassy heath to the south, the armbands of the two goblin veterans giving a white and red sparkle in the sun with the tall shining armour clad elf in between. As their figures dwindled into specks, the elves watching thought they saw another figure join them and the four seemed to disappear.

Something caught his eye and the King glanced down to the heath in front of him. Standing very still near the castle was an armoured Knight, rubbing around its legs was a small black animal. All of the Knights were gathered elsewhere on the heath at that time. "It's a cat!" The Queen exclaimed.

---0---

The story of the Knights of the Star and the Lost Queen is to be continued in volume two. The Legacy of the King

Made in the USA
Charleston, SC
25 September 2014